"K'wan has really outdone himself on this one. *Street Dreams* is a must-read for any fan of urban fiction."
—Shannon Holmes, national bestselling author of *Bad Girlz*

"K'wan has done it again with another bangin' tale of the streets. . . . This is by far K'wan's best work. The game is over!"
—Joy, *Essence* bestselling author of *Dollar Bill*

"K'wan promises to bring the good ol' days back to literature . . . when authors existed who wrote such gripping tales that you never had to question whether or not you should cop their books. K'wan's stories are always satisfaction guaranteed, with characters that you can see and feel. With *Street Dreams* he is set to take over the griot of a new generation. Make way for the Donald Goines/Iceberg Slim of our era."
—Tracy Brown, author of *Black*

"If you thought *Gangsta* and *Road Dawgz* were bestsellers . . . wait until you read this! K'wan is raising the stakes for all of us. He's a triple threat to the industry."
—KaShamba Williams, author of *Blinded* and *Grimey*

"*Gangsta* was hot and *Road Dawgz* hushed any and all who thought K'wan was just a passing thing. But *Street Dreams* is a classic. The kid has got a story to tell."
—Darren Coleman, *Essence* bestselling author of *Before I Let Go*

"K'wan delivers another classic. . . . You won't be disappointed."
—Mark Anthony, *Essence* bestselling author of *Paper Chasers*

STREET Dreams

Also by K'wan

Gangsta
Road Dawgz

Anthology

The Game

K'WAN

STREET DREAMS

St. Martin's Griffin ▲ New York

www.stmartins.com

Design by Jamie Kerner-Scott

Library of Congress Cataloging-in-Publication Data

K'wan.
Street dreams / K'wan — 1st ed.
p.   cm.
ISBN 0-312-33306-4
EAN 978-0312-33306-5
1. Harlem (New York, N.Y.) — Fiction.   2. African American men —
Fiction.   3. Abused women — Fiction.   4. Ex-convicts — Fiction.
5. Young men — Fiction.   I. Title.

PS3606.O96S74   2004
813'.6 — dc22

2004046805

D   20   19   18

ACKNOWLEDGMENTS

'll begin with thanking God. Twenty-seven years strong and I'm still here. I know my hand called for it more than once, but you spared me. Thank you.

My mother, Brenda Foye, whom I'm sure you're all familiar with by now. This is her gift, I'm just a vessel.

William Green, my father. Looks like we've finally managed to come to a common ground. I'm thankful for that. Life is too short to hold grudges.

My greatest accomplishment, Ni' Jaa'. You are the purest part of me and my constant motivation. Until I saw you, I never knew I could love something so much. Even though you're still little, you've taught your old man quite a bit. Restraint, patience, and how to change a Pamper and talk on the phone at the same time.

Denise, the mother of my child and oil to my water. We fight like cats and dogs and say some hateful things to each other, but it's all love.

I wish you nothing but the best and you're still my peoples. Watch over mine and I'll watch over you.

Dajanae & Ty' Dre Joseph. You might not understand it now, but I do what I do for a reason. When you're older and you reflect on judgments that I have made you will understand and appreciate it.

My kin: the Greenes, the Crockers, and the Foyes; Nana (our backbone); Tee-Tee (our strength); my aunt Leslie; my uncles Eric, Darryl, and Frankie.

Charlotte, my walking dictionary and intellectual sparring partner. I see such great things in your future, you just need to stop thinking so much. I guess that statement is why you call me "Conundrum." Still my nigga, though.

"For My Team"

My agent, Vickie Stringer: thank you for helping me determine my worth and get a step closer to the brass ring. My nigga Shannon Holmes, who helped me learn to be patient and respect this blessing of mine. My career began when the two of you decided to take a gamble on a kid with a wild imagination. It's been a long hard road and I know that my education is just beginning. I thank you for supporting my dream and also allowing me to grow as an author. I only hope to make you both proud of my accomplishments. That's from the heart!

St. Martin's Press—Sally Richardson, Matthew Shear, George Witte, John Cunningham, Matthew Baldacci, Anne Marie Tallberg, and John Karle, for accepting me and making me feel welcome. Monique Patterson, you get a special shout, 'cause I know editing this book had to be a pain in the ass, but you did it and helped me to make it beautiful.

My Folks at Triple Crown: Tracy Brown (where that brotherhood at, girl?), Kashamba Williams, Trustice, Joylynn Jossel, T. N. Baker, and the rest of y'all. Couldn't leave out Ms. Nikki Turner (you still Bonnie, ma. Keep chin-check'n that best-seller list). Thanks, Shannon.

On the Hood Side of Things

My nigga Ty (keep ya game strong, 'cause we got work to do, fam), T.M., Party Tyme (help you spend it like it's his), Shae, all my li'l cousins (there's too many of y'all to name), Li'l Shae, Kai (Koo-Koo come home), Boo, Mark the Shark, Jay Betts (silent assassin), A.C., Queen, Mike Sap, Al (aka "White Chocolate" Justice), Ke-Ke, Shirley Johnson, Ida Johnson, Donovan, Derrick Johnson, young Kris, my man Rob Cash, PT2, JB (we gotta hit Cali again), Star Stringer, all the street vendors, *King* magazine Don Diva, FEDS, Dangerous Music, Los Don, Darren Coleman, Eric Gray, Mark Anthony, Anthony White, Thomas Long, Wahida Clark, Kwame Teague, and anyone else whose path I might've crossed, but forgot to mention.

Something I Wanted to Say

Wow. This is the third go-round and the readers are still with me. That's what's up. I can't thank you enough. It makes the headache of going through the edits worth it.

This road that I have traveled has been filled with bumps. A while back, an O.G. in this game sat me down and talked to me about what was ahead of me. At the time, I listened, 'cause he knows what he's doing, but I didn't really understand it. As I grow as an author and a person, I'm beginning to understand what he meant.

Y"'all niggaz line the fuck up. Everybody gonna get served, just hold ya head." The corner managers barked their instructions and the fiends did as they were told. That's just the way it went in the hood.

Darius, also known as Rio, stood against the project building puffing his Newport, dark eyes constantly scanning the block for police. Rio was a handsome young cat. He was about six-foot-three with pretty raven-colored curls decorating his crown. The girls at his high school would always mess with him, saying he was a dark, pretty nigga. But he felt he was just him.

By most standards, Rio was a good kid. Smart, well educated, and soft-spoken. He was respectful to his elders and fair when dealing with people on the streets. From speaking to him, you couldn't tell that he was an on-again, off-again field lieutenant for the local drug czar. The title he held was a "manager." What a manager did was just make sure that things went smoothly while he was on shift. It wasn't a glamorous job, or even the highest position in the chain of command. But Rio was content to do his little part. It was just to keep money in his pocket or food on his table, until he could secure a legit job.

Rio spotted his man, Shamel, and moved to greet him. Shamel was a short fat nigga with a lazy eye. His lips were too big for his small face and often hung down when he talked. Shamel's razor-bump-ridden, brown face bore scars that were the result of fights on the streets as well as in the system. Shamel might've been ugly, but he was a bull waiting to charge. Niggaz in the streets gave him his space. He was Rio's right-hand man.

"Sup, my nigga?" Shamel asked, placing his fist over Rio's heart.

"Another day on the grind, kid," Rio said, returning the gesture. "The block is a li'l slow this morning. Ma fuckas act like they don't wanna get high."

"Walk with me, yo?" Shamel said as he started off toward the ave. Rio looked at the dwindling flow of addicts and figured, why the hell not? After finding someone to relieve him, he strolled with his man to the ave.

The after-school program was letting out, so 104th and Columbus was flooded with little kids running back and forth. Rio and Shamel posted up by the courts on 104th between Columbus and began the day's politics.

"What's new, player?" Rio asked.

"Ma fucking same thang different day," Shamel said, lighting a cigarette. "I just came from seeing one of my baby mamas and shit."

"Who you was laid up wit, big-boy?"

"Man, Meeka crazy ass. I ain't been wit her like that since Shawn was like two, and he's five now. Fuck is that telling you?"

"Man, but you be leading them bitches on."

"How the fuck you figure, Rio?"

"Because, you still fucking em. You say you don't love em anymore, but you still answering them four A.M. phone calls when them sack-chasers ring you."

"Fuck you, Rio," Shamel said, blowing out a smoke ring. "Pretty ma fucka, always think you know some shit. We can all be like you and Trinity. Leave-it-to-Beaver ma fuckas."

"Nigga, don't hate cause my boo-boo down for me. Trinity is my A-like and I'm hers."

"What the fuck ever wit that ABC shit. You know what I mean. These bitches is too full of game for my taste."

"Then stop raw dick'n em."

"Whatever, nigga. What that block like?"

"It's a slow go, dick. But I cope wit it."

"Fuck that. Y'all niggaz be out here twenty-four/seven any weather clicking. You might as well get a job for all that. A nigga like me," Shamel said, beating his chest. "I'm gonna get my marbles regardless."

"Fool, you make your living by force, mine is by choice. We don't put a gun to nobody's head and make 'em buy this shit. Ma fuckas get high in the hood cause they want to."

"Same shit, punk. We both doing dirt."

"Ah," Rio said, shrugging his shoulders. "We make the best out of what we have."

The two friends popped a little more shit and watched the day go by. Rio and Shamel had been friends since grade school. Rio was a grade over Shamel and used to tutor him in the after-school program. People used to make fun of Shamel and call him stupid, when he was actually quite the opposite. Shamel was a wiz with numbers, he just had a problem with reading and writing. The problem wasn't stupidity, it was dyslexia.

"What's on for the night?" Rio asked.

"It's Thursday, kid," Shamel said. "You know niggaz is probably gonna roll through Vertigo. What up, you trying to go?"

"Nah, not tonight."

"Yo, Rio, you need to get off that bullshit. You don't never go nowhere anymore. Fuck, is you a hermit or something now?"

"Nah, I'll probably chill wit Trinity tonight."

"Let me find out you sprung. Nigga, it's wall to wall pussy in the club, yet you content wit the same ol' cracker. What up wit you, Rio?"

"Y'all niggaz just got the game fucked up, Shamel. Wit me it ain't really about how many bitches I can fuck. I been through all that shit already. I can be content wit one girl, cause me and Trinity is like that. She's more than just a lover, she's my friend too."

"Fuck outta here," Shamel said spitting. "You expect me to believe that shit?"

"Believe what you want, kid. It is what it is wit us."

Their conversation was interrupted when a Benz truck pulled to the curb. The Benz was forest green with 22-inch chrome rims. All the windows were tinted, totally concealing the occupants of the truck. But everyone in Douglass knew who the vehicle belonged to.

The driver stepped from the truck, first giving a brief look around. He was a fifty-something slim cat, with skin the color of a moonless night. His processed hair shone like a waxed floor in the afternoon sun. A passing breeze pushed the jacket of his gray suit open, just enough to expose the butt of the 9 in his belt. His birth certificate read James Woodson, but the streets called the five-foot-five man Li'l J.

Li'l J went around to the other side and opened the door for his boss. The man who stepped from the truck was an even six feet. He had brown skin with salt and pepper hair. His royal blue suit was custom-made to fit his lean frame. With both his fists flooded with diamonds, he looked more like a retired movie star than a drug lord. His name was once Teddy Brown, but now he was known as Prince. Lord of the crack game.

Li'l J started in Rio's direction with Prince bringing up the rear. Something about Prince always made Rio uneasy, but he tried not to show it. He didn't want the big man to think he was some starstruck punk. But still, an air of greatness clung to Prince like a second skin.

"Sup, li'l nigga," Li'l J said, giving Rio a pound. "What it look like?"

"Ain't nothing old-timer," Rio said. "I'm just trying to make a dollar like everybody else."

"I hear you, kid. Fuck you doing round here?" Li'l J asked, directing his attention to Shamel. "I know you ain't bringing that bullshit round here."

"Damn," Shamel said in an annoyed tone. "Ain't nobody doing nothing. Why don't you be easy, J?"

"What?" Li'l J said, reaching for his pistol. "I know you ain't getting smart? What you say?"

"I ain't say nothing, man." Shamel said in a submissive tone.

"Punk ma fucka. I know you didn't," J sneered. "Why don't you take a walk, kid? Prince wanna holla at ya boy."

Shamel wanted to say something slick, but thought better of it. J might've been getting on in years, but he was still a dangerous cat. One day Shamel would have a surprise for the old bastard, but not today. Shamel slapped his man five and bounced.

"Was that Shamel?" Prince asked, strutting over.

"Yeah," J said, watching the big man depart. "That was him."

"Why you hang wit that kid, Rio?" Prince asked, concerned. "Fucking thief. Niggaz like him is only destined for the penitentiary or the grave."

"Maybe," Rio said in a serious tone. "But nine times outta ten the same rewards wait for most of us who play the game."

"You sure is a philosophical ma fucka, Rio."

"Hey, I can't help the way life is. I just call it like I see it, Prince."

"Sure ya right, kid. Come on and walk with me."

Prince started off toward Central Park West with Rio at his side and Li'l J bringing up the rear. They strolled past the end of the projects and across Manhattan Avenue. The walk from Columbus to Central Park was like walking through an evolutionary scale. Where the projects ended, walk-ups and little town-house-like structures began. The town houses ended making way for the luxury apartments. It was like stepping into a whole new world in a few short blocks.

Prince stopped near the mouth of the park and took in the scenery. White folks were walking their dogs, riding bikes, and doing all sorts of outdoor activities. All carrying on as if they were oblivious to the fact that there was a crack-infested housing project a block away.

"Look at this shit," Prince said, motioning toward a young white couple strolling through the park. "Strangers in a strange world. Few years ago you wouldn't have seen no shit like this. This whole area was black and Spanish. Now we got the 'Caucasian invasion.'"

"I feel you," Rio said, lighting a cigarette. "Hood don't seem the same, do it?"

"Hell, nah. Man, we had all this shit in the smash, now the crackers done took over."

"Can't really blame the white folks, Prince. Like you said; we had all this shit in the smash. The thing is, we let it slip away like everything else. Look at Harlem. We had a good run wit that and ain't do shit but fuck it up. Black folks act like they ain't used to nothing."

"Li'l nigga, don't you go trying to tell me about the civil rights. I was around in the sixties, remember?"

"Sorry, Prince."

"Yeah, back in the day we had a li'l more pride bout our shit. Now ma fuckas act like they don't care 'bout nothing. They just content to do without. But not ol' Prince. From the day I left that damn shit hole in North Carolina, I made myself a promise. No matter what I had to do to survive, I'd never go without again."

"I hear you on that," Rio said, sitting on one of the wooden benches. "A nigga trying to get his weight up."

"Bullshit," Prince said, elbowing Li'l J. "You hear this, kid? Rio, you ain't really trying to be on top of ya game. If you were, you would've accepted my offer."

"And a generous offer it was, Prince. But this shit ain't for me."

"What you mean it ain't for you? Nigga, you'd rather be out here getting part-time money, instead of trying to climb the ladder?"

"It ain't like that. I just don't wanna be a hustler."

"News flash for ya, kid. Every successful person in the world is a hustler in one way or another. We all hustle to get where we need to be. Only a fool would sit around and wait on another man to feed him."

"I hear where ya coming from, Prince, but I ain't hard to please. I'd be content to get a decent li'l gig and a crib of my own. As long as I ain't starving and my bills are paid, I'm cool."

All Prince could do was shake his head. He had been trying to get Rio back to working for him full-time ever since he came home from lockup. But every time he propositioned Rio, he would always go into his speech about getting a nine to five. He had been on countless interviews with no luck, but Prince still tried him every chance he got.

Before Rio went away, he was getting heavy in the game. The kid ate, slept, and shit money. That's the main reason Prince had taken a liking to him. Rio would be the first nigga on the block and the last nigga to leave. Everyone thought that when he came home, he would be right back on the grind. But Rio had changed while he was away. He wasn't a coward, but he was much more serious about his life and not wasting it. Some people took this as Rio going soft, but Prince knew better. The kid was just growing up.

"Rio, I'm gonna give you some advice," Prince said. "You're a good kid, but you got low expectations for ya self. All through school you got good grades, even managed to get ya self a li'l degree. But where has it gotten you? Yo ass ain't no closer to a plush pad on Park Ave. You still out here playing corners like the rest of these ma fuckas."

"In due time, Prince."

"Due time, my ass. You better wake up and smell the green. Only a man willing to take his destiny into his own hands is ever gonna make something of himself. Food for thought, hear?"

Prince made more sense than a li'l bit. Rio had indeed finished his education and tried to take his life a step beyond the expected. But so far he didn't have shit. Rio had gone on at least seven interviews in the last few months. All of them turned up dead ends. Ever since he took a fall, people began to treat him as if he had the plague. No one wanted a convicted felon working for them. Sure he had a degree, but it was from a two-year school. Nowadays, that wasn't even good enough. He had high hopes for an interview that he would be going on that week, but part of him expected to be passed over. Becoming a member of the working class was beginning to look dismal for him. So he had to hustle until things changed. If they changed. Rio wanted more from his life, but fast cash was the order of business.

"Anyhow," Prince continued, "let me tell you why I came down so I can get from round you sorry ma fuckas. I'm having a li'l thang tomorrow night, at the Cotton Club. My son, Truck, is finally getting his stupid ass outta the clink. Let's hope he can stay out this time. It's by invite only and you invited."

"Thanks, Prince," Rio said, shaking his hand. "Is it all right if I bring people with me?"

"Yeah, it's cool. Just don't bring none of them hood niggaz you hang with."

"Why you always gotta rank on my friends, Prince?" Rio asked, frustrated.

"Cause you too smart to be running round with assholes. You better listen to an old-timer, Rio. Cut them hard luck niggaz loose."

"I hear you, Prince."

"Don't just hear me, listen, too. Them niggaz is trouble waiting to happen. Here," Prince said, peeling off five hundred dollars, "take ya li'l girlfriend out, or buy ya self something."

"I can't take this from you, Prince."

"See, that's what I mean by you being stupid. You never turn down free money. Now get up off this hot-ass block. School Boy can finish out ya shift."

"A'ight, Prince. Thanks again."

"No problem, kid. I expect to see you tomorrow night. Bring li'l Tiffany wit you."

"Her name's *Trinity*. And I just might do that."

"Whatever, Rio. Just have yo ass there." Prince nodded at Li'l J and they made their way back up the block. As Rio watched the duo leave, he couldn't help but think, *Prince sure has had it together*. Rio promised himself that one day he'd be holding his own paper. It was hard eating from the hands of another man, but sometimes you had to do what you had to do.

2

Trinity sat inside the library on 100th Street, trying to make heads or tails out of the GED prep book. She did okay with the reading part; it was the math that frustrated the hell out of her. The more Trinity thought about it, the more she wished she'd finished high school when she had the chance.

It's not like she was a bad student, or she wasn't smart enough to keep up, but circumstances had sidetracked her. To be so young, she had a lot of responsibilities weighing on her. She had to take care of both her brothers and her father. When her mother was alive, things were much simpler, but after she died, everything went downhill. Trinity's grades began to slip and she became more and more distracted. Eventually she just stopped going altogether.

Trinity decided that she was long overdue for a smoke break. She stretched her five-foot-four frame and felt a little better. She snatched up her knapsack and headed for the exit. As she walked out of the library, she could feel people watching her. That's what happened when you were young and beautiful.

Trinity had a cute round face and the most alluring hazel eyes. When Trinity entered a room, people couldn't help but stare. Not only was she pretty in the face, but she had a body for days. Nothing on Trinity was too large or too small. Everything was just right. Her wavy black hair stopped around midback when she let it hang down loose, but she mostly wore it in corn rows, or box braids. It was easier to keep that way.

Trinity managed to ignore the stares instead of lashing out, as she was known to do. She knew a man was going to be a man, but she didn't like to be gawked at. By the time she made it outside, she decided to extend her smoke break indefinitely.

She strolled up 100th Street in no particular hurry. Before she got to the corner, she heard someone calling her name. She turned around to see Alexis and Joyce waving at her. Trinity stopped and allowed the girls a chance to catch up.

Alexis was a pretty Trinidadian girl from the projects. She had a caramel complexion with hair almost as long as Trinity's. Alexis was one of those girls who looked more Spanish than black. Many a time they had been out and dudes would roll up on her speaking Spanish. Trinity used to laugh but it frustrated the hell outta Alexis. The only thing that really gave her away was her ass. Alexis's booty looked like two basketballs tucked in her jeans.

Joyce was just a girl Trinity tried her best to be nice to. She wasn't as pretty as the other two girls, but she still walked around like her shit didn't stink. She was a dark-skinned girl with short nappy hair, which she mostly wore in a weave. Joyce was also a notorious busybody. She was always gossiping about who got what and who was fucking who. It irked the hell out of Trinity but she was nice to the girl because she was Alexis's friend.

"What up, bitches?" Alexis asked, hugging Trinity. "Where you been hiding?"

"Please," Trinity said. "I been trying to get ready to take this GED."

"Again? Damn, this is the second time. Girl, I hope you pass it."

"Me, too."

"Well," Joyce cut, "you asked me, I'd say the hell with it."

"Well," Trinity said, cutting her eyes, "nobody asked you, Joyce."

"Damn, Trinity. Let me find out you light-skinned bitches is sensitive."

"Joyce, I've asked you time and again, stop calling me out my name."

"Gosh, Trinity. I didn't mean it like that. Shit, Alex can call you out ya name and you don't chew her head off."

"Cause, that's my bitch and I fucks wit her like that. I don't fuck wit you like that."

"Why don't the both of you bitches knock it off?" Alexis said, trying to avoid the drama.

"Whatever, Alex. So, where y'all just coming from?"

"Oh, we went to the movies with Tommy and his man Dave."

"Oh, y'all fucking wit them niggaz?"

"Hell yeah," Alexis said, giving Joyce a high five. "That nigga Tommy is fine."

"I hear that," Trinity said, pulling out her pack of cigarettes. "But mister fine also got a crazy baby mama."

"Shit," Alexis said, helping herself to a cigarette. "That's his problem. I ain't got nothing to do with that."

"A'ight. One of these days you gonna fuck with the wrong bitch's man."

"Well, I'll cross that bridge when I come to it. And who the hell are you to preach? Trinity, yo trifling ass used to play the game right along with me."

"Yeah, I had my fifteen minutes of fame, but that was before. Things are different now, Alex."

"Um hmm. The only difference is Rio is blowing ya back out now."

"That nigga is fine," Joyce said.

"Joyce," Trinity said, lighting her cigarette. "Don't get fucked up, a'ight?"

"There you go wit that shit, Trinity. I was just trying to give you ya props. Please, don't nobody want ya man," Joyce lied.

"I'll bet." Trinity knew damn well that Joyce would fuck Rio in a heartbeat. She wasn't fooling anybody with that fake sisterly love shit. A girl from 112 Street had whipped Joyce out over the summer for fucking with her man. Joyce was grimy like that.

"So, what's up for tonight?" Alexis asked.

"I dunno, girl," Trinity said. "I'll probably just kick it wit Rio."

"I hear that shit," Joyce said. "I heard it's gonna be some ballers in Vertigo tonight. I'm trying to get up in there."

"That's ya problem right there," Trinity said with attitude. "All you ever think about is dick. Life has more to offer than a nut."

"Shit, I can't tell." All the girls laughed at that one. "But, seriously T. You need to roll wit us."

"I dunno, Joyce."

"Bitch, knock it off," Alexis said. "Rio's still gonna be here. Why don't you come shake ya ass a li'l? Maybe it'll bring you out of ya slump."

"I ain't in no slump, hoe. I just like to spend time with my man."

"Which is all the more reason why you need to come with us. You and Rio are together twenty-four/seven. Give ya selves a chance to miss each other."

Trinity thought about it for a minute. It had been quite some time since she went clubbing. Since she got with Rio she saw less and less of her girls. When she was with Rio she felt safe, but those times when he wasn't there she felt more alone than a little bit. She missed kicking it with her bitch, Alexis. What could one night hurt?

"A'ight," Trinity said, tossing her cigarette. "What time we rolling?"

"That's the Trinity I know," Alexis said, hugging her girl. "I'll be by to pick you up at about eleven."

"Oh, you pushing?"

"Girl, you know how I do. That nigga Church is letting me hold his jeep. Let me worry about the details. Just have yo ass ready by eleven."

Rio stepped off the elevator and exhaled. The smell of the projects was bad enough on its own, but niggaz pissing up the tiny elevators didn't help. It seemed like you couldn't ride the elevators anymore, without stepping in piss or being overwhelmed by the stench of it.

He strode down the hall past the graffiti and other scribbling until he reached his apartment. Before putting his key in the lock, he listened at the door. The sounds of Harold Melvin blared through the door. This meant two things. His mother was home and she was drunk.

Rio entered the apartment and looked around in disgust. There was a week's worth of laundry scattered all over the floor. He thought that buying a washer and dryer would put an end to the buildup, but it didn't. He walked into the tiny, yellow kitchen and saw the same dishes in the sink from three days ago. He loved his mother dearly, but her utter laziness turned him off.

Rio walked into the living room and there was Mama. Sally was already a naturally thin woman, but the drinking had her looking damn near skeletal. Her once smooth skin was now splotchy from constant abuse of her body. At one time Sally had been a beautiful blues singer. Now she looked more like a walking corpse.

"There's my boy," Sally said, exposing a near-toothless grin. "What's up, baby?"

"Hey, Ma," Rio said flatly.

"Boy, don't you see nobody else in here? Come on in and speak to Willie."

Willie was Sally's on-again, off-again boyfriend. He was a dark-skinned dude with salt-and-pepper hair that had began to grow thin on the top. Willie was an alcoholic/crackhead. Back in the days he was a big player in the game, but now he was just another hype. Somebody must've forgot to tell Willie that he wasn't a star anymore, because he still tried to act like he was balling.

"Sup, Willie?" Rio said.

"Mister-man," Willie said, standing. "What it be like, young blood?"

"I'm chilling."

"How we looking out there?"

"Excuse me?" Rio asked, frowning.

"I say, how we looking? Ya know, on the block?"

"I couldn't tell you, Willie." Rio shrugged. "Seeing how I'm in here instead of out there, I wouldn't know. But don't worry, you'll be the first to know when things pick up."

Rio was sure that Sally knew about his side activities, but he didn't like to throw it under her nose like that. And Willie was always trying to drop little hints for her to pick up on. He called himself trying to be funny, but Rio called it dry snitching. As opposed to choking Willie's skinny ass, Rio went into his room and slammed the door.

He kicked off his shoes and tossed his coat over the back of his computer chair. His answering machine boasted four new messages, but he didn't feel like being bothered. He started to call Trinity until he remembered that she was studying at the library.

Rio picked up the small picture frame from his dresser and wiped away a thin layer of dust. Rio was the spitting image of the man in the picture. They had the same curly hair and sharp chin. The man was dressed all in black, holding his fist high in the air. Sally was at his side, playing the proud wife.

Rio didn't really remember the man who had fathered him, but he'd heard many stories. He was a legend in the streets but not from being in the drug game. Rio's father had been a Panther. The way Sally told it, Rio's father, whose name was Amir, was a respected man amongst his peers. He was down for what he believed in until the day the justice system took him from the world.

Back in the late '70s Amir and some of his comrades attempted to break an inmate out of the Atlanta Federal Pen. The inmate had been an eighteen-year-old boy on death row awaiting execution for a murder he hadn't commited. During the attempted breakout, ten people were injured and three were killed, two of whom were law enforcement agents. The entire team was captured and charged with treason and murder. The other men copped out, but not Amir. He stood strong behind his cause and his pride. He ended up riding that pride straight to the gas chamber. Amir was one of the last men to be executed in the state of Georgia.

When Rio's father was killed, Sally went downhill. In her depression, she turned to the bottle to ease her hurt. But no matter what, Sally never let Amir's memory die. She made sure that Rio knew what kind of man his father had been. A champion of the people.

Rio turned on his CD player and flopped down on his futon. He lit a blunt and let his mind coast while TQ crooned about wanting his girlfriend's sister. And in sleep, Rio's mind found a temporary escape.

Trinity entered her three-bedroom apartment and found it silent for once. That meant her brothers weren't home and her drunk-ass father was either passed out or running the streets. It didn't matter to her either way. The important thing was she could have some quality time to herself.

Trinity tried not to feel sorry for herself most of the time, but she was only nineteen and life had seen fit to thrust her into the role of homemaker way before she was ready. When her mother was alive, life hadn't been too bad. They were still poor and her father still drank uncontrollably, but at least there was someone in the house who actually cared about her.

Trinity was barely fourteen when her mother contracted the HIV virus. By the time she turned fifteen, she was gone. Her mother didn't do drugs or sleep around on her father. She was just misfortunate enough to get a raw deal on a blood transfusion. Janice was Trinity's best friend as well as the person who brought her into the world. Losing her mother, coupled with everything else that was going wrong in her life, was almost too much for Trinity to bear. She had considered taking her own life, but she knew her family would need her.

When her mother passed, it had been up to her to take care of her father and two brothers. She didn't mind at first. Taking care of the house kept her mind off the loss of her mother. She was even able to put up with her father's drinking. Everything was all good, until the touching started.

Her father would pinch her developing breasts and tease her about how she was getting old on him. Then he took to rubbing himself against her ass when he would pass her in the hall. Still Trinity tried to tell herself it was nothing. In her mind, she made a million excuses for her father. But the excuses ran out the night her father came into her room drunk.

Her mother had been gone maybe four or five months on that horrible night. Trinity had been sleeping when her father's sobs woke her. She opened her eyes and saw him standing in her doorway holding a fifth in one hand and a picture of her mother in the other. He was crying like a baby, talking about how much he missed his wife.

Trinity's father sat on the edge of her bed and patted her leg. Trinity, trying to be the good daughter, sat up and held her father in her arms and tried to console him. After a while his sobbing stopped. She continued to pat his back comfortingly, feeling good about being there for her father in his time of need. Then she felt his hand slide up under her nightgown. He turned his head to kiss her, and she tried to push him away. He kept slurring about how pretty she was and how much she looked like her mother, Janice. Trinity tried to fight but he had been too strong for her. The next thing she knew he had his hand clamped over her mouth and was penetrating her.

Trinity just lay there crying while her father pumped away. Then he released inside of her and rolled off. Blood and semen were running down Trinity's legs and onto the sheets. Instead of trying to make excuses for what he did, the sick bastard slapped her face and cursed her for seducing him. He told Trinity that no man would ever want her because she was "spoiled goods." Trinity believed him, believed that she was the one who had done something wrong. As she got older the raping became less frequent, but he still came calling when he wanted to release some stress. Trinity just took it as one more reason to want to end her life.

Shaking off the memories, Trinity took the opportunity to take a shower. With any luck she'd be dressed and gone by the time her father came home. After her shower Trinity wrapped herself in a towel and went back into her room. She curled up on her bed with the extra-large stuffed animal Rio had won for her at Coney Island. She kept one of his T-shirts on the doll so it would always smell like him. She missed her boo-boo.

Trinity picked up her Mickey Mouse phone to call Rio but decided against it. She knew he'd been on the block all night, so if he was home he'd probably be asleep. She walked over to her CD player and hit PLAY. She lit some scented candles and listened to Mary and Aretha singing about not wasting their time on no-good men. Trinity loved the song, but it really didn't apply to her. Rio was a good man. Trinity's mind finally began to relax and everything was all good. Until she heard her father's voice.

"*Trinity!*"

3

The line outside Club Vertigo stretched nearly half a block. Women were on the line wearing next to nothing, hoping to get someone's attention and make their way in without paying. The fellas were doing just as much fronting as the ladies. Each man trying to out-stunt the other and look like the stars they knew they weren't.

Rio just looked at the circus of people and shook his head. It was amazing what people would go through for a li'l attention. To Rio, it was all wack. You could be the flyest nigga or have the hottest car, but what did it all amount to if you still lived at home with your moms?

Even though Rio wasn't really into material possessions, he was still a sharp dresser. He was rocking a Sean Jean denim jumper with a crisp pair of constructions. Every curl on his head was in place and looking like a million. His man Chris had laced him with a fresh lineup before he left for the club. Rio was ready to party.

Originally he had planed on spending the evening with Trinity, but that had changed. When he woke up he checked his messages. None were from Trinity. He checked his cell and got the same thing. He didn't worry though. Trinity was probably just in one of her moods.

Every so often Trinity would just draw in on herself. For days at a time she would just lock herself away and shut everybody out, including Rio. She wouldn't see him or take his phone calls. When Rio would ask her what it was all about, she would get all emotional on him. Sometimes it would be a fit of crying, while other times she'd bark his head off. When Trinity closed him out like that, it pissed him off. She was his girl and if she was going through something, he wanted to be there for her. Hopefully she would open up in time.

"You about ready to go in?" Shamel asked.

"Waiting on you, kid."

Rio was so wrapped up in his own thoughts he'd almost forgotten his friend was there. Shamel was dressed to impress. He wore a loose-fitting black sweater and some blue Parasuco jeans. He wore the laces of his black suede Timb's slightly untied, giving him that hood effect. The iced-out cross bounced off his chest every time he moved, casting a hell of a glare. Shamel was ready to bag something.

Shamel knew the bouncer so they didn't have to wait on line. The two youngsters made their way through the angry crowd and into the club. The flashing lights and blaring sound system played havoc on Rio's senses. He had to stand still for a minute to let his eyes adjust to the lights. Inside, the club was jumping off. Ladies crowded the dance floor, bouncing their asses, while the guys played the bar getting saucy.

Shamel greeted a few of the other roughnecks and ballers, while Rio played the background. He was never big on crowds or people. Rio nodded to a few of the cats he knew from the hood, but other than that he kept to himself.

Shamel was on the dance floor "doing him" with two females, while Rio played the bar. He knew how to dance, but rarely did he show it. He mostly came to the club to get "mopped" and listen to the music. He was content to leave the flashing to cats like Shamel.

As Rio sat at the bar nursing his Long Island iced-tea, he found his thoughts drifting back to Trinity. He knew she needed her space when she got in her moods, but he still didn't like not hearing from her. He would feel better if he at least knew she was all right.

Rio thought about the way he was acting and felt a little embarrassed. Here he was in a club with his right-hand man and about three hundred females and he was thinking about Trinity. Maybe the stories of him being whipped were true.

Rio's thoughts were interrupted when someone tapped him on the shoulder. He turned around to find himself face-to-face with a chocolate dream. She was a cute li'l thang, with a pretty mouth and a fat ass. The tight-fitting black dress she wore looked like someone painted it on. She brushed a lock of her auburn hair from her face and smiled at Rio.

"How ya doing?" she asked.

"I'm cool," he said, a little shy.

"You're Rio, right?"

"How you know that?" he asked with interest.

"Ya man told me."

Rio looked over to the dance floor and saw Shamel smiling at him, waving a bottle of Moet in the air. Rio should've known that this was his handiwork. He'd check him about that shit later.

"I'm sorry," she said, extending her hand. "I'm Precious."

"Nice to meet you, Precious."

"Is it a'ight if I sit by you, or are you expecting someone?"

"Nah," Rio said, clearing out a space at the bar for her. "Get ya sit on."

Precious squeezed into the little space Rio had cleared for her and sat on the stool. As she was sliding in, she made it a point to rub her ass on his lap. "Sorry." She giggled. Precious was a bad chick, but she had sack-chaser written all over her.

"So," she began, "why you sitting over here all lonesome instead of getting ya groove on?"

"I dunno," he said, smiling.

"You shy or something?"

"Something like that."

"Well," she said as the bartender slid her a drink that Rio didn't remember her ordering. "You ain't gotta worry about me. I'm harmless."

"I find that a little hard to believe."

"Come on now, Rio. Do I strike you as that kinda girl?"

"Nah, shorty. I'm fucking wit you."

"Better be careful how you phrase your words, Rio."

Rio continued to sit at the bar talking to Precious for lack of anything else to do. Dudes was trying to throw blocks left and right, but she was shooting them down. Her focus was on Rio. He knew Precious was trying to holla and he damn sure wouldn't have minded blazing her, but he couldn't seem to focus. His mind was on Trinity.

The DJ slowed it down and played an old Tony-Toni-Tone jam. "That's my shit," Precious said, grabbing him by the hand. "Come dance with me, Rio?"

"Nah," he said blushing. "Do you, ma."

"Cut it out, Rio. I'm not asking you for ya soul, just a dance. Please?"

Rio started to shut her down until he spotted Joyce. He'd know that gorilla-looking bitch anywhere. After scanning the crowd he saw Alexis and Trinity coming out of the ladies' room. Rio's mood suddenly darkened. He'd been worried sick about her and she was out shaking her ass. Well, if she wanted to play it like that, he could too.

"A'ight," he said, leading Precious by the hand. "Come on."

Rio led Precious to the middle of the dance floor. Without hesitation, she locked her arms around his neck and placed his hands on her ass. Precious's ass felt like the softest cloud. Rio felt his little man wake up and stand at attention. When she felt his hardness against her leg, she smiled and pulled him closer. The group sang about the weather in Southern California as Rio enjoyed the feel of Precious's body against his.

Three songs later Rio felt as if he had proven his point and made his way back to the bar. Precious followed closely on his heels. The whole time he danced with Precious he felt Trinity watching him. Served her right for making him worry. He had used Precious to make Trinity mad but it seemed Precious wanted a little more out of the deal.

"You sure know how to make a sister sweat," Precious said, fixing her hair.

"Thanks for the dance," Rio said, hoping she'd catch on.

"Listen Rio, let's cut the bullshit shall we? I mean, we're two adults, so we should be able to just say what's on our minds, right? I wanna fuck you and I'm sure some part of you wants to fuck me," she said, looking at his crotch. "So let's skip all the bullshit and go get a room."

Rio stared at her in surprise. The way Precious was eyeballing him, he felt like the female. Rio didn't know what to say. But thanks to Alexis he didn't have to say anything.

"What's up, Rio?" Alexis asked, eyeing Precious. "You was gonna sit up in here all night and not say hi to a sister?"

"What up, Alex?"

"That's what I'm trying to find out. Who's ya li'l friend?"

"I'm Precious," she answered before Rio could say anything. "And you are?"

"A concerned citizen." Alexis said, rolling her eyes.

"Well," Precious said, matching her attitude. "Rio and I were just leaving."

"Oh, really?"

"Really. Rio, who is this, ya girl or something?"

"No," Trinity said, grabbing Rio by the arm. "But I am."

Precious looked back and forth from Rio to the angry young females. "Listen," she said, adjusting her purse. "I ain't got time for this. Rio sweetheart, youz a classy nigga. When you get tired of doing the R. Kelly thang wit these li'l bitches, you holla at me, okay?"

"Bitches!" Trinity snapped. "Oh I got ya bitches! Bitch!"

Trinity started taking off her earrings, but Rio grabbed her up. Alexis and Joyce called Precious all kinds of bitches as she left, but neither one tried to flex. Now Rio had to deal with Trinity and her wild-ass temper.

"Fuck is up wit that shit, Rio?" she snapped, pushing him. "You was gonna slide wit that bitch?"

"Trinity," he said, holding her at arm's length, "you bugging out. I wasn't going nowhere with that girl."

"So, what the fuck was she talking about?"

"Look, all I did was dance with the girl."

"Somebody's lying," Joyce butted in.

"What?" Rio snapped. "Joyce, mind ya fucking business. This ain't got nothing to do with you."

"Come on, Joyce," Alex said, seeing all hell about to break loose. "Trinity can hold hers. Let's go get a drink." The two girls walked off leaving Trinity to handle her business.

"So, what you got to say for ya self, Rio?"

"What? I ain't got shit to say, cause I ain't do shit."

"Nigga, you got cold jokes. I watched you rubbing all on that bitch and you gonna try and tell me you ain't do shit?" Trinity began to remove her jewelry. "Me and you is about to have a misunderstanding."

"Trinity," he said, backing out of arms' reach. "You better not start acting all crazy."

"Fuck you, Rio. I should cut yo punk ass for trying to play me."

"Play you? Trinity you know how many times I tried to call you? I ain't even wanna come up in this ma fucka, but you was off doing you. I think you got it backward."

Trinity glared at him. She knew Rio had a point. She hadn't called him or answered her phone. Even though he was right, she still had an attitude.

"Well," she said, sucking her teeth. "I was going through some shit. But that still don't make it okay for you to be in here jumping off wit these nasty bitches."

"Trinity," he said, stroking her cheek. "You know that the only two women I love in this world are you and my mama. Don't none of these other bitches count to me. Besides, shorty breath was cold stinking."

"You stupid," she said giggling. "I'm still mad at you though."

"Aww," he said hugging her. "I'm sorry, ma. Let me make it up to you?"

"Oh, don't worry, you will. Can we get outta here?"

"A'ight. Let me just find Shamel and tell him I'm leaving."

"No need," Shamel said, slapping him on the back. "What up, T?"

"Hey, Shamel."

"So, you bailing on me, Rio?"

"Yeah man," he said, hugging Trinity. "I got me a slide, kid."

"Do you my nigga. Y'all be safe."

Shamel watched the two lovebirds leave, and what passed for a smile sprang to his rugged face. He was glad his man had someone he cared about in his life. Maybe one day he'd find someone special for himself. But not tonight. Shamel had half a bottle of "Mo" left and was on his way to being drunk. The club was still full of sack-chasers and he intended on taking one home.

Rio sat in the back of the taxi listening to Trinity bark. She had been running her mouth nonstop about the sack-chaser from the club. She had calmed down a little, but once you got Trinity's mouth going it was hard to shut her up.

"That was some real crab shit, Rio," Trinity said. "I'm supposed to be ya girl, but you hugged up on that skanky weave rocking bitch. What kinda shit is that?"

"Trinity," he said, exhaling. "Why you gotta drag shit on? I told you that I wasn't sliding wit her. I saw you in the club and I was trying to get back at you for 'looping' my calls."

"Yeah right, Rio. That's a lame-ass excuse. You gotta come better than that."

"T, I'm a grown-ass man. Fuck I gotta lie for? You should already know how I'm rocking. You my boo. Ain't nobody else, ma."

"Whatever, Rio. I'm still mad at you."

"Okay," he said, reclining in the backseat. "Since you mad at me, I guess you don't wanna go to the Cotton Club wit a nigga?"

"Rio," she said, turning to face him, with attitude etched across. "That's some lame shit. They don't even have events at the Cotton Club anymore," she informed him.

"They do if your name is Prince."

"Prince is throwing a party?"

"Yep. His son Truck is the guest of honor."

"Truck? I thought dumb-ass Melvin was his only son."

"So do most people. Truck just did damn near ten year on a body."

"Damn, I know that's gonna be the jump-off. Fuck, I got a fit, but a bitch ain't got no footwear."

"Baby, I got you. When I go see my P.O. in the morning, I'll hit the village and cop you some nice li'l joints."

"Thank you, baby," she said kissing him on the lips. "You know what size I wear, right?"

"Trinity, how many pairs of footwear have I bought you? Of course I know what size you wear. I just don't know what color."

"Oh, you can cop me some black riding boots. Just make sure the heel isn't too high."

"I got you, ma. It'll be nice to see you dress like a lady for a change."

"Oh, you trying to say I'm not a lady?"

"Nah, I ain't mean it like that. But you know how you are."

"No, how am I, Rio?"

"Trinity, keep it funky. You know ya M.O. is boots and jeans."

"Fuck you, Rio. I dress to be comfortable, not to impress these low-life ma fuckas in Douglass. I dress up sometimes."

"Yeah, when you going out wit ya hood rat-ass friends."

"You back on that shit, huh?"

"Them bitches is funny style, Trinity, and you know it. Especially Joyce. I can't stand that bitch."

"Joyce is a'ight. Sometimes."

"Fuck that nickle-grabbing bitch. She ain't nothing but a sack-chaser."

"Well, I don't really fuck wit her like that. Alex is my bitch."

"Yeah, that's my girl, too. But Alex is loose in the drawers."

"You're so judgmental, Rio. You out there doing ya dirt like every-body else."

"Yeah, but it's different. Wit me, the end justifies the means. I'm just hustling till I get on my feet, girl. You think I like being out here like that? Hell nah. Prince is always coming at me about getting down full-time, but I ain't gonna do it. I mean, the money would be all that, but it ain't worth it. I can't bring myself to be the kinda nigga it takes to grind full-time. I'm sure most niggaz would jump at the chance to be the man next to the man, but not the kid. I'm my own man."

"Yeah, I hear you, Rio," she said, sucking her bottom lip. "But . . . you ever think about the benefits of having that paper?"

"Oh, yeah. I thought about it plenty of times, boo. Who wouldn't have? But in the long run, is it worth it? Sure, I might be able to ball a li'l harder, but for how long? We both know it's only two ways out that game there."

"But you ain't like most niggaz, Rio. You're smart."

"Trinity, you know how many niggaz that came before me thought they was smart? Nah, matter of fact let's count the niggaz that actually were smart. In the streets it's really about who's the coldest. I thought about it, Trinity. Many a night a nigga be counting up that cheese and thinking, 'This is all mine, if I chose to seal the bargain.' Tempting, but I ain't quite ready to sell my soul."

Trinity just stared at Rio while he aired his thoughts. Prince would gladly set him out as his right-hand man. Rio was the kinda nigga who was worth his weight. He was book smart and knew what time it was on the block. He was the reason Prince was able to move his product in some of the white neighborhoods. Rio plugged Prince to some white dudes from his school who liked to buy in bunches at a time. In time they told their people, and so on and so on. Prince could clear at least ten to twenty thousand on a good weekend. Rio still did his little side-thing with the cats, but he never asked Prince for PC on the hookup. He was just the kind of dude to leave every man to his own devices.

"I feel you, pa," Trinity said, staring out the window. "Whatever roads you take in life, I wanna take them with you."

"That's why you'll always be my down-ass bitch," Rio hugged her to his chest. "We in it together, ma." The two lovers interlocked fingers and prepared to exit the cab as it pulled up on 102nd street.

Rio escorted Trinity to her building and kissed her good night. He stood in the doorway of 845 and watched her until the elevator came. He really didn't need to watch her. Trinity kept a blade of some kind on her person at all times. It was unnecessary, but he was protective of her. The vultures of the jungle they lived in were always searching for new prey.

Rio took a stroll to his building, puffing a cigarette and feeling pretty good about himself. He had a decent hustle and a pretty bitch. Compared to a lot of niggaz, he was doing okay. Let Trinity have her dreams of a palace in the sky. He would give her a house in the suburbs. He intended to get right off hard work, not drug money. It served its purpose for the moment, but it was all for the greater good in his mind.

Rio gave dap to some of the local hardheads and kept it moving. He dug his hand inside his jacket pocket in search of his keys. He felt a paper towel mixed in and took it out to wipe his nose. As he brought the tissue to his nose, he saw something scribbled on it. It was a 718 number with the name "Precious" written in purple ink. Rio smiled and tucked the number back in his pocket. He figured, *A man gonna be a man.*

❏ ❏ ❏

Shamel staggered into his building on 107th and Manhattan feeling like the luckiest dude in the hood. He had a liver full of liquor and a bad broad on his arm. Monique was a twenty-something-year-old paralegal from West End Avenue. The youngest child of a Trinidadian father and a Korean mother, she had the appearance of a five-foot-nine China doll. She had the body of a sista with bronze Asian features. Shamel kept his face buried in her silky black hair most of the night.

After a brief altercation with his keys, he managed to get his door open. He had a modest apartment decorated in black and white. He eased her down onto the checkerboard love seat and began unbuttoning her top. His tongue explored her dark nipples like a hungry child. Monique moaned softly as he did his thing. Shamel might not have been the prettiest dude, but he was an expert at the forbidden arts.

Shamel snaked his tongue from her throat to her vagina. He sucked greedily at her clit, while she squirmed in ecstasy. She turned Shamel over and began to undo his pants. When she popped his dick out, she got even more excited. She slid her mouth over his ten-inch log and stepped to her business. To his surprise she was able to fit most of his shaft into her throat. Monique was maintaining eye contact the whole time she was "topping" Shamel. She was definitely a bitch who got down for her crown.

Monique slipped the prophylactic on his wood and took her position. She bounced on his dick like it was a twenty-five-cent pony ride. Shamel held fast to her waist, trying to match her fury. She cocked her ass up a little higher and grabbed his neck. Once they established a rhythm Monique did her. She bucked at one hundred miles a minute, causing him to bust a little sooner than he expected.

Monique climbed off Shamel and pulled her skirt back into place. She didn't have to worry about finding her panties cause she didn't bother with them. Monique fixed her hair and blew Shamel a kiss. She pealed off three hundred from the wad of bills on the coffee table and bounced. Shamel didn't really mind the exchange though. For a few dollars a nigga could take a trip to paradise.

Rio found himself up with the chickens. He had a full day ahead of him and he needed it to go right. Instead of his usual street gear, he was sporting a cream turtleneck sweater and black slacks. Before he was to see his P.O., he had a job interview downtown. This was his second interview with them, so things were looking good.

He came out of his building and got on the good foot to the train station. He said what's up to a few of the heads on the block, but didn't stop to chat. After waiting on an elderly lady to figure out that her metro was supposed to be swiped along the strip, Rio went through the turnstile. He missed the first C train, but another one came right behind it. Another good sign.

After riding on the musty-ass train for what seemed like forever, Rio found himself on Fifty-ninth Street. The fight against the flow of the crowd was a brutal one, but Rio managed to get to the exit without killing anyone. The walk along Seventh Avenue was a short one. The building he was seeking was only a block or so from the station. Rio glanced up at the office building and took a deep breath.

Burns & Taylor was a small marketing firm that was slowly on the rise. A friend who worked there had submitted Rio's resume for him. A week later Rio got called in for an interview. After impressing the Human Resources director he was called back for a second interview with the vice president. Rio really needed the job to come through in the worst kind of way. It only paid twenty thousand dollars a year to start, but it was better than flipping a burger or scrubbing a toilet. Besides that, this job would allow him to get out of the streets and go back to school for his bachelor's.

Rio squeezed into the little chrome elevator just as the doors were closing. He hit the floor he was going to and took up a spot in the corner. Rio could feel his palms sweating as the elevator approached his floor. The disapproving looks he got when he stepped into the small waiting area didn't help his nerves any. There were five or six other people sitting around with resumes or other such documents in their hands. Rio assumed that they were also seeking employment. The difference was that he was the only black face in the room. He tried to nod at a Spanish-looking cat sitting by the door, but the cat just rolled his eyes.

Rio brushed off the insult and walked to the small window on the other side of the room. Behind the glass sat a thin white girl. Her blue eyes didn't hold a drop of intelligence as she twirled a golden lock of hair around one finger. Rio walked up to the window and flashed his whites. "Darius Santana to see Ron Silver," he said pleasantly.

The white girl stopped clicking her gum long enough to size Rio up. The way she looked at him you'd have thought that he had just climbed out of someone's gutter. Rio ignored her stare and kept his composure. "And may I ask what this is in reference to?" She asked a little too stink for him.

"I'm here to interview for the marketing position," he said, still trying to be pleasant.

"Oh," she said as if she didn't believe him. "Were you aware that the position requires a degree?"

"I sure am. As a matter of fact I showed mine to Miss Chelsea when I came down for the first interview. Now, if you're done interrogating me, could you tell Ron that I'm here?" Rio walked away leaving the receptionist looking stupid. He could've said a few more slick words that she probably would've had to look up later on, but for now the look on her face was reward enough.

Rio sat in the waiting area thumbing through a book he'd just bought. When he first bought the book he had been skeptical about reading it. Rio mostly read self-improvement books, but *Road Dawgz* turned out to be a good read. After a few moments, the white girl came for Rio. She led him down a hallway to a door marked R. SILVER VICE PRESIDENT. Rio knocked on the door and a deep voice bade him enter. What happened behind that door would be a defining moment in his young life.

Rio stuck his chest out and went through the door. The office was a little more modest than Rio would've expected. The walls were painted an eggshell white with wall-to-wall gray carpet. Posters and other promotional material hung on the walls and were stacked in corners. A simple wooden desk cluttered with papers sat in the middle of the office. Behind the desk sat Ron Silver.

Ron wasn't quite what Rio expected. Over the phone, he sounded like your typical stuck-up white dude, but in person he seemed the opposite. Ron was wearing a blazer over a pair of blue jeans. When he came around to greet Rio, the laces of his white tennis shoes flopped around his feet. Ron brushed his red hair from his high forehead and extended a hand to Rio.

"Darius," he said, smiling. "Good to meet you."

"Thanks," Rio said, taking his hand. "Same here."

"Come on and have a seat," Ron said, leading Rio around the desk. Ron waited until they were both seated before he started speaking again. "So, Darius, what brings you to B and T?"

"Employment, Ron."

"Oh," Ron said, chuckling. "I know that part. I mean, what made you decide to apply with us?"

"Oh, okay. Well, I guess because you guys are up and coming, just like me."

"Good answer, Rio. I also read on your application that you have a degree?"

"Yep, I have an associates degree in computer science and I've been taking marketing courses off and on for a while now."

"Quite the full plate, huh?"

"I try, sir. When you keep yourself busy it allows you less time to get into trouble."

"Words to live by, Rio. Now, B and T is still a relatively small company, but we're on the rise. A lot of people are trying to get with us."

"I know. I saw quite a few people in the reception area."

"Yeah, mostly college kids. They're trying to get their feet wet then move on to a bigger company."

"I hear that, but my plans are a little different, sir. I'm looking for a company that I can not only grow with, but will also provide some sort of stability."

"That's why we're having this conversation, Rio. Personally, I like you. I like how you present yourself and you're smart. I wanna hire you."

"That's what's up." Rio said, enthusiastically.

"Hold on, Rio. I said I *wanna* hire you, but my boss gets the final say. Everything looks good. All we're waiting for now is your background check to clear."

At the mention of a background check, Rio felt a lump build in his throat. He had lied on his application when he first applied to B & T. When he was called down for a second interview, he figured he had beat the background check. Now his little white lie could end up biting him on the ass.

Rio answered a few more questions for Ron. Nothing really job related, mostly stuff about his personal life. Ron was cool as hell for a white dude. He even listened to rap music from time to time. Talking to him was like kicking it with an old friend. Then the phone rang.

Rio tensed up as Ron reached for the receiver. When he first put the phone to his ear, a smile spread across his face, but as the speaker continued, Ron's face became more grim. "But," he protested, "let's just think about this . . . but . . . okay. No, I'm in with him now. Yes, very pleasant young man . . . I understand." Ron hung up the phone and slouched in his chair. It didn't take a rocket scientist to know that the phone call was about Rio's background.

"Everything okay?" Rio asked casually, praying for good news.

"Afraid not," Ron said, his expression grim. "It's about your background."

"Damn," Rio said, lowering his head.

"Jesus, Rio, you should've told me that you had a record."

"I know, but I didn't wanna risk not getting the job."

"I understand why you did it, Rio, but you probably jammed yourself more by lying."

"What was I supposed to do?" Rio asked, watching his chances at getting the job become slimmer and slimmer.

"You could've told me. At least I might've been able to try and sell my boss on you."

"Mr. Silver," Rio said formally, "we both know that the working world got no place in it for a felon."

"Rio, that's true in some cases, but not all. We stand by the phrase *equal opportunity*. Believe it or not, I have a record, too. I did a little time as a juvenile, but nothing major."

"So how did you land this job?"

"Because I learned to put the bullshit behind me. I learned to stop using my criminal record as an excuse and let it motivate me."

"Okay, I know I was wrong for lying, but I'm qualified to do this. I *need* this job, sir." Rio pleaded.

"I know Rio and I'd like to give it to you, but . . ."

"You ain't even gotta tell me," Rio said, standing. "I can't get the job because I got a record." He frowned, already knowing how it would play out.

"No, Rio. You can't get the job because you lied about having a record. Makes it look like you've got something to hide. I'm sorry."

"Not as fucking sorry as I am," Rio said, storming out the door. He pushed the office door with so much force that one of the letters cracked. As he passed the reception area, he noticed the blonde trying to cover up her grin with her hand. At first he was going to let it go, but the devil in him wouldn't allow it. As Rio passed the booth, he leaned in and hog-spit in the girl's face.

"Laugh about that shit, cracker-bitch!" Rio said. The white girl sat in the booth with spit running down the side of her face, as he stormed out of the office. This was the third job Rio couldn't get because of his record. Truthfully, the shit was downright depressing. In today's world a blemish on your record could follow you for the rest of your life. With a need for income and lack of opportunity, some youths turn to the streets to get on. At that moment, the streets didn't seem like a bad idea to Rio.

The day seemed to drag by at a snail's pace for Trinity. She worked the register at the discount store where she made her so-called living, but her mind was hardly on the ninety-nine-cent items they peddled. All she could think of was the baller affair she was to attend with her boo. The manager's menacing glare brought her back to the here and now. It was business as usual at Happy Jack's.

Trinity hated working at the discount store. Sure, it was a paycheck, but $6.75 an hour wasn't worth the bullshit she had to put up with. Happy Jack's was hood in every sense of the word. It was a hood store that sold goods to hood people. All kinds of people came into the store to get what they needed. From TVs to Du-rags, they had it.

The girls that worked at the store were cool for the most part, but between the manager and the customers, Happy Jack's left a lot to be desired. Loupe Garcia had been managing the store since his father, Juan, had purchased the spot two years prior. Loupe's people were from San Juan. Real old school. They were among the upper crust in Latino society, but Loupe was a different story. He was just one of those people that couldn't figure out where he belonged in the social spectrum. One day they might see him in a pair of baggy jeans. Then others, they'd see him in suits.

Loupe had an attitude like he was king shit cause his people were holding. He would always crack on the girls about how gangsta his cock game was, or what he could do for them. The girls that had been there for a while knew what was up with Loupe, but some of the newer ones got caught up in the hype. They learned sooner or later that all that glitters ain't gold.

Loupe came strolling into the store like he was little Napoleon. His mop of oily hair glistened in the flickering sunlight, looking like an extra in *Goodfellas*. The legs of his tan polyester suit whistled as he made his way past the disposable cameras. With 10k gold shining in the store lights, you couldn't tell Loupe he wasn't the shit.

"Whaz up, baby?" Loupe asked, adjusting his crotch.

"Ain't nothing," Trinity said, clicking her gum and glancing at his crotch. "I see you still trying to make small talk."

"Ha, ha. Youz a funny bitch, Trinity."

"Listen," Trinity said, stepping from behind the register. "I could've sworn I told you bout calling me out my name. Keep playing wit me, Loupe, and you gonna catch a bad decision."

"Come on, Trinity. It's okay for y'all to call each other bitches, but I can't?"

"Hell no! I don't fuck wit you like that Loupe. Ma fucka do you call ya momma a bitch?"

"Watch ya mouth!" Loupe said angrily.

"Fuck outta here, Loupe! You always coming out ya face."

"Cause I'm the boss. You keep running your mouth and you won't have a job, bitch."

Trinity had heard him use that word one time too many. Without chipping a nail, she slapped the cold shit outta Loupe. He staggered from the slap in shock, but recovered quickly and lunged at her. With speed almost faster than the eye could follow, she removed a switch-blade from her pocket and drew steel to Loupe's neck. All of Loupe's courage drained out of him and into the blade.

"Go ahead, nigga," Trinity hissed. "I'll dice yo chilly bean–eating ass six ways to Saturday."

"T," Rashawn pleaded. She worked the register next to Trinity's. "Be easy. You know Loupe don't mean nothing by it."

"Fuck that, Ra," Trinity barked, still clutching the blade. "I'm tired of this nigga's mouth."

"T-Trinity, baby," Loupe stuttered. "You know I was just playing, right?"

"Say sorry."

"Huh?"

"You heard me. I want you to apologize to every female in here that you've ever disrespected."

"Come on Trinity. I . . ."

"Come on, my ass. Yo ass has been in need of checking for some time now. Say it, Loupe."

Loupe looked into her eyes and didn't see any sign of humor. He wanted to spit one of his snappy comebacks, but he didn't want to trigger the crazy bitch into sticking him. "Okay," he said humbly. "I'm sorry."

"Please, that shit was lame. Say it with some feeling." she said in a forceful tone.

"Okay, okay. I apologize to all of you ladies for—"

"Beautiful black queens."

"What?"

"Don't play wit me, Loupe," she said, adding pressure to the blade.

"A'ight. I apologize to all of you beautiful black queens."

"For being an asshole."

"Come on, Trinity. Why you gotta OD?"

"Loupe, you say it or so help me . . ."

"Okay, just be cool. I apologize to all of you beautiful black queens for being an asshole."

All of the female workers applauded as Loupe ate humble pie for the first time. For as long as they could remember, Loupe had used his clout to degrade them and crack for sexual favors. Now he was eating his words. Trinity had become the Angela Davis of Happy Jack's.

"Very good, Loupe," Trinity said, tucking her blade. "Was that so hard?"

"Fuck you," Loupe spat, his eyes watery. "You yellow bitch. You've just fucked yourself out of a job. Bitch, pack ya shit and get the fuck out."

Obviously Loupe rediscovered his courage now that he didn't have a blade pressed against his throat, but Trinity didn't give a shit what he said now. Loupe had proven himself to be a coward in front of the same women he had been taking advantage of. That was reward enough. Trinity grabbed her Coach bag and headed for the door. As she was leaving she fake lunged at Loupe, causing him to jump back. The sight of his cowardice gave her a good laugh all the way to the train station.

Rio was feeling the pains of frustration tingling at the back of his head. It seemed like every time he tried to make some sort of forward progress, someone or something was pulling him back. The job interview had turned out to be a waste of time, and to add insult to injury, now he had to go and see his P.O.

Rio was walking up Leonard Street smoking a cigarette when he heard someone calling his name. When he turned around, he saw a thin man walking in his direction. Rio didn't recognize the man right off, but he figured he knew him from back in the days because he was calling out Darius instead of Rio.

"What it is, young brother?" the middle-aged man asked as he caught up to Rio. "Boy, it's been a while since I last saw you."

Rio stared at the man, but still couldn't place him. He was a dark-skinned man who appeared to be in his late thirties to early forties. He wore a pair of no-name jeans and scuffed combat boots. Rio examined the various political buttons that decorated his second-hand jacket with two swords crossing it. The symbol of an activist group called M.E.M. (Minority Education Movement).

"Jamal?" Rio asked, finally placing the face.

"Yeah," Jamal said, flashing a yellowed grin. "In the flesh, baby."

"Damn," Rio said, shaking his hand. "How you been, man?"

"Up and down, brother. You know how it is."

"For sure. So, what you been up to?"

"Man, the pigs had me in custody. Gave me eighteen months on a bullshit charge."

"Damn, sorry to hear that, Jamal."

"Ain't about nothing, brother Darius. I'm back in the world now and still doing my part in the movement. What's up with you? I ain't seen you down at the rec center in a while."

"You know how it is," Rio said, looking at his shoes. "Been a li'l busy."

"I hear that," Jamal said, looking at him suspiciously. "So what's been keeping you from the tutoring sessions?"

"Ripping and running. Just trying to keep my head over water like everyone else."

"Brother Darius, you know you can't bullshit me. Before I joined the movement, I was a stinking ass dope fiend. I know every con in the book. You back on them corners?"

"A nigga gotta eat." Rio said flatly.

"Come on, Darius. That's a poor cop-out and you know it."

"Take it for what you want, Jamal, but real is real. I've been out here for months trying to find work. Ain't nobody in a rush to hire a felon. You don't expect me to starve, do you?"

"Darius, there's plenty of things you could do other than hustle. Down at the center we're hosting a job fair. We've gotten quite a few people jobs recently. Even sent me out on an interview."

"Listen," Rio said, "I don't knock M.E.M. for what they're doing and if I works for you, cool. But on the real, that ain't for me."

"So, you trying to say that you're too good to work an honest job?"

"Nah, I ain't saying that at all, Jamal. What I'm saying is that it ain't for me. I want more for myself, man. I don't knock anybody's hustle, but I can't see myself working a job for five-something an hour and being content."

"What's gotten into you, Darius? You were one of the few young brothers who were really down for the movement and what we were doing."

"And I still am. I think what the movement is doing is a beautiful thing, man. I'm just doing other things right now. Trying to better my situation."

"Man, that's jive. How the hell is slinging poison gonna help better your situation?"

"Truthfully, it won't. I don't advocate hustling, but it's keeping a roof over my mother's head and food in our bellies. I believe in what the movement is doing, but I also believe in survival."

Jamal looked at Rio with saddened eyes and shook his head. "Man, if your father was here he wouldn't dig what you're talking about. He was for the people."

"Well, my father ain't here and I ain't him. I'm Rio."

Rio stormed off and left Jamal standing there. Jamal was a little upset about Rio's attitude, but he couldn't be too mad. He understood what it was like in the streets. You had to get it on your own because no one was going to hand it to you. He felt for Rio. It seemed like more and more kids were succumbing to the call of the streets. All he could do was respect Rio's space and say a prayer for him.

❏   ❏   ❏

Rio entered the department of probation and went through the usual hassle. Since the 9/11 attack, security had been very tight. Before it you could just walk into the building and just get searched when you reached the probation floor. Now you had to remove your belt and go through a metal detector upon entry. It was more like a prison than a government building.

After nearly an hour in the waiting room, Rio was called to see his probation officer. Mrs. Ortega was a motherly looking Puerto Rican woman who wore purple cat-eyed frames. Rio was lucky to have been assigned to her. She was one of the more easygoing P.O.s. Her visits were pretty basic. Have you been rearrested, are you employed or going to school, and do you still live at the same address? After answering her questions, Rio was free to go. After he picked up Trinity's boots, he was going to be on the next thing smoking back to the hood.

Rio clutched his package tightly as he jogged up the steps of the 103rd Street station. One more month of freedom. Going to see his P.O. always made him feel uneasy for some reason. He guessed it was the thought of another bid looming over his head brought it on. Rio's bid had been a short one, but it was long enough to teach him that he didn't like jail. That shit was wack, with a capital W.

As Rio crossed Manhattan Avenue, he spotted two of New York's finest muscling some of the home boys. Rio hated the police. Not only for what they helped do to his father, but because of what they were doing to hoods all over the globe. They were supposed to be the protectors, but they were more like overseers. N.Y.P.D. became more like the S.S.

The neighborhood elders just kept it moving, while the police were slapping the youngsters up. Rio had a few minutes to kill, so he decided to have a little fun. He calmly walked over to the stoop and took a seat. When the police noticed him sitting there, he pulled out his cell phone and began scribbling something on a paper bag.

"Fuck are you doing?" a tall white cop barked. Rio ignored him and kept writing. The tall white cop snatched the bag and flung it into the bushes. "Didn't you hear me, boy?"

Rio looked at the white cop and smiled. "Of course I heard you," he said politely. "By exercising my right to remain silent, I chose not to answer you."

"Oh," the white cop said, putting his boot up on the stoop. "You're a smart one, huh? If I bust that big brain of yours outta your black-ass skull, how smart will you be then?"

Rio scratched his chin as if he was thinking. "Well," he said, standing to face the officer, "there ain't no doubt in my mind that you'd *try* to make good on your threat, Officer Nelson. But what do you think I'm gonna be doing while you're trying to make a vegetable outta me?"

"You challenging me?" Nelson asked.

"Never," Rio said, maintaining eye contact. "Only a fool fights a battle he can't win. I didn't come over here to bust up ya party. I just wanted to make sure that those young men get a fair shake. You know, by the book and all?"

Officer Nelson weighed his options. He could just beat the hell out of the nosy kid, but there was something different about him. He knew Rio was from the hood cause he had seen him around, but he wasn't like the rest. Rio was a smart nigger. The kind of kid that knew the law and could cause a potential problem. In the long run, it wasn't worth it just to jack a few dollars.

"They dirty?" Nelson asked over his shoulder.

"Nah," the Puerto Rican cop said. "They're clean."

"Okay," Nelson said, backing up. "Let's get outta here. I'll see you another time," he told Rio.

"I'll be looking forward to it," Rio said smugly. On the outside Rio looked confident, but on the inside he had been holding his breath throughout the whole confrontation. He'd taken a big gamble with those cops. They could've whipped his ass and taken him in. That would've been a violation and sent him right back to jail. All cause he wanted to prove a point.

"Yo, kid," Mark said, getting up off his knees. "That was some cold shit, Rio. You played crazy brain game on that pig. Good looking." Mark extended his hand, but Rio just shook his head. "What up wit you, Rio?"

"Y'all," Rio said flatly. "Fuck is you niggaz doing?"

"Getting money."

"Mark, who hit you?"

"Come on Rio . . ."

"Fuck that shit, Mark. When I'm on shift, do I ever hit y'all wit work?"

"Nah, but . . ."

"Nah but my ass, Mark. I told y'all, you're too young to be out here. It's fucking eleven-thirty in the morning and you out here getting searched. You need to have ya ass in school."

"School ain't gonna pay the bills, kid."

"Bills? You only twelve, Mark. You still live wit yo mama, what bills you got?"

"You know what I mean, Rio."

"Nah, I don't know what you mean. This shit is wack out here. Give it up while you still can."

"Rio, you're still out here on the grind, so how you gonna tell us not to be?"

"Let me tell you something, my man," Rio said, getting angry. "Don't compare my ma fucking situation to yours, cause they ain't hardly the same. I been doing me to feed me since I was a shorty. My pops is dead and my moms is a wine head. Nigga, you still got both ya parents, they ain't strung out, and they both got city jobs."

"Rio," Mark said, not trying to hear it. "You used to be one of the wildest niggaz out here. My older brother used to talk about you all the time. Everybody out here knows whose project this is. Shit, Prince might hold it in name, but this shit is yours. All you gotta do is reach for it."

"Wow," Rio said sarcastically. "I got a little street fame, big fucking deal. All my rep did was make me hot in the hood and catch me a bid. You think that shit is a badge of honor, then you're mistaken. My one and only dream is to get up outta this shit and be something. Getting out these streets, that's my dream."

Mark still didn't seem moved. "I hear what you saying, but technically you set the standard for a lot of niggaz out here."

Rio's face went completely blank. Mark's words were like a slap in the face. At first Rio was offended, but as he thought on it, was it that far from the truth? Rio had never really thought about how his actions affected those around him. Was he truly some street legend that all of the kids aspired to be like?

"Fuck it," Rio said, walking off. "It's your life, Mark, but you better find a purpose for living. This shit out here," he motioned to the buildings around them, "it's a death sentence one way or another."

Mark watched Rio walk up the hill and shook his head. How could a nigga that had so much potential prove to be such a lame? Mark's level of respect for Rio dropped a few notches. In his mind jail had made Rio a weak nigga. What kind of hustler were you when you have the world at your fingertips and you close your hand? Mark was determined to come up in the game. When his time came, he would take what was his.

Later on that evening, Mark was caught transporting two ounces of powder. All he would be taking now was the five to fifteen the judge was going to hand him. Just goes to show. Every nigga thinks that he's smarter than the ones that came before him.

Prince sat in his plush Harlem apartment staring out of his picture window. He loved to watch the sun set over the city of broken dreams. His city. He had come a long way from his days as a stable boy back home. He used to tend the horses of the white family that he and his mother worked for and dream of owning one. Forty-something years later, he owned his own stable and five fine horses.

The sound of someone knocking on the study door brought Prince out of his daze. Prince turned around in his wing-backed chair and saw Li'l J standing in the doorway. With the wave of a jeweled hand Prince waved Li'l J inside.

"What it is, my man?" Li'l J asked, flopping on the love seat.

"Just thinking," Prince said, offering J the bottle of rum.

Li'l J poured himself a drink and returned to the love seat. From the deep crease in his brow he could tell that something was bothering Prince. After being as thick as thieves for over thirty years, the two knew each other's moods pretty well.

"What's on ya mind, Prince?" Li'l J asked.

"Nothing, man," Prince said, sipping his drink. "Trying to figure this damn Rio kid out. What's his angle, J?"

"How do you mean, Prince?"

"Look at it, J. A few years ago, Rio was my number-one man. I was grooming him to be the next big thing. Then he does a bid and comes home with his head screwed up. Talking about going legit. As sweet as this money is, he must've fell and bumped his head. I just can't figure him, J."

"Well," Li'l J said, lighting his Salem. "As long as we been down I ain't never questioned your judgment, but I gotta ask. Maybe you fingered Rio wrong?"

"Bullshit, J. That kid is it. You know it as well as I do."

"Yeah, Prince. He's a bright kid, but he ain't built for the streets. I tried to tell you when you first recruited him, but you wouldn't listen. You figured because he was so young you could program him. If a nigga ain't street, he just ain't. I don't care how much you try to brainwash him, you gotta be born with it."

"I dig where you're coming from, J, but I don't agree. I know Rio ain't the killing type and I'm cool with that. Hell, we got soldiers for that. But this kid has got his marbles in order in a major way. Rio's little spot always checks in the most scratch when he's on shift. Wanna know why? Cause he's on his job. That kid has got a nose for money. But I need a way to pull him in totally. I even offered him the Columbus side of the projects and threw in Manhattan Avenue. But still he refuses me. What can I do, J?"

"Well, you could always muscle him."

"Nah, can't do that. You try to muscle a kid like Rio and one of two things is gonna happen. Either he ain't gonna perform at peak efficiency or he's gonna make it so you don't wake up in the morning. You can't back a guy like him into a corner. I need another angle."

"You could always run the con on him, Prince."

"Yeah, that could work. But if he wakes up to it the whole thing could sour. Just give me some time, J. I'll rope that kid in. Everyone's got an itch. Rio's got an itch, I just haven't figured out what it is. But when I do, I'm gonna be the one to scratch it. You watch."

5

The party at the Cotton Club ended up being a big turnout. It was mostly full of older players, but a few of the up and coming were also invited to attend. The D.J. played a blend of music to accommodate both crowds. The booth blared out everything from "Lonely Girl," to "Ya Birthday." Prince had thrown quite the little shindig together.

Trinity looked around in awe. Prince's party was like the prom she always wondered about. People were dressed in all kinds of fits. She couldn't remember ever having seen so many diamonds and gold in one spot. Not wanting to come across as a bird, Trinity refrained from staring.

She wasn't looking half-bad herself. Trinity had selected a cute little outfit for the event. Her tight-fitting stretch shirt showed off her tiny waist as well as her 36D bustline. The short leather vest she wore over that went perfectly with her snug leather miniskirt. The skirt was tight enough to show off Trinity's apple-shaped booty, but it wasn't tight to the point where people would've called it trashy. Her midcalf leather boots capped the fit off nicely. Trinity might not have been the most glamorous female in attendance, but she still managed to turn quite a few heads.

Rio was dressed in a similar fashion. He stepped in looking like a runway model in his loose-fitting leather pants, with matching three quarter leather jacket. The white mock-neck shirt he wore hugged his torso, showing off his lean frame. Rio wasn't a health nut but he did work out a few times a week. The ladies in the spot sized the young player up as he moved through the crowd with Trinity on his arm.

Rio noticed the men in the club eyeing Trinity. He didn't get mad though. The way they were lusting over Trinity filled him with pride. Trinity was a bad young chick and she belonged to him. Those other cats might look, but she shared her body with him. They made quite the cute couple in their leather ensembles.

"Rio," she whispered. "This place is off da hook. Look at all the minks floating around this joint. I feel so outta place."

"Please," he said hugging her. "Ain't not a one of these broads can touch you, ma. You the baddest thing in here."

"You always know how to make me feel better, pa."

"What kind of man would I be if I didn't? Here," he said handing her a fifty. "Why don't you go to the bar and get us some drinks while I see if I can find Prince?"

"Rio, I'm only nineteen. They ain't gonna serve me."

"Trinity, you're in a room full of hustlers. Do you think they really abide by the state drinking age? Go on to the bar and stop talking crazy. I'll be back in a second."

Rio went off in search of Prince while Trinity bumped her way to the bar. The fellas in the club were like octopuses. It seemed like every few feet someone was trying to grab her arm or cop a feel. After slapping a few hands and cursing a few people out, Trinity made it to the glass-topped bar. The bartender was a tall dark man who wore a patch over one eye. When he got to Trinity, he glared at her with his one good eye.

"Ah . . ." she stuttered. "Can I get a Hennessy straight and an apple martini?"

The brutish bartender went off to make Trinity's drinks leaving her alone among the wolves. Trinity ignored the advances and tired come-on lines while she bobbed to the rhythm of "To Be Real." After a few minutes the bartender returned with her drinks. When Trinity reached in her purse to pay for the drinks, a huge hand reached over her shoulder and placed a hundred-dollar bill on the bar.

Trinity turned around to see who the latest sorry-ass cat was trying to get a rap. To her surprise she found herself staring at a belt buckle. The man standing before her had to be one of the largest she'd ever seen. He stood at least six-foot-seven without even trying. His bald brown head looked like a dented mailbox atop his shoulders. His broad chest fought to escape the confinement of his blue suit. The hulking man smiled at the bartender, exposing two rows of gold teeth.

"Keep the change." the big man said in a baritone voice.

"Nah," Trinity said, trying to force the fifty on the bartender. "I got it."

"Easy, shorty," the man said. "It's on me."

"Ah . . . thanks." Trinity picked up the drinks and tried to keep it moving, but he blocked her path. "Excuse me."

"Hold on a sec," he said, smiling at her. "Think I can get a dance?"

"Nah, I'm wit somebody."

"It's cool. I just wanna dance, not ya soul. What's ya name, shorty?"

"Trinity. Now, if you'll excuse me." Trinity tried to brush past him, but the big man grabbed her arm.

"Wait up, Trinity," he said, steering her back to the bar. "Damn, girl. Whoever you wit must be a hell of a nigga. Shit, you damn near running back to him. Who you wit, ma?"

"She wit me," a voice to his rear said. The big man turned around and found a familiar face staring at him. He started to bark on the kid, but there was something familiar about him. After a brief stare down, the big man's memory cleared.

"Get the fuck outta here," the big man said. "Little ass Darius. Is that you?"

"Sup, Truck," Rio said, moving between him and Trinity. "I see you met my wife?"

"What up, kid," Truck said, hugging Rio. "Shorty wit you? Man, you got refined taste, kid."

"I know," Rio said, taking his drink from her. "Welcome home, big boy."

"Man, it's good to be home. Them shit holes they use to *reform* us ain't nothing nice. But shit, I ain't gotta tell you, right?"

"Man, I only did a year. That ain't even a quarter of ya bid."

"Yeah, but time is time, right? So, Darius. Or should I call you *Rio?*"

"Rio is fine. Darius is for my fam."

"Right, right. My pops used to tell me about this up-and-coming kid named Rio, but I never put two and two together. I hear you leading in MVP votes?"

"Nah, man. I'm just out here trying to do me."

"Bull shit, li'l nigga. My pops told me he offered you a spot on the team and you turned him down."

"Yep. This ain't a lifetime thang for me. I plan on retiring, not getting retired."

"Yeah, you was always a li'l scary and shit. I remember we used to chase ya li'l bookworm ass around the hood. Hey, you remember that time we dumped you in the garbage?" His comment was directed at Rio, but he kept his eyes on Trinity.

"Yeah, I remember," Rio said, tightening his jaw. "Y'all used to give a nigga hell."

"Shit, we never meant nothing by it. We was only trying to toughen you up. But the way I hear it, you one of the toughest ma fuckas in the hood now."

"You heard wrong, Truck. I'm just me."

"You a class act, Rio. Most niggaz would've jumped at the chance to be a capo in a million-dollar-a-year operation, but not you. Yeah, you content to be a spot runner."

"It serves its purpose, kid. I do what I do and I'm good with it."

"Yeah, okay. If I was you, Rio, I'd be doing all I could to keep this fine young thang living like a queen. You know some niggaz would sell their souls to be wit a piece like this here. You better be careful, son. I'd hate to see a more qualified player snatch her from you. Y'all enjoy your night."

Rio just stared at Truck as he shoved his drunk ass back through the crowd. Truck called his self playing Rio in front of Trinity. Rio's body temperature rose about one hundred degrees. At that moment nothing would've pleased him more than to take Truck's life. Rio was so lost in his thoughts he almost didn't feel the glass crack in his hand.

"Damn," Trinity said, taking the broken glass from him. "You a'ight?"

"Yeah," Rio said, looking at his soaked hand. "I'm cool."

"So, that was Prince's kid?"

"Yeah. Good old Truck."

"That guy gives me the creeps. I can believe that he done killed a few niggaz."

"Fuck that nigga," Rio said coldly. "He bleeds like everybody else. I don't wanna see you around that nigga, Trinity."

"Please, you know I like pretty niggaz like you," she said jokingly.

"I'm serious," he said, glaring at her. "Stay the fuck away from Truck. I don't want him around you and I don't want you talking to him."

"Okay, okay. Damn, what's up wit y'all two?"

"Nothing. Just do like I say."

"A'ight, damn. Did you see Prince?"

"Yeah, I saw him. Kicked it for a few, while you was over here wit ya peoples."

"Come on, Rio. Don't even go there. He was trying to get at me. I didn't even know who he was."

"Oh, so you talk to strange men on the regular, huh?"

"Rio, knock it off. You know I ain't trying to fuck wit none of these cats. I'm happy with you."

"Whatever. Look, let's just get outta here."

"But we just got here."

"I got a headache. You can stay if you want, I'm out."

Rio made his way to the door, leaving Trinity standing at the bar. She didn't know what the deal was between him and Truck, but there wasn't a whole lot of love between them. Trinity downed her drink and followed her man.

Truck sat at a private table in the back, watching the couple and grinning. He knew he'd gotten under Rio's skin. When Prince had written him about his idea of promoting the youngster, Truck had flipped. Who the fuck was Rio to share in the wealth that was promised to him? Truck just laid in the cut and bided his time.

Now that he was home, shit would be a little different. Prince was getting on in years and didn't understand the new age hustler. It was a savage time for the street hustler. Only the most brutal or cunning man could hold sway in the jungle. Truck was a combination of both.

Prince sat in a booth across the room, watching the exchange. When he had seen Truck approach Trinity he had started to intervene. At the last minute, he changed his mind and decided to see how it played out. Truck was an asshole as usual, but Rio handled himself like a stand-up dude. As Prince watched Rio leave, he knew something would come of the altercation. Truck thought Rio was still the same punk kid from back in the days. If he kept pressing the issue he'd find out different.

6

Rio and Trinity sat on the jungle gym, feeding each other fried chicken. It was a nice night so the "hawk" wasn't too bad. Since they had been together Rio and Trinity had spent many a night just sitting outside, talking under the stars. Looking into Trinity's eyes, Rio thought she was still as beautiful as the day they met.

Rio had been walking up Columbus Hill, trying his best not to freeze. He had been a college graduate for two whole months and still found himself broke as a joke and unemployed. He knew his old position on the block was still there for him, but that was a last resort. He had gone through all the trouble of getting a degree and he wanted to put it to some use.

While Rio was making his way up the hill, he noticed a pretty little light-skinned girl, struggling with a shopping cart in the snow. The girl had made it almost all the way to the top of the hill when her cart fell over, scattering all of her goods on the sidewalk. People were just passing her by like they didn't even see her. Rio, being the kind of fella he was, rushed to help her.

"I got it," she had snapped, throwing cans into the cart.

"Damn, shorty," he said, ignoring her protest. "Don't bite my head off. I'm just trying to help."

"Sorry. I didn't mean to snap. It's just that I'm just so pissed off."

"I would be too if I was trying to play a superhero and do it all myself. Why ya man ain't out here pushing this cart?"

"Ain't got one, don't need one, don't want one."

"Yeah, right. Every good woman needs a good man. Or at least should have one."

"And what makes you think I'm a good woman?"

"Your eyes. They say that the eyes are windows to the soul."

"Really? Well, what do you see in my eyes?"

"I see a future where all of the days are sunny. Where the flowers never cease to blossom and hunger doesn't exist."

"My eyes tell you all that?" she asked suspiciously.

"And then some. I left out the most important part."

"Oh, yeah? And what's that?"

"The part where you and I are standing in a stony creek," he said with sincere eyes, "under the spray of a waterfall. I reach into the clear water and pull a ring from the bottom. The ring is made of the rarest stones that shine like tiny suns. I place the ring on your finger and ask you to be my wife."

Trinity turned beet red. She usually didn't talk to strange guys, but there was something different about him. She didn't know if it was his beautiful words or the sincerity in his eyes, but there was something about this man that was special. After he helped her get the groceries back into the cart, they continued to walk and talk. Since that day the two had never left the other's side.

"What you thinking about?" Trinity asked, wiping a smear of grease from Rio's cheek.

"Ain't nothing," he said, snapping out of it. "Just daydreaming."

"Rio, it's two A.M. How could you be daydreaming?"

"Don't be a smart-ass, Trinity. You know what I mean."

"I know, Rio."

"We've been together for a while, huh?"

"Yep. Over a year now, boo," she said smiling.

"One of the best years of my life, ma."

"And many more to come."

"Fo sho."

Trinity got silent for a while. She was just staring up at the moon wondering what it was like up there. Were there ghettos in space?

"What *you* thinking about?" Rio asked.

Trinity thought about it for a moment then said, "Tigers."

"Tigers?"

"Yeah, tigers. Something wrong with that?"

"Nah, nothing wrong with that, T. What is it with you and tigers?"

"I don't know. I just like em. Tigers are beautiful animals. They're so free, ya know? They go where they want and they don't answer to anyone."

"Plus they'll gobble yo ass up."

"You're so silly, Rio. But I do love tigers. I've never seen one up close."

"You've never seen a tiger?" he asked seriously.

"No, what's so hard to believe about that?"

"Nothing, I guess. Just thought that it was a little odd. You've never been to the zoo?"

"Nope. My family isn't the most highly functional one. When I was a little girl, I used to always watch National Geographic and hope to catch a glimpse of a tiger. They just fascinate me."

"Maybe one day I'll buy you one," he said seriously.

"Rio, you're sweet. But I don't think people are allowed to own tigers. Especially not in the projects," she responded in a defeated tone.

"When you got money you can find ways around just about any-thing, T. One day I'm gonna be a rich dude."

"I believe you," she said, stroking his face. "I believe you." They both fell silent again. "Rio," she said, laying her head on his lap. "Can I ask you something?"

"Anything, T."

"Do you love me?"

"Is the sky blue? Is water wet?"

"Stop playing, Rio. I'm serious."

"Me, too. You're the best thing that's ever happened to me, Trinity. I would declare my love for you from the highest mountain. Well, project building in this case. I love you now and I will love you always. Be it in this life or the next."

"If you really knew me, would you still say that?"

"Trinity, I do know you. I know your heart as well as I know mine."

"What if I had a secret?" she asked hesitantly.

"Trinity, unless you were born a man there's no secret that could make me stop loving you." Rio rubbed his hand across her breast and was surprised when she jumped. "What's wrong?"

"Nothing," she said, sitting up. "It's nothing."

"Trinity," he said, turning to face her. "Why do you always shut me out?"

"You don't understand." She sighed.

"Then make me understand. I wanna help, T, but you gotta let me in."

"Rio, sometimes I don't know about us."

"What you talking about girl? We're soul mates."

"Rio, I love you more than waking up in the morning," she said passionately. "If I had it my way, we'd be together for a long time. But you deserve better."

"Trinity, you're talking crazy."

"No, no, Rio. You don't know what you're saying. I'm damaged goods. You deserve someone more like you."

"Trinity, I don't care nothing bout them other niggaz you been with in the past. You're with me now. If I couldn't have you, then I wouldn't want nobody."

"Rio, I want you to understand what you're getting into before—"

"Shhh," he said, placing his finger over her lips. "I know just what I'm getting into. My heart tells me you're right and I'm co-signing it."

Rio pulled Trinity to him and began to kiss her softly. He started at her forehead and worked his way down to her stomach. Trinity moaned in ecstasy as Rio fondled her breast. He used his index finger to play with her clit, while he sucked her nipples like a starved puppy. Rio was about to slide her skirt up, when it started raining.

"Ain't this some shit?" he said, looking up at the sky.

"No." She pulled him on top of her. "Don't stop. I've always wanted to make love in the rain."

Rio lay his leather jacket on the floor of the jungle gym and placed Trinity on top of it. He removed her panties and slowly slid her skirt up to admire her nudity. Trinity had the perfect body. Not a scar or blemish on her. Just as soon as he had the thought, he noticed the bruise on her thigh. He hesitated to ask her about it, deciding to let it slide.

Rio balanced his weight on his palms and slid on top of Trinity. Between the warmth from her body and the cool rain on his back, it was a euphoric feeling. Rio aimed his penis and penetrated Trinity. Her vagina was as warm as beach sand on a summer day, but something was different. It had been about a week or so since they had sex. Yet he slid right in. Usually they had to work on it for a second or two, but not tonight. Something nagged at the back of Rio's mind, but he couldn't put his finger on it.

"Darius," she moaned. "Make love to me. Make me feel like I'm special to you."

Hearing Trinity's sweet voice made Rio forget about everything except giving Trinity whatever she desired. He tried to be a gentleman about it at first. He wanted to take his time and do it slow, but Trinity wasn't having that. She wanted to fuck, not make love. The two went at it for a good half hour. The harder Rio pumped, the louder she screamed. He had to put his hand over her mouth to keep her from waking the whole project up. When it was all said and done, the two lovers lay holding each other. The only sounds that could be heard were their heavy breathing and the last droplets of rain hitting the monkey bars.

Rio lay on the wet steel looking up at the smoke rings his cigarette was giving off. When he was with Trinity he felt like the luckiest man alive. She was everything a man could want. Beautiful, intelligent, and dead nice with her hands. Trinity had quite the reputation as a boxer.

Rio looked over at Trinity and noticed that she was shivering. He moved to comfort her, but she turned away. He loved the shit outta Trinity, but the girl had major issues. Then he heard her quietly sobbing.

"Trinity," he said, sitting up. "What's wrong?"

"I'm okay," she said, sniffling. "Just got a lot on my mind."

"Come on, girl," he said, standing. "Time to get you indoors."

Trinity allowed Rio to help her up without wigging out. The two lovers dressed in silence, each lost in their own thoughts. After they finished dressing they hopped off the jungle gym and headed toward Trinity's building. When they were about halfway there, Trinity's father came staggering out of the building. By the way he was tripping all over himself they could tell he was tore down.

"Shit," Trinity mumbled. "Just what the fuck I need."

"It's okay, boo. He just a li'l tipsy, that's all."

"Well, well," Baker said. "What do we have here?"

"What up, Mr. Baker?" Rio asked. "How you doing?"

"Nigga," he slurred, "how the fuck you think I'm doing?"

"Enjoying your night, sir?"

"Yeah, but probably not as much as you, huh? Trinity, what the hell you doing out this late?"

"Me and Rio just came from the club. He was just walking me home."

"Fuck, I look stupid?" he asked in a threatening tone. "I know what y'all been doing. Trinity, you dropping ya drawers for this nigga?"

"Please, Daddy," she pleaded.

"Please, my ass. You know you hot in the pants and so do this slick-talking li'l ma fucka. Rotten li'l cunt, you been out here fucking this nigga?"

"Mr. Baker," Rio said, cutting in. "I think you've had a little too much to drink. Why don't I walk both of you home?"

"You ain't got to walk me nowhere," Baker said, raising his voice. "Fuck, don't you think you've helped enough? All I know is, that li'l bitch had better not pop up pregnant. If she do, that's yo ass and hers."

"Damn," Trinity said, sucking her teeth. "I'm so sick of this shit."

"You watch your cum-drinking mouth," Baker said, grabbing her arm. "Bitch, I'm ya father. You gonna learn to respect me."

Out of nowhere Baker slapped fire out of Trinity. She staggered backward, but managed to stay on her feet. Baker raised his hand to deliver another blow. His wrist was caught midswing.

"Now, you listen," Rio snarled angrily. "This might be ya daughter, but she's my girl. Trinity ain't no goddamn punching bag. *Please*, don't put your hands on her again."

Baker tried to break Rio's grip, but the man had him in a vise lock. The more Baker tried to struggle, the tighter Rio squeezed. The pressure got so intense that Baker dropped to one knee.

"Rio," Trinity said, placing her hand on his shoulder. "It's okay, boo," she insisted, trying to calm her man. "I'll just go with him."

"Trinity," Rio said, squeezing tighter. "He's got no right to put his hands on you."

"It's okay, baby. I'll be okay."

Rio waited until he had a few feet between them before he let go. Baker staggered drunkenly to his feet. He rubbed his sore wrist and shot daggers at Rio. Rio turned to Trinity and was about to hug her, when he caught a flicker of steel. Baker rushed Rio with switchblade drawn and murder in his eyes. Rio easily sidestepped the drunk's lunge and went into a defensive position. Baker turned to attack again, but the sound of a hammer cocking froze him.

"Fuck is the deal?" Cutty asked, stepping out of the darkness. Cutty was a friend of Rio's.

He was a short, dark-skinned kid with his hair in corn rows. The black army suit he wore made him almost invisible in the darkness. But the chrome 9 he waved was very visible.

"Yo, Rio," Cutty said, moving closer. "You straight?"

"Yeah," Rio said, looking at Baker. "I'm cool."

"Rio," Trinity said. "I'm gonna take him home."

"You sure, ma?"

"Yeah," she said sadly. "I'm sure. I'll call you, okay?"

"A'ight, T. Hit me on the cell if you need me tonight."

"Punk-ass niggaz," Baker mumbled. "Pull a gun on me? That's a'ight. You ain't gonna never see my daughter. Ma fucka if I ever see you around my li'l girl again, I'll kill yo punk ass."

"Keep it moving, old man," Rio hissed. "I'm letting you slide off the strength of Trinity. But, if you keep shooting ya mouth off, I'm gonna let Cutty pop yo ass."

Rio stood there and watched the father and daughter depart. He didn't relax until they were out of sight. When Baker had hit Trinity it took every ounce of self-control in his body to keep from killing the man. People often underestimated Rio because he was skinny. Rio had always known how to box and had been taking lessons in martial arts for the last couple of years. If he really wanted to kill Baker it wouldn't have been hard.

"Fuck was that all about?" Cutty asked, putting his gun away.

"Hood shit, my man. Pure, unsaturated, hood shit."

"Bitch," Baker screamed, when they entered the apartment. "You fucking fast-ass bitch. You and ya li'l drug dealer boyfriend think you're hot shit, huh?" He grabbed Trinity by her blouse, ripping the neck line. "I'm gonna teach you, whore!"

"Daddy!" Billy pleaded. "You're gonna kill her!" Billy, was Trinity's youngest brother. He bore a resemblance to their father, sharing his brown skin and high forehead, but he was slim like their mother. The boy was only thirteen, but he was very protective of his sister. Billy only weighed one hundred pounds on a good day and really didn't stand a chance against the 260-pound Baker. Still, the boy grabbed at his father's arm.

"Unass me," Baker said, slapping Billy to the ground. "I'll kick ya li'l ass for you next. And you, li'l bitch," he growled, turning back to Trinity. "I'm gonna show you how niggaz like him do whores."

"Daddy," she pleaded, "don't, please?" Trinity tried to struggle, but the drunk had her beat. Little Billy lay on the floor and cried as Baker carried his sister into the bedroom.

Baker threw Trinity down on the bed and began to undo his pants. "Little slut whore," he slobbered. "Open up for daddy."

"Please, Daddy," Trinity cried. "This ain't right. We ain't supposed to be doing this."

"Oh, yeah? But it's okay for you to give it to that punk-ass hustler?"

"Daddy, Rio's my man. We're in love."

"Shut up," he said, slapping her. "You keep running ya mouth and I'll put something in it, bitch."

Baker wiggled his little penis out and climbed on the bed. He fondled her breast with one hand and tore at her leather skirt with the other. He groaned like a wild animal as he forced his way into his only daughter.

Trinity closed her eyes as tight as she could and tried to relax. She had learned over the years that if she didn't fight, he came quicker. As Baker pumped away, Trinity wondered how anyone's God could let something like this go on? If only Rio could somehow take her away from this place, she might know what it was like to be happy for more than just a few stolen moments. But that was a fantasy. Trinity's only thoughts now were to let God take her painlessly.

"Yo, y'all niggaz know y'all violating," barked Knowledge. His short, skinny ass looked like a brown Jiminy Cricket. He was a member of the notorious Thieves' Clique. Although Knowledge was one of the smaller members of the clique, he was by far one of the most vicious.

"That's my word," he continued, "y'all niggaz ain't even from over here, how you gonna try to just post up like that? Where's the respect for the block, son?"

"Man, fuck you," Divine said. Divine was an up-and-coming dealer, looking for a block to call his own. He had a medium build with squared soldiers. Divine looked like a Tasmanian devil high on chronic. "Y'all niggaz ain't got no claim to this stoop. This shit says 104th and Manhattan, not Douglass. Fuck outta here." Divine went back over to his peeps and laughed Knowledge off.

"A'ight," Knowledge said, walking away. "Have it ya way, kid."

Knowledge disappeared around a corner. He came back a few minutes later with Shamel and Slugger in tow. Slugger was Shamel's *little* brother. Even though most people wouldn't call his six-foot-four, 250-pound frame little.

"What up?" asked Shamel with his arms spread.

"Ain't nothing, God," Divine said.

"Gotta be something. I know my li'l mans and them wouldn't come get me for nothing?"

"Just a li'l block squabble."

"Block squabble? Fuck it's a block squabble and y'all is from like 110th?"

Normally Divine would've said something slick, but that would've been a fool's move. He knew who Shamel was and what he was about. Violence. Best to bow out gracefully. "You got that, dawg," Divine said humbly. "We up outta here. Peace, God."

"Peace," Shamel said with a disgusted look on his face. "Ain't shit peace." Shamel reached under his jacket and produced a Desert Eagle. "Fuck the dumb shit. Y'all niggaz empty ya pockets."

"Yo, Shamel," Divine pleaded. "This shit ain't—"

"Fuck up," Shamel barked, clocking him with the gun. "Peel, you bitches." Reluctantly, Divine and his crew gave up their shit. They had come down the way trying to open up shop, but ended up getting rode on by one of the most feared and brutal stick-up kids in the hood.

"Big man," Shamel said to one of the boys. "Run that chain, son."

Trinity sat in the tub letting the scalding hot water wash over her. Her eyes were swollen from crying and her face throbbed from the beating. As she sat there under the water, her eyelids began to get heavy. "Soon," she whispered, looking at the empty pill bottle. "Soon."

The little altercation with Trinity's father had Rio pissed. He'd never really liked the man, but he tolerated him because of Trinity. But Baker had taken Rio's kindness for weakness and almost got the business end of the deal. There was no doubt that if Rio had given him the nod, Cutty would've gladly aired Baker out. That wouldn't have really helped much though, and Rio decided just to let the matter slide.

That still didn't change the fact that he was pissed off. Rio genuinely loved Trinity, but sometimes she could be a little much. She could have mood swings and shut him out whenever she wanted, but flipped on him when *he* would withdraw. Another man would've been long gone, but Rio was different in that way. Their relationship, in addition to his own personal problems, was a strain on him. What he needed was to let off some steam. Just then a light went off in Rio's head. He pulled out Precious's number and smiled. It was at that moment he could feel little horns sprouting from his head. When Rio called Precious, she was thrilled to hear from him. After a bit of small talk he cut to the chase. Precious agreed to rendezvous with him.

She originally wanted him to come to her apartment in the Bronx, but Rio didn't feel like going up there. She offered to come to his house, but he was hardly a fool. All it would've taken was for some loud mouth to see them together and he would've been in the doghouse with Trinity. Caution was in order.

Rio told Precious to meet him at a hotel on Fourteenth Street. After he hung up with her, he hopped in a taxi and headed uptown. His first stop was at the bootlegger. He purchased a bottle of champagne and a pint of cognac. Next he went to see Dread to cop some dro. After all that was accomplished, Rio snatched a box of condoms and shot downtown.

It took him about half an hour to make the preparations for his little meeting. He figured that he had a little time to kill since Precious had to come down from the Bronx. To his surprise, she was already waiting in the hotel lobby. She was looking quite sexy, wearing a three-quarter lavender leather jacket and matching riding boots. Her hair was pulled back into a ponytail, exposing her cute face.

"What's up, girl?" Rio asked, spreading his arms for her.

"What's good, sexy?" she said, hugging him around the waist. "I was a little surprised to hear from you after that li'l thing in the club."

"That wasn't about nothing," he lied. "Let me go see what they've got available."

"No need," she said grabbing his crotch. "I already took care of that. We're in 224."

"You're on top of things, huh?"

"Yep," she said, licking her lips. "Hopefully I'll be on top of you before the night is over."

"Be careful what you wish for," he said, leading her up the narrow stairway.

Rio held the staircase door open for Precious to pass. When he looked at her body he couldn't help but to whisper, "Damn." Precious had it. She unlocked the door and went in, with Rio on her heels. The rooms at the hotel weren't the most plush, but they were clean and cheap. Besides, it wasn't like they were vacationing. The room would only be needed for a few hours, if that.

Rio opened the bottle of yak and plopped on the bed. "Here we are," he said, grinning.

"Indeed," she said, sitting in the wooden chair opposite the bed. "You don't know how much I've thought about you since that night, Rio."

"I feel you," he said, taking a sip. "You've been on my mind, too."

"Oh yeah?"

"No doubt. You left a lasting impression on me, girl."

"What was up with those chicks at the club?"

"Oh, I told you that wasn't nothing."

"Yeah, right," she said, twisting her lips. "Red bone looked upset. Was that your girl?"

"Why you ask me that?"

"Come on, Rio. We're both grown. Ain't no need to lie, boo."

"Yeah, that was my girl."

"I figured that," she said, putting one leg up on the chair, showing him that she didn't have on any panties. "It's all good though, baby. Shorty can have you for the long run. I just want you for a little while."

Precious slowly licked her index finger and slid it between her legs. Rio sat on the edge of the bed with his tongue hanging out of his head as Precious began to massage her clit. At first she was just rubbing it with her finger, then she slid it inside her vagina. First one finger, then two, then three. Precious was moaning as she fingered herself for Rio's viewing pleasure.

Rio absently began to rub himself as he guzzled the cognac. Precious stood up and walked over to the bed. Rio reached for the tie on her leather jacket, but she pushed his hand away. She laid him back on the bed and popped the bottle of champagne. Precious began to drink greedily from the bottle while she wiggled out of her leather jacket. Just as Rio had suspected, she was nude beneath it. Precious continued to chug, letting the champagne spill freely down her breasts and stomach. When the bottle was about halfway finished, she put it to the side and began to undress Rio.

She slowly removed his mock neck and began to lick his bare chest.

Precious then proceeded to slide Rio's pants and boots off. She looked at his throbbing penis and found herself getting more excited. She opened her mouth as wide as it would stretch and made Rio's penis disappear.

Feeling the heat from her mouth, Rio almost came. She began to lick and suck him viciously, trying to get him to come, but he held fast. Seeing that this tactic wasn't working, Precious took it to another level. She raised up from Rio and retrieved the champagne bottle. Rio looked at her puzzled as she walked back over to the wooden chair. When Precious placed one leg on either side of the chair he understood what was going down.

Precious licked the mouth and neck of the bottle, making sure she had it good and moist. After lubricating the bottle she slid it inside her. Rio looked on in amazement as Precious began to work the bottle in and out of her vagina. She bucked wildly as she came over and over again.

"You like this?" she asked. All Rio could do was nod dumbly as Precious fucked herself with the bottle.

Rio couldn't hold his composure any longer. He snatched Precious from the chair and threw her roughly on the bed. She tried to claw at his chest, but he slapped her hands away. The last thing he needed was evidence of what he was about to do. After he put the condom on, he jammed himself inside Precious.

Precious felt good to Rio, even through the condom. He stroked her like a wild man as she threw it back at him. After a few minutes in the missionary, he flipped her over and began to stroke her from the back.

"That's what the fuck I'm talking about," she huffed. "Take this pussy, daddy! Take it!"

Rio continued to pump away, trying to smash out Precious's insides. The whole time she cursed and cheered him on. Just as Rio was about to come, she jumped up and pulled the condom off. Rio released himself in Precious's mouth and on her face. She lapped up every bit of it like the good little freak that she was. When it was all said and done, Rio collapsed on the bed feeling ten pounds lighter.

"Damn," she said, wiping her mouth on the sheet. "That shit was the bomb."

"You ain't never lied, girl," he agreed. "We need to do this more often."

"I don't think so, Rio."

Rio looked at her with a confused expression. "What you mean by that?" he asked, sitting up. "Wasn't I good?"

"Oh yeah," she assured him. "You were the best. The thing is, you've got baggage, Rio."

"Baggage?"

"Yeah, you've got a girl."

"That didn't seem to stop you from fucking me just now."

"Listen, Rio, you're everything a girl could want. You're fine, smart, and getting money. Another place and time and I would've loved to have you as my own, but this can't be. You've got a girl and I ain't into breaking up homes. That just ain't my style. I wanted to fuck you, so I did. Now that I've got it out of my system, it's a done deal. No offense, baby, but it ain't that serious."

Rio watched Precious dress and didn't know what to think. He wasn't sure if he should be offended or flattered. It was nothing really, though. He was winning all the way around the board. He had fucked a fine broad and she didn't want any strings attached. He could go back to his life with Trinity and no one would be the wiser. Pretty good deal if you thought about it.

"Thanks, Darius," she said, blowing him a kiss. "Another place, another time." Precious flashed Rio a smile and walked out of the hotel room and his life.

7

Rio sat on the benches in front of 875, watching the flow. It was check day, so the block was jumping. Crack heads of all shapes and sizes shuffled back and forth, trying to get their fifteen minutes of fame. It fucked Rio up to see what a little white rock could do to a nigga's character. People that used to be on top were sucking dick and selling ass to get they high on. It was sad, but a grim reminder of how fucked up it was to be a product of the ghetto.

The way Rio saw it, the whole hustler fiend relationship was a cycle of sorts. A lot of the people who made up the fiend population, sold it at one point or another. They traded their souls for the very illusion they were pushing. Rio watched countless faces in his hood take a fall from the poison. It was sad how something man-made could decimate an entire community. Those who sold the product were harbingers of death. But a good few of them answered to Rio, so where did that put him? Rio knew that what he was doing was wrong, but survival won out over morals.

"What it is, young blood?" asked Sonny. Sonny was a booster from around the way. The hustlers would place orders for certain things they needed. Sonny would steal them from the stores and sell them at a discount or trade them for rock. He was a tall fella, with skin that looked like a Nestle's Crunch. Little pus-filled bumps were scattered on his face, making him quite a sight. Rio hated talking to the man, but he always spent money with him.

"What's up, Sonny?" Rio asked.

"Shit, these niggaz acting all kinda funny with me, man. So you know I had to come to see the man in charge."

"What can I do for you, Sonny?"

"Man," he said, scratching his bumpy face. "A nigga trying to cop a few of them joints."

"So, you know where we clicking, yo. Take yo ass on and cop."

"A nigga a few dollars short, Rio."

"A few dollars short? What the fuck you trying to cop?"

"Dawg, I need two twenties, but I only got thirty-three dollars."

"Nigga, you seven dollars off."

"I know it, brother, but I'm good for it. Check cashing was closed by the time I got out, so I'm hit."

"Sonny, why you always gotta come at a nigga wit a story?" Rio said irritated.

"Man, you know I'd never try to put shit on you, Rio. I've known you since you was no bigger than this damn bench. Check it though. You let me slide this time and I'll hook you up wit this brand new hair dryer I came up on." Sonny pulled a brand-new blow dryer from his bag and held it out for Rio to inspect.

"Go head wit that shit, Sonny," Rio said, pushing it away. "Fuck am I gonna do wit that?"

"Dry yo hair wit it."

"I'm good, Sonny."

"Rio, don't do me like that. You know a nigga gonna be sick. I need to get right."

"If that's the case why don't you just buy what you can afford?"

"Shit, you know how my wife is? Bitch got an oil burner and a half. Check it, if you can't use it, get it for ya girl."

When Sonny mentioned Trinity, Rio realized he hadn't spoken to her in two days. It had gotten pretty ugly the other night, but Baker had it coming. That ma fucka rubbed Rio the wrong way. The only reason he hadn't let Cutty blast on him was cause Trinity had been there. Other than that, Baker's ass would've been stinking. Cutty loved to bust his gun. That's part of the reason Rio kept him around. Why get his hands dirty if he had someone who was more than happy to do it for him?

He didn't like the time lapses between him and Trinity, but that's just how she was. That girl was in dire need of counseling. Rio was no stranger to hard times, but Trinity grew up rough. Ever since her mother died she had to hold her family down. Usually Rio just waited her depression spells out, but this time something didn't feel right. When his shift was over, he was going to make an unannounced visit to her house. Fuck what her daddy said.

"A'ight, Sonny," Rio said. "Give me the damn dryer and go cop."

"Thanks, man," Sonny said, passing the bag off. "You know you my favorite nigga, right?"

"Sonny, get yo conning ass away from me and go ahead. Don't smoke it all up before you get home."

Sonny went into the building and came out smiling like a shire cat. He knew he really didn't run game on Rio. The kid had just given him a play. Rio was the kind of cat that if he could help you out, he would. He was a good dude like that. Even though he only had one foot in the game, the hood loved him more than they did Prince.

Rio watched Sonny disappear into the hood, on his merry way. Suddenly Rio felt cold steel against his ear. He almost shit his pants at the touch of the gun barrel. He'd know that feeling anywhere.

"Break yo self, nigga," a familiar voice joked. Rio turned around slowly and found himself face-to-face with a smiling Cutty. Rio was pissed that his friend would play like that, but he didn't get mad. That's just how Cutty was.

"You was cold scared," Cutty said, tucking the gun back in his waistband.

"Fuck you, Cutty," Rio snapped. "You play too fucking much."

"I'm just trying to keep you on your toes. You're lucky it was me and not another ma fucka."

"Yeah, well, another ma fucka wouldn't be playing with a hammer in broad daylight."

"You still missing my point, Rio. You out here on the grind unarmed like it's sweet. If a nigga comes through here dumping, you hit."

"Man, ain't nobody round here busting nothing."

"You still missing the key phrase here, kid. *What if?*"

Before Rio could continue the argument, Alexis came out of 865. She was looking real good in her short denim skirt and matching top. Alexis was a bad chick. If she wasn't such a sack-chaser, she might've made some nigga a nice wifey.

"What up, shorty?" Rio said, smiling. Alexis just looked at him and sucked her teeth. "Oh, it's like that now, Alexis?"

"Rio," she said, stopping short. "I ain't got no rap for you."

"Alexis, I know you ain't still salty over what happened in the club?" he asked, sounding very confused.

"The club? No-the-fuck-this-nigga-didn't. Rio, fuck what happened in the club. Ya girl is laid up in the hospital and you out here fucking wit these low-life niggaz?"

"Hospital," Rio asked, getting off the bench. "Fuck is you talking about?"

"You serious?"

"Alexis, this ain't even the time for you to be playing. What you talking bout?"

"Rio," she said, covering her mouth. "I'm so sorry. You really don't know."

"Know what?" he asked nervously. "Alex, quit with the riddles. What's going on?"

"Trinity tried to kill herself the other night."

At that moment it felt like God had reached down and caved Rio's chest in. He collapsed on the bench in a heap. He had just been with Trinity and now this?

"Alexis," he said, grabbing her arm. "How? What happened?"

"I don't know, Rio. They said she took a whole bottle of sleeping pills. They pumped most of them out of her stomach, but she's still in pretty bad shape."

Rio's body began to shake. He tried to formulate a coherent thought, but his brain wouldn't work. He couldn't lose Trinity. Not now, not ever. He couldn't take it. Before he realized what he was doing, he had Alexis by the arm and was dragging her to a taxi. Fuck the block. His place was with Trinity.

The cab stopped in front of St. Luke's Hospital on 114th and Amsterdam. Rio tossed a wad of bills through the little window space and hopped out, still holding on to Alexis's hand. He was moving so fast that she almost fell twice. The security guard tried to question Rio about where he was going, but he just kept moving. All he could think of was Trinity.

They finally made their way to the floor where Trinity was being kept. Rio looked around at all the people in the waiting room and noticed they all had one thing in common. Each wore his/her own mask of despair. God have mercy on him if he was too late.

Alexis led him down the long corridor to Trinity's room. Rio just stared at the door, trying to get his emotions in check. He had no idea what to expect in the room so he tried to prepare himself for anything. When Rio finally pushed the door open, he felt his heart explode in his chest.

Trinity was laid out in the single bed with all kinds of IVs running in and out of her arm. From the bruises on her face and arms he cold tell someone had worked her over. Young Billy sat at her bedside reading the Bible. When he noticed Rio in the doorway, he stood up and led him back into the hallway. Billy's face was a combination of worry and anger.

"What happened?" Rio asked in a cracking voice.

"She tried to off herself, man." Billy said, tearing up.

"Oh, man," Rio sobbed. "This is all my fault. If I hadn't gotten into it wit ya pops, this shit wouldn't have happened."

"Rio," Billy said, touching his shoulder, "this ain't got nothing to do with you. You're the one bright spot in my sister's life."

"If it wasn't that, what made her do it?"

"Guess you got a right to know. Alex," Billy said, wiping his swollen eyes, "could you sit with her while I talk to Rio?" Alex nodded and went into the room.

Billy started off down the hall with Rio on his heels. Billy was only thirteen, but he carried himself like a little adult. The kid had been through some shit but he still carried himself like a trooper. Rio had a lot of love for the li'l nigga.

"So, what happened, Billy?" Rio asked.

"This shit is fucked up," Billy said, crying again. "So fucked up, man. I couldn't do nothing for her, Rio."

"Billy, just tell me what happened!"

"She got raped, yo."

"What! Fuck you mean raped?"

"He raped her, man. My sister ain't never did nothing to nobody. From my drunk-ass daddy, to my crack-smoking brother, Rich, she held it down. She always took care of us. That nigga ain't have no right to do what he did."

"It's on," Rio said, trying to control his growing rage. "On my life, I'm gonna kill the nigga who did this, Billy."

"Yeah, you kill that ma fucka, Rio. Kill him and make us orphans. I'll probably have a better life in the system."

"Orphans? Billy, what are you telling me?" Rio asked, grabbing Billy by the shirt.

"He did this, Rio," Billy said, crying harder. "Our father raped Trinity. He's been doing it for years, but I've been too scared to say anything. I'm sorry, Rio. I should've told somebody. It's my fault."

Rio suddenly found himself overcome by a wave of dizziness. He loosed the youngster and fell back against the wall. He played the conversation back over in his head, hoping that he had heard wrong. He knew Baker was a dirty ma fucka, but he never imagined he would do something like this. He should've let Cutty pop him and now he would pay the price for his weakness.

Rio left Billy crying in the hall and wandered back to the room. Trinity was sitting up, talking to Alexis when he got there. When she saw him, she turned away and tried to hide her face. Rio walked over to the bed and took her hand. When he looked into her eyes, all her pain became his. He cried just as hard as she did.

"I'm sorry, Rio," she sobbed. "I'm so sorry."

"Trinity," he said, stroking her hair. "You ain't do nothing wrong. None of this is your fault. If anything, I'm to blame. I should've been a better protector. How could he, well . . . you know?"

"Oh," Trinity said embarrassed. "So Billy told you, huh?"

"Yeah, but don't be mad at him. He was just trying to look out for you."

"I wanted to tell somebody, Rio. But how would people have looked at me?"

"Trinity, I could give a fuck how people look at you. It's how I see you that's important."

"And how do you see me now, Rio?" she asked with tear-filled eyes. "You probably think I'm some kinda freak."

"Never, T. No matter what, you're still my heart," he said seriously.

"You don't have to try and be nice about it, Rio. I'm a big girl. If you don't wanna see me anymore, it's cool?"

"Picture that," he smiled. "How could I live without you?"

"Just stop it, Rio. I'm damaged goods. I could never make a man happy. It's like my father said. 'I'm a filthy whore.'"

"You stop that talk, Trinity. I don't wanna hear it! It's his fault, T. That drunk ma fucka is gonna answer for this!"

"Rio, please. Hurting him isn't gonna solve anything. All you're gonna do is get ya self in trouble."

"It don't matter, Trinity. You're my life. Be it man, woman, or anything living. If it harms you, then I will harm it," he said with a chill to his voice.

"Rio you don't have to prove anything. I just want you to be here for me. Promise me you won't follow up on this."

"I can't make that promise, T. I failed you once and it won't happen again. On everything, I'm gonna make this right."

Rio kissed her forehead and walked out. Trinity called after him but he ignored her. Thoughts of revenge clouded his mind and his judgment. For a long time the beast in him had lain in the cut, waiting for someone or something to wake it. Baker had done just that. The poetic young man was gone, leaving only the monster Rio had tried so hard to keep at bay.

Rio's visit had really upset Trinity. It took a while, but the nurses were finally able to calm her down. They gave her something to help her sleep and escorted her guest out. Trinity lay there looking up at the ceiling and thinking. She didn't want Rio to get himself locked up over her, but it was nice to know that he cared. As if there was any doubt.

Rio was the best thing that ever happened to her. He loved her as no one had before and he showed it every day. Trinity knew that Rio hated hustling, but he did it to take care of his loved ones. She wasn't fond of his career choice, but she didn't knock him for it. His hustle wasn't just for him, it was for them. Rio promised to deliver her from the ghetto and she believed him, so she would stand behind him. Rio hustling wasn't the wisest choice, but it was a way out. As the medication began to kick in, Trinity wondered if Rio killing her father would be such a bad thing.

"You a Gangsta Now"

Rio decided walking home would help him to clear his thoughts, so he set out down Amsterdam Avenue. He walked through the streets in a dreamlike state. Trinity was Baker's daughter, but that didn't give him the right to do that to her. When Rio worked in the Big Brother program at the M.E.M. center, he had met many victims of incest. He wasn't feeling it then and he sure as hell wasn't feeling it now that it was affecting him directly. All he could think about was revenge.

His first stop was the liquor store on 105th. He copped himself a fifth of Hennessy and cracked it before he got out of the store. Rio walked down Columbus guzzling from the bottle, with total disregard for the public drinking laws. The law didn't do shit to help Trinity, so why should he give a fuck about it?

As Rio was crossing the street, Shamel came from behind the center. He called to his friend, but Rio kept stepping. Shamel sensed something wasn't right and jogged to catch up with him.

"Yo," he shouted. "Hold on, kid!"

Rio stopped and turned around. He looked at Shamel as if he hadn't noticed him before. "What up, God?" Rio asked.

"Shit, you. You ain't hear me calling you?"

"I got a lot on my brain right now, Shamel."

"Tell me about it. You looking like you lost ya best friend. Everything cool with you and Trinity?"

"Nah, she in the hospital, kid."

"Hospital? She a'ight?"

"She tried to kill herself the other night."

"Fuck she go and do some dumb shit like that for?"

"She got raped."

"Oh," Shamel said, a little embarrassed. "My bad, Rio. Police catch the nigga?"

"Fuck the police!" Rio shouted, taking another swig.

"Easy, my nigga. You know you can't hold ya liquor."

"Fuck the dumb shit, Shamel. I'm gonna kill me a nigga."

"Rio, now you talking out ya ass. You know damn well you ain't no killer. Chill wit the crazy talk."

"Shamel, I ain't never been more serious about anything in my life. I'm gonna body this nigga."

"Rio, murder is not something to take lightly. Talking bout it ain't the same as doing it. When you see the life draining from a nigga that shit stays wit you, man."

"You see," Rio said, taking a long swig, "that's niggaz problem now. Everybody thinks it's something sweet about me cause I'm a book-smart nigga. After tonight, niggaz is gonna respect me. That's my word."

"A'ight, *killer*. If you determined to roll on the nigga that did this, cool. But I'm rolling wit you. Who is the cat?"

"Her father."

By the time Rio got home his bottle was almost empty and he was pissy drunk. He walked into the apartment and found his mother and Willie on the couch watching television. He nodded in their direction, but didn't speak. He was just gonna go to his room and think. But of course, Willie had to open his mouth.

"Kingpin," Willie said. "What it is?"

"Chilling," Rio said flatly.

"Yeah, yeah. Just coming in from a hard day's work, huh?"

"Yo, stop playing wit me, Willie," Rio said through clenched teeth.

"Aw, somebody's in a fucked-up mood," Willie teased. "What happened, that fine young girl of yours find another nigga to milk?"

"Let me say something to you, Willie," Rio said, standing in front of the television. "Fucking with me is one thing, but don't let me ever hear you talking about Trinity. Don't say her name or even make a reference to her. Do we understand each other?"

"Ain't this some shit," Willie said, standing up. "Li'l nigga get some liquor in him and he grow a spine?" he said in a mocking tone.

"Y'all cut it out," Sally cut in.

"Nah, baby," Willie protested. "I think this li'l nigga trying me. You trying me, boy?"

"Go head, Willie." Rio stood there opening and closing his fist. He tried to calm himself, but the liquor was whispering in his ear. He could feel the beast daring him. Rio turned to walk away and Willie grabbed his arm. The beast leapt into action.

Rio grabbed Willie's arm and hurled him across the living room. Willie fell through the dining room table, sending glass flying everywhere. He tried to stagger to his feet, but Rio tore into him, kicking and punching. By the time Sally was able to pull him off, Willie was a mess of glass and blood.

"What have you done?" Sally screamed. "Oh, Willie," she said helping him up. "Are you hurt bad? Rio, you just like yo damn daddy! Y'all always putting your hands on somebody!"

"But, Ma, I—"

"But my ass. You ain't have no right doing this to Willie," she snapped.

Rio just looked at the two in disgust. That crack-smoking ma fucka came at him, but he was the bad guy? This was some bullshit. Rio took one last swig from his bottle and smashed it against the wall.

"There y'all go," he snapped. "If you hurry, you can catch the last few drops before the carpet soak em up." Rio gave a drunken chuckle and stormed into his room.

Rio ignored the curses Sally slung at him and slammed his door. After making sure he locked it, he moved to his bed and got out his lock-box. He opened the box and looked at the chrome 9 inside. When he bought the gun he never expected to use it, but that was before. As soon as the sun set, his little pretty bitch was going to earn her keep.

Truck hopped out on the corner of 107th with a baseball bat resting on his shoulder. The dudes he had working were standing around looking sus-pect. Truck sized the soldiers up and went to stand in the center of their circle. All three of the men tensed up, but none of them moved.

"Fellas," Truck said, flashing his freshly polished golds. "What's good?"

"Ain't nothing," said Link, who was a skinny light-skinned kid. "We just out here grinding."

"Fo sho," Truck said, spitting on the ground. "How we looking?"

"Everything is straight on my end," Joe said, handing Truck a wad of bills. "That's good money there, Truck."

"Right," Truck said, thumbing through the bills. "What you got for me, Cee?"

"I got eight for you now and the rest when it's finished," Cee said nervously.

"Y'all niggaz ain't finished up here?" Truck asked, scanning the trio.

"My peoples is done," Link said, handing Truck his money. "You know I come on time, every time."

"My nigga," Truck said, accepting the tribute. "You check on that thing for me, Link?"

"Yeah, daddy."

"What was the verdict?"

"Bogus as hell."

"Damn. Oh, well, can't win em all. Yo, Cee," Truck said, switching the bat to his other shoulder. "Let me ask you something and I'm only gonna ask you once. You switching my shit with yours?"

"What?" Cee said, startled. "Hell, nah, Truck."

"I think you lying, man. See, I set yo punk ass up. I kept getting complaints about the quality of our product. At first I wasn't even gonna follow up on it, but something about the complaints nagged at me. That's when it hit me," Truck said, switching back to the other shoulder. "All of the complaints were coming from the times you were on shift."

"Nah," Cee said, backing up. "I wouldn't come at you like that."

"Bullshit," Truck said, punching him in the mouth. Cee staggered but stayed on his feet. "Youz a creep-ass nigga, Cee, and you're gonna answer for it."

"Wait, Truck!" Cee pleaded. "I got yo money, I swear."

When Truck swung the bat it whistled through the air. Cee tried to move, but he was too slow. All you could hear was a sickening crunch. Blood splattered on Link and Joe as Cee's skull caved in. The young man lay on the floor twitching, but Truck wasn't done yet. He continued to rain blows on Cee's back and legs. Only when the twitching ceased did Truck's beating end.

"Punk ma fucka," Truck said, spitting on the corpse. "Y'all niggaz get rid of this body."

Rio woke up that night with a headache and a half. With all the liquor he had consumed, he was lucky he woke up at all. He checked his 9 to make sure it was loaded and cocked. After changing to darker colors, he was ready to hit the streets.

Rio carefully made his way out of his bedroom with his gun in hand. He was in no mood to talk. If Willie came at him for round two, he was going to get one hell of a surprise. The time for petty chatter was over. Any more talking would be done over gun smoke. Fortunately, Rio was able to make it out of his house without incident. Neither Willie nor Sally appeared to be home.

Rio stepped out of his building and took a deep breath. The cool night air seemed to clear his still drunk mind. It was early and Rio had a little time before Shamel would pop up. His stomach was flip-flopping from the booze so he took the time to put something in it.

Rio walked up Columbus Ave lost in his own thoughts. He hated Baker for what he had done to Trinity, true enough. But murder wasn't truly in his heart. Rio was a dreamer, not a killer. He'd leave it to those who were best suited to it. If Baker didn't answer to Rio then he would answer to another later.

Rio made his way to the chicken store on 105th Street, where the entrance and sidewalk held a sprinkling of neighborhood kids. Some were hustling while others were just standing around socializing. Rio slapped palms with those he was cool with and nodded at the cats he just knew by face. After ordering his snack box, Rio stepped outside to smoke a cigarette.

Rio stood outside of the chicken joint, his mind on Trinity. He needed to find a way to get her up outta her house and away from her father. A flicker of motion caught Rio's attention. A young girl was walking up the block with someone who looked familiar to Rio. The figure kept to the shadows, making it difficult for Rio to get a good look at him. As Rio squinted against the glare of the streetlights, the man's features became a little more visible. It was Baker.

As sure as Rio's ass was black, Baker was walking up the block with a girl that didn't look to be more than fourteen or fifteen. The sight of the rapist with the young girl sent Rio's mind into a frenzy. Against his will, his hand dipped under his jacket and clutched the 9. It took all of his strength to keep the heater from barking too soon. Rio decided it would be best to just follow them and confront Baker in a quiet spot.

Baker hung a right on 104th Street and headed toward Amsterdam Avenue. Rio followed almost an entire block behind, watching and waiting. Halfway down the block, Baker and the young girl cut into P.S.145's park. Rio peered from behind the brick wall as Baker led her into the shadows by the benches. Baker disappeared from sight, but it was no secret as to what he was up to. Rio had no intention of letting that monster take advantage of yet another girl. Baker's run would end with Trinity.

Rio took the long route and slipped over the brick wall so he could creep on them. His palms were sweating so bad that he almost lost his grip on the pistol. As he neared the end of the park where Baker had disappeared, he could hear muffled whispers and giggling. He peeped around the final bend in time to see the young girl putting her mouth on Baker's penis. She worked her mouth up and down his shaft like a pro. The reality of it all was the girl was underage, and Baker was disease and Rio was the antidote.

Rio eased along the wall until he was within spitting distance of Baker. He stared at the older man with pure hatred. Baker eyes rolled back in ecstacy, grunted and hissed as the girl sucked him off at various speeds. He was so caught up in the rapture that he didn't even see Rio standing over him. The sound of Rio's hammer cocking split the darkness and caused Baker's head to snap to attention.

"What the fu—" Baker began, but was cut off as Rio aimed the 9 at his heart. The girl looked at Rio wide-eyed, but eased backwards.

"Shut up, nigga," Rio hissed. "What we got here? Oh, you got you a young thang, huh?"

"Li'l nigga," Baker barked. "You better put that rod away, before I fuck you wit it."

"Big talk, you fat piece of shit. I think you'll find that I ain't as submissive as these li'l girls you take advantage of, chump. On ya feet, *Chester.*"

Slowly and very carefully Baker eased his pants up and got to his feet. Baker had considered rushing the smaller man, but the shaky trigger finger and stench of liquor changed his mind. He just stepped to the side and glared at Rio.

"You know," Rio said, "I used to respect you, Baker. Now I see you ain't nothing but a fucking monster. Why you like the babies, huh? You can't get it up for bitches your age or do they laugh at ya li'l dick?"

Baker laughed sinisterly. "What's the problem, Rio? Oh, you mad cause I'm fucking ya bitch? Boo hoo, nigga."

"Watch ya mouth, porky," Rio said angrily.

"What you gonna do?" Baker asked, pulling his knife. "Youz a gangsta, nigga. Do something."

"Put that knife away, Baker."

Hearing the shakiness in Rio's voice, Baker began to inch closer. "Come on, Rio. Buck!"

When Baker thought he was close enough, he lunged for the gun. Baker slapped Rio's firing arm away, sending a wild shot off into the air. When Rio tried to bring his gun around, the unexpected happened.

The young girl jumped on his back and locked her arms around his neck. The whole situation was going to shit.

Baker used the girl's distraction to try and wrestle the gun from Rio's hand. The two struggled for control of the weapon and it suddenly went off. Baker's eyes bugged from his head as he spat blood in Rio's face. Baker made a muffled sound and collapsed. Rio just stood there staring as blood poured from Baker's gut and mouth. He had seen dead bodies before but never this close up. It was a sight that would stay with him for the rest of his days.

Trinity jerked awake from a nightmare. She stared around her hospital room as if she was seeing it for the first time. A ghostly breeze materialized out of thin air sending a chill down her back. Something in the world was terribly wrong and Trinity felt it.

A shriek behind him caused Rio to spin around with his pistol raised. The young girl was wailing at the top of her lungs about how he had killed her man. Rio tried to calm her, but she was past the point of reasoning. When he tried to clamp his hand over her mouth, she tried to take a chunk out of his finger. Seeing no other option, Rio grabbed the girl by her hair. Her brown eyes glazed over as he put the hammer to her chin and pulled the trigger. The girl's body jumped from the impact of the bullet that slammed into her skull, and she died in Rio's arms.

Rio dropped the body and jumped back. He kept looking from the smoking gun to the two victims on the ground. His brain raced in every direction but the right one as he tried to understand what he had done. He was standing in a schoolyard with two dead bodies and the murder weapon. He was shocked, but he wasn't stupid. Rio took off running.

He found a pay phone on Amsterdam and tried to call the one person who could help him. His hands were shaking so violently, he almost couldn't dial the phone. It took him three attempts, but he finally reached the person he was looking for. "J," he said, out of breath. "Let me speak to Prince."

❑ ❑ ❑

A few miles north, Prince sat on the phone listening. The more the panicked Rio became, the broader Prince's smile got. Prince hung up with Rio and reclined in his seat. Li'l J stared at his friend in utter bewilderment.

"What's up, boss?" he asked. "You smiling like the cat who swallowed the canary."

"That was our boy, Rio."

"What he rapping bout?"

"Hmm . . . seems like he's had an itch. Why don't you go pull the Lincoln around? While you're at it, call them Grave-Digger Boys and have them bring a kit to 105th and Amsterdam."

When Li'l J pulled the car up on 104th he spotted Rio standing across the street looking suspect as hell. He kept pacing and his cigarette shook whenever he tried to take a pull. All J could do was shake his head. In all truthfulness, he felt bad for Rio. That's the real reason he kept trying to sway Prince from recruiting Rio. The boy reminded him of his youngest son, Johnny. Johnny had been killed over a whore and a fifth of liquor.

Li'l J idled the car and looked at his friend in the rear view. Prince licked his money-hungry chops at the thought of finally being able to rope his number one pupil. Rio had no idea what plans Prince had in store for him. Rio would play the game now whether he wanted to or not. Even though J felt bad for him, this was the price you paid when you slept with the streets. She was a jealous bitch who would always find a way to bind you to her. Rio would learn these lessons and more as he walked the road of the damned.

J stepped out of the car and held the door for Prince. Prince adjusted the .45 that hung from a holster under his overcoat and moved to greet Rio. Rio hugged Prince back tightly when the two embraced. From the distraught look on his face, Prince knew he had him.

"What's up, son?" Prince asked, grinning like a proud father. "What troubles you so much that you call me out of my house tonight?"

"My bad," Rio said sniffling. "I didn't mean to take you from what you was doing, but I didn't know who else I could call. Man . . . I did some dumb shit, Prince. Can you help me fix it?"

"Rio, I got pull in this city and I can make a lot of shit happen, but these things cost."

"Prince, I feel you. I got some money saved up and I could—"

"Rio," Prince said, cutting him off. "I seriously doubt if you got problem-fixing money. Even if you did, I wouldn't take it. You are as much a son to me as Truck or Melvin. If I can do this thing for you, then I will."

"Good looking, Prince."

"Where?"

"In the schoolyard. Down by the end."

"J," Prince said, with a nod of his head. Li'l J made his way across the street and into the schoolyard. After what seemed like hours, he was back with a grim look on his face.

"Well?" Prince asked.

"It's a bad deal," Li'l J said. "One fat stud and a young girl. Ain't too much of a mess, but it's ugly."

"Prince," Rio said nervously. "Let me explain . . ."

"Baby boy," Prince said, cutting him off again. "You ain't gotta explain nothing to me. I know your heart was in the right place regardless of what you done. Get in the car and wait on me." Rio bowed his head and got into the Lincoln. Prince started across the street and motioned for J to follow him. When they were out of earshot, Prince spoke.

"Dig it, J. Call them boys and have em clean that shit up. We gonna take Rio and get him cleaned up." J nodded his head and went off to fulfill his boss's wishes. Prince took a slow stroll to the car and mentally went over his plan to bind Rio to him.

After receiving Prince's orders, Larry and Lester Batis, aka the Grave Digger Boys, set out to do their work. The twins strolled around to the rear of their fifteen-passenger van and began to unload their supplies. They removed two dollies and two large boxes from the truck. They wheeled the dollies over to the area J had directed them to and began with their task.

The first thing they did was get each body into one of the boxes. The girl went in easy, but Baker's bulk required both their efforts. Once the bodies were packaged, they began to work on the crime scene. They each pulled out packages of baby wipes and ninety-nine cent bottles of bleach. They throughly doused and scrubbed anything Rio might've touched and scrubbed all traces of blood away. The area didn't really require much cleaning though. Come sunrise, the whole park would be teaming with students and faculty. Even if the police were to discover that something had gone down, there would be way too many sets of prints to trace back. After the clean up, the Grave Diggers wheeled their packages back to the van where they were loaded and transported back to the spot to be dismantled.

Rio seemed a bit more relaxed on the ride back. Prince had handled his little problem with no questions asked. It takes some kinda cat to help you cover two murders and not even ask you why you did it. Rio knew he owed Prince a great debt, but he was yet to find out how great.

"What's up, baby boy?" Prince asked.

"Nerves a li'l bad, that's all," Rio responded. "I ain't never . . . well . . . you know?"

"Sure, kid. It creeps all of us out at one point or another. Once you get over the initial shock, you'll be peaches again."

"I dunno, Prince."

"Trust me, kid. You ain't did nothing wrong. I blame that poor slob for getting himself croaked. If he hadn't done what he done, he wouldn't be stiff."

"I guess you're right, Prince."

"Sure I am. Don't worry about nothing, kid. A few greased palms and everything will be square."

"I owe you, Prince. Big time."

"Glad you feel that way," Prince said with a grin. "Now let's discuss the method of payment. Getting something that big covered up don't come cheap, kid."

"I got ya, Prince. I told you I had some money saved up and I could work the rest off."

"Not quite what I had in mind, but close." Rio didn't like where this was going. "Rio," Prince continued, "you've been a good earner for a lot of years. I think it's time you stepped up."

"Prince, you know I ain't trying to—"

"Nix that shit," Prince barked with a wave of his hand. "You clean your ears out and listen to me, kid. You in a whole different league now. Ain't no more part-time hustler. You're in now. On this level we play by different rules. You asked me for something and I gave it, now I'm asking you for something. What's it gonna be, kid?"

Rio heard the question, but it was more like a statement. Price had him by the balls in the worst kind of way. Becoming a Capo was never something Rio wanted for himself. But now it seemed as if he had no choice. If he refused Prince there was no telling what could happen. Prince could very well expose the murders he had just committed. What choice did he really have?

"A'ight," he said sadly. "I'm in."

Li'l J watched the exchanged with a heavy heart. He felt bad for the young boy. Prince was a sly character. He had walked Rio to the gates of hell and ushered him through. J had seen so many youngsters get roped up by slick-talking niggaz like Prince. It was sad to see one black man contribute to the decimation of another, but that was the game.

Rio walked into his apartment building about three A.M. He walked down the hall and put his ear to the door and listened before entering. Through the fire door he could hear a soft melody floating on the air. He slipped into the apartment and spied his mother sitting on the couch. Willie's bandaged head rested on her lap as she stroked it lovingly. Sally was bent over Willie crooning a beautiful Billy Holiday classic. No matter what she did or who she chose to love, it wasn't anybody's business but hers.

He started to apologize to Sally but decided against it. Best to let sleeping dogs lie. Instead Rio crept through the darkness to his room. Rio locked his door, flopped down on his bed, and closed his eyes. No sooner had his eyes closed than they fluttered back open. The faces of those bodies in the park haunted him. He got up, shuffled through his jacket pocket and fished out a pill bottle. He looked at the purple and white tablets and shook his head in frustration. Prince said that just two of them would make you sleep like a baby. Rio had already downed four and still couldn't relax.

Then he noticed the digital readout on his answering machine signaled four messages. Rio didn't feel like talking to none of his peeps, but he checked his messages in hopes that Trinity had called. The first message was from Shamel: YO GOD . . . WHAT'S REALLY GOOD WITH YOU? I THOUGHT WE WAS GONNA HOOK UP, SON. HOLLA AT ME WHEN YOU GET THIS. Rio mashed the ERASE button. Shamel was probably somewhere laid up with a girl at that hour of the morning.

The next message was from Cutty: WHAT UP, MY NIGGA? I JUST CALLED TO CHECK WITH YOU. NIGGAZ SAID YOU WASN'T FEELING SO HOT. HIT ME ON DA JUMP OFF. ONE. Damn, word in the hood traved fast. Rio wondered how many other niggaz would call to give their grief-ridden speeches? Of them all, Cutty and Shamel are the two he felt the most love for.

The next was a hang-up. As the fourth message began to play, Rio was going to just cut the machine off. The familiar voice that came from the speaker froze his hand. RIO . . . AH, THIS IS . . . IT'S ME . . . TRINITY. I CAN'T TALK LONG CAUSE THE SECURITY GUARD IS LETTING ME USE HIS CELL. LISTEN . . . I JUST WANTED TO SEE HOW YOU WERE DOING. THEY SAY I CAN COME HOME TOMORROW MORNING. YOU CAN COME GET ME . . . WELL, IF YOU WANT? IF YOU DON'T WANT TO . . . I UNDERSTAND. BYE.

Rio played the message two more times before he blinked. The sound of Trinity's voice seemed to pull some of the tension out of him. She wasn't there with him in body, but she rode with him in spirit. He wondered how she would take the news? He felt like such a hypocrite. He was always pushing Trinity to do well and make something of her life, but look at the rotten mess he had made of his. Most cats would look at being a Capo in Prince's crew as a badge of honor, but to Rio it was a badge of shame.

No point crying about it now though. Rio had shot dice with the devil and crapped out. He had to ride it out now no matter what the outcome. One thing was for damn sure, Rio might not have wanted to play the game, but he'd be damned if he was gonna lose. He would milk Prince's little circle for all it was worth and do the right thing with his money. He had taken Trinity's father from her, so the least he could do was make sure that she was taken care of. She would have the cleanest living from the filthiest money.

Truck fidgeted on the bar stool as Li'l J applied stitches to his damaged hand. Skin hung loosely from his knuckle, but the bleeding seemed to slow from a spill to a trickle. Li'l J looked at Prince's eldest boy and shook his head. Truck's hand was busted up pretty good, but he had managed to avoid serious injury. If he had lost any of its mobility, it would've served him right because he had done it to himself.

After J dropped Rio off, he had escorted Prince back to his plush apartment to meet with Truck. Prince broke the news to Truck about the young soldier's promotion. Needless to say, Truck hadn't taken it well. He had thrown a fit, cursing and smashing things in his daddy's office. It was slamming his fist through the glass bar that caused the injury to his hand.

Prince had made it clear that no matter how much of a fit Truck threw, Rio would be Capo of Douglass projects. This was his will and Prince's will was law. It wasn't as if he had left Truck out of the loop. Prince had given his eldest sole control of his crack houses from 105th and Amsterdam to 112th and Morningside. Truck still wasn't content with this. Douglass was one of Prince's most profitable spots and Truck felt as if it was only right that he have it. The nine-block kingdom that Truck was given produced enough paper to keep everyone happy, but in Truck's warped mind it didn't compare to controlling a city housing project. Truck felt that it was a slight to his honor. A slight that wouldn't soon be forgotten.

Rio arrived at the hospital bright and early the next morning. When he walked into the room, Trinity and Alexis were sitting on the bed chitchatting. "Sup, y'all?" Rio mumbled.

"What up, Rio?" Alex said. Rio walked over and kissed Trinity on the forehead. She held his face in her hands and he pulled away slightly. Knowing what he had done to her father, Rio couldn't look her in the eye. She noticed his strange behavior, but didn't comment on it.

"Thanks for coming," Trinity said, trying to muster a smile.

"Ain't nothing," he said, hugging her. "You my girl and I'd do anything for you, ma. You heard? *Anything.*"

Something about the way Rio said that bothered Trinity. She had known Rio long enough to know when he wasn't himself. There was something very peculiar about the way he was acting. When he touched her there wasn't any warmth behind it. And as much as they loved to gaze into each other's eyes, he would barely meet hers. There was a small part of Trinity that wondered if Billy's phone call had anything to do with Rio's strange behavior.

Billy had phoned Trinity earlier that morning with disturbing news.

Their father had pulled another all-nighter. From time to time Baker was known to disappear overnight on one of his drinking binges, but they would always be able to find him somewhere in the hood. This time was different. Billy had been to all of Baker's haunts, but could find no sign of him.

Billy, having an overactive imagination, feared the worst. He ran down the line from kidnapping to abandonment. All in a quest to justify their father's disappearance. One theory had offended Trinity personally.

Billy wondered if maybe Rio had something to do with their father's untimely vanishing. At the time, Trinity had dismissed the idea and made Billy promise never to speak of it again. But with the way Rio was acting, maybe Billy wasn't so far off? The situation would definitely bear some looking into.

"You bout ready?" Rio asked, breaking into her thoughts.

"Ah . . . yeah. Just let me get my paperwork." Trinity busied herself gathering up the release papers and tried to push thoughts of foul play from her head. But no matter how much she tried, she couldn't stop thinking the worst. What if Rio and Baker did get into it and Baker got killed? There were ups and downs to this. She could finally stop playing the twisted game her father had subjected her to for so many years. And she could finally commit herself totally to Rio. But then . . . if Rio had kill her father he would surely get the chair if it ever got out. And what about Billy? Would he end up a product of the system?

Trinity knew she had to step to Rio about this, but how to approach him? There was no doubt in her mind or heart that she was gonna ride with her boo. Whether he did it or not she knew he could justify it. Her man's word was good enough for her. Trinity's only problems now was, keeping her man out of jail and her little brother out of the system.

Cutty peeped from the lobby window of his bulding, scanning the block for possible trouble. After seeing that all was well, he stepped from the shadows and into the noon sun with a light bop. He had nabbed a quick $3,700 from a sting he had pulled that morning. He was going shopping on the niggaz he had robbed on Ninety-fourth Street.

As Cutty came through the parking lot of the projects, he spotted his niggaz Boo and Kev. Those two jokers were the Mutt and Jeff of the stick-up game. They were determined to become notorious, but just couldn't seem to get it right. They got a big *E* for effort though. These cats would bust you frame if they thought you had some change. Cutty respected their gangsta and they respected his.

"Fuck you two criminals doing in the good part of town?" Cutty asked playfully.

"Oh shit," Kev laughed. "My nigga Cutty. What it be like?"

The three thugs exchanged hugs and insults. It was good like that between them. If the two had a leader, it would've been Kev. He was a tall handsome kid with copper-colored skin. Kev was one of those kids who didn't have to do dirt. He was educated and had a nice little place on the lower end of town. He did dirt cause he liked to. Kev was fucked up like that.

Boo was a bit different. He was a wide-bearded dude, who wore his hair in a large nappy fro and had limbs like tree trunks. Boo constantly scanned the area with his good eye in search of enemies or a possible vic. Boo was a mad dog that could never get full. He was one of those dudes that was on some *"Fuck you, ya momma, and yo kids. Gimmie mine, nicca!"* The only thing he respected was paper. Wasn't nobody in the hood crazy enough to hang with Boo other than Kev. He had a way with the big man.

"What up, Cutty?" Boo said in his raspy voice. When he spoke, it sounded like someone firing up the engine on an old junker. This came from the scar he sported across his throat. Boo had the scar, but the kid that gave it to him was wearing wings.

"Chilling," Cutty responded. "Just came out."

"Us, too," Boo said, looking around. "Say Cutty, you fuck's wit these niggaz over here. Who's winning?"

Cutty looked at Boo and shook his head. The youngster was always looking to come up. "I can't call it, Boo. I do me and they do them. As long as you ain't fucking wit none of my people, do you."

"Drop a nigga a hint or something. I know you know who's clicking?"

"Come on, Boo. You know I don't rock like that, son. Finger-pointing ain't my thang."

Boo started to press the issue but Kev cut him off. "Come on wit that, yo," he warned his friend. "No disrespect, Cutty. My man ain't mean nothing by that."

"Don't sweat it," Cutty said. "I ain't offended. So other than trying to bang a ma fucka, what y'all up to?"

"Shit," Kev said. "We just out here trying to come up, you know?"

"Fo sho."

"Nigga, you need to get back in and give some of us undereducated ma fuckas some direction."

"Nah, Kev. They giving out too much time for that shit, kid."

"Fuck, Cutty . . . nigga, I know a bid ain't made you chicken-hearted?"

"Li'l nigga, don't even come at me like that. My gun hotter than ya momma house on a summer day. I'm the kinda dude that'll do whatever I gotta do to get some. I've just found that there's mo money in one game than the other. I'm good with my choices in life, kid."

"I know that's right," Kev said, giving Cutty dap. "You always was a hustling nigga."

"And I'm always gonna be, Kev. Take the advice of a nigga who knows. Always have a hustle to fall back on. A true get-money nigga will always know of other ways to clock cheese. If one well goes dry, drink from another one. Simple as that."

"Water and cheese," Boo mumbled. "We out here thinking about money and this nigga planning a picnic?"

Kev and Boo looked at Cutty dumbfounded. Most of what he had said went over Boo's head, but Kev was the smarter of the two. Kev listened to what Cutty had dropped on him and cracked a half-smile. Kev understood what the older head was talking about. Cutty was a gangsta, there was no doubt about that. But more than anything he was a thinker. His only problems were, he was always thinking on how to gain profit from negative shit. Rio had often tried to sway him, but some people were just set in their ways.

Kev tapped Boo and started walking up the block. It was always good talking to Cutty. The boy had a lot of wisdom to be so young. Sometimes he and Kev would bump into each other on the streets and talk for hours. Nothing in particular, just swapping knowledge. It was all good, but it still didn't change the fact that Kev's pockets were leaning. After checking his weapon he and his partner went off to catch a vic.

Trinity put her key in the front door and prepared herself for the worst. Surprisingly enough, the house was empty. She walked inside and held the door for Rio. He paused for a long moment before he crossed the threshold. The funnier Rio acted, the more afraid Trinity became.

"Looks like no one's home," Trinity said, trying to strike up a conversation.

"Guess not," Rio said, looking around. Being in the house of a man he had killed was creeping him out in a major way. Rio kept feeling like Baker was going to spring out of a closet and grab him. Between the bodies and the pressure of his new career move he felt like he was going to wig out any minute. He needed to clear the air and see just where he stood with Trinity. Before Rio could open his mouth, Trinity began speaking.

"Rio," she began slowly. "We need to talk."

"I was just going to say the same thing, T."

"Oh, okay. Well . . . look, I guess you deserve some sort of explanation."

"Trinity, it's cool. If you don't wanna talk about it, I'm fine with that."

"No, Rio. I think I need to talk about it. The thing with me and my father . . . well, I don't know exactly how it started, but it's been going on for a while. When it first happened I thought it would be just a one-time thing, but it wasn't. He . . . it went on for years. The older I got the more often he tried." Trinity paused, trying to gather herself. "I'm sorry I didn't tell you. I was just so ashamed."

"Trinity," he said, putting his arms around her. "You ain't do nothing wrong. Your daddy was just sick, that's all."

"I know, Rio. I just always hoped it would get better." Rio held her close to him for a long while. Trinity lay with her head on his chest as he rocked her. She felt so safe in Rio's arms. It was a feeling she wanted to go on forever. Then it hit her that Rio had spoken about her father in the past tense. Before Trinity ask him about it Rio broke the silence.

"Trinity," he whispered. "I got something I need to tell you. I'm trying to get my thoughts together, but it's hard."

"Take your time," she said, patting his hand.

Rio looked around the living room, trying not to make eye contact with her. After taking a breath, he continued. "Remember how you used to sometimes ask me if I would reconsider Prince's offer?"

"Yeah, and I'm sorry, Rio. I had no right to suggest that to you. I know how you feel about that kinda stuff and I should've never even brought it back up. Rio—"

"Hold on, T," he said, cutting her off. "Just listen for a minute. I know I'm the one always taking about doing the right thing and doing something more with my life. See . . . the thing is, sometimes life deals you a bum hand and you gotta play it out. Even if it means going against what you believe in."

"Rio, what are you saying to me?" she asked nervously.

"I took it, T."

"Took what, Rio? What are you talking about?"

"I'm in. Prince made me a Capo," he said, sounding defeated.

"A Capo," she asked in disbelief. "What do you mean, a Capo? Rio, tell me you didn't?"

"I'm with Prince, now."

Trinity was overcome with both fear and anger. She couldn't believe that he would go and do something so drastic without consulting her. Trinity had been a little selfish when she first suggested he take Prince up on his offer. It's not that she wanted to see him in harm's way, but the way she was living threatened to drive her crazy. If Rio was on Prince's payroll, they'd be able to move a whole lot sooner. After seeing how adamant he was about not doing it, Trinity deaded the subject and tried to figure something else out. Now Rio was telling her that he had had a change of heart? Something was definitely not right. There was no way Rio would've made this kind of move. Unless he had no choice.

"Rio," she said, grabbing his arm. "Are you fucking crazy? Tell me you're playing."

"Nah, T. A nigga got into a situation and ya man helped out. I owe him."

"Owe him?" she barked in a heated tone. "Rio, you don't owe that nigga shit. You ya own man, Rio, and that's why I fuck with you. You standing here saying that you just became a part of one of New York's largest drug cliques, cause you owe a nigga? I don't buy that, Rio. Come wit the real."

"A'ight," he said, steering her toward the sofa, "sit down, boo." When Trinity was seated, he said, "I don't know how you're gonna take this."

"Rio, I'm down for you from now till the day I shut my eyes. Just keep it real."

"A'ight. After you told me about . . . well, you know? Anyhow, I didn't take it so good. Trinity, I love you as much as a dude can love his own mother. My feelings for you is deep like that. For your father, or any other nigga to do something like that . . . I couldn't accept it, Trinity. It ate at me until I couldn't control it. I felt what he did to you was the most heinous of crimes. A crime punishable by death."

Trinity sat there stone-faced. She knew what he was saying, but her brain couldn't translate it to her. Until that moment she had only entertained the thought in her mind. Now, as her lover spilled the truth at her feet, she knew.

She just sat there looking at Rio's tear-streaked face and said nothing. She felt a strange mixture of utter shock and joy. The weight she had carried for so long was now lifted. Her father was gone, but there wouldn't be much of a difference in her day to day life. Trinity always kept a job and pulled her own weight. She hadn't asked her father for money since she was sixteen. She didn't need him financially and she damn sure didn't need him morally. What's done is done. Baker was gone and hating Rio wouldn't bring him back. In a strange way, she felt like thanking him.

"Trinity," he said, touching her cheek. "You understand what I'm trying to tell you?"

After a long pause, Trinity found her voice. "Yes, Rio. I heard you."

"Listen, T. I'm sorry, God knows I am. But I wasn't in my right frame of mind. Trinity, I swear to you—"

"Rio," she said, cutting him off. "I . . . I kinda knew. The other night I had this weird dream. I can't remember what it was about, but I woke up thinking about my father. Rio, I know you didn't kill my father cause you're some kinda monster. You did what you did because he hurt me. I know I should be cursing you or trying to turn you in, but I'm not. I understand, baby. I understand."

Rio exhaled and wiped his face with the back of his hand. He hadn't known what to expect when he had dropped the bomb on her. But Trinity was gangsta with hers. He didn't think it was possible, but at that moment he found himself loving her a little harder.

"It's gonna be okay," she said, rubbing the back of his head. "But what should I do if the police come around?"

"Just be cool," he told her. "Prince's people took care of everything. When you wake up tomorrow, call down and report the old man missing. Even if his body turns up, which I doubt, you got an airtight alibi. You was laid up in the hospital when he caught it. Everything is gonna be fine."

"I hope so, Rio. And speaking of Prince, what up wit that situation?"

"It is what it is, T. I made a deal with the devil and now I gotta ride it out."

"Ride it out? Nah, you thinking too small. I don't agree with what you've managed to get yourself into, but we gotta deal with it. If we gonna play the game, we gonna play to win. Forget riding it out, ride this bitch to the top."

"So you wit me, ma?"

"That ain't even a question, Rio. All we got is us."

10

Because of the nice weather the corner of 104th and Columbus was packed. People were just out talking shit and enjoying the weather. Shamel was posted up off to the side with his man, Knowledge. They passed a bottle between them trying to size up a potential victim. Their attention was temporarily drawn away when Freddy came from behind the center looking all crazy.

Freddy was just your average dude from round the way. He didn't hustle or anything, he was a working dude. He usually kept his appearance up, but today was different. His hair was uncombed and it looked as if his clothes had been slept in. His eyes were red and sported circles like he had been crying.

"Sup, y'all?" Freddy asked.

"What up," Shamel responded. "You a'ight, kid?"

"Nah, man. A nigga fucked up. Me and Moms was worried cause Tracy ain't come home from school since like yesterday."

"Fuck outta here? Ya sis only like thirteen or so and she hanging like that?"

"Nah," Freddy said, lighting a cigarette. Which was odd because he didn't smoke. "That's just it. Tracy doesn't stay out. Plus this lady from my mom's church said she thought she had seen Tracy walking toward Amsterdam with some dude."

"Wow, that's some heavy shit, Freddy. I'll keep my ear to the dirt for you, kid. I hope she comes home soon."

"Me, too, Mel. Me, too." Freddy continued on his way, leaving the two crooks to ponder the latest news.

"That's fucked up," Knowledge said, shaking his head.

"Ain't it though," Shamel co-signed. "You hear anything on the Vine?" The Vine was a network of people from various neighborhoods and cliques that swapped info. Shamel and his people had set that up to keep tabs on who was getting money and where they were laying their heads. The Vine was mostly composed of big-mouth chicks who liked to stay in some shit. Some of the dough getters got hip and tried to shut it down, but that proved to be damn near impossible. All people in the hood did was gossip.

"Nothing really," Knowledge said. "Not that I could think of. Oh . . . matter fact, I did hear some shit, but I ain't follow up on it. That big-butt bitch, Jasmin, from up the way was telling one of her girls how she though she seen a nigga get his shit split. She goes and gets her brother to walk her back to where she knew the body was so they could call the news or some shit. The thing was, when the brother goes to peek ain't nothing there."

"Fuck outta here," Shamel said, waving him off. "I wouldn't follow up on nothing that pothead bitch says. She's the only female I know that blow trees before she do anything else in the morning."

"I don't know, Mel."

"Whatever, kid. I'll be back in a few. I'm going down the block to see if I see that nigga Roger. Ma fucka owed me three hundred dollars for a minute. I'm popped and I need mine." Shamel hauled himself off the gate and disappeared in back of the center.

Rio got Trinity settled and decided to hit the streets. The fresh air would help clear his head, plus he needed a chance to check his new territory. Actually calling the shots was going to be way different from being a spot runner. As a spot runner, he was only in charge of a single spot and maybe a few workers. As Capo he was in charge of all the neighborhood spots as well as being responsible for Prince's money.

Before Rio made it to the steps, Shamel was making his way across the park. He was dressed in dark colors and looking suspect. Rio knew his friend was on the grind. Between Cutty and his itchy trigger and Shamel with his sticky fingers, Rio had his hands full.

"Sup, God?" Shamel said.

"Chilling, man," answered Rio.

"I know that's right, dog. Oh, yeah, congratulations on the promotion."

"How the fuck you know?"

"Come on, kid. I'm plugged into the Vine."

"Yeah, I stepped up to the plate," Rio answered modestly.

"What brought on the career change?"

"Time to come up," Rio lied.

Shamel looked at him sideways, but didn't comment on it. "I hear that, Rio. What happened to you last night?"

"Oh . . . I got sidetracked, ya know? Nigga just kicked it in the crib and meditated."

"Word? I went to ya house. Sally said that you wasn't there."

"Me and my mom's boyfriend got into something. She was probably still mad."

"I can dig it. So, what you wanna do about the Baker situation?"

"Ain't nothing, man. I ain't gonna wet that shit. Somebody will end up killing his ass sooner or later."

"Oh, last night you was bout ya business, now you on some live-and-let-live shit?" Shamel questioned.

"Damn," Rio snapped. "Fuck is up with the questions and shit? You wired or something, nigga?"

"Easy, son. I ain't the enemy. I'm just fucking wit you."

"I got a lot of shit on me right now, dog. I just ain't in a joking mood."

"I feel you, Mr. Grinch. But on a sadder note, Freddy's sister is missing."

"Who the fuck is Freddy's sister?"

"Tracy. You know her. The young'n wit the big titties?"

For a minute Rio couldn't quite figure who his man was talking about, but then it hit him. That's why the girl from the other night had looked familiar. Rio could recall days when he would give Tracy and her little friends dollars. He hadn't seen her in quite some time, so he hadn't recognized her. Suddenly his heart felt heavier.

"That's fucked up, Mel," Rio said.

"Fucked up ain't the word. I'm hoping the little heifer got hot in the pants and stayed out with a boy."

"Yeah, that's probably what happened." In his heart Rio wanted what he had told his friend to be true, but she wasn't coming back.

"So," Shamel continued. "Where you headed?"

"Up the block, man. Walk with me."

The two hiked up the steps talking shit. As they passed, a group of girls were pointing at Rio and smiling. He smiled back and kept stepping. While he walked toward the building, he could feel them still staring at him. Rio just shook his head and thought about Trinity.

All of the homeboys were assembled in front of the building chilling. When Rio walked up, they all started clapping. Rio was taken back by the response. He knew that now that he was a Capo things would be different, but he never expected an ovation. One by one they gave Rio dap and wished him well. He was definitely a hood favorite.

The little ceremony was broken up by a commotion in the lobby. Rio jogged to the building followed by the soldiers. When they got inside, a kid named Cory was beating fire out of one of the workers. Cory was about six feet tall and about 220, while the worker was maybe 125. Rio didn't like to see shit like that, especially where he was clicking.

"Yo," Rio said, grabbing Cory. "Fuck is you doing, kid?"

Cory started to swing again, but when he realized who was talking to him, he froze. "Oh," he said out of breath. "What up, boss?"

"Fuck is up wit you? You pounding this li'l nigga out in the lobby and shit. You know that ain't kosher."

"My bad on the scene, Rio. But not for nothing, this li'l nigga had it coming. He ran off with two packs from Truck's spot on 110th. He's the one that told me to come down here and handle him."

"Look," Rio said, upset at hearing Cory drop Truck's name. "This ain't 110th. This nigga wrong and I can respect you wanting to make it right, but this ain't how you do it. I'm sure you know I'm holding this down? You could've come to me first."

"I dig where you're coming from, Rio. I ain't mean no disrespect, but that's what Truck wanted."

"A'ight, Cory. But you tell ya man Truck that, next time, he comes to me." Rio helped the young boy to his feet. "Look at me," he said, grabbing the boy's face. "You can't get money no where, no more, my man. From now on you work for free and you pitching. Cory," Rio tossed Cory a wad of bills. "Tell Truck his problem is solved. The boy owes me now."

"Truck wants me to bring him up the hill."

"Cory, what I just tell you?"

"A'ight, Rio. Truck ain't gonna like it, but I'll tell him." Cory shot an evil glance at the worker and left. Once Cory was out of earshot the worker got his voice back.

"Good looking, Rio," He said over a bloody lip.

"Fuck outta here," Rio barked. "I ain't did shit for you. Nigga, youz a thief and a traitor. I ain't got no love for you, chump. You gonna work day and night till you get my paper up. Now get the fuck out my face and tell Tommy to give yo sorry ass a pack."

The worker looked at Rio with a mixture of hurt and anger. Rio had played him in front of his crew and destroyed his street credibility. It was some bullshit, but he brought it on himself. He should've been thankful that Rio stepped in and saved him, but he wasn't. All his petty mind would allow him to feel was jealousy and animosity toward Prince's newest Capo. He would do as he was told for now, but Rio would answer for playing him. Had he been a man about his shit, he would've spoken up. But because he was a coward he left and did as he was told.

"Umm, hmm," Shamel mumbled.

"Fuck is you mumbling about?" Rio asked.

"Nothing, Rio. I was just thinking that for someone who don't want shit to do with the game, you sure nuff got the role of boss down pat."

"Fuck you, Shamel. What was I supposed to do, just let Cory keep beating the nigga up and fuck up the flow?"

"Oh, nah player. You handle things how you see fit. This ain't my game so it don't make me no never mind. I was just pointing something out to you."

"Thank's for the advice, Maury."

"Make all the jokes you want, Rio. The sad fact is, you on a high road to hell and I think you know it. It was different when you were just holding the block down. Now you the man. What you do and say from here on out affects others as well as yourself. You bout to step waist-deep in some shit, baby boy. I just hope you're ready for it."

"I'm cool, Mel. I can handle it."

"Let's see if you feel that way when one of these niggaz decides to try you."

"It ain't that serious, Mel. I ain't trying to get involved in the politics of this shit. I'm just out here trying to do me."

"It ain't that serious? Rio, I don't think you understand the full weight of what you've gotten yourself into. You've chosen a side in this Rio. Because you're with Prince, his enemies are now your enemies. When they come for him, they'll come for you."

"Don't worry about it, Mel. I'm a big boy."

"A'ight, Rio. You my man and you know I got ya back either way. All I'm saying is, you've become a key player in the very thing you've sought to distance yourself from. The genocide of your own people. When the times comes, and believe me it will come, are you ready to spill or shed blood for this thing here?"

"Come on, Mel."

"I'm serious, Rio. When you're married to the streets, you can't get a divorce. I'm always gonna go to the hammer for my nigga. Right or wrong, daddy, I'm wit you. But prepare yourself, my nigga. The storm is coming. Just don't get caught out in the rain."

Trinity sat in her room, staring out the window. The last few days would've been enough to drive any other girl crazy, but not Trinity. She was built from stronger stuff. As she thought about her life's turn of events, she tried to decide her next move.

She didn't totally agree with Rio for killing her father, but she understood. In a way, she loved him more for it. It was one thing for a guy to say that he loved you, but how many were willing to body something to prove it? Rio was a classic nigga and she felt blessed to have him in her corner.

Trinity's thoughts were broken by the sound of the front door opening. It was probably Billy. She still hadn't figured out when and if she would tell him about their father. Rio had suggested that she just dummy-up and never tell him what happened, but she wasn't sure if she was comfortable with it.

Trinity came out of her bedroom and saw that it wasn't Billy, but her brother Richard. She hated seeing him almost as much as she hated seeing her father. Richard had always been book-smart, but didn't have a drop of street knowledge. It was absurd for a kid who knew nothing about the streets to always want to be in them. This would ultimately be his undoing.

"Sup, sis?" asked Rich. By the way his eyes were all glazed over and his jaw stiffened, she could tell he was high. Looking at her elder brother she felt pity for him. The drugs had distorted his once handsome golden face and caused skin discoloration. His formerly chiseled body was now just skin hanging off bone. Richard had made the mistake of falling under the thrall of the "white lady."

"Hey, Rich," she said dryly.

"Ain't nothing, just came to change my clothes. Didn't think anybody was home." Which meant, *I was coming to see what I could steal, and you fucked it up by being home.* "What up wit you, T? Billy told me you was in the hospital. Everything cool?"

"Yeah, big bro. I was just a little under the weather. I'm okay now." Trinity felt bad about lying to her brother. The two of them used to be thick as thieves when their mother was alive. Richard and Trinity were only about a year and a half apart, but he was still her hero. Rich had always been there when she had a problem. When she needed help with something, he always had the right answer. But that was a long time ago. Ever since Rich had sold his soul for a fix, she couldn't stand the sight of what he had become. It reminded her of what he used to be.

"Say, T," Rich asked. "You seen Daddy?" At the mention of her father Trinity turned white as a ghost. "Trinity, did you hear what I asked?"

"Oh," she stammered. "Yes. I mean, no. I mean . . . yes I heard you and no I haven't seen Daddy. You're the one always in the streets with him. You haven't seen him?"

"Nah, and I been to all of his spots. They said the last time they saw him, he was with some young girl. I think that kid Freddy's sister?"

Trinity frowned at this. Rio had never mentioned another victim. Maybe she hadn't been with Baker when it went down? Trinity knew she was just fooling herself. With Baker's fetish for young girls it's a good bet that he was with Tracy. If she knew Rio as well as she thought she did, that's probably what set him off.

"I dunno, Rich," she said. "Well, if he don't pop up by tomorrow, we can file a missing person's report."

"Shit." Rich chuckled. "Daddy ain't hardly missing. Our luck couldn't hold together so well. He's probably shacked up with some-one's little girl. Shit, maybe little boy? Ol' Daddy's probably having a real live time right now."

Trinity laughed with her brother, but her shit was as phony as a three-dollar bill. Baker's time would be anything but live from then on. As Trinity turned to walk back in her room she couldn't help but won-der how her brother would support his habit or shelter himself now that Daddy was gone. That wasn't Trinity's problem anymore. He was a grown man and had to fend for himself. As everyone had to at some point.

A few days later Rio had an unexpected surprise for Trinity. He came and scooped her up for a kind of surprise date. She asked him where they were going, but he wouldn't tell. When she got outside he already had the cab waiting. During the cab ride, he made her wear a blindfold so she couldn't see where they were going. The ride took a while so Trin-ity figured that they were in another borough. Rio helped her out of the cab and led her by the hand. When he finally removed the blindfold, Trinity gasped.

She almost broke down and cried as she looked out at the beautiful trees and greenery. There were hoards of people moving about the open area. Couples, families, and children on a field trip from one of the local schools. She smiled broadly at the sign that read BRONX ZOO.

"Surprise," he said, smiling.

"Oh, baby," she said, hugging him. "I've always wanted to come to the zoo."

Trinity had lived in New York for her entire life and never made it to the zoo. The Bronx was only a stone's throw from Manhattan, but she had never made it there. It wasn't that she couldn't go, she just never seemed to have the time or a reason. A trip to the zoo might've seemed like something simple to most people, but to Trinity, it was one of the greatest gifts anyone had ever given her.

"I figured it would pick your spirits up," he said, with a grin.

"Oh, it did. Come on," she said, grabbing him by the hand. "Let's go see the animals." The two lovers ran off like school kids into the zoo. As they toured the zoo, Rio schooled Trinity on the different animals. She admired him and how he was so knowledgeable but could still be street. Trinity knew that she would win with Rio.

They spent the day walking through the zoo and being silly. It was like the first time they met all over again. Rio fed her cotton candy as he explained the mating habits of Bengal tigers. Unbeknownst to her, he had spent quite a few hours studying them, just so that he would be able to narrate the tour for her. The zoo also had a petting section where Trinity was allowed to hold a tiger for the first time. It was against the zoo's policy to let people hold the more exotic animals, but Rio had slipped the keeper two hundred dollars to make it happen. Trinity looked like she wanted to cry when she saw the baby tiger. She instantly fell in love with the cub.

"I think he likes you," Rio whispered in her ear.

"Rio," she said, smiling as she scratched the tiger's head. "This has been one of the best days in my life."

"Just one of many, ma. We're doing everything first class from now on." As the sun started to set, Trinity knew that her fantasy date was coming to an end. Night was approaching and Rio had money to make. The block needed him, so they headed home. They got out of the cab together on 101st Street and kissed good night. Rio promised to call her as he headed up the block. Trinity watched her man as he walked off and wondered what she had ever done in life to be so lucky?

Darkness had come to the projects and with it the creatures of the night. The working class were locking themselves away within their safe lives, preparing to bed down, while the hustlers were just rising. As the inky blackness covered the streets, the children of the night crept from their hiding places.

Rio sat on a far bench hunched over in the shadows. With a pen in hand, he scribbled away in his notebook. The little tattered black and white was one of Rio's most prized possessions. It was his book of thoughts. He would often spend hours pouring his soul onto its pages. Aside from Trinity, it was one of the few things in life that brought him peace.

Suddenly, Rio heard the rustling of leaves behind him. As he turned to see what it was, cold steel touched his cheek. Rio sighed deeply and cut his eyes. Cutty stood dressed in his usual black, smiling at his friend.

"You still slipping, huh?" Cutty hissed. "When you gonna learn about these streets, my nigga?"

"Don't be so quick to judge," Rio said, looking at Cutty's crotch. Cutty looked down and saw that Rio had a 9 under his jacket and it was honed in on Cutty's manhood. "I take notes from time to time," Rio quipped with a slight smile.

"That's what the fuck I'm talking about," Cutty said, putting his pistol away. "I see your promotion got you thinking better?"

"You know it, dog. I gotta be a li'l tighter wit my shit, ya know?"

"That's what I been trying to tell you all along, dog. You playing for big paper now. Who you got wit you?"

"Wit me?"

"Yeah, square-ass nigga," Cutty said, playfully. "Who watching ya back?"

"Me, I guess. I ain't never gave it much thought, know what I mean? I'm a man just like the next nigga. Ain't no fear over here."

"Rio, it ain't about being scared, it's about being smart. Your eyes can't be everywhere at once, kid. Now that you wit the big man, you gonna be handling a lot of paper. You need a nigga to hold you down."

"And that's you?"

"Come on wit that shit, Rio. You know we peoples, dog. I don't wanna see you gobbled up out here by some thirsty young nigga trying to come up."

"You got a point, Cutty. Niggaz do be funny style."

"Please, you forget who you talking to? I'm one of the grimiest niggaz on the planet, but I'm loyal to my fam."

"A'ight, Cutty. You my nigga, so I'll give you a play. Just let me get wit Prince and let him know what the deal is. I don't want him to feel funny about seeing you around all the time."

"Cool, cool. We gonna get this money and everything is gonna be gravy."

The two men's conversation was broken up when Li'l J appeared. The sneaky little bastard had this habit of popping up outta thin air. He was dressed in a midnight-blue suit with a diamond stickpin that looked more like a flashlight. His overcoat looked like a death shroud flapping in the night air. Li'l J patted his perm with one hand and tucked the other into his pocket. No doubt clutching a pistol.

"Sup, kid?" J rasped. He addressed Rio but was looking at Cutty. "I need to holla at you."

"A'ight," Rio said. "What's good?"

"Nah, I don't know this kid to be talking in front of him."

"Oh, this my man, Cutty. He cool."

"He cool wit you, but I don't know him."

"Cutty's gonna be holding it down wit me, ya know? Kinda like a bodyguard."

"*Bodyguard?*" J chuckled. "Sure kid. Let's take a walk."

J placed a firm hand on Rio's shoulder and steered him toward the steps. Cutty took a step, but Rio waved him off. Rio strode off with J, leaving Cutty standing there puzzled. He wanted to check J, but something in the old-timer's face told him not to.

When they were halfway to the avenue, J began speaking. "Who was that punk?"

"Oh, that was my man, Cutty. I told you, he's cool."

"Look, kid. You might have a little position now, but you don't call the shots. Prince decides who comes into the fold and who doesn't. As far as cool, ya little green-ass nigga, we decide who gets that label. What's his name?"

"I told you. Cutty."

"Not his street name, Gilligan. His real name."

"Oh, Curtis. Curtis Turner."

"That's better. I'll get him checked out later on. Should have something on him by the morning. Until then, you don't tell him dick. Get me?"

"Yeah, J. I got you. So, where are we going?"

"Meeting. Prince wants to get all his people together. He usually has his Capos meet every so often. Tonight's a little special."

"What's the occasion?"

"You. Ya made ya bones, kid. Tonight's the night we bring you in."

Rio was a little puzzled. He thought that once Prince had passed the word down of his promotion, that would be it.

"Hold on," Rio said. "I ain't even dressed for nothing. I got on a sweat suit."

"Just come on." J kept it moving before Rio had a chance to protest any further. Rio went to get into the passenger side of the Caddy, but J directed him to the back. Rio climbed into the backseat of the car, where he noticed a bag with his name on it. Inside the bag was a pair of wool slacks, a black turtleneck, and a pair of black suede shoes. Rio smiled. The ensemble was along the lines of his tastes. Maybe working for Prince wouldn't be so bad after all.

J pulled the hog up in front of a brown brick building in the block of 128th. The building was formally one of those clunkers that the city lets someone fix up for a small fee, then charge a grip on the mortgage. From the picture windows and marble stairs, Prince must've been getting hit for a bit on this little gem.

Rio stepped out of the whip looking like a totally different cat. The hustler garb was shed and out stepped a respectable looking young man. He wasn't dressed up, but he could've passed for a middle-class working nigga. This was the way Prince wanted it. Rio thought that his benefactor was just showing love, but the clothes were just a front for the neighbors. Prince wanted to come across as one of them. Just a working-class Joe. A working-class Joe wouldn't have people coming to his house rocking trump jewels and tipping bottles.

J made his way up the stairs with Rio on his heels. When they reached the door, Rio noticed a huge man standing between the outer gate and the actual door. He hung back in the shadows like a wraith haunting some forgotten square. The guard nodded his ebony dome and bid them to enter. J slipped through the foyer and made his way to the main house. With a nod of his processed head, he motioned for Rio to follow him.

Rio proceeded into the lair with caution. The huge guard stared down at the shorter Rio. Rio returned his glare. He hadn't come looking for trouble, but Rio was the kinda dude that wasn't gonna let anyone punk him. No matter how big or small, Rio would bang out with you if it came to that.

As Rio squeezed past he and the guard found themselves eye to eye. The guard puffed out his chest in an attempt to mark his spot. Rio felt his heart start beating a little faster, but held his head as best he could.

As the guard raised his hand, Rio tensed, preparing himself for combat. The guard laid a paw on Rio's shoulder and grumbled a word. "Congratulations."

Rio stared in surprise, the statement catching him totally unprepared. He nodded his head and gave the big man a brief smirk. Rio kept it moving to the front door. Li'l J must've picked up on the exchange because he was smiling as he held the door open for Rio.

J led him through the first-floor entrance where they hung their jackets. Then they walked down a staircase to the lower levels of the house and across the living room. About six or seven men were lounging, sipping drinks, and watching the basketball game. Rio recognized a few of them from the hood. They were lieutenants and enforcers for Prince's Capos. Rio nodded to those he knew and continued on his way. As they approached the basement door J stopped short. "Listen, kid," he started, "what you're about to see and hear is for your eyes and ears only. Can you dig it?"

"Sure, J," Rio said, sounding more confident than he actually was. "I ain't some chickenhearted kid."

"Man, cut that bullshit. I'm trying to help yo thinking ass. This is the big-time, kid. I'm about to take you down to the very bowels of hell. You think you can play the hand fate dealt you?"

Rio paused making sure he had J's full attention before answering. "Let's do it."

J sighed deeply and pulled the door open. Rio stepped across the threshold and damn near gagged on the stench of cigar and weed smoke. He descended the stairs to the basement where everyone was waiting. He took a deep breath before stepping through the final door to embrace his destiny.

Shamel stood in the shadows of a building entrance scanning the block for movement. His black hoodie and jeans made him hard to spot in the dim light. Shamel's mind should've been on the business at hand, but he couldn't help but think about his partner's strange behavior. Things just didn't add up. The day before Rio had seemed hell-bent on putting

Baker out of his misery. Now he had a change of heart? The shit just didn't make sense.

Then there was the mysterious disappearance of Freddy's sister. It had come down the wire that she was last seen with a character matching Baker's description. It would've been real simple to just ask Baker, but no one had seen him in a day or so. Coincidence? Not likely. Somehow all of it tied in together. Rio knew something, but he wasn't telling. Shamel would get to the bottom of it sooner or later.

Shamel was so caught up in his fantasizing about playing Sherlock Holmes that he almost didn't see his mark. Ed strolled down the street as if he didn't have a care in the world. He greedily stuffed pork rinds into his mouth, letting the crumbs drop freely on his shirt. Back in the day people had high hopes for Ed. Some even said he would go pro. Ed was one of those dudes that used to be built, but with age came flab. Now he was just a cat that used to play college football.

Shamel let the bigger man pass before creeping behind him. Ed was headed up 105th going toward Amsterdam. If luck held out, the block would be dead and Shamel could take him quietly. It didn't. Some of the homeboys were standing around hollering at a group of females. This shit threw a monkey wrench in his plan, but he would not be deterred. When Shamel made up his mind to get you, you were as good as hit.

Ed gave dap to the fellas and started to get his mack on with one of the females. A fine chocolate sister, sporting a peach sweat suit. Ed had just about roped shorty in when he felt a tap on his shoulder. When Ed turned around, his eyes nearly sprang from his head.

"What up, Ed?" Shamel asked with a grin.

"Yo . . . my nig . . . I mean, my man Mel. What's the science, God?"

"Oh," Shamel said, running his hand over his face. "Now you wanna get cute?"

"What up, Mel? What up wit that rah-rah?" Ed asked with an attitude.

Ed was trying to be cool in front of the girls, which only made Shamel angry. At first he wasn't gonna clown, but now he felt that he had to teach Ed a lesson. "Oh word, Ed? Look, nigga . . . you got mines?"

"Come on, Mel. You ain't gotta be coming at me like that." Ed said, folding his arms.

"My bad," Shamel said with a grin. "You're right. I should've respected your square and came correct. My bad," Ed smiled long enough for Shamel to knock out his two front teeth with the butt of his desert. Ed fell to the ground, holding his bloodied mouth.

"Pussy nigga!" Shamel barked. "Fuck is you to talk to me like you a gangsta?" Shamel kicked him in the ribs. "Fucking bug nigga. I'll squash yo bitch ass!"

Ed curled up on the floor while Shamel rained kicks on him. By now the big man's face was a crimson mess. Shamel reached down and ripped off the two front pockets of Ed's jeans. Kids were gathered around, just watching him get the shit stomped out of him. Some of them felt bad for Ed while others were just glad it wasn't them.

Shamel shook the torn fabric, dropping their contents to the ground. Using his foot he sifted through Ed's personals until he found the bread. He picked up the only bill in the mess and frowned. Without warning Shamel kicked Ed viciously in the gut. Ed looked at his attacker in wide-eyed shock as he tried to gasp for air.

"Ten dollars, nigga," Shamel snarled, kicking him again. "You made me go through all this bunk shit and all you got is ten?" Shamel gave him one more kick to the head, knocking Ed unconscious. "Be a while before you'll be able to eat anything solid, let alone some pork. The only reason I ain't gonna do you dirty is cause you owe me cheese. A dead man can't pay his debts." Shamel stuffed the bill in his pocket and walked off. Once outside, he came across cool, but inside he felt like the biggest dick in the world. His quality of life was slipping. That dumb shit he did could've landed him right back in the joint on attempted murder. All for what? Ten—fucking—dollars! Sometimes Shamel wondered if it was even worth it.

When Rio stepped into the basement, he was transported into another world. Rio had thought that the inside of the house would be as nice as the outside, but it wasn't shit compared to the basement. The whole thing was a replica of a seventeenth-century war chamber. Gray brick covered the walls and high ceiling of the room. Plush brown carpet lined the floors. Along the walls were various weapons from the period that the room was made to resemble. Upon closer inspection, Rio noticed that the array of battle-axes and other blades were the real deal. He wondered to himself if his boss had ever used any of the weapons on a living person.

Prince and about a dozen or so others sat around a large conference table drinking and talking shit. The heavy hitters from all over Manhattan and the Bronx were gathered there. Rio tried his best not to look like a starstruck kid in front of them. Not only were there Willies in attendance that he knew Prince dealt with, but there were some cats there that Rio knew of, but never knew that they were tied to Prince.

Prince spotted his newest Capo and motioned for him to come over. Rio took a deep breath and descended into the sea of sharks. As he approached the table, all eyes were on him. Some of the other Capos nodded in greeting, while others just mean mugged him. But no matter the response, Rio kept his game face on. This was too big to let emotions fuck it up.

"My man, Rio," Prince said, standing. "What it is, man?"

"Chilling," Rio said, nodding.

"Chilling? Well, bring ya cold ass in here and take a seat. We been waiting for you." Rio took the chair at the opposite end of the table from Prince and gave him his undivided attention. "Well, now that the guest of honor is here, we can get started. Now, as all you niggaz know, I done brought some fresh blood to the family. I had my eye on this kid for a while, but he just decided to move where the grass was greener. Most of y'all know him, but for those of you who don't, this is Rio. He'll be running thangs down in the projects from now on. Maybe in time I'll step down and let Rio get a piece of what I got. Between him and Truck, they can't fuck it up too bad," Prince joked. "Y'all show that man some love."

The basement suddenly erupted with claps and clanging glasses. Rio was playing it cool, just nodding and smirking, but inside he wanted to grin from ear to ear. For so long he had steered clear of people like Prince and what they represented. But strangely, he seemed to be getting more love in a room full of associates than he would've from his own family. He was still uneasy about working for Prince's organization, but the more he saw of their world, the more intrigued he was by it.

"Okay, okay," Prince barked. "Y'all can do the meet and greet later. Let's get down to business. Now, Rio's taking over in the DP. He's been working for me on and off for a while, plus he's from the hood. That should work out nicely. This kid has got a head on his shoulders and he's a hell of an earner. I'm sponsoring him personally on this. Anyone object?"

Rio looked out at the sea of faces in astonishment. No one uttered a word in protest. These were all hardened and dangerous men, but none would go against the will of their prince. What he said was the law.

"Good," Prince continued. "Rio, I'm gonna run it down the line as to who these cats are. Just pay attention cause I'm only gonna say it once. From right to left we got, Big Paul from Hell's Kitchen, Marco from Webster Ave, Breeze and Jake from Queens, and Gino from the Lower East Side. These are my eyes and ears in Manhattan as well as other boroughs. The gentlemen with them are their . . . advisors of sorts. These are your brothers at arms. Each and every one of them is loyal to this organization, as you will be. You might all be on my payroll, but you're the masters of your own destinies. Y'all know how I do. You run your spots as you see fit, I don't care. As long as you got mine when it's time to ante up, we ain't gonna never have no misunderstanding. Do you understand, Rio?"

Rio nodded his head. "Good," Prince said. "Now, before we get on with the drinking and get back to the game, I got something to add. Rio, you pay special attention. I love you all like, sons, but I won't have the bullshit. The price of wealth is loyalty. The price of betrayal is death."

Rio absorbed Prince's words with a heavy sigh. He was getting in over his head, but what could he do? He had fucked up and Prince fixed it for him. Now he was indebted to the crime lord. He brought it on himself and now he had to carry the burden.

Rio's mental debate with himself was broken up by the sound of footsteps from above. Rio looked to the door just in time to see Truck coming through it.

"What up?" Truck slurred. "How y'all niggaz gonna have a party and not invite me?" Truck lumbered over to the conference table where the Capos were seated. Of all of the places to stand, he decided to stand near Rio. As the big man stared down at him he could smell booze seeping out of him.

"Sorry I'm late, fellas," Truck said. "I had some shit I had to take care of. But now that I'm here, let's get it started. Raise up, lil nigga. You in my seat."

Rio started to get up, but Prince waved him back down. "You keep ya ass glued to that chair, Rio. Truck, you know what time we do our thang, so keep your excuses."

"Come on, Daddy," Truck whined. "I had a situation that demanded my personal attention. I get here a li'l late and find the young boy all cozy in my spot. Fuck, you bringing him in to replace me or something? Well, if that's the case you've wasted your time. There's only one me, baby."

"Son, why don't you go ahead and talk out ya ass somewhere else. This gathering is for gentlemen, not street punks. You wanna carry ya self as such, go upstairs and hang out with the rest of the gun clappers."

"A'ight, Daddy. Damn. All I was trying to do was let Rio know he had taken the wrong seat."

"Truck," Prince said, getting to his feet. "You done already fucked up by coming up in here drunk. Don't push your luck by trying me, ya hear? I call the mutha fucking shots round here. Ain't nobody replacing nobody. Rio's got his spot and that's just the way it is. If you felt so strongly about it, you should've had ya ass here to cast ya vote. Now, shut the fuck up about the seat and let us continue with our business."

Truck wanted to keep it going, but decided to let it slide. He knew that if he got his father started they might all be there for hours. Instead of making everyone else suffer, Truck just grabbed a folding chair and sat down. *Weak-ass niggaz*, Truck thought to himself, *None of you niggaz got a spine.* Let his father do him while his so-called Capos bowed and kissed his ass. It was only a matter of time before Truck would set his plan into motion. Then he would show the *Capos* what real power was about. All would bow before Truck or die. Especially Rio's punk ass.

Rio silently watched the exchange between father and son. He knew the whole seat thing was an attempt to punk him, but he didn't feed into it. He remained the poised gentleman and was offered the seat to his senior Capo. Rio didn't know what it was that made Truck hate him so. This was the second time Truck tried to come at him sideways in as many meetings.

Gentleman that he was, Rio wasn't going to let too much shit slide. He was the greenest of the group so he played his position, but he wouldn't be green forever. Niggaz in the hood already had love for Rio. Now that he was the nigga running things in his hood, that love would double.

Rio really had no stomach for the grind and in many ways it would work to his advantage. While most of the Capos were known to be brutal and ruthless in their hoods, Rio would rule with fairness. He was going to make sure that everyone down his chain of command saw paper. Even if you were just a pitcher you could eat if you remained loyal to Rio. If he played his cards right, he could have quite a little following.

Until he got his weight up Rio would just do his part and remain silent. Once he had a solid team of soldiers behind him, it would be a different story. *Let Truck get crazy*, he thought to himself. The fact that he was Prince's son gave him a lot of leeway, but not enough to keep shooting his mouth off. One thing killing his wifey's father had taught him was that if pushed, there was no telling how far a man would go.

Trinity sat in her bedroom puffing yet another cigarette. The Neo–Soul CDs that usually picked her spirits up did nothing more than aggravate her at the moment. Billy had been quizzing her all day about where she thought their father might be. For every excuse she gave him, he came up with two more questions. When he asked about Rio she nearly bit his head off. Since then the questions had stopped.

Trinity felt as if her bedroom walls were beginning to close in on her. The very air itself seemed to be trying to strangle her. She decided that a breath of fresh air might do her some good. She threw on some old jeans and wrapped her hair in a scarf. After grabbing her leather jacket, Trinity was out the door.

As soon as she got into the night air she began to feel better. The streets were empty aside from a few crackheads trying to score a fix. Most people steered clear of the streets at that hour of the morning, but Trinity liked to take midnight strolls. She wasn't worried about anyone trying anything. Most of the people in the projects knew her. If someone did decide to get crazy, they were in for a rough time. Trinity was hardly ever without a blade.

She strolled through the projects taking in the sights and scents of the ghetto. To some people the projects were a horrible and unwelcome sight. Crack infested the streets and the kids pissed in and destroyed the very buildings their families had to live in. Trinity didn't quite see it that way. I mean, sure the projects were falling apart, but she remembered a time when they weren't. Believe it or not her projects weren't always that way. Douglass project was once a nice place to live. Trinity could remember a time when her mother used to leave the front door unlocked. But that was a time long ago. Just like most of the other hoods, Douglass was street-poisoned.

Trinity looked over near the grassed-in area and saw a familiar figure swaying on the iron bench. At first Trinity was just going to keep walking, but decided against it. She bit her bottom lip and headed in the direction of the benches. Looking at Sally in the moonlight she realized for the first time just how beautiful she was.

Sally had a sharp jawline and thin nose making her look slightly mixed. She wasn't light-skinned, nor was she as dark as Rio. She was a smooth butterscotch. Even though it had been slightly discolored from years of drinking, her skin still held a certain glow. Her once beautiful hair hung down her back in a tangled mess.

Trinity couldn't help but feel sorry for Sally. Back in the later '70s she was a pretty popular blues singer. People would come from all over and pack the lounges to hear Sally-May do her thing. She had even recorded a gold album. That was big back then. Old Sally was on top of her game until Rio's dad came along. The young militant got her knocked up and that pretty much put her singing on hold. Then he got in all that trouble with the Feds, which only made matters worst. When Rio's dad went away, Sally turned to the bottle for comfort. It had been downhill ever since.

Sally must've felt Trinity because she turned around suddenly. At first her face was twisted in a mass of anger but after seeing who it was, she softened it. She smiled at her son's girlfriend and motioned for her to sit down. Trinity hesitated for a moment because she really didn't feel like talking, but if she didn't she would've seemed rude. Trinity decided to spare the old singer a few ticks and sat down.

"Hey, Trinity," Sally said in a raspy voice. "What you doing out here at this hour?"

"Hey, Ms. Sally," Trinity said, smiling. "I was just out getting some air."

"Girl, you better be careful in these streets. These crazy-ass crackheads will steal the clothes off yo back."

"I don't worry about stuff like that. I mean, I know the streets are dangerous and all, but danger lurks everywhere. If I can't feel safe in my own projects, I can't feel safe nowhere."

"Hmpf, say what you want. You better take it from a gal that's been around for a while."

There was a brief silence then Trinity picked up the conversation. "So, how's Rio?"

"Shit," Sally said. "I was gonna ask you the same thing. I don't see *our* boy like that. He spends more time with you than he does at home. Had the nerve to jump on Willie the other night. Willie was just joking with Rio and he went all crazy."

Trinity raised an eyebrow at this new bit of information. She knew Willie was an asshole and probably said something slick. Slowly but surely the pieces were starting to come together. Rio wasn't a punk, yet he wasn't the kind of person to just snap like that. It seemed as if the last few day's turn of events led him to what he had done.

"I don't know what's gotten into that boy, Trinity," Sally said sadly. "Lately he's been so . . . I don't know? It's like the older he gets, the more he reminds me of his father. He was so damn bullheaded."

"Don't worry about it, Sally," Trinity said, patting her hand. "Rio's just going through the motions."

"I know, Trinity. A man is gonna be a man, but I still worry. Does he ever talk to you?"

"Well . . . sometimes. But you know how he is. He keeps everything bottled up. But it's like I said. Rio's just going through the motions. He's down about a lot of stuff. You know with being unemployed and—"

"Oh, knock it off, Trinity," Sally interrupted. "We're both adults, so let's keep it real. I know what my son is out here doing. I don't condone it, but he's grown. I've been running the streets longer than both of you have been alive. I know the havoc she can play on a person's soul. Rio is strong and smart as a whip. I'll give him that. But I know my son, Trinity. He ain't built for what they serving out here. I ain't saying that he can't handle his business, but . . . I dunno. The game has a strange way of corrupting a man. I don't want that for my boy."

Trinity just sat there and absorbed what Sally was saying. If she had been drinking, they'd have hardly gotten this deep. Strangely enough, the sober side of Sally held the wisdom that comes with age. It just goes to show how much a dependency could alter a person's mind.

Before the conversation could go any further, Willie came staggering up from the parking lot. His head was wrapped in a dingy bandage, but that still didn't keep him from his nightly lurking. From the shape of the package in his hand Trinity knew what time it was. She could hardly tolerate Willie sober so there was no way she was going to sit around him drunk. Trinity took that as her cue to leave. As soon as she stood to leave, Willie started in.

"Well, well," he said, licking his lips. "What's going on, li'l lady?"

"Chilling," Trinity said, walking off.

"Hold on, T. You ain't gotta leave on my account. I brought a li'l taste for me and Sally. You're more than welcome to join us."

Trinity looked at him as if he had lost his mind. He was playing himself by flirting with her in front of Sally. If he knew like she did he'd be easy. With the way Rio had been acting lately he could very well find himself missing for it. "I'm good," Trinity said graciously. "I'll talk to you later, Sally." Trinity headed for the ave when Sally called out to her.

"Trinity." Trinity stopped short and turned around. "Take care of our boy."

"I will," Trinity said, smiling. "I will."

12

Rio was awakened early the next morning by Sally banging on his door. "Darius!" she shouted. "You hear me, boy? Somebody's on the phone for you."

Rio sat up, rubbing his eyes. He wondered who it could be calling him on his mother's phone? Anyone who needed to reach him could call his cell or the phone in his room. Rio slid out of bed and made his way to the door. Might as well get the phone. Sitting there wondering who it was wouldn't satisfy his curiosity.

Rio opened his door and faced his mother. It was the first time they had seen each other since the fight the other night, so a bit of tension hung in the air. As Sally handed him the phone, she cast a puzzling glare. Rio caught his mother's look and felt a little guilty. He figured she was still salty from the other night. As he took the cordless from her outstretched hand, he made a mental note to apologize to her. Little did he know Sally's worries ran deeper than a few words.

Rio cradled the phone to his ear and closed his room door. "Who dis?"

"What up, youngster?" J said on the other end.

"J? How the hell you get this number?"

"Don't sweat the small stuff, kid. We got ways. Listen, I got the run-down on ya man. He checks out, but that don't mean shit. Douglass is your thing so that's your decision to make. But, if you bring this nigga in, then you're responsible for his actions."

"A'ight, J. I can dig it."

"I hope so, youngblood. Really I do. Your man is gonna meet you in front of your building in about half hour. Time to punch in."

"Punch in? J, it's like seven-thirty."

"And? You better nix that small-time thinking kid. What you *used* to do, was part-time. This here is a full-time gig. You gotta know what's go-ing on in ya hood twenty-four seven. Now, you can do what you like, but my advice for you would be to get yo ass up and hit the streets." Rio was about to protest further, but J had already hung up. Rio was tempted to get back in the bed but decided against it. He probably wouldn't be able to go back to sleep anyhow. Might as well hit the block.

Rio sifted through his closet to find a fit for the day. After a brief glance out the window, he saw mister sun peeking back at him. The outfit he selected was a white, hooded sweat suit. He looked at the rack in his corner, which held at least ten fitted hats. A black Sox hat was his choice for the day. He wasn't really one for hats, but he felt like wearing one. After pulling his black and white timbs out of the box he was set.

Rio showered as quickly as he could, jumped into his clothes and headed for the door. He glanced at his mother's closed bedroom door and was tempted to knock. They had both said and done a lot of things they shouldn't have. One day they would make it right, but it could wait. Rio had to go to work.

Rio stepped out of his building and inhaled the morning air. The slight chill felt good in his chest. He looked at the sky and smiled. He spent so much of his time running around at night that he had almost forgotten how beautiful the sun was. He used to get up and go job hunting a few times a week, but he hadn't done it in a while. Hustling to make ends meet had consumed quite a bit of his time.

Rio felt someone standing behind him, causing him to spin around. He was relieved to see that it was Cutty. Cutty was dressed in black jeans and a black Fubu sweatshirt. Rio made a note to himself to take Cutty shopping for some brighter colors.

"Sup, boss?" Cutty asked sarcastically.

"Oh, you got jokes, huh? You the street legend, Cutty."

"Nah, I ain't got nothing on you, big-time."

"Fuck you, Cutty." The two men danced around and threw fake punches. After the ritual greeting, Rio said. "Say, I hear you got a call from ol' J?"

"Yeah, kid. I was gonna ask you about that shit. You gave them dudes my number?"

"Hell, nah. Cutty, you know I don't rock like that. Ol' boy said he was gonna run a check on you before I put you down. You know I spoke positive in ya favor, but these old-timers . . . they second-guessing everybody. Ya know?"

"I feel you, Rio. I guess that's why they've been on top for so long."

"That's for damn sure. Them niggaz is like the Feds. Not only did they get your number, but they called my mom's line a li'l while ago."

"Fuck outta here?" Cutty asked in shock.

"Straight up," Rio said seriously. "J is the one that told me you were out here. Seems like them old niggaz got a line on everything. Fuck it, let's hit the block."

The two young men strolled up the block to oversee their operation. The ave was filled with the working class and the schoolkids making their way to wherever they had to go. Rio, nodded to those he knew and kept it moving. As the duo reached the corner of 104th they spotted the shift manager, School Boy. School Boy was a tall, light-skinned kid who wore his hair in a close fade. He got his name because of the way he was known to dress. Button-up shirts and cardigan sweaters. The wire-rimmed glasses that sat on the bridge of his nose made him look more like a teacher than a spot runner. But as they say, "you can't judge a book by its cover." School Boy had a nose for money and his till was hardly ever short. Even when it was over, he never cuffed any of the money. School Boy was a good dude.

"Sup, my nigga?" School Boy said, extending his hand.

"What it is, baby," Rio responded, giving him dap. "How we looking out here?"

"Well, we had some trouble finding someone to pitch, but we got it squared away. George is holding it down in back of the center."

"George," Rio said with raised eyebrows. "What happened to that other kid, the one Cory was whipping on? Nigga know he got a debt to work off."

"Oh, I forgot. You disappeared last night so you didn't hear."

"Hear what, School Boy?"

"Some niggaz who work for Truck came through here last night and snatched him. I tried to tell them that you had him out here, but they wasn't trying to hear me. They said that if you had a problem with it that you should see Truck."

"Mutha fucka," Rio mumbled angrily. Truck was out of line with this stunt. He knew that Rio had the boy out there trying to get his money back and he touched him anyway. Rio had no doubt Truck had done this to try and undermine Rio's authority. The difference this time was that Rio intended to step to him behind this shit.

"Where Truck at now?" Rio asked.

"I think he's over on 107th," School Boy answered.

"A'ight, School Boy. Hold the block down for me. I'll be back in a few." Rio tapped Cutty on the arm and headed north on Columbus.

Trinity sat in the lobby of the Twenty-fourth Precinct, waiting to speak to an officer. As Rio had instructed her, she went to file a missing person's report on her father. She looked around at the officers doing this and that and felt her stomach flip-flop. *What if they know I'm lying?* she thought to herself. Rio had killed her father, but what had happened to the body? She knew if she wanted to keep her man out of jail as well and not incriminate herself, she had to keep her game face. As Trinity sat waiting, a dark-skinned man wearing blue jeans and a white T-shirt walked past her on his way to the back. The young-looking officer spared Trinity a brief smile. She smiled back and turned her head away.

An officer came out of the back room holding a clipboard. He was a tall brown-skinned man with a short Afro. He didn't look all stiff like the rest of the officers. This young man had a sort of laid back air about him. Something about the way he looked at her made Trinity feel a little easier.

"Ms. Baker?" the officer asked. Trinity nodded. "I'm Officer Brown. What can I do for you?"

"Well," Trinity began, "it's my father, Steven Baker. He's missing."

"I see," Brown said, scribbling something on the clip board. "How long?"

"Excuse me?"

"I meant how long has he been missing?"

"Oh, I'm not sure cause I was in the hospital. But I would say . . . two to three days."

"Umm hmm," Brown said, scribbling again. "Does your father do this kinda thing often?"

"Well . . . he drinks a lot, so he does tend to stay out. Sometimes. But not usually for this length of time. He'll usually call or send word through someone."

"Has anyone come by or seen him?"

"No. My brother checked some of his hang outs but no one has seen him."

"Do you know who he was last seen with?"

"No," she lied. "I don't. It's like I said, I've been in the hospital for the past few days, so I really don't know." As the lies rolled from Trinity's mouth, her conscience banged away at her. She thought of the little girl's family and how worried they must be. She hoped that one day they would be able to bury their child properly and put their minds to rest, but at the moment the only thing that mattered was her and Rio's future.

"I see," Brown said, looking at her quizzically. Something about the young girl's story didn't seem right to him. He didn't sense that she was lying, at least not totally. But he felt as if she was holding something back. "Okay," he continued. "I don't wanna scare you, but I have to ask. Did your father have any enemies or someone that might've wanted to see him harmed?"

"Well . . . I . . ." Trinity took a deep breath. "Listen, Officer Brown. I don't wanna lie to you. My father did a lot of shit to a lot of people. He is a notorious drunk and the people he hangs around ain't about shit. Could someone have wanted to harm him? Maybe, I can't say for sure. He hasn't been the best father in the world, but he's the only one me and my brothers have."

Officer Brown looked at the young lady as her eyes began to glass over. From the way she broke it down he could tell she was going through something emotionally. But as emotional as she might have seemed, Brown knew there was something wrong with her story. He couldn't put his finger on it right away, but he vowed to figure it out.

"Well, Trinity, I'm going to file this report and put your father's description out over the air. You go on home and I'll call if I should happen to come up with anything."

"Thanks," she said, standing to leave. "Please let me know if you should hear anything." Trinity turned and headed for the exit. Officer Brown seemed like he believed her story, but Trinity wasn't stupid. She was very good at reading people. She knew that he wasn't totally convinced. Nothing she could do about it now except hope she hadn't just indicted herself on a conspiracy charge.

As Trinity was leaving, a plainclothes detective was coming in. The balding white man moved over slightly to let her pass. However, he made sure that she had to brush against his potbelly to get by. He stared at her shapely rear and licked his lips. Something about the girl struck a cord in his head. He couldn't place her at the moment but he knew he would eventually. With an ass like hers, how could he not?

"Well, well," the detective said, grinning. "If it isn't *Officer* Brown. What's shaking on the streets?"

Brown nodded to Detective Stark and continued filling out the missing person's report. Not so long ago Brown had also been a detective. While trying to apprehend a suspect he had accidently shot him. What he thought had been a real gun had turned out to be a toy. Brown had managed to keep his badge, but the captain had him busted down to beat-walker. Brown vowed to one day get his badge back.

"Say, Brown," Detective Stark said. "Who was that fine young thing?"

"Oh," Brown said, closing his folder. "That was a young lady by the name of Baker."

"Baker," the detective said, as the light went off in his head. "Trinity Baker?"

"Yeah, you know her?"

"You could say that. I locked her up a few years ago for cutting some girl. But she wasn't built like that. What'd she come in for? Her boyfriend's luck finally run out?"

"No, nothing like that. Seems her father's gone missing. Why'd you ask about her boyfriend? He somebody I might know?"

"What?" Stark asked, surprised. "Brown, you patrol this hood and you don't know? Her boyfriend is Darius Santana. Known as Rio on the streets."

"Yeah, I think I know who you're talking about. He got picked up a few years ago on a gun charge."

"Yep, that's him. Did a year on that and hasn't been in trouble since."

"Well, if he's kept his nose clean, why the sudden interest in him?"

"Brown, just because the slick fuck hasn't been rearrested doesn't mean he ain't doing dirt," Stark insisted. "Until recently, he was hitting the block part-time, ya know? A shift here and there, but nothing major. That is, until a few days ago."

"What happened?"

"Well, it seems as if our young friend is moving up in the world. Seems as if he's no longer just a spot runner. I heard through the grapevine that he was just recently promoted to Capo."

"No shit?"

"That's the way I hear it. We been trying to bring Prince and his crew down for a while now."

"I know," Brown said, filing his folder away. "We were trying to get him when I still had a shield. Prince is slicker than oil. I'd love a chance to knock him on his dope-pushing ass."

"Hmm," Stark said, scratching his bald spot. "That doesn't sound too impossible. We just need a way to get someone inside. As a matter of fact, I think I got a plan and you might be able to help."

"Well, I can't do it," Brown said. "If Trinity is his girl, then she would blow my cover the first time she spotted me around him."

"I know it, Brown. But I got another way you can help out. Get me Officer Jenkins," Stark said, turning to the desk sergeant.

"Jenkins," Brown asked, confused. "What do you want with my partner? He's just a rookie."

"Jenkins might be a rookie, but he looks just like one of them. I've got a surefire plan that'll get your shield back and earn me a promotion. Are you game?"

"Okay, I'm listening."

Mikey crept slowly down Eighty-sixth and Broadway, tailing his prey. He had been shadowing the tall white man ever since he had seen him come out of the bank. He knew the dude had some type of money on him, because he came out tucking an envelope into his suit jacket. No matter how much it was, Mikey was going to relieve him of it.

Mikey was your typical wannabe. He had been trying to hook up with the thieve's crew for the longest and they had finally given him a play. Shamel's people had put him down on the trial basis. Mikey had finally gotten his chance and was determined to prove to the rest of the clique that he was a top-notch thief.

The white guy banked a left on the corner of Eighty-sixth and headed down into the 1 & 9 station. Mikey decided that this was the perfect time to strike. He ran up behind the white dude before he had cleared the first landing and spun him around. The white dude looked at Mikey as if he had lost his last mind.

"Gimmie yo shit, cracker!" Mikey barked.

"Listen, kid," the white dude said in a calm voice. "I don't think you know what you're doing."

"Oh, I know what I'm doing. Now come up off that bread you just got from the bank and un-ass ya wallet."

"Listen kid, I'm trying to tell you—"

"Shut up," Mikey said, slapping him. "You ain't telling me shit. Now come up off ya wallet."

"Okay, kid. I tried to tell you." The white man handed Mikey the wallet and folded his arms. Mikey greedily flipped open the wallet and nearly shit his pants. Inside the wallet, next to a miniature family portrait, was a shiny gold shield. Mikey's dumb ass had just tried to rob a cop.

Mikey looked around wild-eyed. He knew he had fucked up, *big time!* He pushed the detective down the last few steps and took off in the other direction. As he hopped up the last step, someone sucker punched him in the stomach. Mikey collapsed onto the ground, holding his gut. As he looked up teary-eyed, he could make out the shape of a potbellied white man standing over him.

"Well, well," Stark said. "Looks like you're having some trouble, Tommy."

"Fucking shit," Detective Thomas White, aka Tommy, said. "This coon fuck tried to rob me."

"Is this true?" Stark asked, looking down at Mikey.

"Nah," Mikey stuttered. "I mean yes . . . but it wasn't like that. I didn't know he was a cop. Let alone your friend, Stark. I swear!"

"Bullshit," Tommy cut in. "I tried to give your ass a play, but you wouldn't listen. Now you're going to jail. Well . . . after we kick your nigger ass."

"Hold on," Mikey pleaded. "Maybe we can work something out?"

"Fuck you, shit-bird," Stark barked. "You ain't in no position to make deals. Tommy, what do ya say we take ol' sticky fingers down by the peer and see if shit floats?"

"Sounds good," Tommy said, grinning. The two detectives grabbed Mikey and lifted him to his feet. Mikey's brain started spinning at one hundred miles a minute. He needed a way to get up outta this, but how? Then it hit him.

"Okay fellas," Mikey said. "Y'all got me dead to right, but you might wanna rethink my offer. I know things."

"What kinda things?" Stark asked, already knowing where this was going.

"Well . . . there's these kids in the project getting money."

"What the fuck else is new?"

"Nah, Stark. I'm dead-ass. I got a direct connect to the whose who in the hood. Square biz."

"Li'l nigger, we already know who's who in the projects. If you can't deliver me Prince on a platter we ain't got nothing to talk about."

"Well, I can't get you Prince, but what if I could give you one of his peoples?"

"Fuck do we want with some petty-ass street runner?"

"Nah, man. I ain't talking about some nickle-and-dime hood. What if I could get you one of his captains?"

"Okay," Stark said, pausing. "I'm listening."

"I swear to you guys if you give me a little time I'm sure that I can cut into one of Prince's Capos."

"And we're supposed to just take your word for it?"

"My word is all I have."

"Not good enough," Tommy said. "We need a show of good faith."

"A show of good faith? Like what?"

"Like . . . who can you give us right now?"

"Right now? I ain't got nobody."

"Oh, you better get somebody," Stark said, "if not, your black ass is going to jail."

Mikey began to skim through his mental Rolodex trying to think of someone he could give up. Just any old body wouldn't do, he needed someone juicy to get the two dicks up off his back. Suddenly an idea formed in his head. It would be risky, because the people he was about to snitch on would surely murder him if they found out. Risky as it was, he had to do it.

"Say, y'all interested in some robberies?"

13

io and Cutty stepped onto 107th Street in search of Truck. They spotted a few cats shooting dice over in the cut. Although they didn't see Truck among them, these guys were sure to know where to find him. As Rio approached the group one of the kids, whose name was Slim, turned to greet him.

"What it is, big-dog?" Slim said, flashing his gold caps.

"Ain't nothing," Rio said, giving him dap. "Just came to see Truck. He around?"

"I just saw that nigga a few minutes ago," Slim said, looking around. "Check the corner store." Slim pointed to the bodega down the street. Rio thanked him and kept it moving. As Rio crossed the street, Truck came out of the bodega, smoking a black and mild. The orange Atlanta Falcons throwback he was wearing made him look like a fat-ass pumpkin. Truck noticed Rio and smiled menacingly.

"Sup, Rio?" he asked.

"Ain't nothing, Truck. I just needed to talk to you about something."

"Well, talk about it."

"Well, it's like this. I heard somebody that I had on the block owed you some paper. I paid the debt outta my pocket and had him out there working it off. But you still had him snatched. Why is that?"

"Oh, you mean the li'l nigga with the sticky fingers? I was wondering when you would come around and ask about him. Come on."

Truck led the two men down 106th Street into a walk-up apartment building. The trio hiked up the three flights of stairs, to a beat-up brown apartment door. Truck removed a key from his pocket and opened the door. Rio's senses were bombarded by a variety of smells. The most pungent was that of chronic. Inside the apartment there were a few cats lounging around playing PS2. Rio didn't see anything unusual in the living room, but when Truck led him to the back his mouth dropped wide open.

The walls and floor of the back room were covered in black garbage bags and the windows were taped up. A young man stood in the doorway smoking a cigarette, watching the show. Rio remembered him from Prince's house, but he didn't know his name. A metal chair sat in the middle of the room. Strapped to the chair was the young boy Rio was seeking. His face was a mess. One of his eyes was closed and he was covered in bruises, but Rio still recognized him.

"Truck," Rio snapped. "What's all this about?"

"Oh, you ain't know?" Truck asked with a smile. "We've decided to take disciplinary action against our thieving-ass friend here. Mmm hmm. Been working him over for a few hours now, but I don't think he's sorry for what he's done."

"Truck, you're going too far. I don't think—"

"That's my fucking point," Truck said, cutting him off. "You don't fucking think. This ain't no nickle-and-dime shit here, Darius. We play for keeps around this ma fucka. If you wanna play with the big boys, you gotta think like us. These streets ain't nothing nice. You let one ma fucka skate and they all gonna try you.

"Barney," Truck said to the kid in the doorway. "Let me get that." Bone handed Truck a chrome 9. "Listen up, li'l nigga," Truck said, glaring at Rio but aiming the pistol at the thief's face. "I'm about to give you ya first lesson in the game. Rule number one, never let a nigga put shit on you." Before Rio could protest, Truck pulled the trigger.

❏   ❏   ❏

A few blocks away, Shamel stepped on the block where his peoples held it down. He had been having a funny feeling in his gut ever since he woke up. He knew something wasn't right, but he couldn't put his finger on it. His first clue was when he called the clubhouse and got no answer. The clubhouse was an abandoned building where he and his peoples hung out. It didn't belong to anyone in particular, it was just a place where they could hang out and stash their stolen goods. Even though it was technically abandoned, there was always someone there.

Shamel began walking toward the clubhouse, but was stopped short by a "pssst" noise. He immediately reached for his hammer, but breathed a sigh of relief when he saw Knowledge creeping from the direction of the park. Even though he knew Knowledge wasn't a threat, something still wasn't right. The worried look on his protégé's face only filled him with more dread.

"What up, God?" Shamel asked suspiciously.

"Let's take a walk." Knowledge responded nervously.

"Hold on," Shamel said, grabbing his arm. "I was just about to go through the spot and pick up some paper."

"Nah, Mel. You don't wanna go round there."

"Fuck you mean I don't wanna go around there? Nigga, Burger owes me for them rims I set him out with."

"Shamel, listen to me, man. You don't wanna go around there."

"Knowledge, you been smoking wet?"

"Man, why the fuck ain't you listening to me?" Knowledge asked, raising his voice, which was unusual for him. "You don't want to go to the clubhouse, cause there ain't no more clubhouse."

"Knowledge, fuck is you talking about?"

"Shamel, use your eyes!" Shamel looked down to the corner where the clubhouse was, for the first time noticing the crowd of onlookers. Against Knowledge's wishes, Shamel walked to the corner. What he saw almost made him break out into a run. There were police cars and paddy wagons everywhere. One by one the members of the thieves' clique were brought out of the building in shackles.

Shamel couldn't believe what he was seeing. For the last two years the thieves' clique had operated out of the clubhouse without incident. Now, it was all over. Shamel personally had close to fifty thousand dollars worth of hot items stashed in the spot. Those items along with all his comrades were being dragged from the building. He suddenly felt sick to his stomach. He almost passed out, but Knowledge caught his arm.

The little man steered Shamel in the other direction. Once they were a good distance away, Shamel allowed Knowledge to sit him down on a park bench. Shamel couldn't believe it. The money that he had stashed in the clubhouse was the bulk of his paper; now it was gone. He had a few dollars put up, but it wasn't much compared to the amount that would've been pulled in by what was in the house. All that was gone. At that moment he decided he needed a different hustle.

Trinity stood in her kitchen watching the soap bubbles swirling in the sink. Her hands were washing dishes, but her mind was elsewhere. She pondered her life and wondered why things were so hard for her? She wasn't a saint, but was she that bad of a person? None of it made sense anymore.

Billy came into the kitchen and stood in the doorway. She had been ducking her little brother's questioning eyes for the past day or so. She really didn't know what she could tell him to put his mind at ease. No matter how much she danced around the issue, she knew she would eventually have to tell her youngest sibling that their father would not be returning.

"What's on your mind, sis?" Billy asked.

"Huh?" Trinity said, caught a little off guard. "Oh, nothing. Just daydreaming."

"Umm hmm. Care to share?"

"Not really."

"Listen, T. I know you might not want to admit it, but Daddy's disappearance has you spooked. Don't feel bad, it has me a little shaken, too. But don't worry, T. He'll be back soon."

"I'd like to think so," she said, rubbing her cheek. "But . . . what if he doesn't?"

"What do you mean, sis?"

"Well . . . what I mean is, what if he doesn't come back this time?"

"Trinity, you're talking crazy. Daddy's probably out somewhere drunk as hell."

"No, Billy, seriously. Did you ever stop to think what we're gonna do if he doesn't come back this time?"

"Well . . . no. I never considered it. I mean, would it really make a difference? Trinity, you've been taking care of us since Mommy died. Dad hasn't ever been much help. At least not like a father should be."

"Yeah, you're right. But I still think we need to have some kinda plan just in case. Ya know?"

"I guess that makes sense. But do you really think he might not come back?" Her silence was answer enough. After a few awkward moments Billy said, "Trinity, I wanna say something to you. Look . . . I'm sorry. You know, for what I said about Rio. He's a good dude. For me to even suggest that he might've done something to Daddy . . . well, I'm sorry."

Trinity gave her little brother a phony smile of thanks, but deep in her heart she knew that he wasn't that far off. Rio was a good dude, true enough. But he had everything to do with their father's disappearance. Her lover had been the one who pulled the trigger and took their father from them. As noble a gesture as it was, did that make it okay?

"Well," she began, "let's try not to dwell on it, Billy. We'll leave it in God's hands and hope everything works itself out."

"You're right, sis. As usual." Billy grabbed an apple from the fridge and went on about his business. Trinity watched her little brother leave and felt a heaviness in her heart. She hated lying to her little brother, but the ends justified the means. She had to protect her man at all cost. Rio, her darling Rio who would make everything right. In time he was sure to make everything okay. He had to.

As soon as Trinity was done with the dishes, she heard her Mickey Mouse phone ringing. She had no idea who it could've been since she had been ducking just about everyone since she got out of the hospital. She jogged down the narrow hallway to her room. The lights were off so she couldn't see the caller ID. As soon as she picked up the phone, she wished she hadn't.

"What's up, girl?" Joyce asked. "Where you been hiding?"

"Hey, Joyce," Trinity said in a phony sisterly voice.

"Girl, I thought you up and dropped off the face of the earth. I asked Alex what was up with you, but you know how she be on it? Bitch acting all tight-lipped and shit, like she don't love drama."

"Ain't nothing, Joyce. I just been taking it easy, ya know?"

"Yeah, I feel you. I heard you was in the hospital?"

"Yeah, I'm fine though."

"I know that's right. You a trooper girl, so you always gonna come out on top. I was gonna come see you, but this nigga Max just came home. You know how that shit go. Had to get that three-year nut up out him."

"Umm hmm," Trinity said dryly. "Listen, I was just about to cook dinner for me and Billy, so . . ."

"Oh, I feel you. I just called to tell you the latest gossip."

Trinity didn't really feel like hearing any gossip, but if she humored Joyce, maybe the mouthy bitch would get off the phone. "Okay, spill."

"Well, you know about them boys from the clubhouse?"

Trinity knew that she was referring to Shamel's thieves' clique, but she played stupid. "Who?"

"Oh, Trinity. Girl, you ain't been gone that long. Them niggaz steal whatever the fuck ain't nailed down. Cars, jewels, whatever. You knew who them thieving niggaz that Rio's peoples run wit?"

"Oh, okay. What about em?"

"Girl, they got busted!"

"Busted? Which ones?"

"The whole squad. Bear, li'l man, Stink, all them niggaz. Cold busted."

Trinity began to think the worst. She knew that Shamel was one of their leaders and always in the center of what went on among them. He was like a brother to both her and Rio. If something were to happen to him, she'd truly be hurt.

"Damn, Joyce," Trinity sighed. "That's fucked up."

"I know it, girl. Them niggaz was getting it, now they ain't. I heard the police was bringing all kinda shit outta the clubhouse. Money, jewels, you name it. Them kids was sitting on some paper."

"What about Shamel?"

"I don't think he was one of the people who got caught. But I heard he had some dough stashed up in there. All them niggaz kept money and hot shit stashed around that house. They didn't even try to keep it a secret. Everybody knows what happens to people stupid enough to cross them rowdy ma fuckas."

"Damn, I gotta go find Rio and let him know what happened."

"Please, girl. Rio probably already knows what went down. The way I hear it, he's that nigga now."

"What you mean by that, Joyce?"

"Trinity, you ain't gotta front for me. I know what's up."

"Oh, yeah? Well, why don't you tell me what's up?"

"Trinity, all the girls at the nail shop was talking about it. They say that Rio got a promotion. Douglass is under new management. Youz about a lucky bitch, cause Rio is about to see major paper and you wit him, so you know he gonna look out. If you was smart you'd put a baby on that nigga."

Trinity felt her anger getting the best of her. It would be a no-good bitch like Joyce to be thinking scandalous. Bitches like her were the reason that there were so few niggaz like Rio. Before things got ugly, Trinity decided to end the conversation. But not before she put Joyce in her place.

"Listen, Joyce," Trinity began in an even but firm voice, "them bitches in the hood ain't got nothing to do but gossip. Rio doesn't sell drugs," she lied. "Them bitches don't know me or my man, so they need to keep both our names out their mouths. I'd hate to have to come up there and clown. And on a parting note, if you were as much my friend to me as you claimed to be you'd check these bitches instead of following up on the bullshit." Trinity hung the phone up before Joyce could respond.

Trinity threw on her sweatpants and got ready to head out in search of Rio. She had to put him up on the latest turn of events and see how she could use it to their advantage. One thing Trinity had learned from spending so much time on the streets was that one man's misfortune is easily turned into another man's fortune. Well, in this case, woman's.

14

Rio sat in the little Spanish restaurant on 104th picking at his food and punishing a Corona. Cutty had begun to worry about his friend. Rio had hardly said anything since he saw Truck blow that boy's brains out. Cutty agreed that it was overdoing it, but he understood why Truck had done it. He was sending Rio a message. To play in this game you had to play dirty. Sometimes you had to make an example out of a ma fucka.

"You a'ight?" Cutty asked, tapping Rio's arm.

"I'm cool," Rio said, ordering another beer. "Just a little shaken, that's all."

"Don't feel bad, kid. It threw me a li'l, too. That boy Truck is a fucking monster. Blew that poor kid's head all over that spot."

"That shit was wack, Cutty. Real fucking wack."

"Yeah, man. It was wack all right. But that's the game. That might've been the first body you've seen, but it won't be ya last kid. When it's all said and done, you might end up catching one yourself."

"Man, I don't know if I got the stomach for this shit."

"Rio, don't start talking crazy. I don't wanna hear no shit like that coming outta ya mouth. You ain't 'small Paul' no more. Youz an official big dog. Ain't no turning back at this stage of the game."

"Fuck, I know. It's just that I hope I haven't bitten off more than I could chew."

"Rio, it is very important that you don't doubt yourself. Not to others and for damn sure not to ya self. People who are in it halfway, get buried all the way. You gonna fuck around and get locked up or get ya brains blown the fuck out. Either way ain't no future for those who doubt their own ability."

Rio nodded, letting Cutty's words sink in. What he was saying might've sounded a li'l off, but it was dead true. Many a man had come and gone in the game, only to fall victim to their own worst enemies. Themselves. Rio vowed that this was something that would not happen to him. Whatever adjustments he had to make would be handled. He had to get his head right if he intended to make it through the storm to come with his skin intact.

The two men sat and discussed their plans for the immediate future. Rio was a master schemer and Cutty was a case waiting to happen. They were like oil and water, but the two had each other's back. Their little meeting was interrupted by a chorus of "damns" and "good lords." They turned to see what the commotion was about and found Trinity at the center of it.

Trinity stood in the doorway of the little diner looking like the star that she was. Her tan Lady Enyce sweat suit hugged her body, showing off a shape that she couldn't hide if she wanted to. Her long corn-rowed hair hung down to her shoulders, making her look like Bo Derrick in her prime. Trinity strode confidently through the onlookers and thirsty niggaz to greet her man. When Rio stood and embraced her, most of the men quickly turned their heads. No one really wanted to earn the displeasure of the hood's newest superstar.

"Hey, boo," she said, kissing him on the mouth.

"What's good, ma?" he responded, palming her phatty with both hands, not out of disrespect, but to let the rest of the vultures know whom she was rolling with. "What you doing up this way, Trinity?"

"Looking for you, daddy. I haven't seen you all day."

"My bad. A nigga been running and shit, trying to get my affairs in order. Ya know?"

"Yeah, I know. But a bitch was lonely."

"I know, ma," he said, kissing her cheeks. "I'm sorry. I'll make it up to you."

"I know you will," she said, punching him in the arm.

"Sup, Trinity?" Cutty asked.

"Hey, Cutty," she responded with a half-smile. Trinity and Cutty had never really seen eye to eye on anything. He had never done anything to her personally, but he had a reputation as being a snake. He was one of Rio's closest friends, so Trinity gave him that, but he wasn't Shamel. There was just something about the young man that rubbed her the wrong way.

"Well," Cutty said, standing. "I'm gonna go get some smoke and leave you two alone. Rio, you want something?"

"Yeah," Rio said, peeling off a bill. "Snatch me a 'dub.' Don't bring me none of that green shit you smoke either, nigga."

"I got you, big-dog." Cutty took the bill and left.

"You hungry, ma?" Rio asked.

"Nah, I'll get something later. Let's take a walk. I wanna talk to you about something."

"Okay, ma. Let's boogie."

Trinity took Rio by the hand and led him out of the diner. Outside people were buzzing back and forth doing their thing. Those who Rio knew, he gave dap. Those he didn't know turned their eyes away. This was one aspect of being connected that Rio didn't like. To be respected on the streets was all fine and good. But with power came fear. Rio was always a dude that got love from everybody just about everywhere he went. He didn't feel comfortable with people being afraid of him. A wise man once said that "a scared nigga is the quickest to kill you, just cause he's scared."

Rio and Trinity took a slow stroll down Columbus Ave, shooting the breeze. It had been a while since he had been able to just chill with his lady. Truth be told, he hadn't had a chance to really kick it with her since her father's . . . accident. He couldn't help but to wonder what was going through her mind. He wanted to reach out and try to offer her some sort of comfort, but he knew that wasn't her way. Trinity would open up when she was ready. When that time came he would be there for her.

"So, what's good, T?" he asked, breaking the silence. "What's so important that you came out here looking for me?"

"Damn," she said playfully. "You so anxious. Nah, but on the real though. I wanted to talk to you about Mel."

"Shamel? What about him?"

"You ain't hear what happened to the clique?"

"Nah, I been running around with Cutty for most of the day."

"Well, you know I ain't one for the gossip, but I thought this might interest you."

"Okay, I'm listening."

"Joyce's nosy ass called me at the house earlier. She was basically trying to be up in the mix, but she did pass some info along to me about the clique. It seems that they all got knocked."

"Get the fuck outta here," he said, shocked. "T, them niggaz is like thirty deep and they all run in different circles. How the hell they all get knocked?"

"I don't know the details, Rio. I'm only telling you what I heard. Well, like I was saying, the police ran up in the clubhouse and snatched whoever was laid up and all their goods."

"Damn, my nigga Mel locked up?"

"I don't think so. She didn't say anything about Shamel. But a good handful of them took a fall."

"Shit, that was my nigga's bread and butter right there. Everybody either used the clique's services or fenced hot shit through them. I know he's gonna be uptight."

"That's my point," Trinity said slyly.

"What you talking about, T?"

"It's like you, Rio, said. The whole thieving thing was Shamel's hustle. I'm sure he could do okay independently, but without the clique, business is sure to be slow."

"And?"

"And, that's where his main man Rio comes in."

"Trinity, you know damn well Shamel don't fuck wit drugs in no kinda way. He ain't gonna go for that shit."

"Rio, I love you, but at times you can be a silly goose. A desperate man will do anything to keep his head above water. Bring Shamel into the fold. Not on the drug tip, but make him part of your little entourage. Kinda like a bodyguard."

"I got Cutty for that."

"Rio, Cutty's cool, but the boy is a loose cannon. Shamel is more of a thinker. A street-wise nigga like him can point certain things out to you that Cutty couldn't. Besides, in your line of work you never can have too many sets of eyes behind your head."

Rio started to protest further, but the more he thought about it the more sense it made. With Cutty and Shamel with him, his clique would be a lot tighter. Cutty was the more vicious of the two, but Shamel wasn't no slouch. With a three-headed monster like that, how could they lose.

"Damn, Trinity. Youz a smart chick."

"I know, baby," she said, kissing him on the cheek. "That's why you love me. Now, make it your business to find Shamel and lay your offer out."

"That's easier said than done. That boy is like a ghost. I wouldn't even know where to look." The sounds of shouting and breaking glass gave him a good idea where to start.

Shamel came out of the corner store clutching a forty of that eight-ball. It was his third in as many hours, but he didn't intend to slow up. He had short paper and needed to get wasted. If anything could do it for little money, it was Old English. As he staggered across 100th Street, he could make out two figures moving his way. After fighting with his eyes for focus, he recognized the figures as Kev and Boo.

Shamel sucked his teeth at the sight of his two rivals. Because of the fact that they were all stick-up kids, their paths had crossed before, but there was no love lost between them. The duo didn't like Shamel because he was a beast and rolled with the Thieves' Clique. Shamel didn't like them because they were rouges. The clique had certain codes that they wouldn't violate, but the rogues respected nothing. All that mattered to them was paper.

"What up, Mel?" Kev asked, smiling.

"Sup," Shamel responded, not bothering to slow down.

"What's really good wit you?" Boo spat. "You ain't got time for old friends?"

"Fuck outta here," Shamel said, stopping short. "Nigga, we ain't never been friends."

"Come on, Mel," Kev interjected. "We ain't come on no bullshit. We just wanted to talk to you."

"Talk to me about what?"

"Look, we heard about what happened with ya team."

"Terrible, just terrible," Boo cut in.

"And?" Shamel asked, swigging his beer.

"And," Kev continued, "we wanna make you an offer."

"Listen, man, y'all ain't got nothing I want."

"Come on, kid," Boo said. "We know what happened to the clique. It's a wrap for them cats man. What you gonna do, starve? You might as well stop bullshitting and come on it. Me, you, and Kev can start another clique on some new and improved shit. We the cream of the crop, baby. With us three together, we can kill em. Shit, you look like you could use the money. Running round drinking Forties like we still in the fucking eighties."

"Hold on, hold on," Shamel said, putting the top back on his beer. "Let me put you niggaz up on game. The God always has and always will be his own man. My team is gone, but that ain't gonna stop my shine. I've always held my own. Matter of fact, why am I even talking to y'all?" Shamel tried to walk away, but Boo wasn't finished.

"Hold the fuck on," Boo said, grabbing his arm. "We ain't finished wit—" Before he could finish his sentence, Shamel smashed him in the side of the head with his forty. Boo stumbled twice and crashed head-first into the ground. Shamel followed up with a kick to the side, sending him crashing into the small gate.

"Is you fucking crazy?" Shamel barked. Kev had managed to pull his Glock while his man was getting whipped out. He was trying to ease up behind Shamel to lace him, but changed his mind when the darkness exploded with flashes of gunfire. Rio came charging toward the scuffle spitting rounds from his hammer. Kev ducked behind a car and took off running through the parking lot. Boo took one in the shoulder, but managed to pull his ass up and follow his man into the night. Rio hadn't intended on hitting anyone, but fuck it. His man needed him and he was there.

Rage and anger had taken over Shamel, causing him to wild out. Without looking to see who it was, he took a swing at Rio. Rio managed to avoid most of the blow, but still got nicked on the chin. As Rio tried to get out of the way Shamel drew his weapon. Trinity saw what was about to go down and got on the good foot trying to catch up to them. Rio also saw what was about to go down and didn't like the idea of getting shot. He could've easily gunned Shamel down and saved himself, but he needed another way. Shamel was drunk and really didn't realize what he was doing.

As Shamel brought his shooting arm around, Rio ducked and advanced on him. He made sure that there wasn't enough space for his friend to pop him. "Shamel!" shouted Rio as he grabbed the big man in a bear hug. Shamel outweighed Rio by quite a few pounds, but it wasn't that easy to take him down. Shamel thrashed and tried to break the smaller man's grip, but had a very tough time of it. Bellowing out in rage Shamel tried to throw his weight on Rio. Even though Rio was smaller, he was learned in various fighting techniques—jujitsu being one of them.

Rio let Shamel think that his plan was working and then turned the tables on him. He loosed his grip from the man's waist and grabbed him by his shooting arm. Using Shamel's momentum against him, he tossed the big man over his hip. Shamel skidded a good three feet before crashing into the concrete steps. The impact caused Shamel to lose his grip on the P89. Unarmed and embarrassed, Shamel pulled a dagger out of his boot and got up to charge Rio. Rio decided that if he wanted to get out of the situation uninjured he was going to have to shoot his man.

Before either of the two men could jump, Trinity said in a firm voice, "What the hell is y'all doing? Shamel, I know you ain't about to get at ya man."

Shamel turned on Trinity as if he were going to attack, then suddenly froze. Slowly the glare of madness started to fade from his eyes. He blinked twice and slurred, "Trinity?" Shamel looked from Rio to Trinity as if seeing them for the first time. Shamel looked at the blade in his hand as if it were a viper. Suddenly the realization of what he had almost done became painfully clear. Shamel collapsed on the ground with his hands on his face.

"Fuck am I doing?" he whispered.

"I was gonna ask you the same thing," Rio said, sitting beside him. "What's really good with you, fam? I come through here to check you and it's like Vietnam out this Bitch."

"I . . . yo Rio . . . you know I would never . . ."

"Don't worry about it," Rio said. "You were going through something, my nigga. I respect that. But make me understand what's going on with you, God. This here ain't you."

"Gone," Shamel said. "All gone, kid."

"What you rapping about?" Rio asked. "You talking about the clique?"

"Man, fuck the clique, Rio. I mean, I'm gonna miss my comrades, but fuck that shit. I had a gang of shit tucked away in there. I figured it was smarter to keep most of my shit up in the house instead of at my spot. But look what the fuck happened."

"Don't wet that, Mel. I could shoot you a few dollars till you get on your feet, man. Plus I know you had some paper put up."

"Paper," Shamel asked chuckling. "Baby boy, ain't no paper. I got a few dollars put up at my mom's house and a few 'ones' at my spot. I had close to forty thousand in cash and stolen goods tucked at the clubhouse. I'm hit, baby."

"Shamel," Rio said, lighting a cigarette. "As long as you been robbing and stealing, you really ain't stash no bread?"

"Rio, I really don't feel like hearing that old 'I told you so' shit. I was balling outta control. A nigga always had money coming in, so I wasn't thinking about saving. As long as it was niggaz around for me to rob, I figured I'd always be good."

"So, what if you just went back to freelance jacking?"

"Rio, I wish it were that simple. The clique was supposed to have been shut down because of a snitch. Nobody knows exactly who it was, but ain't none of the fences trying to fuck with us right now. Nobody knows who pointed the finger, so everybody from the clique is getting fed with long-handled spoons. It was hard before, but without the help of the fences, it's damn near impossible to move quality shit. Shit, I'd probably be better off getting a job."

Trinity gave Rio the eye without letting Shamel catch it. Rio frowned at her but figured what the hell? The worst Shamel could say was no. In which case, he'd still have Cutty. "Look homey," Rio began. "What if I told you that I had a way for you to still keep ya head over water?"

"Rio," Shamel said, pulling himself up. "Unless you know of a good fence or a nice mansion I can take off, I don't think you can do anything for me."

"See, there you go. Ever since we was young, you've been quick to jump to conclusions. I ain't asking you to sling no drugs. I know that ain't your thing. What I'm asking you is to become a part of my team."

"So, you just gonna pay me for nothing?"

"Oh, hell no. Ain't nothing in life without a price, dog. You taught me that. I need loyal niggaz around me that I can trust. Cutty is my nigga, but you like my brother. I know if I can put my life in anybody's hands, it's yours."

Shamel scratched at his beard and weighed his options. The stickup-kid thing was slowly dying out. True, there was still money in that game, but they were giving out too much time for it. The amount of time that it would take to get another operation going like the one he and Burger had set up would take too long. Rio was surely on his way to the top of the crack game and he would make sure Shamel ate. If all he wanted Shamel to do was watch his back or slap a few niggaz up, why not? He was doing it for free, so if Rio was willing to pay him for it then so be it.

"A'ight my nigga," Shamel said. "You my peoples, so you know I'm gonna look out for you. This ain't really my game, but I'm willing to play."

Trinity had to turn her head so Shamel couldn't see the grin that spread across her face. Just as she had said everything was falling into place. Rio now had a solid team, each with his own special usefulness. Cutty would kill without question, but Shamel would kill with efficiency. Rio was her boo and she loved him dearly, but sometimes he needed a little direction. She remembered something her mother used to tell her: "Behind every good man is a cunning woman."

Truck sat in the rear of Prince's Caddy, fuming. His father had been screaming on him for the last twenty minutes without so much as taking a breath. It seemed that someone had told Prince about the little show he put on for Rio. To say that Prince was upset would've been an understatement.

"I just don't understand you, boy," Prince scolded. "You think you can just go around killing people and it's all good?"

"But Pop—"

"But Pop, shit, Truck. It don't work like that. This is my ma fuck'n setup and I call the shots," Prince said, jabbing his index finger into Truck's chest. "I decide who lives and dies."

"Pop, all I was doing was trying to show ya little protégé what time it is."

"Fuck you gonna show somebody what time it is and you don't know? Rio is a good kid and a damn good earner. I don't need you cramming his head with that bullshit you laying down."

"I hear you, Pop, but the boy is soft. He needs heart."

"Heart? Truck, you don't know Rio as well as you think you do. He's a stand-up dude."

"Just because he did a little time doesn't make him a stand-up anything," Truck insisted. "Plenty of niggaz in the hood did time and I don't see you pampering them."

"Oh yeah, smart ass? Well, tell me this then, how many niggaz done time for someone else?" Truck remained silent. "Just like I thought," Prince continued. "You really don't know the score, son. That gun they pinned on Rio wasn't even his. My 'protégé,' as you call him, took that charge for one of my boys."

"Damn," Truck asked in disbelief. "You serious?"

"As a heart attack. You remember Go-Go, don't you?"

"Yeah."

"Well, ol' Go-Go had an open case and decided that it was a smart thing to be running around holding heat. When the police rolled up, Go-Go wanted to shoot it out. A gangsta-ass thought, but a dumb-ass move nonetheless. Had he shot it out wit them people, he would've gotten himself as well as everyone else in front of the building killed. Rio, being the kinda nigga he was, came up with a plan to save everyone's skin. Everyone except his."

"What he do?" Truck asked.

"Rio told Go-Go to pass him the heat."

"Why did he do a dumb-ass thing like that? He could've just stepped off."

"Because, you selfish bastard, Rio is a smart nigga. Go-Go was one of my top dogs back then. He brought me a lot of paper during his run. Rio knew that Go-Go had a jacked-up record, whereas he had none. The police would've fried Go-Go, but they could only do so much to Rio. So he took the fall to save Go-Go. Everybody thought they would give Rio probation, but he ended up getting some time on top of that."

"So that's how he ended up doing the thirteen months?"

"Umm hmm."

"Shit, that li'l punk was probably scared to death, huh Pop?"

"Yep, heard he damn near cried his first night on the island. But the funny thing about it all was that boy never once spoke my name or anyone else in the organization."

When Prince mentioned the "Snitch Factor," Truck tensed up a bit. The cocaine he had been sniffing was telling him that Prince knew what he was doing in the joint. Truck didn't consider himself a snitch by any stretch of the word. He looked at it more like good bargaining. While he was behind the wall, he would feed the guards from time to time. Nothing heavy though. A buy here, somebody holding a shank there. They would piece him off from some of the bust in addition to shaving his time. He might've been able to skate by on that shit while he was inside, but the streets were ignorant to such mercies.

"That's some deep shit," Truck said, lighting a cigarette. "The boy got a li'l heart. But all that proves is that he was stupid."

"Truck," Prince sighed. "You still don't see the big picture and that's probably why you'll be middle management for the better part of your career. To some niggaz, what he did might've been considered stupid, that's the truth. But to me and the type of players I deal with, that was noble as hell. He sacrificed his freedom for the love of his man and the good of the organization. The whole time he was locked down, he never asked me for a dime. Not one fucking cent, Truck. He put his self there, so he held that time on his own. That's a stand-up nigga, Truck. You see, son, I got big plans for both of you boys. You're my son, Truck, so it's only natural for me to want you to succeed me. But you need a nigga like Rio to be like a second brain, catching things that you might've missed. If you wanna do it the right way, Truck, its gonna take a team effort."

Prince's words both enlightened and hurt Truck. Taking a charge of any kind for someone else, let alone a gun charge, took balls. He could kinda see why his pops fucked with Rio like that, but he still didn't like him. Truck might not have been as smart as Rio, but he wasn't no dummy either. Team effort his ass. He saw just where his father's twisted little mind was going with all this. He was grooming Rio to be his successor.

Just thinking about it made Truck want to reach over and choke his sperm donor. He might've tried it, but there was no doubt that if he did, J would pop him. Truck eased back, trying to calm himself. Prince could pop all the shit he wanted, for now.

"Okay, Pop," Truck said, sliding out of the hog. "I fucked up and I won't let it happen again."

"You damn right," Prince snapped. "You better be cool, Truck. Hot-headed cowboys don't last long in this here. You let me worry about Rio. Ya hear?"

"A'ight Pop. I got you. But why—" Before Truck could pose his question, J pulled the hog into traffic. Truck just stared at the taillights in disgust. Prince's fifteen minutes of fame would soon be over. Truck was going to see to that personally. Regardless of what Prince wanted, Truck was going to be the next king.

15

After walking Shamel home, Rio dropped Trinity off and hit the block in search of Cutty. The li'l sparring match with Shamel took a lot out of him, but he was still in pretty good shape. Shamel never really drank like that, let alone forties. What went down with the clique must've really had him down. Whoever the snitch was, Rio would've bet his life that it wasn't Shamel. After hearing that, Rio understood why J made him hold off till he checked Cutty out.

Rio's attention was drawn to the sound of a blaring car horn. When he turned around, he saw Prince's hog coming his way. As the Caddy eased to the curb, the back door swung open. Rio already knew what time it was, so he just got in. Prince greeted him with a warm smile.

"What it is, youngster?" Prince asked.

"Chilling," Rio responded. "What brings you down here, Prince?"

"I wanted to rap wit ya about some bread."

"Bread? You ain't get the take money for this week?"

"Oh, I got it. Everything is right on time, kid."

"Okay, so what bread you talking bout?"

"Here," Prince said, tossing him a heavy envelope. "That's for you."

Rio skimmed through the bills and shook his head. "Hold on, Prince. There's like eight grand in here."

"Ten. That's your paycheck."

"But Prince, I was only getting a few hundred before."

"I know it. But that was before I brought you in. You checked in a hundred grand. Ten percent goes to you. As you get ya weight up, you'll buy from me and just kick something back to the home team."

"Damn," Rio said, smiling. "I keep getting hit like this and I'll have my weight up in no time."

"I told you, Rio. You'll win fucking with me. The more you check in, the more you'll make. Think about that the next time you hit the block. Now, get up outta here and spend some of that bread."

"Thanks," Rio said, getting out of the car. "But I think I'm gonna put this up."

"Have it your way, kid. It's your paper. But take some advice from an old player. If you gonna be a big dog, you gotta dress the part. Try trading in the sweat suits for some nice slacks?"

Rio looked at his getup and shrugged. "Nah, I'm good, Prince."

"Have it your way, kid. But remember what I said about 'big dogs.'" Prince winked at Rio and the Caddy took off.

Truck strolled down the Avenue of the Americas with his man Slim. Slim was unlike the other cats that Truck surrounded himself with. Slim actually had class. He was a brown-skinned dude that stood an even six feet. Standing next to Truck he still looked like a midget. Slim had thick black hair that he kept low and waved out. His Gucci jumpsuit was identical to the loafers he wore on his feet. Slim might've looked like a pretty boy, but he was by far one of the most dangerous men in Harlem.

"Damn, my nigga," Slim complained. "How fucking far you gonna walk me?"

"Be easy," Truck barked. "We almost there. We gotta meet these niggaz in the park on the side of McDonald's."

"It better be worth the trip, Truck. You got me down here with these crackers, knowing damn well I don't fuck with white people."

"Man, these folks ain't thinking bout you. Just bring yo ass on."

Truck understood where his friend was coming from. They had traveled a good distance to find someone to perform a service for him. Everyone else that Truck tried to get at turned the contract down. Prince had a lot of love in the streets so no one wanted to take the contract. As a last resort Truck sought help from outsiders. The two men walked the last few blocks to West Fourth without further debate. When they got to the park, it appeared to be empty. Truck moved warily into the park, followed by Slim. Truck had the meeting set up through a third party. He had never actually met the man he was coming to meet, but he had heard that he was one of the best.

"Fuck is going on," Slim whispered. "This cat ain't coming?"

"Hold on, son," Truck said. "He's still got a few ticks."

A flicker of movement caused Slim to spin around with his gun drawn. Slim's muscles relaxed a bit when a teenage boy stepped out of the shadows. The boy was tall and thin with dark shiny skin. His brown eyes seemed to burn with an unnatural glow. At first Slim was going to say something slick to the boy, but something in the back of his mind told him to let the boy be.

"Beat it, kid," Truck barked. "It's dangerous in the park after dark."

"Danger only finds those who try to avoid it," said the boy in a voice that hardly matched his young face. "I should be telling you the same thing about the dark, my friend."

"I ain't ya fucking friend, shorty. I got business down here and you holding that up."

"I know about your business, Truck."

"Man, how you know me?"

"Because, I'm the person that you're waiting for. I'm Kane."

Truck looked at Kane as if he were lying. As far as he knew, the man he was supposed to meet with ran with some of the best killers around. The scrawny punk in front of him couldn't be Kane. Could it?

"Look, kid," Truck said, getting frustrated. "You ain't but maybe twenty or so, the guy I'm waiting for is an older dude."

"Truck," Kane said, stepping closer. "You shouldn't believe everything you hear. I think my reputation had been a little overexaggerated. Trust me, I am Kane. Now, we can sit here and keep talking shit back and forth or we can do some business."

Truck noticed that Slim hadn't moved since the kid stepped out. He just kept staring at him like he was in love or some weird shit. He was definitely going to get an earful about it later. Right now, Truck was going to test the waters with this Kane.

"Okay, shorty," Truck said. "If you're Kane, then you already know why I'm here?"

"Yes. If my information is correct, you need someone to die. Am I right?"

"Right as rain, baby. I need someone to get gone. Permanent like. I hear you get down for yours, shorty. Can you do it?"

"Hold up, man," Kane said, raising a gloved hand. "First things first. Let's talk paper."

"Oh, for sure, man. How much you gonna charge me for the job?"

"One body . . . gimmie a hundred thousand dollars."

"One hundred grand. Man, you can't be serious? I ain't asking you to kill the pope."

"Shit, you might as well be. Truck, I ain't never been stupid. I know just who you want dead. Why you want Prince dead isn't my concern, but that's the price. Take it or leave it."

Truck was a little disturbed by the youngster's vast knowledge for his business. He always played his hand close to his chest, so having a stranger be so knowledgeable of him didn't bode well. It was too late to turn back now.

"A'ight, Kane," Truck sighed. "I can get the money up, but how do I know you're as good as they say?"

"First of all," Kane said, plucking an imaginary piece of lint from his sweater. "I don't know where you got your info, but I don't go on jobs anymore."

"So, what, you just popping all this shit for nothing?"

"Never for nothing, Truck. I just said that I don't go on jobs anymore. I never said it wouldn't get done."

"Come on, dog. You bringing other niggaz to the table that I don't even know?"

"Oh, you can meet him anytime."

"So, where the fuck is he?"

"Right behind you."

Truck turned around and scanned for the so-called killer. At first he didn't see anybody, but as his eyes strained into the darkness they picked out a shape coming toward them. He stepped into the light so Truck could get a good look at him. When Truck took in the full scope of the young man, his hopes fled.

The man that stood before him looked more like a skeleton than anything else. He was tall, but not as tall as Truck. He had a long thin face that gave him a caninelike appearance. His black eyes looked Truck up and down, but didn't show one drop of emotion. The three-quarter leather jacket did little to hide the form-fitting body armor he wore. The stranger's fingers looked like worms hanging from the sleeve of his jacket as he looked from Truck to Kane.

"Truck," Kane said, stepping forward. "This is the man who will do the job. This is the Hound."

Truck wanted to explode but managed to hold his temper in check. "The what?" He snapped. "Kane, what the fuck are you trying to pull? This nigga looks like he just staggered out of a meth clinic. If he's gonna go at Prince, he's gonna need an army behind him."

"Don't be so quick to judge, Truck."

"Quick to judge, my ass. Fuck makes this nigga so special?"

"Maybe a demonstration? Hound," Kane said in a commanding voice.

The man known as Hound stepped forward, showing Truck his palms. Hound rubbed his palms together and spread them again. When he held his hands out, in his palms he had two star-shaped blades that looped around his middle fingers like rings. With a flick of his thumbs, Hound set the blades to spinning.

Truck was so fascinated by the demonstration that he almost didn't see Hound whip one of the blades in his direction. The blade whistled past Truck's ear. If Hound had wanted to hit Truck, there would've been nothing the big man could've done about it. Truck was very impressed with the young man's speed. Before anyone could say anything, Slim spoke up.

"What the fuck!" Slim yelled, grabbing his ear. The blade had whistled past Truck and nicked Slim's left ear. "What the hell is going on?"

Truck just looked at Slim slack jawed. If he wasn't sure of Hound's qualifications before, he was a believer now. The Hound was the truth.

"I take it by the look on your face that you're impressed?" Kane asked.

"Yeah," Truck responded. "But a fancy knife trick ain't gonna kill Prince."

"Don't worry, Truck. You'll get your body, as soon as we get our money."

"You'll get ya money, Kane. I wouldn't cross you."

"I should hope not, Truck. Round here, we take it in blood. Ya heard?"

"You threatening me?"

"Nah, I'd never threaten a dude that owes me a hundred grand."

"Well, Prince ain't dead yet, so I don't owe you shit."

"Like I said, you'll get your body. By the end of the month, Prince will be no more."

With their business conducted, Truck and Slim got up outta Dodge. Kane and the Hound watched them leave before speaking. "So," Kane began, "what'd you think?"

"I don't like that cat," Hound said, speaking for the first time. "Something stinks about him."

"Yeah, him and his weak-ass man."

"Nah, Kane. Don't sleep on the other kid. That boy had killer written all over him."

"I know you ain't scared, H?"

"Fuck outta here. You talking to the Hound, remember?"

"Yeah, I remember, nigga. You tried to come at me once, remember?"

"Yeah, I remember. You were the only person to ever get one up on me. That seemed like so long ago."

"I know it, man. So what now?"

"Shit, I'm hungry. I ain't eat all night."

"Me either. I got it, let's hit that party over by NYU."

"Yeah, that'll work. Probably gonna be a lot of honeys up in that joint."

"So let's do the damn thang, baby."

"Say, Kane," Hound said, pausing, "what was all that shit about?"

"What?" Kane asked.

"You know what I'm talking about. All that, 'Danger only finds those who seek to avoid it?' What was that all about?"

"I always wanted to say some shit like that to a nigga, Hound. You know I love the drama."

"Do you. Spitting proverbs and shit."

"*Me?*" Kane asked, smiling. "What about you with the little knife trick?"

"He wanted a demonstration."

"Fronting ass nigga," Kane said, playfully punching Hound. The two killers traded fake punches and giggled their way east.

Truck was feeling good because he just knew he had a bad-ass dude working for him now. Little did he know, he had just released hell up in Harlem.

Rio and Trinity stood on the observation deck of the Empire State Building, looking out at the city. The lights against the night sky were quite a sight to behold. New York might have been a virtual concrete jungle, but its skyline was a marvel. The array of lights and structures that danced in the distance were beautiful indeed, but only a rouse to hide the madness that infected the streets below.

"It's beautiful up here," Trinity said.

"I know, ma," Rio said, pulling her closer. "Sometimes I come up here to think, ya know? Something about being way up here gives me a feeling of peace."

"Yeah, I see what you mean. You can even see the stars from this high up. It's almost like you can reach up and touch them."

"You like the stars?"

"Yeah, even though I don't get to see them very often. I remember when I was little, my mother would take us to her sister's house upstate. You can see all of the stars in that clean country air. I used to lay out on her lawn and stargaze for hours."

"Well," Rio said. "Since you like the stars so much, pick one."

"Quit playing, Rio."

"I'm serious. Pick one."

"Okay," Trinity said, scanning the sky. "How about that one there?"

"Ah, good choice. That star there is actually one of three that make up Orion's belt."

"Orion?" she asked, confused.

"Yeah. He was a mythological hero of sorts. But since you like the star so much it's yours. Fuck Orion," he said playfully. "From now on we'll call it 'Trinity's heart.' One star for each of us. You, me, and Billy."

"You're so silly, Rio," she said, pushing him. Trinity's smile slowly faded and gave way to silence.

"What's wrong?" Rio asked, concerned for his boo. "Did I say something to upset you?"

"No," she said waving him off. "Just remembering the dreams of a foolish young girl. It's silly."

"Trinity, ain't nothing silly about dreaming. What we dream and strive for makes us unique."

"I know, Rio. Sometimes I just wonder if I'll ever get to live in a house of my own where I can stargaze all I want?"

"If I have anything to do with it, you will. T, we ain't gonna live in the projects forever. I plan to make a life for us. Each and every one of us in these streets has a dream. Mine is to be free."

"Then I guess we share the same dream, Rio."

"A dream that will one day become reality. I promise, ma. One day we'll live out our dream and be free of this bullshit. I promise, Trinity. Just have a little faith in your man."

"Rio, you're about the only thing in this world that I still have faith in. When everyone else abandoned me, you were in my corner."

"And I always will be. Trinity, I love you in this life and I'll love you in the next. We'll see our dream come to life and be free of these streets. Just keep your faith, ma. Keep your faith."

16

Trinity strolled across 125th Street with her girls Alex and Joyce. The sun was shining and her boo-boo had given her three thousand dollars to go get herself some items for the summer. The streets had been good to Rio over the last few weeks. He in turn was good to her. His career change was benefiting both of them nicely.

"Girl," Joyce said. "You got a rack of shit."

"I know it," Trinity said, shifting one of her bags. "I really appreciate y'all helping me with all this."

"Trinity," Alex said. "Cut it out. You know you my girl and I'm gonna hold you down."

"I know that's right," Joyce butted in. "And the Coach bags you bought us didn't hurt none."

Trinity caught Joyce's slick-ass remark, but didn't follow up on it. Rio showed Trinity love and she in turn showed love to her peoples. That's how it went with Trinity. Alex was her girl, so she was gonna live regardless, but she bought Joyce a bag just for being there. The comment she made just proved what Trinity already knew. Joyce was a low-end bitch who wasn't used to anything.

"T," Alex said. "You sure know how to shop."

"I had a lot of catching up to do," Trinity said. "It's been so long since I been shopping, I needed a little bit of everything."

"Shit, I think you got that and then some."

"I know that's right," Joyce said. "Rio is setting you out, girl. Since he hooked up with Prince full-time, he's that nigga. You better get him for all he's worth before some other bitch try and slide up in your spot."

"Look, Joyce," Trinity said, a little irritated. "Just because Rio's had a little good fortune, don't move me. We've been down for each other since before he was getting money. Our relationship ain't hardly based on material things. I would love him if he didn't have a pot to piss in. Sure, the money helps, but that ain't what we about. And as far as another bitch sliding up in my spot, I ain't worried about it. Cause even if he did decide to play his self and slip one of these bitches a little dick, they ain't me. Ain't a bitch out here that can take my spot." Trinity made sure she was staring directly at Joyce when she said the last part.

Joyce caught the venom in Trinity's voice, but let it ride. Trinity might've thought she was the queen, but a nigga was going to be a nigga regardless. She could prance around and act like she had her shit tight, but Joyce was an authority on other people's men. Once a bitch came along with a fatter ass or a better head game, Rio's tail would be wagging like the rest of them.

Trinity and her team made another pit stop at Dr. Jay's, off of Seventh Avenue. Trinity needed a pair of Timbs to go with the jeans she had bought. When they got upstairs there was a group of guys doing a little shopping of their own. As the Trio passed they drew stares from the fellas, but kept it moving. The dudes were all wearing trump jewels, so it was a good guess that they were getting money. Joyce wanted to holla, but Alexis pulled her along so as not to seem too thirsty.

The girls busied themselves trying on different boots and sneakers, while the guys looked on. One guy in particular seemed to take a liking to Trinity. He was tall, although not as tall as Rio. He had a handsome cinnamon-colored face, with a thin beard lining his jaw. His long dreads hung down his back and were held together by a white bandana. The tight shirt he wore showed off his lean but healthy frame. Trinity caught the Dread's stare but didn't acknowledge him. The dude was fine as hell, but she was good with Rio.

After a brief bit of debating, the guys decided to approach Trinity and her team. As soon as Trinity saw them walking over, she gathered her things and headed for the register. While his boys were trying to get their mack on, Dread continued to stare at Trinity from a distance. Trinity placed two pairs of boots on the counter and reached into her Gucci purse to pay for them. Before she could pull her money out, Dread stepped up.

"Hold on, ma," he said in a deep voice. "What you doing?"

"Excuse me?" Trinity asked in a stink voice.

"I asked what you're doing?"

"I'm bout to pay for my boots. Is there a problem?"

"Actually, yes. Your money's no good here, ma," he said, pulling out a large bank roll. "I got this."

"First of all," Trinity said. "My name is not ma. Second of all, I got my own," she said, pulling out her knot. "I'm good."

"Damn," Dread said, putting his hands up submissively. "I ain't mean no disrespect. I was just trying to be courteous."

"Well thanks, but no thanks."

"Hold up, ma . . . I mean miss. Maybe we started off on the wrong foot? My name is Baron. And you are?"

"Her name's Trinity." Joyce said, butting into yet another conversation.

"Okay," Baron said, licking his full lips. "Pleased to meet you, Trinity."

"I wouldn't call Joyce telling you my name us meeting."

"Well, it's a start. Listen, I know I don't know you and I really don't be rolling up on strange females like this, but when I saw you, I couldn't help myself. If it's okay with you, I'd like to maybe take you out to dinner and pick your brain a little?"

"Well, Baron, I'm flattered by the offer, but I can't."

"Word?" Baron asked surprised. "Damn, I just came from Crab Inn so I know my breath might be a little hot, but I didn't mean to completely turn you off."

Trinity giggled a little. "No, Baron. Your breath is fine."

"So what's really good?"

"I got a man, Baron."

"And?"

"And that means I'm loyal to him."

"Check it out, Trinity. I hear where you're coming from and I respect that. But I think you got it all wrong. I'm just trying to get to know you. I don't wanna step on nobody's toes. All I'm asking is for dinner and a little conversation."

"Thank you, Baron, but no thanks."

"Well," he said, pulling out a white business card. "If you change your mind, give me a ring."

"Baron, I told you I got a man."

"She'll call," Joyce said, snatching the card. "As a matter of fact, your peoples invited me and my girl Alex to that party y'all throwing. How bout if we bring Trinity along?"

"Sounds like a plan," Baron said, smiling at Trinity.

"Then it's settled." Joyce said, grinning like she had just done a good thing.

"A'ight," Baron said. "So I guess I'll see you there?"

Trinity mustered a phony smile at Baron as he left followed by his entourage. That bitch Joyce had really played herself this time. Not only had she put Trinity in a compromising position, but she made her team look wack. Baron and his peoples probably thought that they were a bunch of sack-chasers, the way Joyce was acting all thirsty.

"Joyce," Trinity said with attitude. "What was that shit all about?"

"Girl," Joyce began, "why don't you just be easy? If anything, I did you a favor."

"How do you figure you did me a favor?"

"Trinity, I know you don't get out much, but do you mean to tell me that you don't know who that was?"

"Should I?"

"Hell, yeah! That was Cedric Baron."

"And?"

"And? Trinity, think about it. Cedric Baron aka Baron is holding.

He getting it with them niggaz on 155th. Last time I was at the Rucker this nigga pulled up in a CLK."

"So?" Trinity said, shrugging. "And that means what to me? He ain't the only nigga with a CLK."

"T, he hit the streets with one two whole years before it came out. That boy wipe his ass with big faces. I don't think you know what you got on your hands. First Rio and now Baron. You winning right now, T."

"Joyce," Trinity said, rolling her eyes. "You be killing me with that shit. Everything is about paper with you. Money doesn't buy happiness."

"You're right, Trinity," Joyce smiled. "But it can buy a nice fit with the matching shoes. You better get up on it."

Rio hit the block feeling pretty good about himself. Since he had started fucking with Prince, the streets had been good to him. He was getting money and was making sure everyone else ate. Rio wasn't the type of cat to want it all for himself. By making sure the niggaz that he was fucking with was eating, it kept them happy. Besides that, it took some of the light off him.

Rio and Cutty were coming from the chicken store, talking shit, when School Boy came riding up on his mountain bike. As he got closer, Rio could see the grim look on his face. He knew that he was bringing bad news.

"What da deal, School?" Rio asked.

"Not good," School Boy said, coasting alongside the two. "We lost another one, dick."

"Fuck," Rio said, slapping his palms together. "That's the second time in as many days. What was he holding?"

"The boy had a half a pack and about five hundred bucks on him."

"This shit is getting fucking ridiculous. Every time the police run up on us, we lose. We lose a worker, work, and paper. This shit here has got to stop."

"What you wanna do, Rio?" School Boy asked.

"I'll tell you what. Ride on ahead and close up the shops. Tell every-one that's working to meet me in back of the center, right now. I don't give a fuck if they're in the middle of serving a customer. Have them ma fuckas over here within the next ten minutes."

"You got it, boss." School Boy quickly rode off on his bike to do as he was told. He didn't want to get caught in the backlash of Rio's anger. Over the last few weeks, School Boy had noticed a change in Rio's demeanor. It was like the game was making Rio bitter. He used to always smile and joke around with the homeboys, but there wasn't much of that going on lately. Rio was a money machine and paper chasing had become all consuming. One thing School Boy knew was that if anyone could come up with a scheme to fix their police problem, it was Rio.

"What you gonna do?" Cutty asked, strolling alongside Rio.

"Fuck you think I'm gonna do," snapped Rio. "These niggaz is slipping and I'm gonna get their minds right."

"That's what the fuck I'm talking about, Rio. You gotta rule this ma fucka wit an iron fist," Cutty said excitedly.

"Easy, Wild Bill. You know that ain't even my style. I'm a kind general. Our soldiers just need to think a little smarter." Rio was about to add onto his wisdom when his cell went off.

Trinity was sitting on the bench in front of her building with Alex, smoking a joint and enjoying the weather. It was nice to just kick it with her girl and not have to hear Joyce's annoying-ass voice. Alex was her best friend while Joyce was just a bitch she tolerated. She didn't hate the girl, but she wasn't too fond of her either.

"This is some bomb shit." Alex said, accepting the joint.

"I know it," Trinity said, exhaling a cloud of smoke. "Rio sent Cutty uptown to get us an ounce of this shit. This is one of the few kinds of weed that he'll smoke."

"Umm hmm. Speaking of Cutty, where he at now?"

"Probably up the block with Rio. Why do you ask?"

"No reason."

"Yeah, right," Trinity said, nudging Alex. "Let me find out?"

"Please Trinity. Find out what?"

"That you feeling Cutty."

"He a'ight," she said shrugging. "But he ain't nobody."

"Alex, I know you."

"Okay, so I might've been thinking about hitting him off. I know if he's fucking wit Rio, he's caked up."

"Yeah," Trinity said, taking the joint. "The boy is on a come up. But I don't know, Alex."

"What you mean by that, T?"

"I ain't trying to scare you off, but something about Cutty gives me the creeps."

"Girl, you tripping," Alex said, waving her off. "I know what Cutty is out here doing and it don't bother me. That nigga out here getting it and I want some."

"You starting to sound like Joyce."

"Never that. I got too much class with my shit. By the way T, what's up with you and her?"

"Ain't nothing up. Why?"

"I don't know, it's like there's some tension between y'all."

"Nah, Alex. I wouldn't call it tension. We just don't click. I ain't feeling how she gets down. Look how she did with Baron the other day?"

"Now, I gotta disagree with you on that one, Trinity. Baron is large in the game. I wish he would've tried to holla at me."

"But you know I ain't on it like that, Alex. Rio takes care of me just fine."

"No disrespect, Trinity, but Rio ain't seeing paper like Baron. He's just starting out, while Baron has been doing this for a while."

"Money don't make or break me, Alex. Now y'all got me all caught up in this party bullshit with Baron and his team. I ain't trying to tip out on Rio."

"Trinity," Alex said, snatching the joint. "It's only a party. Ain't like you sliding with the nigga. Besides, when is the last time *we* went out?"

"I don't know, Alex. Let me see what Rio's doing first?"

"Trinity, you know I love Rio like a brother, but fuck that. If it's okay for him to go out with his peoples, why you can't do it with yours?"

Alexis raised a good point. Rio went out with his peoples just about every weekend and Trinity never beefed. She just sat in the crib and waited on him. Maybe she should attend the party. Before she could ponder it further, a police cruiser pulled up. Trinity tossed the joint, but the cop had probably seen it. When the officer stepped out, Trinity thought he looked familiar too.

"Hello, Trinity," Officer Brown said, smiling. "It's Officer Brown. Do you remember me?"

"Oh," Trinity said, casting her glare to the still-burning roach. "Yeah, I remember."

"Don't worry about that," Brown said, following her gaze. "I'm not here to bother you about a bag of weed. I actually came to see how you were doing?"

"I'm a'ight, I guess."

"Did your father come back yet?"

At the mention of her father, Trinity's palms began to sweat. "Nope," she said a little nervously. "I thought y'all was supposed to be looking for him?"

"And we have been," Brown said, leaning on the fence. "But we haven't had any luck. We've checked all the hospitals, rehabilitation centers, homeless shelters, and morgues. All turning up zero. It's as if your father has disappeared from the face of the earth."

"I'm not surprised," Trinity said in a stink voice. "Seems like the NYPD ain't good for shit except giving niggaz a hard time."

"Hey," Brown said, holding his palms up. "I'm on your side, Trinity. Don't let a few rotten ones turn you off from eating strawberries."

"I'm sorry," Trinity said. "I just haven't been myself lately."

"It's cool," Brown said, waving her off. "I know it's a lot on you, with taking care of your little brother and all, huh?"

"Yeah, it's a struggle. But somebody's gotta do it."

"That reminds me," Brown said, turning more serious. "I need to talk to you about that. Alone," he said, cutting his eyes at Alex.

"I gotta 'burn it' anyway," Alex said, standing to leave. "Call me later on, T."

"Later, Alex," Trinity said, waving. "So," she said turning her attention back to Brown. "What's up?"

"Well," Brown said, sitting on the bench beside her. "I think the best way to tell you this is to just come out with it. There's a very good possibility that your dad might not be coming back. You're nineteen so you really can do for yourself. But your brother Billy is still underage. As a minor he has to have some type of adult supervision."

"What are you trying to tell me?" she asked in a worried tone.

"What I'm trying to tell you is that Children's Services has decided to step in."

"What? I know y'all ain't trying to take my little brother?" she said defensively.

"Be cool, Trinity. It ain't that serious yet. They'll probably be contacting you sometime soon about coming out to the house to discuss the matter with you. Being that Billy does have relatives, there's a chance for him to stay home. Is there anyone in your family that might be able to take him?"

"Damn," Trinity sobbed. "It's just Billy, Rich, and me. We ain't got no other family."

"I know the situation with your brother Rich, so that one ain't gonna fly. Is there anyone else you can think of?"

"Nope. The only one left is me. Why couldn't I do it?"

"I don't know," Brown said, scratching his head. "That's a lot of responsibility, Trinity."

"It ain't no more than what I'm doing now. I been taking care of my brother since I lost my mother."

"Good point. But I gotta tell you, Trinity, you have to seriously step your game up. Them people ain't gonna just let you keep Billy because you're his sister. You have to show them that you can provide a stable living environment for the boy. You're gonna have to show them that you receive some kind of income and are at least pursuing a diploma. Do you think you can do that, Trinity?"

"I don't really have a choice, do I?"

All Brown could do was shake his head. Trinity had real character to just go hard for her brother like this. In a way he felt bad about the way he was stringing her along. Children's Services had been contacted because Billy was a minor, but the situation wasn't as serious as he was making it out to be. He was just trying to gain the girl's trust by seeming to look out for her. She was a good kid who just happened to get mixed up with a bad apple. Brown's number one priority was to assist in the downfall of Prince's crew. Rio was a part of that and Trinity was just a way to get to him. But when it was all said and done, Brown really intended to help Trinity.

"Okay," Brown said, pulling out a white business card. "Here's my number. Call me if you need anything, Trinity. I don't care what time of day or night, my cell is always on."

"Thanks," Trinity said, dabbing at her eyes.

"I'm serious, Trinity. You really gotta step it up. If not for you, then for your brother. All this sitting on the bench and smoking weed crap has gotta stop."

"I feel you, Officer Brown. And thanks."

Trinity got up off the bench and started walking toward her building. She remembered what she had first thought of the brown-skinned cop and felt a little remorseful. Perhaps Brown wasn't a dick like the rest of New York's finest? He actually seemed like he wanted to help. But friendly or not, he was still the enemy, so he had to be fed with a long-handled spoon. Her man was on one side of the line and Brown was on the other. That's just the way it had to be.

Trinity spared a glace over her shoulder to see Officer Brown still watching her. Something in his eyes told Trinity that he was sharper than most. Rio would have to be careful of him. She reached into her pocket, pulled out her phone, and autodialed Rio.

Rio listened carefully as Trinity relayed the conversation she'd had with the officer. He instructed her to keep her head and he'd meet up with her later on that night. Rio tried to sound confident so he wouldn't scare Trinity, but truthfully he was nervous. Prince was thorough when it came to making problems disappear, but what if the police did find out what went down? He wasn't too worried for himself. His mother used to always tell him, "Don't do the crime if you can't do the time." He had committed murder and if worse came to worst, he'd hold the time as opposed to incriminating anyone else. His biggest fear was that Trinity might somehow get roped up in it all. She hadn't done anything herself, but she had knowledge of the crime. With the judicial system being the way it was, having the knowledge was almost as bad as doing the dirt yourself.

"Yo dawg," Cutty said, tapping Rio. "Everyone is here. You ready?"

Rio cleared his throat and focused on the business at hand. He had assembled all of his workers behind the center for this important meeting. Rio had dozens of people under him, but there were about ten of them gathered behind Frederick Douglass center. All employees of Prince and soldiers in Rio's army. Things in the hood were not going as they should and Rio intended to nip it in the bud.

"Excuse me," Rio said, trying to speak over the crowd. The soldiers kept talking and doing whatever they were doing. "Yo," Rio said a little louder. Still, no response.

"Yo!" Cutty barked. "Y'all niggaz shut the fuck up and pay attention!" At the sound of Cutty's booming voice, the crowd got quiet. "That's more like it. Go ahead, Rio."

"Good looking, Cutty," Rio said, smiling. "A'ight y'all," he said, addressing the now silent crowd. "I ain't gonna keep you long, so I'll get right to it. We been losing money over the last few days and I'm not feeling it. We been losing good people and good money. This shit can't go on, fellas."

"Yo Rio," said Paul, a brown-skinned hustler from the Amsterdam side of the projects. "It ain't our fault. Police been jumping out from everywhere, kid."

"I hear that, but what do you expect? We out here slinging stones, B. Ain't like we licensed to do this shit. Truthfully, a lot of y'all niggaz been out here for too long to fall victim to the dumb shit."

"So what do you suggest, boss?" School Boy asked.

"I'll tell you, my nigga," Rio said, putting his hand on School Boy's shoulder. "We gonna do our shit a little different from now on. Instead of just having a pitcher and a lookout, we'll add a money man to the mix."

"Money man?" a soldier named Sean asked.

"Yep," Rio said, looking him in the eye. "A money man. He'll be the dude that collects the money from the hype and signal the pitcher. This way if police do snatch a nigga, they don't get everything."

"But that's another nigga you gotta pay," School Boy said.

"Not really. See, the way it works is, the pitchers and the lookouts will each donate a portion of their scratch to pay the money man. So if you look at it like that, it all works out." A few cats mumbled under their breath, but Rio quickly put it to rest. "I don't know why y'all niggaz is even mad when y'all the ones out here slipping. I'm trying to make it so we can all keep eating. If we don't get knocked then we can keep bubbling. Until y'all get it together that's the way it's gonna go. If y'all don't like it, step the fuck off. This is a business. Use ya head, fellas." Rio's tone had no malice in it, but everyone knew he was giving an order. Prince's newest Capo was exercising his authority.

With that being said, the mumbling stopped. They knew what Rio had said made a lot of sense. Having a third party in on the transactions would make everyone else's job easier. Each man could focus on a specific task. A money man would also provide an extra set of eyes for the lookouts. It was times like those when they were glad Rio was running things. He was a dude who knew how to get money.

17

io and Trinity sat snuggled in the last row of the Magic Johnson theater. They had been able to catch the opening night of a movie called "Amor Negro." It was a classic tale of four friends, all in search of a different kind of love. It was a good movie, but the book had been better. None of that really mattered, however, because they barely watched the movie. They were too caught up in each other. Rio's new position demanded a lot of his time and Trinity had been busy herself studying for her GED. She needed to pass it now that Children's Services had come into the picture. She had to get her shit together.

"Penny for your thoughts?" Rio whispered in her ear.

"Oh," she said, "Nothing. I was just thinking about Billy."

"Don't fret that ma. Billy ain't going nowhere. This whole shit is gonna blow over. You watch."

"I hope so, Rio. I need to get it together so I can take care of my little brother. These people want proof, not words."

"Ma, I told you got you. I got the hook up for these under-the-table apartments uptown. I'm gonna get a nice two-bedroom for me, you, and Billy, but it's gonna be in your name. That takes care of the living environment. You take your GED in a few weeks and I know you're gonna pass it this time. Then you got your job down at Happy Jack's. It ain't much, but it's yours."

At the mention of her job, Trinity got quiet. She hadn't told Rio about her losing her job yet. She had been so preoccupied, she hadn't really thought about it. "Rio," she said timidly. "I gotta tell you something. But you gotta promise that you ain't gonna get mad at me?"

"Trinity, why would I be mad at you."

"Because I quit my job at Happy Jack's."

"Damn," he said, relieved. "That's all? I thought you had some heavy shit to drop on me, ma. That sets us back a bit, but it's all good. You can get another job, but you know I'm gonna take care of you, ma."

"I know," she said, kissing his lips. "And that's why I love you."

The movie was over and the lovers followed the crowd out to the avenue. Rio was standing off to the side with Trinity, talking on his phone. She had her back to him, lighting her cigarette. As Trinity exhaled, she noticed a familiar figure coming out of the theater. His dreads were pinned up and he wore a heavy medallion, but she was sure it was Baron.

As if he felt her watching him, Baron turned around and looked at Trinity. He smiled, but didn't approach her. Then he winked his eye. Trinity cracked a half-smile and finger-waved at him. Baron's man came out of the theater and whispered something in his ear. Baron nodded at his man and followed him to the cherry-red Benz truck that was waiting on him. The big truck bent the corner with 23-inch chrome rims sparkling in the moonlight.

Trinity spared a last glance at the taillights and shook her head. "Another place another life, but not this one," she said softly to herself.

"What did you say?" Rio asked, startling her.

"Oh," she said cooly. "Nothing. Just thinking out loud."

"Okay. Well, the cab should be here in a few. You wanna go eat or you wanna call it?"

"Nah, I think I'm gonna go home and study."

"A'ight, I'll take you home."

The cab pulled up and beeped its horn. Rio took Trinity by the hand and led her to the Lincoln. As she was getting into the cab, he stopped her short. "Trinity," he said suspiciously. "Who was that cat with the dreads?"

Prince came out of his apartment building wearing a purple suit and matching gators. He had a twenty-something young lady, who looked like a Jet beauty of the week, on his arm. He was stepping out to take the young lady on a dinner date. J held the back door open while Prince helped the young lady inside. After a brief look around, J and the brute from the meeting got in the front of the tank. The Hummer pulled out into traffic and took off down Fifth Avenue.

As the taillights of the Hummer faded into the distance, a figure looked around carefully before stepping from the darkness. Hound knelt down on the ground and ran a gloved finger over the tread marks the vehicle had left. He scanned the area once more and slithered back into the darkness. Prince was only prolonging his life at best. Once the Hound was set on your trail, death was a stone's throw away.

Trinity, Alexis, and Joyce stood outside the club, trying to look cute. They were all dressed in eye-catching gear and dying to show it off. Alex was wearing a white leather skirt and go-go boots. The drop-neck blouse she wore showed off just enough cleavage without looking trashy. Joyce had on a black leather skirt that was cut a little shorter than Alex's. With the matching vest. The outfit was cute, but Joyce had to throw a little slut in the mix. Under the vest, she wore a see-through top and no bra.

Trinity wasn't really the dress-up type, but she could kill em when she wanted to. The tight leather pants she wore left very little to the imagination. She had on a white dress shirt that she had trimmed and tied off in the back to show off her six pack. The little half-tie she wore gave the outfit a certain effect that made many a head turn. As she moved through the line, her Shirley Temple curls bounced on her head. Trinity was definitely winning.

Originally she wasn't even gonna come to Baron's party. She was just gonna keep it local and kick it with her boo. But when she asked Rio about staying with her, he said he and his boys already had plans. Trinity figured she'd be a fool to waste another weekend in the house while her man got his party on. She hit the hair salon on 109th Street and got her wig tightened up. Her next stop was 125th to get a manicure. Once all the pieces were in place she called her girls and they set out for the party.

Trinity nearly gagged when Rio had asked her about Baron. She hadn't done anything with him, nor did she plan to, but she was overwhelmed by guilt when Rio had asked her. She made up a story about him being some cat that Alexis was fucking and brushed it off as nothing. He looked at her as if he didn't believe the story, but he let it go.

"Damn," Joyce said. "It's niggaz out here tonight."

"Yeah," Alex joined in. "I see quite a few ballers out here. Girl, I'm trying to snatch something."

"Y'all need to quit." Trinity said, lighting a cigarette.

"You need to quit." Alex said, slapping the cigarette.

"Bitch," Trinity snapped, lighting another one. "These shits is eight-cash."

"So, you got it. Rio ain't hurting."

"Fuck you, bitch." Trinity said, laughing.

"Yeah," Joyce cut in. "I know that's right. But I don't understand Rio. Now, regardless of what you say T, I know Rio getting it with Prince, but he don't act like it. You don't never see him sporting jewels or nothing. What up with that?"

"Here we go," Alexis exhaled.

"Look Joyce," Trinity began. "The niggaz who flash and act all crazy be the ones to catch football numbers. How could a guy that's supposed to have a minimum wage job afford a fifty-thousand-dollar medallion? And while I'm thinking about it, why you so worried about Rio's finances?"

"Trinity, it ain't even that serious," Joyce told her. "Girl, you know we're bigger than that."

"Yeah, a'ight. Let me find out, Joyce."

"Come on y'all," Alex said, stepping between them. "Let's just go up in there and get our drink on."

Trinity reluctantly allowed Alex to lead her into the club. She shot Joyce a mean look on the way in. Joyce was a bitch that was gonna need some watching. She came wearing a smile, but Trinity knew that she had larceny in her heart. At the minute Joyce got out of pocket, she was gonna smash her.

Rio stepped out of the green jeep flanked by Cutty and Shamel. He was dressed in a pair of black linen pants and a cream shirt. The diamond name bracelet he had on caught the eye of many people, but no one would dare rob Prince's boy. Besides that, niggaz knew what time it was with Cutty and Shamel. The Trio moved toward the line and it parted like the Red Sea.

"Membership has its privileges, huh?" Cutty asked.

"You silly," Rio said, nudging him.

"Damn," Shamel said, looking at a scantily dressed girl on the line. "It's some hoes in this house. I'm trying to get my freak on."

"You shameless," Rio said, lighting a cigarette. "All you think about is pussy."

"You got that fucked up, Rio. I think about money *and* pussy." Shamel corrected him.

"I know that's right," Cutty said, slapping Shamel's palm. "You better follow suit nigga. You spend all yo time wit ya head up Trinity's ass. Don't you know she ain't got the only pussy in the world?"

"What would the world be without hating-ass niggaz?" Rio asked sarcastically. "Apparently you don't know me as well as you think you do. I love my girl with everything that I am and I ain't afraid to show it. But don't get it fucked up, I still do me. Shit, I boned that chick Precious a while back."

"You lying," Shamel said, sucking his teeth.

"Nah, I took her to the ma fuck'n Liberty. That bitch fucked and sucked me like a pro. After I bust that pussy, she bounced. I only sleep next to one bitch and that's Trinity."

The trio made their way to the front of the crowd where a mountain stood between them and the club entrance. The mountain was just informing a well-known boxer and his crew that they would have to wait an hour before they would be allowed into the club. Cutty and Shamel hesitated for a minute, but Rio never broke his stride. He slapped a hundred dollar bill in the mountain's paw and kept it moving. The people looked on in astonishment as the unknown young player breezed into one of the city's most exclusive clubs.

Rio got inside and paused to let his eyes adjust to the darkness as he scanned the club. Lately he was becoming increasingly paranoid. But when you live in the streets you had to be. A nigga could be waiting to get you at any given time. Rio waited for Shamel and Cutty to catch up, then the three moved to the bar area.

Trinity and her crew sat at a table in the back of the club. They were laughing and sipping Crystal. All courtesy of their host, Baron. When they had arrived, he showed them to their table. He had been the perfect gentleman. Even when they were sitting at the table, he wasn't trying to be all up on her. Baron seemed to be pretty cool.

"You having a good time?" Baron asked, leaning toward Trinity.

"Oh, I'm having a ball, thanks," Trinity said politely.

"So why you not acting like it?"

"I didn't realize I was that transparent."

"Only to someone who knows what to look for."

"Wow, you got like X-ray vision or something?"

"Something. You're not that hard to read, Trinity, and I don't think you're having a good time."

"I'm sorry. I'm probably messing up everybody's groove."

"Nah, you cool. But what's bothering you?"

"I'm just thinking about my man. Me and him usually go out on weekends."

"So what happened?"

"He and his boys had plans."

"Shit, then he must be a fool." Baron said in disbelief. "What kinda nigga would put his boys before his lady?" Baron stroked Trinity's cheek with his index finger. The way he dragged his manicured nail across her skin, barely touching it, made her shiver. She pulled her face away and slid over a bit.

"My bad," Baron said, folding his hands. "I just got a little caught up, ya know? Can you imagine how it feels to want somebody, but you can't have them because they already belong to someone else? Then on top of that, the person they belong to don't know how to treat em?"

"I'm sorry, Baron, I don't. I'm perfectly happy with the man I'm with. You're very sweet though." Trinity reached out to give Baron a friendly pat on the cheek and all hell broke loose.

Rio was posted up at the bar with his crew, getting his drink on. When Cutty had told him about the party he didn't really wanna come. He had been thinking about taking Trinity to dinner or something. But the more he heard about the party the more he wanted to come. At the last minute he said fuck it and changed his mind. Now that he was there, he was glad that he had come. Everybody was in the joint. Rio was clocking the honeys, but he was more occupied with networking. There were quite a few underworld figures there as well as some square pegs. It was always good to know people, as long as you were careful of who knew you.

Rio was leaning against the bar tapping his foot and enjoying the show two lesbians were putting on in the corner. As Rio scanned through the crowd, he thought he caught a glimpse of a familiar face. He had to blink twice because he knew that his eyes were lying to him. Sitting in the back of the club sipping champagne was Trinity and the kid from the movies. Something had told Rio that the boy was shady when he first saw him.

He saw through a haze of red as he stormed through the crowd. He didn't even bother to tell his peoples. Rio got to the back just in time to catch Trinity stroking the dude's cheek. He walked calmly over to the table and leaned on his knuckles. "Sup, T?" he asked, staring.

When Trinity looked up and saw who was addressing her, everything in her stomach turned to liquid. Of all the rotten-ass clubs he could've picked to go to, Rio had to pick the one her girls dragged her to. She wasn't doing anything, which was a plus for her, but Rio probably took the cheek thing the wrong way.

"Rio," Trinity said perkily. "What you doing here, boo?"

"I should be asking you the same thing, shouldn't I?" he said coldly.

"Chilling. Me and the girls decided to come out tonight and get a few drinks."

"I see," Rio said, eyeing the glass as if it were poisoned. "Who ya peoples?"

"Oh, this is Baron. It's his party."

"What's good?" Baron asked extending his hand. Seeing Rio wasn't in the friendliest of moods, Baron dropped his hand. "I hear that hot shit. So, this ya *boyfriend*, Trinity?"

"Yeah, this is Rio." Rio didn't say a word. He didn't blink, he didn't breathe. All he did was stare. "Rio," Trinity said, trying to break the tension. "Baron brought us a bottle of champagne to help celebrate his birthday. You want some?"

"I'm good," Rio said through clenched teeth. "Matter of fact, I think I'm gonna keep it moving. Y'all have a good evening." Rio turned and walked off. By this time Shamel and Cutty had come over. Trinity got up from the table and went after Rio. She could've kicked herself for letting Baron get to her. It wasn't that serious, but Rio's pride was hurt.

"Hold on," she said, grabbing his arm. "What's wrong with you?"

"I told you, I'm good," Rio said, jerking away. "Go back to ya table and do you, ma."

"Oh, I know you ain't tight about a nigga buying some liquor? Boo, it ain't like he just bought it for me, We're all drinking."

"T, I told you, I'm good. You go be a fucking jump-off like ya friends."

"No-the-fuck-you-didn't," she said, placing her hands on her hips. "Darius Santana, for as long as you know me, you better never speak to me like that again. You over here clowning over some nigga that I don't even know."

"Fuck," he barked, "I couldn't tell. You stroking his cheek and shit."

"Rio, how many times I gotta tell you that you're the only man I want in my life? Remember the promise? Through good and bad. You remember?"

"Trinity, I'm tight right now and I ain't really trying to talk to you." Rio tried to walk away, but Trinity grabbed his arm again. This time when he jerked away he put a little too much force into it. Trinity staggered back and bumped into an approaching Baron.

"Yo a'ight, Trinity?" Baron asked, catching up.

"Yeah," she said, straightening herself up. "Thanks."

"Yo, money," Rio said, moving toward Baron. "What's really good with you? You want my girl or something?"

"Actually, yeah," Baron said, looking Rio square in the eye. "You in here stunting like uptight about something?"

"Fuck you," Rio growled. "Ain't nothing sweet over this way." Baron's crew drew their weapons at the same time that Cutty and Shamel drew theirs. Baron and Rio stood toe to toe, neither man flinching. "However you wanna do it, money," Rio said, grinning. "Y'all niggaz ain't the only ma fucking gangstas uptown. If you want it, then buck, nigga."

The club-goers were climbing over each other trying to get out of the way. No one wanted to catch a stray bullet. But before the violence could erupt, Truck, of all people, muscled his way through the crowd, followed by Slim. When he made his way to the center of the disturbance, he was quite surprised by who was standing in it.

"Well, well," Truck said, smiling. "If it isn't my two favorite rising stars. What's going on, boys?"

"Truck," Baron said, without taking his eyes off Rio. "You know this clown?"

"Hey, watch what you say, Baron. He's with us. This is Prince's new protégé, Rio."

"Hold up," Baron said, tilting his head. "This is *that* Rio? Truck this ain't that Rio. That Rio is supposed to be a businessman and a gentleman. This nigga here is a street punk."

"Watch ya mouth," Cutty said, tightening his grips on the two 9s.

"Easy fellas," Truck said, stepping between the gunmen. "All this cowboys shit ain't called for. Plus I ain't gonna have you two niggaz shooting my place up."

"A'ight Truck," Baron said, waving his men off. "Yo an OG, so I'll respect this call. But you really need to teach this li'l nigga some manners."

"No harm no foul," Truck said, patting Baron on the back. "You boys go on and have a bottle on the house."

Baron spared one last angry glance at Rio and sucked his teeth. As he was walking away, he winked his eye at Trinity. Rio started to pursue, but Truck stopped him. He knew that Rio really didn't know who he was fucking with. Baron was a ghetto superstar and had people that would gladly kill for him. He couldn't have his father's newest Capo getting himself bodied over some dumb shit in the club. Besides the pleasure of killing Rio would be all his.

"So," Truck said, turning to Rio. "Seems as if you ain't so laid back after all."

"Fuck that nigga." Rio spat.

"Easy, youngster," Truck said, pulling Rio out of everyone else's earshot. "Do you know who that was that you were about to lock ass with?"

"Don't need to know. He can get it just like anyone else."

"That's the problem with you young cats. Y'all always wanna rush into shit half-ass. If you plan on going to war you gotta do it right. The first rule of thumb is, know your opponent. You're becoming a big man on the street Rio, that's true enough. But you're still green. Baron, he's on the come up, same as you. The only difference is, he's been in the game a little longer than you have. Experience will usually win out over a fast trigger."

"I'm good, Truck."

"Say what you want, Rio, but you better try listening to someone other than Prince and J."

"That nigga was trying to play me, Truck. Clawing all over my girl and shit."

"I told you about that girl before, kid. When you got a lady as fine as Trinity, you gotta put a lock on her. Every nigga wit a few dollars is gonna be looking to holla. If yo shit ain't tight, the girl is gonna be tempted. Temptation usually leads to actions, if a ma fucka ain't strong in the mind. Think about what I'm telling you."

Rio watched Truck as he walked back through the crowd. What Truck was saying only made Rio tighter. Trinity was his girl and supposed to act accordingly. Having some nigga pawing over her in the club wasn't keeping it funky. Especially one of Rio's rivals. Rio took a deep breath. Truck might have been a bullshit nigga, but what he said made sense. Trinity was the kinda girl that needed to be treated like a queen. Rio was getting money, but his heart really wasn't in it. A regular nine-to-five nigga couldn't get it done.

"We out," Rio said to his entourage. He stormed for the door while his men watched his back. Trinity continued to call after Rio, but he ignored her. His pride and the alcohol wouldn't allow him to think straight. All he knew was that his pride was hurt and Trinity was the cause of it. If she wanted a baller, let her have Baron's punk ass. Rio was a stepper and you can't stop a stepper.

Trinity stood in the middle of the club feeling hurt and embarrassed. What was supposed to be a night out with the girls had turned out to be a complete disaster. She knew that she would never stray from Rio, but she'd done a poor job of showing it. Her friendliness had caused a rift between her and her lover. A rift that would take some time and understanding to fix.

Alexis and Joyce just played the background while Trinity got herself together. Neither of them had ever seen that side of Rio. They had always known him to be a fun-loving and laid back dude. The man who had broken up their little party was a stone gangsta. It goes to show how enough time in the streets can bring out the worst in a person. Alexis was shaken by the whole incident, but Joyce found herself strangely turned on.

Rio and his crew left the club and hit the block. Shamel and Cutty wanted to stay with their friend to make sure he was all right, but he wasn't trying to hear it. Right then, Rio didn't need friends, he needed isolation. The only things that could bring him peace at that moment were his poetry and the fifth of liquor he had tucked under his arm. Against their better judgment, Shamel and Cutty left their friend alone to gather his thoughts.

Rio took his bottle and notepad to the roof of his building. This was his special place. He would sit up here for hours, just writing and looking at the sky. It was in this place he found temporary peace. A peace that brought on creativity.

Rio staggered over and leaned against one of the ventilation shafts.

In the night air, his head didn't spin as much, but the fire still burned in his chest. He had almost lost control of himself inside the club. Seeing his wifey touching on that nigga put him in a killing mood.

Rio peeled the cap off of his bottle and took a long swig. The cognac burned his insides, but it calmed him a bit. This was just what he needed. Rio looked down at his blank notepad and tried to find that special place he needed to be. As he stared intently at the blank page, words began to form in his mind. He touched his pen to the paper and let his creativity take over. Rio began to write. The story that began to unfold was a sad one. It was a story of a flower. A flower that everyone sought to have for their own. Every time the flower began to blossom and take root, someone always came to try and uproot it. It was as if no one wanted the flower and the earth's nurturing soil to develop the relationship they both needed to truly bloom. Eventually the flower began to wilt and it died. It was a sad, but familiar story. The story of his and Trinity's love.

Trinity and her girls made it back to their hood not long after Rio and his boys had parted company. Alexis had tried to be supportive of Trinity, but there was only so much that she could say. None of them knew what Trinity was going through. Both her friends had been in relationships, but none of them knew what it was to truly be in love.

Trinity cried the more she thought about it. She loved Rio with everything that she was, but dumb shit was always getting in the way. She loved this man hard enough to overlook the fact that he had killed her father, but he couldn't see past a pat on the cheek. There was only so much worrying that she could do though. She knew that his pride was hurt, and pride was something that Rio was very big on. In time he would come around. Or at least she hoped that he would. Trinity and Alexis walked Joyce to her building then headed back up the block to their little piece of the hood. The girls were both tired and wanted the night to end.

Joyce watched the two girls until they were out of sight. When she thought that the coast was clear, she headed back into the projects. She was a little tipsy and had no intention of letting the night end. To her, Trinity went out like a bird. She let Rio leave and didn't try and stop him. Then to make it worse, Baron wanted to slide and she wouldn't go with him either. There was no way a bitch like Joyce would've left the club alone. She was content to let Trinity feel sorry for herself, but she had other plans.

Rio came staggering out of his building, holding his half-empty bottle of liquor. He wasn't as uptight as he had been, but the pain still lingered. That's how it usually goes when you try to escape your troubles through intoxication. You feel good for the moment, but in time it fades and the pain is still there waiting under the surface. And Rio was hurting.

Some of the fellas were in front of the building getting their hustle on, but Rio didn't feel like being bothered. He nodded and bust a hard left in the direction of Manhattan Avenue. When he got halfway down the block, he spotted Cutty talking to a young lady. Rio scratched Manhattan as an escape route and cut south through the middle of the projects.

As he moved down the narrow path, he could feel the liquor trying to steal his balance. He tried to take a few deep breaths, but it didn't help much. He was good and drunk. As he continued through the path, he spotted a female coming his way. The young lady sauntered in his direction, swinging her big ass. Rio eyed the short black skirt she wore and found himself getting aroused. But as he got closer, her face became more visible and his arousal began to die down.

"Hey, Rio," Joyce said seductively.

"Oh, God," Rio said, slapping himself in the forehead. "As if I didn't have enough trouble. I hate to burst your bubble, Joyce, but if you came to deliver a message from Trinity, I don't wanna hear it."

"Damn, hello to you, too. I didn't come to deliver no messages for nobody. Fuck I look like, Fed Ex?"

"So what you want, girl?"

"For your information, I came back through here to see if you were okay."

"Yeah, right. Since when do you show any interest in my well-being?"

"Look, Rio, we ain't never been as cool as you and Alex, but you my friend's man and I care about what happens to you."

"Umm hmm."

"Oh, boy," Joyce said, sucking her teeth, "that's why a lot of y'all niggaz can't keep a girl. Acting like you're too hard to say when you're hurt."

"Joyce, you bugging. You don't know nothing about me or what I'm going through."

"That may be true, Rio. But what I do know is that shit that went down earlier was wack. Listen, can I say something to you and you'll keep it between us?"

"It's a free country, Joyce. Spit it out."

"A'ight. Trinity is my girl and I love her dearly, but that shit she pulled wasn't cool."

"Fuck her and that nigga, Baron."

"I feel you on that, Rio, but it wasn't entirely Baron's fault. He was just trying to be a gentleman and show us a good time. Me and Alex was checking for his peoples, that's why we went through there. Trinity took it upon herself to come with us for whatever reason. Didn't nobody twist her arm and force her to be all up on Baron." Joyce lied.

"Whatever," Rio said walking off. "I ain't really trying to hear it."

"Well, you need to," Joyce said, walking along the side of him. "Trinity is confused right now. She's going through a lot in her life, but that's no reason why you should have to suffer. I ain't got no man, but I'm sure if I did he would've cracked my head open for being up on some nigga. Especially in his people's spot."

"What's your point?" Rio said, slurring his words.

"My point," Joyce said, taking the bottle and drinking from it, "is that some girls ruin it for everyone else. You keep Trinity laced. I ain't saying she was ever a bum, but you keep her in the finest shit. Do you know how many bitches would love to be in Trinity's position?"

"Including you?"

"Rio, I ain't hardly no hater. You my girl's man, so I wouldn't never come at you like that. At least, not while you're with her."

"Well," Rio said, staggering a little, "the way I see it, Trinity's got a new man. I hope her and Baron are happy together."

"Rio, please. You know just like I do, you're talking out your ass. You and Trinity had an argument. That's what couples do. In time this shit will blow over and y'all are gonna be back together."

"I don't know, Joyce," Rio said, beginning to loosen up. "I think it's over between us. The stakes are higher now. I need a bitch that I can count on. Someone that's always gonna be in my corner. You smell me?"

"Yeah, I feel you. Whether you and Trinity fix ya little problems is between y'all. It don't make me no never mind. All I'm saying is, don't be no fool. You're too good for that."

By now the drunk in Rio had overpowered the logic. This bubble-head bitch that he couldn't stand half of the time was actually starting to make sense. Why the fuck should he be all down in the dumps when he wasn't the one in the wrong? If Trinity could do her and not feel bad, he could live it up with a clear head. Fuck it.

Rio walked and listened as Joyce took sips from his bottle and con-soled him. Before he had even realized it, they were in front of Joyce's building. Rio hadn't realized that he had walked all the way to Amster-dam Avenue. As he stood there in front of Joyce's building, the liquor secured a tighter hold over him. His legs wouldn't allow him to move any farther. Against his will his feet led him inside Joyce's building.

"You okay?" she asked, grabbing him by the arm.

"Yeah," Rio said, righting himself. "Just a little tipsy."

"That's what you get for trying to bang yak like it's going out of style," Joyce said, downing the last of it. "You drunk as hell."

"Nah, I ain't drunk, ma."

"Please," Joyce said, putting her arm around his waist. "You can barely stand up on your own. Why don't you come upstairs with me?"

"Nah," Rio said, backing away. "I ain't going up in there. I'm going home."

"Stop acting crazy, Rio. My mom is in Atlantic City for the week-end. Ain't nobody here but me."

"I'm good," he said, beginning to feel faint. "Joyce, I really need to get back up the block."

"The block? Who're you rushing to? Trinity left me and Alex downtown." The last statement reopened the wound Rio sought so desperately to heal. The first thing that popped into his mind was that Trinity had slid with Baron. Jealousy was getting the best of him, just as Joyce had planned it. "Look," she said. "All I'm trying to do is help you sober up a little before you go off wandering the streets. Let me make you some coffee to knock that drunk out. You can chase Trinity later."

"Fuck is you talking about? I ain't chasing a ma fucka. It ain't even that serious."

"That's what ya mouth say," Joyce said, opening the lobby door. "If it ain't that serious, then come on up."

Joyce stepped through the doorway, making sure she shook her ass extra hard. The sober side of Rio screamed for him to turn around and go back up the block. But the sober side wasn't in control anymore. Hadn't been for about the last hour or so. The drunk held sway now and it was telling Rio to let the cards fall where they may. Against his better judgment, Rio followed Joyce and her big ass up the stairs.

Cutty sat on the stoop of 868 smoking a blunt and enjoying the night air. Slowly but surely his adrenaline levels were subsiding. That shit that went down at the club had him tight. "Faggot-ass niggaz," he said to himself. Cutty didn't like the way Baron was trying to play his man, Rio. The cat was coming all kinda sideways as if the niggaz from 103rd didn't get down for theirs. To Cutty it didn't really matter where you were from. Be it 155th or 103rd, niggaz still bled the same.

Rio had surprised him more than what Baron had tried to pull off. Ever since they were in junior high together, Rio had always been the soft-spoken and passive one. Putting in work was left to Cutty. That night at the club was a different story though. Rio was on his flip shit. Wether it was the fact of knowing he had a killer with him or seeing his girl hugged up on some other cat, Cutty couldn't call it. In all truthfulness, he really didn't care. This was the side of Rio he had been trying to resurrect for the longest.

When the two of them first started running together in the late '80s,

Rio hadn't been nearly as laid-back. Some people would've even said he was wild. Cutty didn't buy that shit though. Rio was always just a kid trying to find himself. He knew he had a place in the world, but just couldn't figure out where. Rio had street in him by right of birth. Before his father got on that militant shit he was a numbers' runner on 104th Street. Even his mother was bout her scratch. Sally was one of the first chicks in the hood to go hand to hand, back before the singing calmed her down. She was a wild chick. But somewhere in the equation something went screwy. Rio might've had hustler in his blood, but it wasn't in his heart.

Cutty and Rio had been doing them for quite some time, but where Rio was an on-again, off-again hustler, Cutty jumped into it headfirst. He was always down to do dirt, be it robbing a ma fucka or slinging. He was always gonna make sure he ate. That's just how he was brought up. With no family to speak of, at least nobody who gave a shit, Cutty was forced to take it to the streets to live. He had been putting in work for so long that he didn't see the evil in what he was doing. To him it was just the way things were. He didn't really give a fuck where he ended up down the line, as long as he got to live good when it counted.

For a while, things had been on the downside for Cutty. The number of official niggaz in the streets were dwindling as time progressed. This new breed of hustler had the game all twisted. Everybody was more concerned about getting fresh than longevity. If you had on a platinum chain, but didn't have an emergency stash for lawyers or bail, then you were stupid and had no business in the streets. Cutty was one of the last real niggaz in the hood. The new punks that were running things made him sick.

Just when Cutty was about down and out, Rio came through as usual. He put Cutty in a position to make some real paper on the consistent basis. He never really figured himself as somebody's bodyguard, but whatever put food on the table. At first he was suspect of his old friend. Ever since Rio had come home from his bid, people had been whispering about him. People had been saying that he didn't have it in him to be a Capo in an organization like Prince's. But after seeing the devil peek out of Rio in the club, Cutty's suspicions were laid to rest.

There was a gangsta hiding somewhere in Rio. He just needed a little coaxing to bring him out.

Cutty's thoughts were interrupted when a white Benz wagon pulled up on 103rd and Manhattan. He didn't recognize the car, so he slid his hammer from his jacket. If it was Baron or anybody else trying to come through the hood and violate, they would pay in blood. When Truck hopped from the ride, Cutty allowed himself to relax a bit, but he still kept his gun cocked.

"What up?" Truck asked, showing his teeth. "Fuck is you still doing out here?"

"Chilling," Cutty said, taking a toke on his blunt. "Just chilling."

"Chilling, huh? I hear that. How's *our* boy doing?"

"Rio? Oh, he's good. Left him about an hour ago."

"Say, what was all that shit about earlier?"

"Man, that wasn't about nothing. Niggaz from Fifty-fifth acting like they can't get it."

"Yeah, Baron and them. I know the kid."

"Well, you better holla at ya man. They come at my fam breezy again and it's on."

"Nah," Truck said, sitting on the steps next to Cutty. "It's like you said, 'ain't about nothing.' Some niggaz let pussy cloud their better judgment."

"Pussy?" Cutty asked. "You mean to tell me that all that shit was over a broad?"

"Yep. At least that's the way I heard it. That girl Rio mess with was up in there with Baron and his crew. Ya man Rio caught feelings and wigged out."

"Well, I'll be damned. I almost caught a body in a public place cause of some shit Trinity started?"

"Hey, it's like I said. That's what I was told. Homegirl got our boy's nose wide open."

"That shit is wack, Truck."

"Tell me about it. How does that make our crew look when one of our Capos is letting some chickenhead cause him to forget himself? We supposed to be top of the food chain out this ma fucka. All of us caked up. It ain't nothing wrong with having a little sweetheart, but the number one priority should be your pocket and your credibility. If you running around acting like a bird, ain't nobody gonna truly respect you."

"You got a point, Truck. I be trying to put my nigga up on game, but I don't want him to feel like I'm playing him. I just wanna make sure my fam is good."

"That's what I'm trying to say," Truck said, taking the blunt. "Cutty, niggaz like you is what we need in our organization. You keep it funky and you look out for yo people. That's a true gangsta."

"I am what I am, dawg."

"Fo sho. Man, I just don't wanna see ya boy make no mistakes. You know that any mistakes at this level of the game could prove to be fatal. It's a lot at stake here, Cutty."

"You ain't gotta tell me, Truck. I know what's going on and I'm gonna keep my nigga on point."

"Cutty, you a stand up cat. I was just telling Prince that you're one of the realist niggaz down this way," Truck lied. "Real stand up cat, man."

"Thanks, Truck."

"Listen, you got somewhere to be?"

"Nah, what up?"

"Got a li'l after-party going on over at the strip joint. You feel like rolling?"

"Shit, you ain't gotta ask me twice. Let's bounce."

The two men got up off the stoop and headed to the idling wagon. Truck and Cutty walked shoulder to shoulder like two old friends. As Truck patted Cutty on the back and boosted his ego, all he needed was a knife.

Young Bobby made his way down Broadway, constantly checking his watch. It was his first night working in the projects. After quite a bit of nagging, School Boy had finally let Bobby get some money. He had a few minutes to spare, so he decided to smoke the blunt clip that he had in his pocket from the night before.

Bobby lit the weed and took a deep pull. He continued strolling up the block, never noticing the man in the blue hoodie following him. Bobby had almost made it to Columbus Avenue before Officer Brown made his move.

Officer Brown was dressed in jeans and a varsity jacket. He hadn't yet earned his shield back, but Stark got him authorization to wear plainclothes for the assignment. An officer in uniform was easy enough to spot, but a black officer in uniform stuck out like a sore thumb. Brown walked up to Bobby and tapped him on the shoulder. When Bobby turned around, he found himself eye to eye with a police badge.

"Shit!" Bobby cursed.

"Shit is right," Brown said. "And you're in a world of it. Put your hands behind your back."

"Ah," Bobby pleaded, "come on, brother."

"Brother? Get the fuck outta here. We ain't brothers, punk. You ain't nothing but a dope-pushing snake. But don't worry about it. You're gonna get to do some good for once." As Officer Brown cuffed Bobby, a squad car followed by an unmarked van pulled up. Officer Brown put Bobby in the back of the car and walked to the driver's side window of the van.

"You know what to do?" Brown asked Officer Jenkins, who was behind the wheel, dressed in jeans and a leather jacket.

"Yeah," Jenkins said. "I got this. Let's go, sunshine," he said to Mikey, who was huddled in the rear of the van. Mikey didn't like what he was being forced to do, but what choice did he really have? It was either them or him and he'd much rather save his own ass. Reluctantly, Mikey hopped from the van.

"Listen," Brown said. "You play your cards right and everything will be fine, Mikey. If you try something stupid, my partner will shoot you. Got that?"

"I got it," Mikey said.

"Good. Jenkins, don't worry about a thing. We'll be on you the whole time. At the first sign of trouble, you'll have the whole precinct over here like stink on shit."

"I don't think I'll have any trouble," Jenkins said, checking his weapon. "Me and young Mikey here will get along famously."

"Okay, partner. But don't take any chances."

Officer Jenkins and Mikey made their way toward the projects as if nothing was wrong. Mikey thought about running, but he didn't want to risk the officer making good on his threat. His best bet was to play along for now. He had never considered himself a snitch, but with the threat of jail time looming, a cat found out that he wasn't as tough as he thought he was. Mikey found himself caught up in some bullshit. His only hope would be that the police honored their promise to relocate him. Because he knew that when it was all said and done, his life wouldn't be worth a nickle in New York.

Rio sat on Joyce's couch, sweating like a runaway slave. Between the heat of the apartment and the bottle he had downed, he felt like he was going to faint. The multicolored furniture in the living room made Rio feel like the place was spinning. He spared a glance at the rear of the house and wondered what the hell was taking Joyce so long with the coffee?

As if on cue, Joyce came out of the bedroom. To Rio's surprise she had shed her club outfit for a red silk bathrobe. The soft material clung to her body, giving Rio an eyeful. Joyce might not have been pretty in the face, but she was well put together. She slid on the couch next to Rio, holding two glasses that were filled with a green liquid.

"Here," Joyce said, handing him one of the glasses. "The coffee's on, but I thought you might've wanted something a li'l lighter to sip on while you waited."

"Joyce," Rio said, pushing the glass away. "I think I've had enough."

"Oh, stop being scared," she said, pushing the glass back at him. "This ain't nothing but some puckers and a pinch of vodka. It'll make you feel better than that bottle of yak you been sipping on."

Rio eyeballed the glass before taking it. True, he was drunk as a skunk, but he didn't feel like quitting yet. The yak was sure to make him "earl" eventually, so maybe the puckers was the lesser of the two evils. Rio shrugged and reached for the drink. He downed the green liquid so quickly that he never even noticed the small pill dissolving in the bottom of the glass.

"Feeling better?" Joyce asked with a devilish grin.

"A li'l something. Thanks, Joyce."

"Ain't nothing, Rio. I'm just trying to look out, that's all. So, let's kick it a little while we wait on the coffee?"

"A'ight, but you know I can't stay long."

"I know, Rio. Gotta go chase Trinity, right?"

"See," he slurred, "there you go. Why you gotta come at me like that, Joyce?"

"Like what? I ain't said nothing that ain't true."

"You don't know what you're talking about."

"Whatever, Rio. So, you gonna sit here and tell me that you haven't thought about going by her house?"

"Well . . . no. I mean . . . yeah. I mean . . ."

"What do you mean, Rio?"

"I don't know, Joyce," Rio said, rubbing his forehead. He struggled to keep his thoughts focused. No doubt Joyce's little surprise was kicking in. "I'm all mixed up, ma. I don't know what the fuck I'm gonna do. I love Trinity and all, but the way she do shit ain't kosher."

"Rio, I hang wit her just about every day, so I know." Joyce stretched her arms over her head causing the bottom of her robe to rise just above her waist. Rio looked down and noticed that Joyce wasn't wearing any underwear. The sober side of him screamed, "Run, nigga," but the drunk held him in place. All he could do was stare at Joyce's heart-shaped bush.

"Why you staring at me like that?" she asked playfully.

"Huh?" he said, trying to force his eyes to focus. "Nah, I was just daydreaming. Damn," he said looking at his empty glass. "You sure it was only a pinch of vodka in there?"

"Maybe a dash," Joyce said, moving in closer. "You can handle it, can't you?" Joyce laid her arm across the chair behind Rio's head, and one side of her robe slid down exposing part of her breast. Rio tried not to look, but couldn't seem to help himself.

"See something you like?" Joyce asked, running her tongue across her top lip. Without waiting for an answer, Joyce took Rio's hand and placed it on her breast. He tried to pull away, but the drug and the liquor made him their willing slave. Rio gently rubbed her breast until the nipple began to poke through the fabric. Joyce let out a low moan as his other hand came into play.

"Kiss them," she whispered softly. Rio tried to check himself before he did something stupid, but it seemed to be a little too late for that. He leaned over and kissed the left breast then the right. Every nerve in his body felt like they were tingling at once. His penis began to swell until it felt like it was about to burst through his pants. Joyce reached over and kissed Rio on the lips while using her hand to massage the bulge in his pants. When she touched him, it felt like every nerve in his body came alive at once.

"Do you want me?" Joyce asked as she pulled his penis free of its prison. The living room's colors had become more animated now. The various hues of green and yellows began to taunt Rio as he sat there letting Joyce jerk him off. When she had gotten it good and hard, she placed it in her mouth and took him where he needed to be. Joyce's lips on Rio's wood had the softness of rose petals and the warmth of a summer day. All he could do was let his eyes roll back in his head as she sucked him like a vet. Rio tried to pull away as he was about to cum, but Joyce had a pit bull's lock on him. When he exploded in her mouth, she didn't spill one drop. Joyce threw his cum back like a shot of tequila. When it was all said and done, Rio laid his head back and prayed for the world to stop spinning.

"So," she said, wiping her mouth, "how you like that?"

Joyce wasn't talking that loud, but her voice was like thunder in his ears. "What the fuck?" he cursed, trying to clear his head. "Fuck was in that drink?"

"Don't worry about it, baby. It was just a li'l E."

"A li'l what? Joyce, what did you give me?"

"Ecstacy, silly. Don't worry though, it's harmless."

"My fucking goodness," Rio said, struggling to his feet. "I gotta get up outta here."

"What's the matter, Rio? Didn't I do you good? I know Trinity don't suck you like that, do she? She take all that nut like a good bitch?"

"I shoulda known," Rio said, staggering to the front door. "You talking all this concerned shit when all you wanted was to get a shot of this dick. Trinity's dick."

"And? I don't know why you acting like that now, Rio. Shit, when you busted in my mouth it tasted like my dick."

"Fuck you, Joyce. You scandalous," he said, while zipping his pants.

"Ain't no more scandalous than ya wife. She was the one all up on the next nigga. In front of you at that."

"Joyce, you chasing after something that you can't have."

"Rio, please. Ya shit ain't even that serious. Don't nobody want you like that. I hope you and Trinity are happy together. All I wanted was a nut. Now if you're finished tripping, why don't you come and knock this pussy out."

Joyce began to finger herself while Rio looked on. That little demon inside him said to go over and give the bitch what she wanted. Rio didn't feed into it though. He shouldn't have let it get this far, but he had fucked up. The best thing for him to do was to get the fuck up outta there and sober up. If he stayed any longer he might end up either killing Joyce or fucking her. Either way it was no good for him.

"So," she continued. "What you gonna do, Rio?"

Rio just shook his head and made for the door. "Joyce, you got issues. I'm gone."

"Hold up," she said hopping up. "You just gonna leave me hanging?"

"I'm sorry, Joyce. Me and Trinity on the outs right now, but I still love her."

"After what I did for you? Are you serious?"

"As a heart attack, ma. What we did is wrong. I wish I could take it back, but I can't."

"Darius Santana, you're something else."

"So I've been told."

"So now what? You gonna tell T?"

"Nah, got too much respect for her as well as myself. As far as I'm concerned, this shit never happened." Rio threw two bills on the couch and skated.

Joyce sat on her couch half-naked, feeling played. Couldn't fault Rio though. As it turned out, true love was stronger than any designer drug or conniving bitch. She just had to suck it up. If Rio wanted to be a fool for Trinity then he was welcome to it. Joyce would just have to find herself another vic. It was said that Joyce had the best head in Harlem. If Rio didn't appreciate it, then someone else would.

School Boy paced back and forth in front of 875, checking his watch. He could've kicked himself in the ass for not having someone on standby. Bobby had nagged him about getting a shift and then pulled a no-show. Now School Boy was on the block shorthanded. It was the middle of the night and he would have a hard time finding someone to cover for Bobby.

Mikey and Jenkins came strolling up the block at just the right time. They spotted School Boy in front of the building looking stressed. It wasn't a secret to them why he was stressed. After all the NYPD had set the whole thing up.

"What's up, School Boy?" Mikey asked.

"Ain't nothing," School Boy said, distracted. "I'm just out here trying to do me."

"Have you seen Mel around?"

"Nah, I ain't seen him today. What you need?"

"Oh, he told me that me and my man could come and get some paper on the block," Mikey lied.

"Mikey, I thought that you was a stick-up kid?"

"Man, you heard what happened to the clique. That shit is a dead issue for me. I need for sure money, not maybe money. So, you think we can get a shift in?"

School Boy was leery at first. He knew Mikey from seeing him around the hood, but he really didn't know him like that, and School Boy didn't know the kid he was with from a hole in the wall, but he was in a jam. He figured that his best bet was to let Mikey rock and check him with Shamel later on. It was either let Mikey and his man work the shift or do it himself.

"A'ight," School Boy said. "I'm gonna let you two hold it down. Mikey, you pitch while I hold you down."

"I got a better idea," Mikey said. "Why don't we let my man Jenkins pitch and I'll hold him down?"

"Nah, Mikey. I don't know this cat well enough to let him touch nothing."

"It's cool, man," Jenkins cut in. "I'm out here trying to get some paper, too."

"Listen," School Boy said. "Y'all lucky I'm even letting you pump. Like I said, I don't know you like that. Now, I'm not a coldhearted dude, so this is what I'll do. I'll let you play the lookout while Mikey pitches the stones."

"Thanks, man," Jenkins said, faking gratitude. "I appreciate this. For real." Jenkins could hardly believe how easy it was to get in. They should've been able to take Prince down years ago. The seeds had been planted, now all they had to do was get something solid.

"What can I say?" School Boy capped. "I got a good heart. Y'all go ahead and take your positions so we can open up shop." School Boy walked off smiling as if he did a good thing. Little did he know, he had just invited a weasel into the henhouse.

18

In an attempt to take his mind off all the craziness that had been going on for the last couple of days, Rio decided to hang out with his homeboys. There was a big fight that was supposed to go down, so Rio bought tickets for Shamel, Cutty, and himself. The tickets ran him a good $4,500, but he didn't really sweat it. He wanted to do something nice for his lieutenants. Besides, Rio needed to get out and unwind in the worst kind of way.

The Garden was packed for the event. There were entertainers and athletes milling around the event getting their stunt on. Rio and his clique made their way through the event, taking in the whole scene. It was the first time that any of the young men had ever attended an event of that magnitude, but they did their best not to look starstruck.

"Damn," Cutty said, eyeing a young lady in a sequined dress. "Ain't that shorty from that movie?"

"I don't know," Shamel said, looking at her ass. "Sure looks like her."

"I need to get me a shot of that," Cutty said, licking his lips.

"Don't be acting all crazy when we get up in the joint," Rio said, shaking his head. "Y'all is some vultures."

"Shut up," Cutty said, faking anger. "You act like you the only nigga that's ever been somewhere."

"You know Rio is one of them uppity niggaz," Shamel said playfully. "Where we sitting?"

"Third row back from Ringside," Rio said, looking at his ticket.

"Damn," Cutty said. "I know you had to trick some paper on these."

"Something light. I ain't worried about it though. Y'all is my niggaz, man. If I can't enjoy this paper with y'all, who can I enjoy it with?"

"I know that's right," Shamel co-signed. "Let's go up in there and watch this punk get whipped on."

The inside of the arena was just as packed as the outside. There were people jammed in from the front row to the rear exit. As Rio led his team down the isle, he noticed quite a few familiar faces from the streets. Marco sat in a middle seat with some of his homeys and a few young ladies. The Salvadorian Capo made eye contact with Rio and nodded. Rio tapped his chest once and kept going. It took Rio and his team nearly fifteen minutes to reach their seats.

"You seen that cat Paul back there?" Cutty asked.

"Yeah," Rio said, checking his watch. "I saw him."

"Biker ma fucka in here looking like Mad Max and shit."

"Paul is good people, Cutty. Prince wouldn't have put him where he is."

"Still a cracker."

Rio ignored Cutty's closed-minded comments and began scanning the crowd. There were quite a few famous people in attendance. Sitting near the ring was a player from the Pistons. The ice in his chain looked like tiny flashbulbs. As Rio continued to look over the sea of people, he noticed a familiar face staring at him from across the ring.

Baron sat on the opposite side of the arena, looking at Rio. He was with about six or seven of his soldiers, so he was probably feeling himself. Rio returned his stare. Seeing Baron brought a bitter taste to Rio's mouth. He had developed quite a dislike for his northern rival. Baron looked like a black-ass lion with his dreads hanging freely about his face. Rio envisioned himself choking the life out of him. Rio was more than willing to be the bigger man about it, but if Baron kept eyeballing him, it might have to be something. Rio could put up with a lot of shit, but he couldn't stomach another man getting at his lady. To him Trinity was his alone. To be with her was a privilege. The staring match was broken up by Shamel tapping his arm.

"The fight's about to start, dawg," Shamel said.

The two fighters came out and took their places. At the sound of the bell they came out boxing. The challenger was pretty, coming out with a series of jabs and crosses. The champ got flustered, but managed to keep his wits. This all lasted until the last thirty seconds of the second round. The champ split the challenger's eye and put him down for ten. The crowd flipped out over the bogus fight. Rio just shrugged and chalked it up as a very expensive night with the fellas.

After the fight, Shamel and Cutty wanted to keep the night going and hit the after-party. Rio didn't feel much like partying though. Seeing Baron had taken him out of the mood. He needed to be alone with his thoughts. Rio bid his homeys good night and headed on home.

When Rio entered his house, all of the lights were off. He figured that no one was home, which suited him just fine. As Rio approached his bedroom door, he heard what sounded like voices coming from the other side. He found that strange considering the fact that his room was off limits. Rio cracked the door a taste and peeked inside. Sally was sitting on the bed holding something in her hand. She was rocking back and forth humming a soulful tune. As he looked a little closer he noticed tears sparkling in her eyes.

"Ma?" he asked easing into the room.

"Oh." She jumped. "I didn't hear you come in. Sorry about being in your room, but the door was unlocked."

"It's okay," Rio said, taking off his jacket. "What ya doing?"

"Nothing. Just reminiscing," For the first time Rio noticed what she was holding. It was a picture of his father. "These were the days," Sally said, stroking the picture.

"Word. I heard you and daddy were quite the pair back in the days?"

"Yeah, we raised all kinds of hell back in the seventies. Protesting and acting all crazy."

"I heard stories."

"Rio, I wish you could've really gotten to know your father."

"Daddy was a real gangsta, huh?"

"Yeah, but he was more than that. Your father was a powerful man. He was the type of person that could hold a crowd's attention when he spoke. I remember when he staged a protest in front of the state building. He was pushing for the employment of more blacks on city jobs."

"Yeah?"

"Amir was in all his glory, hollering about the rights of black folks and how we need to be more assertive about ourselves. You know the police locked his crazy ass up. Didn't stop there though. All of them people followed the police all the way back to the station and continued the rally on their doorstep."

"That's deep, ma."

"Amir was deep."

"Do you miss him?"

"All the time, Rio. Willie is good to me, but your father was the only man I ever gave my heart to."

"That's serious."

"No more serious than you and Trinity."

"Nah," Rio said, sitting beside her. "It ain't the same thing. I think Trinity and me are a done deal."

"Nonsense, Rio. You love that girl. You can act tough for your friends, but you can't fool your mother. I see love all in your eyes. Even when you say her name, I see it."

"I love Trinity, Ma, but I can't be weak."

"How does loving a woman make you weak? You young people have some ass backwards views on life. A man can't be truly complete without a woman and vice versa. If that wasn't true, then God wouldn't have made it so it takes one of each to create a life."

"Ma, that's all well and good, but I can't allow my head to be all screwy thinking about some chick. I gotta be focused."

"Focused for what?" she asked, getting serious. "Rio, it doesn't take a whole lot of focus to sling poison."

"Ma . . ."

"Rio," she said, cutting him off. "Don't try to lie about it, okay? I know what you're doing out there. I don't like it, but you're grown. Ain't much I can do to sway you."

"Ma, I know what I'm doing."

"Your father knew what he was doing, too, but what did that get him? Rio, you two are so much alike that it makes my head hurt. Your father could've been somebody big if he focused his energy the right way. When I look at you, I can't help but to see the same thing. You're so talented, but you have a poor sense of judgment. All of that talent going to waste."

"Come on, Ma. I don't wanna talk about this with you right now."

"Why not? We're just two grown folks shooting the breeze. Listen, it's your life, Rio. I raised you to manhood and now it's out of my hands. All I ask is that you use your head. If you wanna run the streets and be like Prince, knock yourself out. But don't be stupid about it. Instead of tricking all of your money off on weed and fight tickets, put something up for a rainy day. You think when we were coming up that Prince was running around buying jewelry and cars? Hell no. Prince was stacking his money and look at him now."

"Yeah," Rio said, lighting a cigarette. "Prince is caked up."

"Because Prince is smart. Don't be a fool like the rest of them, Darius. Take your money and do something smart with it. Why don't you and Trinity move out of the projects?"

"I don't know about that, Ma. Douglass is all I know."

"Then learn something else. Rio, a wise man never shits where he lives. Listen to your mother. Take that money and do something smart with it." Sally took the lit cigarette and strolled out of the room. All the while humming her tune.

Another day, the same hustle. For the last few days Rio had avoided all contact with Trinity. He wouldn't take her calls and when he saw her on the block he ducked her. It hurt him to do her like that, but he felt it was necessary. Trinity had played him and that shit hurt worst. The funny thing is, he didn't know whether he was ducking her because of what happened at the club or because of the bullshit he let Joyce pull. Either way it wasn't a good time to see his boo.

The upside was by him not being around Trinity he had more time to focus on the hustle. Rio attacked the streets with a vengeance. His mind was on scratch twenty-four/seven. His mood showed in the way he began to conduct his business. The happy-go-lucky nigga everyone had known him to be was gone. In his place was a pure hustler. Everything had to go as it was supposed to or Rio was barking about it. If your pack came up short, you put it back out of your pocket. If a nigga ran off with a pack, whoever was on shift at the time would have to work off the debt. That's just how it was.

Rio and Cutty were in back of the center, bullshitting the afternoon away. Rio was tossing a softball while Cutty swung his bat in vain. They were just trying to pass the time. Their little game was broken up when a young worker named Mouse came running down the steps. Mouse was so out of breath that his words were incoherent.

"Calm down," Rio said, grabbing the boy by his shoulders. "Take your time and tell me what went down."

After taking a moment to get himself together, Mouse was finally able to tell the tale. "Stick-up kids," he gasped.

"What?" Rio asked. "What you talking bout?"

"They came through and got us, man."

"Mouse, how this shit happen?"

"It was me, Nate, and Petey on shift. Petey was the lookout, Nate had the work, and I was on the money. Then—"

"Mouse," Rio cut him off. "I know who was responsible for what. I handed out the assignments. Now get to the damn point."

"Okay, like I was saying. We was out there clicking, like we always do. I went upstairs, getting another pack because we had run out of product. Well, while I'm heading into the staircase I hear Nate's voice in the elevator. I know something is funny because the boy is supposed to be in the front waiting on me. I lay in the cut to see what's going on. Nate steps off the elevator looking all shaky and shit. At first I think he's alone, but then I see two niggaz step off behind him holding guns. Right then and there I blow it and come get y'all."

"Hold on, hold on," Cutty said. "You mean to say that you been down here running ya yap, while some ma fuckas is up there robbing our spot?" Cutty cocked his hand back to slap Mouse, but Rio stopped him.

"Hold on, player," Rio said. "How long ago was this?"

"A few seconds," said Mouse timidly.

"A'ight. Cutty, you strapped?"

"Ma-fucking-right."

"Mouse, would you know them niggaz if you saw them again?"

"Yeah. They wasn't wearing masks."

"Come on," Rio said. He jogged up the few stairs leading to the path, but didn't expose himself. He just sat in the cut and watched the building. Most niggaz would've run up in the building blasting, but Rio was too smart for that. He had a plan for this just like every other situation.

After about five minutes or so, they spotted the cats they were looking for. Mouse pointed out two suspect-looking cats coming out of the building carrying book bags. Rio turned to say something to Cutty and noticed an odd look on his friend's face. It wasn't a look of fear, more like shock.

"What up, Cutty?" Rio asked. "You know them niggaz or something?"

"Yeah," Cutty grunted. "I used to know em. Now, they just dead men." Cutty moved toward them, but Rio stopped him. "Fuck is you waiting for, Rio?"

"Hold ya head, kid. We gonna handle it, but not like this. Mouse," Rio said, turning to the youngster, "go upstairs and check on Nate. Once you make sure that he's okay, you go find that nigga Petey. Keep them both here until we get back." Mouse ran off to carry out his boss's orders. "A'ight, Cutty. Let's handle our business."

Rio led Cutty through the path to the parking lot. They made sure they didn't move too fast because they didn't want to get out in front of the would-be stick-up kids. By the time they reached the lot, the stick-up kids were coming down the steps. They were looking around all paranoid as if the boogie man were going to jump out and snatch them.

It was obvious that they were afraid. Didn't count for much though. They should've thought about fear before they tried to rob Rio.

"There they go," Rio said, ducking behind a car. "How well do you know these kids, Cutty?"

"I know em good enough."

"A'ight, this is what we gonna do. You get them niggaz attention. I'm gonna creep further down and come up through the grass in front of 845."

"What we gonna do, Rio?"

"Get our shit back. Quietly if possible."

"And if not?" Rio didn't even have to answer. He just looked at Cutty and crept off. Cutty knew just what was about to go down. Kev and Boo didn't understand reasoning. They were the kinda niggaz to shoot first and negotiate later. He had always been cool with the youths, but this situation was different. They had disrespected his man and indirectly stole from him. If Rio didn't eat, then neither did Cutty. When it came to his paper all that cool shit went out the window. Kev and Boo had to go.

When the two robbers were almost to the area where Rio was hiding, Cutty made his presence known. "Yo," Cutty said, waving. "What's good, fellas?"

Boo and Kev both jumped at the sound of Cutty's voice. He was the last person they wanted to see after pulling off their heist. Even though he worked with Rio, they hadn't stolen from outta Cutty's pocket. It was unlikely that he had found out about it so soon, but if he did then he wasn't there to talk. Their best chance was to play it off.

"What's good, fam?" Kev asked, showing his teeth. "What you doing over this way?"

"Chilling. Trying to find somebody with some weed. Where y'all headed?"

"Bout to go see these chicks. Supposed to take em to the telly." The three of them stood around making small talk as if everything was cool. Cutty didn't seem like anything was wrong, so they figured that they might make it out of the situation yet. That is until Boo spotted Rio hopping the fence.

At that moment all hell broke loose. Boo was the first to react. With his free hand he pulled the 9mm from under his jacket. Cutty was the closest, so he was the most immediate threat. Boo tried to draw on him, but Kev was in the way. He spun around and let off two wild shots in Rio's direction. They missed their target, but provided Boo with the time he needed to make a run for it. By the time Kev realized what was going on, Cutty had a stranglehold on his neck.

"You li'l dumb ass," Cutty snapped. "Thought you was gonna steal from me and get away with it. You're stupid Kev. Real fucking stupid." Kev tried to struggle, but the shorter Cutty had strength and leverage over him. Somehow he managed to free his pistol and bashed Cutty in his head. While Cutty tried to get his focus back, Kev did the hundred-yard dash. Didn't really matter though. Cutty's desert eagle closed the distance with little effort. The first shot hit Kev in the side, while the other one split his skull. Cutty ran up on Kev and put one more in his back. One down.

Rio stood by the fence, watching the carnage unfold around him. When he set Cutty loose he never intended for this to happen. Too late to worry about it now. The damage was done and all Rio could do now was see it through. No matter what the outcome.

"Rio," Cutty barked. "Get his man. The nigga trying to run."

Rio snapped out of his daze just in time to see Boo running across the street. Willing all of his strength to his legs, he took off after him. Boo had a good head start, but fear added to Rio's speed. He knew that if Boo got away, either one of two things was going to happen. Boo would go to the police, and Rio would be tried as an accessory to murder. Or Boo would come back seeking revenge. Either way it wasn't good for business. There was only one thing that Rio could do.

Rio slowed to a trot and aimed his .45. His nerves were so jacked up that his hand kept shaking. Using his left hand to steady his right one, Rio aimed and fired. The cannon thundered to life and spit out two shots. The first one went wild, but the second one splattered Boo's calf muscle. People were running every which way, but Rio didn't pay them any mind. His main focus was to make sure that the stick-up kid couldn't come back.

Boo was on the floor, squirming in pain. Rio jogged up to where he had downed him and flipped him over on his back. As Boo looked up at Rio, a light of recognition went off in each of their eyes. Rio knew the kid from somewhere, but he couldn't remember where.

"Fuck you looking at?" Boo asked. "I see ya aim still ain't got no better, pussy. Yeah, I remember you from the last time. First my shoulder, now my leg. When you gonna get it right?"

At first Rio didn't understand what the kid was talking about, but then it hit him. This was one of the cats that Shamel was beefing with. The same cat that he had popped. Funny how the world is so small. People's paths always seem to cross at the most inopportune moments.

Cutty came running across the street, holding Kev's bag. "Rio," he said frantically. "Fuck is you doing? We gotta get outta here, now!"

"Youz a pussy." Boo smirked. "These ma fuckas running round acting like you God or something. You ain't shit, nigga. Nothing but a pussy."

Cutty leveled his gun, but Rio waved him off. "Fuck him, Cutty. We outta here." Cutty didn't like it, but Rio was the boss. So he followed.

"That's right," Boo continued. "You get the fuck outta here, pussies. Both you niggaz. Hey Rio, you better grow eyes in the back of ya head, nigga. I'm gonna kill you, pussy. If I see you again, it's on. Fuck you and ya team. You a dead man. Dead ma fucka! When I get done with you, I'm gonna get a piece of that fine bitch you run with." This made Rio stop walking. "Yeah, I know ya bitch, nigga. That fine yellow hoe from 845. Yep, gonna get me some of that."

The anger that welled inside of Rio was indescribable. Everything that was wrong with his life danced in his head. His problems at home, the situation with Trinity. It all came to a boil. Rio stood over the fallen man and felt tears forming in his eyes.

"Aww," Boo taunted. "You gonna cry, pussy? Go ahead, nigga. Let it out. Say Cutty, you better find yourself a new employer. This boy ain't built for the streets. Man, if I was you—" That was as far as Boo got. Rio's finger worked of its own accord and squeezed the trigger. Once, twice, three times. Boo wasn't talking junk anymore. He was too busy leaking all over the playground.

❏ ❏ ❏

Trinity sat at her kitchen table, trying to study for her upcoming GED test. She tried to focus on math, but her mind kept wondering. It was hard to think about school when so much in her life was going wrong. She had to worry about what was going to happen to her family when she met with the people from BCW and on top of that, things between her and Rio were going downhill.

It had been almost four days since she had last spoken to him. It was the longest they had ever gone without speaking since they had hooked up. Too long for her. At first she thought he was just being childish, but as she thought about it, she realized that she was the one in the wrong. Rio wasn't a regular dude leading a regular life. He was a hustler. It was bad enough that people were always kicking shit on his name, because they felt like he didn't earn his position. Trinity in all her foolishness didn't help at all. She was supposed to be totally loyal to her man and in his corner at all times. Not popping bottles with the competition. She made Rio look weak by doing that.

Trinity wanted to continue feeling sorry for herself, but Billy had just come in the house. She watched her little brother as he guzzled Kool-Aid out of the pitcher and wondered what she was going to do. Billy always tried to be the strong little man and hold it together, but she knew he was really scared. He was only a child and being made to endure so much. All she could do was put it in God's hands and hope for the best.

"Sup, T?" Billy asked, sitting down at the other end of the table.

"Hey Billy." She smiled, trying not to look worried. "You just getting home from school?"

"Nah, me and some of the fellas went window-shopping downtown."

"You got homework?"

"A little."

"Don't you think you'd better get to it?"

"I am, T. I just got in. Listen to you sounding like Ma."

"Oh, please, boy. I'm just making sure you fly straight."

"I got this, Trinity."

"Actions speak louder than words, Billy."

"I said I'm gonna do it, Trinity."

"Well, maybe you shoulda did it before you went window-shopping? Bullshitting around with ya friends ain't gonna get you into college. You gotta get ya shit together."

"Trinity, you're acting like I'm Richard. I ain't running around trying to smoke my life away. That ain't my thing. Why are you so irritable lately?"

"My bad," she said, closing her book. "I just got a lot on me. This GED is kicking my ass, I gotta find another job. It's a rough on me, Billy."

"I know, Trinity. This stuff is all gonna work itself out."

"I hope so, Billy. I hope so."

"Oh, that reminds me. I just saw Rio."

"Really," Trinity said, perking up. "Where?"

"In the parking lot."

"What was he doing back there?"

"I dunno. Him and Cutty were stooping behind a car looking at something."

"I wonder what the fuck he was doing back there?" Trinity's question was answered by the sound of gunfire.

19

A **group of boys** gathered around in back of the center shooting cee-lo. You could always tell when the weather was about to break, because the gamblers would come out. Don't get it wrong, the bug floated all year around. But the action got heavier when it was nice out. Around a certain time every year the whole city would catch the fever. Gambling fever. In spots, buildings, people's houses. Everyone wanted to gamble. The most popular means of testing lady fate were through dice. Be it with three dice or two, you could always hear them shakers. Dice was where it was, so it was a dice game that Shamel stumbled upon.

"Eight hundred dollars in it," the skinny roller with the gold caps said. "Everything is good if you got money in it." The skinny roller shook the dice in his bony mitt, looking for challengers.

"Stick it!" shouted a kid holding a Heineken.

"Eight to the big man," The skinny roller said, as he went into his mojo. He flicked the dice underhanded, making them dance about like three ballerinas. The trio of dancers twirled about for what seemed like a lifetime. Finally they ended their show and 2-2-6 were the numbers they read. "Head crack, kid. Pay me." Heineken shot the skinny roller a mean look, but reluctantly came out of his pocket. "Sixteen hundred in the bank," boasted the skinny roller.

"Stop that!" Shamel barked, stepping into the circle.

"All money is good," the skinny roller assured, without taking his eyes off the ground. "I ain't got no problem taking ya paper. Matter of fact . . ." When the skinny roller looked up and saw who was addressing him, a die popped out of his hand. "Shamel? Oh, no bet to you, God."

"Word," Shamel said, grinning. "My money ain't green?"

"Come on, Shamel. Look, we out here having a friendly game. Ain't no big money over this way. We got short pockets, man."

"Yo, I ain't on it like that. I made a career change, God. I don't do the jacking no more. I'm just trying to kick it for a minute and roll a few dollars."

"A'ight." The skinny roller sighed. "Sixteen to you." The skinny roller tossed the dice like they sickened him to be in his hand. The dice danced around each other and clanked against the wall. Fever was the point.

"I see you coming wit that heat?" Shamel asked as he picked up the dice.

"What can I say?" The skinny roller asked. "Looks like I'm hot to-night."

"I can dig it." Shamel glanced at the dice and his huge lips parted into a grin. "Five is the point." Shamel let the dice bounce and four was what he rolled. "Looks like you win again, huh?"

"Like I said," The skinny roller said. "I'm hot tonight." Shamel and the skinny roller went back and forth, each winning and losing. But the skinny roller always seemed to be up. Shamel spotted Knowledge creeping on the game so he took a break. The onlookers were pleased because it finally gave them a chance to try and come up.

"What up, sun?" Shamel said, giving Knowledge dap.

"Oh," Knowledge said. "That was you over there at the dice game? Damn, I was thinking I had my car note over here and shit. You working these niggaz or what?"

"Nah, I ain't working em. I'm fucking wit Rio now, remember?"

"Yeah, for sure. But speaking of that cat, you got the latest on him?"

"Nah, I been gone the last two days. Took a ride up north to see my brother."

"Oh, what's up with the God?" Knowledge asked.

"He chilling. But what's this you was telling me about Rio, Knowledge?"

"Yo," Knowledge said in a whisper. "I heard ya man snapped the other night. Murdered them stick-up niggaz from down the way."

"What stick-up niggaz?" Shamel asked, confused.

"Boo and Kev. I heard Rio cold went Stallone out there. Nigga had a .45 in one hand, a desert in the other, and a banger in his ass. Stone cold bugging."

"Hold up, Darius-Rio?"

"Ma fucka, ain't that what I had said? Rio from 875. I heard Boo was talking crazy so Rio aired both of them niggaz out. Blew the back of Kev's skull off and put like six in Boo's face."

Shamel took it all in, but he couldn't comprehend what Knowledge was saying. He knew that Rio was going through some things, but there was no way in the world that he had become homicidal. Rio was a lot of things, but a killer wasn't one of them.

"Knowledge," Shamel began. "Where you getting your facts from?"

"Same place you getting yours. The Vine. The clique might be over, but the Vine is always gonna be."

"You sure about this?"

"Word is bond, God. I told it to you just like I got it."

All Shamel could do was shake his head. If he got it through the Vine then it was damn near accurate. It might not be right detail for detail, but the moral was still the same. Looked like Rio had stepped up into the ranks of the elite. He was really a gangsta now. Regardless of all that get-a-job-and-be-a-husband shit, blood don't wash off.

"I got to go check on my nigga," Shamel said, heading back to the dice game. "Gimmie a sec, God."

The skinny roller had accumulated a fairly large bankroll by now. He was just about ready to step off and trick his money off with sack-chasers. "A'ight y'all," the skinny roller said, tucking his winnings. "It's been real." Just as the skinny roller turned to leave, Shamel stopped him.

"Hold on," Shamel said pleasantly. "Ain't no more money in the bank?"

"Nah, kid. The game is over."

"Nah," Shamel said, pulling his glock. "I think the game is just beginning."

"Come on," the skinny roller pleaded. "You said we was good, Mel."

"You piece of shit, lowlife. You think I don't know when a ma fucka is trying to cheat me?"

"What? I'd never cross you, Mel."

"Roll ya sleeves up, dick."

"Huh?"

"Don't play wit me, duke. I peeped you cuff the dice. Now, roll ya sleeves up or I'm gonna shoot you in the fucking foot."

Everybody at the game knew that Mel was serious. If he said that he was gonna shoot you, then you just might end up shot. Sweat began to pour from the skinny roller as the crowd looked on. He knew he didn't have much choice in the matter, so he did as he was told. Tucked in his shirtsleeve for all to see were the funny dice. One showed sixes on two sides and the other showed four on two sides.

"Dirty ma fucka!" Shamel barked, slamming his fist into the skinny roller's jaw. The skinny roller hit the floor with no resistance. Shamel kicked him in the ribs twice before stripping him of all his clothes. The skinny roller stood there butt-ass trying cover himself with his hat. "Now," Shamel said. "Get the fuck up from around here." To make sure the skinny roller understood him, Shamel gave him a swift kick in the ass. The skinny roller ran down the block crying. Shamel took most of the loot, the rest he tossed into the crowd. He didn't really want the money, but ol' boy had tried to outhustle a hustler. A mistake that he'll hopefully learn from.

"Five-O!" Shouted the lookout in front of 865. All of the workers scattered in various directions. This was nothing unusual. Whenever police came around, the homeboys would make themselves scarce. But when Detective Stark came around, everybody headed for the hills. Everybody except Rio. He was connected now, so there was no more running. He just sat there and continued smoking his cigarette.

"Well, well," Stark said, smiling. "My main man, Rio. What's up, brother?"

"Fuck you," Rio said, spitting on the ground. "We ain't hardly brothers."

"Come on now, Darius. Ain't that how you folks great each other down here?"

"Man, get outta here with that Dolomite shit. Fuck you want with me, pig?"

"Wanna ask you some questions, brother."

"Told you that we ain't brothers. Furthermore, I ain't got shit to say to you, fat boy."

"Oh," Stark said, grabbing Rio by the shirt. "I think you do." Rio swung both of his arms up and out, breaking Stark's hold on him. Stark took an awkward swing, which Rio blocked and countered with a right hook. Detective Stark was out on his feet. Before Rio could take another step, he was swarmed by blue uniforms. The police kicked and beat Rio until the darkness took him.

When Rio awoke, he found himself lying on a concrete floor with one hell of a headache. When he tried to sit up, it felt as if someone had glued his hair to the ground. Maybe it was best for him to lie there for a while. He closed his eyes and tried to figure out exactly how he had allowed himself to end up in this situation. He knew Stark was just trying to get under his skin and he fed into it anyway. That was just plain stupid on his part. Now he had to sit and wait.

After about ten minutes or so, Rio mustered the strength to pull himself up. He was in a holding cell somewhere. Knowing Stark, it was probably the twenty-fourth. The cell was more or less empty. With the exception of Rio, a drunk, and two crackheads, there was no one else in the cell. The crackheads looked like they wanted to say something to Rio, but seeing the look on his face they decided against it.

Rio made his way to the chipped-up mirror that hung on the far wall of the cell. He couldn't help but wonder if he looked anything like he felt? He looked into the mirror and a broken man stared back at him. His face bore the scrapes and bruises of his little scuffle. Nothing that wouldn't heal over time. His lip was swollen and his front tooth felt like it was barely hanging on. Other than that he wasn't hurting too bad. His pride was more damaged than anything else.

Fucking pigs had really tried to do him dirty. "Punk ma fuckas," Rio said, as he spit through the bars. He took one last look in the mirror and shook his head. Rio had always said that he would never be caged again, but here he was in the holding tank with two hypes and a wino. Fuck was he doing to himself? This was hardly his style. His mother always said that his temper would get him into trouble. "So much like your father." She would tease.

Stark came at Rio on some bullshit and that's what got him popped in his mouth from the gate. Talking about they just wanted to ask some questions. Rio wasn't a dummy. He knew just what they had brought him in for. Two dead bodies pop up in the projects and the first person they grab is the one who's running the show. *The cost to be the fucking boss.*

In all truthfulness, Rio didn't even know why he had shot Boo. It was as if all the hate and anger he carried with him had forced its way to the surface. For the briefest instant the rage had been loosed. That one moment of weakness had cost a young man his life. Dumb-ass move. When Rio got in the game, he said that he would change it to suit his needs. But did it end up being the other way around?

Cutty sat up in the spot with Truck, Slim, and another kid that he didn't know. Drinks were being poured and blunts were being passed, as the Lakers put the hurt on the Knicks. Cutty gave Truck dap as he passed him another cup of "Hulk." Truck was an all right dude. Cutty couldn't figure why Rio was so leery of the cat. Sure he was a little shifty, but so were the rest of them. They were all players in a filthy game, fuck did he expect? As far as Cutty could see, Truck showed nothing but love to his peoples.

"How that Hulk got you feeling?" Truck asked, putting the finishing touches on a blunt.

"This shit is alight," Cutty said, taking a deep gulp. "Not bad at all."

"Good, good. I like to make sure that my fam is comfortable. You know you my fam, right, Cutty?"

"Fo sho, Truck. We all play on the same team."

"Nah, I don't mean it like that. I mean, I call you my family, like blood. Fuck this cartel shit."

"That's deep, Truck. Thanks."

"Yeah, you bout ya business, Cutty. That's why I fuck wit you."

"I just do what needs to be done to win, that's all."

"Right. Say, I heard about that li'l work y'all put in the other day."

"What work?" Cutty asked playing dumb.

"Aww come on," Truck said, sliding closer to whisper. "I ain't no square nigga just off the lookout, kid. I know any and everything that goes on in this circle here. You know what the fuck I'm talking about."

"Afraid I don't."

"Anyhow, I'll just put it to you like this; somebody put the hurt on Kev and Boo the other day. Right there on Colombus Ave. Blew the back of Kev's head off and gave Boo a crown of lead and smoke, dig me?"

"Damn, I had heard something about that, Truck. But that wasn't none of my doing."

"Don't bullshit me, nigga. I got eyes everywhere. You shot Kev and Rio put Boo to sleep. Now, when I heard that you caught a body it wasn't no big shock. Youz a trigger-happy young nigga, so I expect shit like that from you. Executions in broad daylight? Heaven help the game. But you know what it was that fucked me up about the whole thing, Cutty?"

"Nah, what was that, Truck?"

"Rio putting in work. That shit just don't compute in my brain. Now, I've known Rio since he was young. He'll scrap with anything on two legs, but killing? I don't believe it, Cutty. The boy ain't built like that."

"Like I said," Cutty grinned, "I really don't know what you're talking about. If it went down like you said, then that was a prime piece of work. But we can't take the credit for it, yo. You're a hellified general, but I see the kink in your armor, player."

"Kink? What kinda shit you talking, boy?" Truck asked, not understanding.

"It's like this," Cutty said. "You underestimate people. You think what you see of em on the outside is what they're made of. It ain't like that, man. You gotta be careful of everybody. Don't never put nothing pass a nigga. Shit, even the prettiest rose has thorns."

Truck rubbed his bumped chin and stared at Cutty. The kid knew how to play it to the chest. Another angle was in order. "I feel you," Truck said, lighting the spliff. "The only reason I asked you was because Rio got locked up a while ago."

"Locked up?" Cutty asked, unable to hide his shock. "For what?"

"For that shit I was just asking you about. Stark came through the hood to pick him up and Rio wigged. Heard he knocked Stark out right in front of 865."

"I ain't know nothing about that. I gotta roll down to see if my nigga is good."

"Don't wet it, Cutty. The lawyer's already on his way. Rio should be out in a few hours. Might as well kick back and enjoy the entertainment."

"What entertainment?" In answer to Cutty's question, the doorbell chimed. Slim hopped up and looked through the peephole. After making sure the visitor was okay, he looked back and smiled at the fellas. When Slim opened the door three fine ladies walked in wearing overcoats. Slim whispered something to the leader of the pack and slipped her an envelope. After conversing with her girls, they simultaneously shed their overcoats. The three young ladies were sporting thongs and stiletto heels. As they began to wiggle and grind for the fellas, Cutty couldn't help but smile. That Truck was sure all right.

Trinity sat up on her bed, trying to make heads or tails out of her math book. She had been studying for the past few days, trying to take her mind off Rio. That was easier said than done. A person's soul mate only came along once in a lifetime and she knew that Rio was hers. As Trinity continued to stare at her book, daydreaming, she could feel her eyelids slipping shut. She tried to fight it, but it was no use. It had been quite some time since she had a good night's rest. She lay back on her pillow and let the sleep take her. As Trinity slept, she dreamed.

Trinity saw herself not as she was, but as she might've looked if she were born two millennia before. She was dressed in peasant's rags, crossing a barren land. At her side was Rio. He too was dressed in a simple robe and sandals. Behind them were the remains of a ruined city.

Trinity spared only a brief glance at the city before Rio pushed her forward. Scratches covered his sweaty face. He looked around wide-eyed. Something had him scared, but she wasn't sure what. Rio continued pushing her along while clutching a small package under his arm. Trinity was about to ask him what they were running from when she heard the charge of horses behind her.

She looked over her shoulder and saw three hooded men, riding black horses. Rio handed Trinity his package and turned to stand against the men, but they overwhelmed him. The hooded men bound Rio in chains and dragged him back to the city. Trinity followed them into the crumbled husk.

The inside of the city looked almost as bad as the outside. Houses and shops were crumbling and acres of crops were rotting away. Skeletal-looking townsfolk were shuffling along in the direction that the horsemen had taken Rio. The people looked malnourished and dirty. The city was more like a ghost town than anything else.

There was a large knot of people gathered in what must've been the town square. They were chanting something in a language that was alien to her. Whatever the words were they weren't nice. Trinity followed the crowd to the center of the commotion. People were screaming and casting stones, but she couldn't see what they were aiming at. By the time she made it to the front of the crowd, she felt her breath leave her body.

In the center of the crowd was Rio. The horsemen had

dragged him into the center of the square and tied him to a large oak tree. A rusty chain wrapped around the tree held his arms spread apart. There were tears in his eyes as he looked down at his lover. Trinity tried to go to Rio, but she found herself unable to move. All she could do was look on in horror as Rio was stoned and spat on.

Trinity sobbed uncontrollably as Rio was tortured. The leader of the horsemen stepped up holding a sword. As he looked out over the mob, his dark eyes seemed to come to rest on Trinity. Something about his eyes was familiar to her. The horsemen removed his hood and he smiled at her. The face he wore was Truck's.

Trinity recoiled in shock as Truck continued to speak to the crowd in the foreign tongue. She still couldn't understand the dialect, but she was able to make out the word "Judas." Truck motioned to another of the horsemen and flashed a wide grin. When the second horsemen removed his hood, he wore the face of Cutty. The nightmare was becoming too much for Trinity.

She looked up at Rio as his tormentors continued to speak to the crowd. There was no hope left in Rio's eyes, only tears. He was trying to say something to her, but she wasn't sure what it was. His lips were moving, but there was no sound. Suddenly the package under Trinity's arm began to pulsate. She looked to Rio and he nodded at the package. Trinity opened the package and found a beating heart inside. When she looked back to Rio, she noticed a gaping hole in his chest. She now understood why the package was so important to him. Her lover had entrusted her with his heart.

Trinity tried to call out to Rio. She wanted to tell him that she was sorry and that she would forever love him, but her words made no sense. The horseman who wore Truck's face raised his sword and turned his gaze back to Trinity. She couldn't bear to watch as he brought his blade across Rio's neck.

Trinity awoke to find herself drenched in sweat. She looked around the tiny bedroom wild-eyed and disoriented. She managed to relax a little when she realized that she was in her room. She knew that she had had a terrible nightmare, but the details were sketchy. The only thing that she was sure of was that Rio needed her. She had almost finished dressing when there was a knock at the front door.

"Got your black ass now," Stark said, leaning on the bars. "Thought you were pretty smart, huh?"

"Fuck you," Rio said as he lay back on the iron bench.

"Hmpf, tough talk, Darius. We'll see how smart your mouth is when you're indicted on murder charges."

"I don't know what you're talking about, Stark. Murder ain't my thing."

"Bullshit! We got witnesses this time, buddy. You shot that boy in broad daylight."

"Stark, you better stop hitting that shit. I told you I don't know nothing about no murder. The charges will never stick."

"Maybe, maybe not. If this one doesn't stick, I'll find something else."

"Now you're fishing."

"Don't think so. I guess you've heard that your girlfriend's daddy has gone missing?"

"What's that got to do with me? I didn't make that cat run off."

"See, that's my point. People like Baker don't just up and leave. That type of guy doesn't move once they root themselves someplace. I think Baker met with foul play. How about you?"

"Fuck outta here. I ain't have nothing to do with that."

"I think you do, Rio. See, a few years back, while I was riding a desk over some dumb shit, I get a phone call. Some kid named Billy Baker says that he knew something bad that he wanted to tell. The little fart goes on to tell me how he thinks his dad is screwing his sister. Me being the prick I am, I tell the kid to quit making up stories and brush him off. I never even thought about it, until we were running a check on the old man to see if we could run him down. Baker, same as little Billy."

"Stark," Rio said, yawning. "You got a point to make?"

"Yeah, Rio. I know what Trinity's old man was doing to her and I think you did, too. You might not have known right away, but you were bound to find out. Too bad it took a botched suicide attempt to bring it out. If I had known that it would lead to you sitting in a holding cell, I'd have put the shit out a long time ago."

"Fuck you," Rio said, sucking his teeth.

"Yeah, you probably got pretty pissed when you caught wind of it," Stark continued. "Pissed enough to do him."

The more Stark talked the more nervous Rio got. Stark had proven to be a little smarter than he had given him credit for. But nervous as he might've been, Prince had taught him a long time ago never to let a person know what he was thinking. Rio kept his game face. "Stark," he said, sitting up. "I already told you that I don't know what the fuck you're talking about. Now, if you don't leave me alone, I'm gonna have you brought up on harassment charges."

"Big talk," Stark sang. "Let's see if you still talk that shit on death row. I'm gonna put the needle in your arm myself, you black bastard."

"That's enough!" barked a voice from behind them. Stark turned around to see Lieutenant Jenkowitz step through the door accompanied by another officer. "Detective Stark, stand down."

"Aw, I was just having a little fun," Stark said innocently.

"That kind of fun can get you brought up on charges. I'll deal with you later. Darius, you're free to go."

"Free to go?" Stark asked in disbelief. "Jenkowitz, what's going on here?"

"His lawyer is here to claim him."

"But—"

"No buts, Stark. Darius Santana," Jenkowitz said, turning to Rio, "this officer will escort you to the front, where your attorney is waiting. He will fill you in on the details of your release. I would like to apologize to you on behalf of this department as well as the NYPD."

The officer opened the cage and Rio stepped out. As he was leaving, he smiled over his shoulder at Stark and said, "See you around, fat boy." With a mocking chuckle, Rio left.

"Jenkowitz," Stark said furiously. "How are we just gonna let that cocksucker walk?"

"Easy, Stark. I want this guy just as bad as you do," he assured him, "but we gotta go about it the right way. What you and your goons did to that boy was stupid. He could sue you as well as the department. I keep telling you about going off to play cowboy."

"I just wanted to ask him some questions. The little shit took a swing at me."

"Stark, I know that kid like I know you. Rio's a lot of things, but he isn't stupid. The only way he would've taken a swing at you is if he was provoked. This thing is bigger than both of us. Bringing Prince down could put me in the running for captain. I don't need you fucking it up playing lone wolf."

"This stinks, Jenkowitz."

"Don't worry, Stark. You'll get your chance at the kid, but we gotta be smart about it."

"Okay. I'll play nice." Stark might've agreed with Jenkowitz vocally, but in his mind he was planning another angle to try and catch Rio. If Jenkowitz thought he was going to steal Stark's shine then he was crazy. He would be the one to bring Rio and Prince down. In a squad car or a meat wagon, it didn't really matter to him. It would be a raise in his pay and two less niggers on the streets.

Slim entered Washington Square Park, clutching a beat-up black tote bag. He looked around nervously before venturing deeper into the park. He was pissed at Truck for giving him the errand to run, but it had to be done. The park was pretty much empty with the exception of a few Goths milling about. Slim moved further into the park in search of his contact.

About ten minutes went by and nobody showed. Slim was turning to leave when he heard leaves rustling behind him. He turned, but didn't see anything. When he turned back around to leave, a young man stood in his path. Slim drew his gun, but held off on the trigger when he saw who it was.

"What's up, Slim?" Kane asked.

Slim damn near jumped out of his shoes when the youngster spoke. "Damn," he said. "Fuck you sneaking up on a nigga like that? Fool, you almost got shot."

"Whatever," Kane said, waving him off. "You got our money?"

"I got ya bread, man," Slim said, handing him the bag. "It's all there, but you can count it if you want."

"Nah, I know y'all wouldn't be stupid enough to cheat us. Tell Truck that the deed will be done."

"When?"

"Slim, no disrespect, but if it ain't your money, then it ain't your business. You just make sure that Truck gets my message. My people stick to their word."

"Man, I'm tired of you coming at me all sideways. Give me the same respect that you give Truck," he said angrily.

"Slim, I'm not the enemy. Instead of you worrying about to whom I show the proper respect you need to be worrying about that cop catching you holding a gun."

Slim turned around to see who Kane was referring to and saw that there was no cop. When he turned around to comment on it, Kane was gone. Once again Slim had been left looking stupid. He made a promise to himself that he and Kane would one day finish their conversation.

About thirty seconds after Officer Brown had delivered the news, Trinity was out the door. She knew that her dream was a bad omen, but she had never imagined this would happen. When Brown had knocked on her door, she figured he had something to tell her about her father. To her surprise he had news on Rio. He had relayed the details of Rio's beating and subsequent arrest. Trinity put her pride on hold and rushed to be with her man.

Trinity shot out of her building like a bolt of lightning. Her every thought was consumed with Rio's safety. She could hardly believe her ears when Brown told her about the shooting, but when she thought back she remembered having heard the gunshots. Had this been a few months ago, she would've laughed if someone told her that Rio had murdered a man. In light of recent events it wasn't funny anymore. The man that Trinity knew Rio to be was slowly fading and the one who replaced him had proven to be very unpredictable. Trinity was in such a hurry that she crashed into Shamel as she turned the corner.

"Damn," he said, rubbing his chest. "If the Jets had a DB that could hit like you, we might've won a Super Bowl already. Where you off to, T?"

"I gotta go check on Rio," she said, out of breath.

"I was looking for that cat myself. You seen him?"

"No, but I heard he's in jail."

"Jail, for what?"

"I don't know, Mel. They said he shot someone."

"Damn. Where they got him?" he asked in a concerned tone.

"At the Twenty-fourth. I'm on my way over there now."

"Come on," he said, grabbing her by the arm. "I'm going, too." When Shamel had first heard the rumor of Rio killing Boo he had thought it was just talk. Now that Rio was actually locked up for it, he cursed himself for not being there to stop Rio and he cursed Cutty for allowing it to happen. They were there to make sure Rio didn't get involved in those types of situations. Regardless of how cool Cutty and Rio were, Shamel would be sure that Cutty answered for his poor judgment.

20

Arnold Epstein stepped from the precinct, followed by Rio. From what Rio had been told, Prince sent the "Little Jew," as he was affectionately called, down to fetch Rio as soon as he heard what had happened. When Rio heard the charges they were bringing against him, he had begun to seriously think about a life behind bars. But somehow, someway, Epstein had managed to free him. Didn't really matter to Rio. He was just glad to be free.

"Thanks, Epstein," Rio said, lighting a cigarette. "I'm glad to be out of there."

"Don't thank me," Epstein said. "Thank Prince. He's footing the bill."

"Whoever. I'm just glad to be out."

"Don't worry about a thing, Rio. I want you to go and get a camera and have someone take pictures of your face. We're gonna sue these pricks. By the time I get finished, they'll all be directing traffic in Alaska."

"A'ight, Epstein. I'll get on it."

"Right away, Darius. I want the pictures while the bruises are still fresh. They're probably gonna be trying to pick you up for any little thing, so you might wanna stay off of the streets for a while. You don't have to be a prisoner in your own house or anything, but stay out of high-traffic areas. You get where I'm coming from?"

"Yeah, I get you."

"Good. You need a ride somewhere?"

"Nah, I live up the block."

"Okay. Prince should be contacting you sometime tonight. Other than that, stay out of trouble." Epstein hopped into his BMW and sped off. Rio walked up the block, rubbing his bruised face. The scratches would heal over time, but the gash on his forehead might leave a scar. It didn't matter though. The pigs couldn't hold him. Just another perk of working for Prince.

Rio got a bottle of water from the store on Ninety-ninth Street and started up the hill. He pondered the things that were going on in his life and wondered what the hell he was doing? Two months ago, he was just a part-time hustler trying to find himself a nine to five. Now he found himself a captain in one of the largest drug crews in New York. He had lost his girl, been beaten by the police, and committed two murders. Talk about a bad run. Rio knew he needed to check himself before the streets got the best of him.

As he was walking up Columbus, he noticed a car coming toward him slowly. Rio immediately tensed up at the sight of the automobile. With the way things had been going lately, his nerves were shot. The car could have just been someone getting dropped off or a death squad sent for him. Rio tucked his hand in his pocket and began to back away.

"What up, kid?" Prince asked, sticking his head out of the rear window. Rio exhaled at the sight of his mentor. It seemed like fear and paranoia had become a constant in his life. As he walked toward the grinning Prince, he couldn't help but think how much the man looked like a tar-black Satan.

"Get in," Prince said, holding the door open for Rio. Rio just wanted to go home and take a shower, but being the loyalist, he got into the car. He slid into the back of the Tahoe next to his employer and it took off. He looked to the front expecting to see J, but J wasn't at his

usual position behind the wheel. Instead Prince had his son Melvin
driving the car.

Melvin was Prince's youngest boy. He looked like a smaller version
of Truck, but with a missing tooth in the front. Melvin wasn't the
sharpest knife in the drawer, so Prince didn't really involve him in major business. He just kept Melvin around to do odd jobs when the need
arose. Melvin also had a drug problem that he thought no one knew
about. Most people didn't, but Rio knew because Melvin had bought
crack directly from him. Normally Rio didn't go hand to hand, but
Melvin would always throw him some extra paper to keep his secret.
Rio stayed true and never spoke a word of Melvin's addiction.

"Where's J?" Rio asked.

"Had some business to tend to in Jersey," Prince answered.

"What's going on, Prince?" Rio asked.

"Not much," Prince said. "Came down to check on my boy. I heard
that you got into a little trouble."

"Yeah, pigs jacked me up pretty bad."

"So I heard. But let me ask you this; have you lost your fucking
mind?"

"What you talking about, Prince?" Rio faked ignorance.

"Rio, don't play with me. You know just what the fuck I'm talking
about. For you to go and shoot someone in broad daylight was fucking
stupid." Prince said seriously.

"Prince I—"

"Let me stop you while you're ahead," Prince said, cutting him off.
"I already know you did it, so if you planned on lying, don't. You and
that fool nigga Cutty shooting shit up like this is the Wild West."

"Prince, them niggaz robbed the spot. I had to show them cats that
we ain't soft."

"Rio, I been filling your head with knowledge all these years and
you still ain't learned shit, huh? Them niggaz who robbed the spot was
supposed to get dealt with. Granted. But you wasn't supposed to do it.
That's what you got soldiers for, kid. You ain't a grunt no more and I
don't expect you to act like this. You got at least thirty to thirty-five soldiers under you. There's no reason that I should get a call, telling me

that my boy shot some dickhead over a few hundred dollars. That's chump shit. You ain't no chump, is you?"

"No, Prince."

"Then show me right, baby. Get it together. I need to know that your head is on straight, Rio." As Prince and Rio continued talking, they never noticed the motorcycle pulling up alongside them. Rio, who was sitting behind the driver, was the first to see the bike. At first he thought it was just someone trying to pass them, but then he saw the gun. When Rio opened his mouth to warn Prince, the Hound opened fire with the P89.

The first bullet hit Melvin in the back of the head. He was dead before he slumped over the wheel. Rio tried to duck down, but two of the bullets still managed to hit him. The first snapped his left forearm and the second cracked a rib. Rio felt the wind knocked out of him as he crashed into the car door. The Tahoe spun out of control and crashed into a streetlight. The Hound dismounted his bike and came to finish his task.

But Prince jumped out firing his colt revolver. Two shots to the chest knocked the Hound on his ass and into the street. Rio managed to get his door open, but didn't have the strength to get away. The loss of blood was starting to make him lightheaded. Rio's legs gave and he collapsed to the ground, but he could still see what was unfolding in the street.

Prince advanced on Hound's prone figure with his gun on the ready. He peered at the black-clad man and saw that he wasn't breathing. Prince was hurt, but he would live. Which was more than he could say for the would-be killer. Then Hound's eyes flicked open and his gun swung up. Before Prince could do anything, the Hound put a single bullet through Prince's skull.

Rio let out an ear-piercing scream as he saw his mentor go down. Prince lay motionless in the streets, dead eyes staring at the sky. Hound got up off the ground and dusted himself off. He plucked the colt bullets from his body armor and shook his head. He dumped two more shots into Prince's lifeless body and came around the truck to where Rio lay.

Rio watched the predator as he moved closer. The Hound smiled and his teeth shone like little knives in the darkness. Rio looked into the eyes of his killer and prepared to meet his fate. Just from the way that the man moved Rio knew he was a pro, and pros didn't usually leave jobs half done. As he lay on the ground leaking, he thought about all the things in life that he had never done and would never get to do. He also thought of the trivial argument he and Trinity had had. He loved her with all of his heart and soul, but would never get to tell her again. He and Trinity would be cheated of that sweet tomorrow. Rio shed one lone tear for the twenty-three years of his life on earth that had been wasted.

Hound held the gun to Rio's head and fingered the trigger. But something about the young man made him hesitate. Hound looked into Rio's eyes and saw no fear, only regret. There was something about young Rio that reminded Hound of what he used to be. A dumb-ass kid trying to find his way in the world. Hound had been snatched from his life and brought into this one at an early age. He felt compassion for Rio. At that moment he decided that Rio would live. Fuck Truck. He had only paid for one body anyhow.

Rio looked up in amazement when Hound turned and walked back to his bike. It was clear to Rio that he would live. He didn't care why he had been spared, he was just thankful for it. The pain in Rio's side got worse as he began to cough. He tried to raise himself, but it was no use. His strength faded and with it his consciousness.

When Trinity and Shamel arrived at the precinct the desk sergeant informed them that Rio had been released. At first they were confused, but when Shamel heard an angry Detective Stark ranting about "some little Jew," he understood. The lion had sent the shark to receive his cub. He led Trinity back out into the streets to plan his next move.

"Do you think it was some kind of mix-up?" she asked Shamel.

"Nah," he said, lighting a cigarette. "Ain't no kinda mix-up. Prince sent Epstein to get Rio out."

"But how? Rio couldn't have been in there more than a few hours."

"That's the kind of power that Prince is working with."

"Damn. So, now what?" she asked, sounding lost.

"You might as well go on home, T. I'll try to call Rio and let you know when I hear something."

"Okay, Shamel. Make sure you call."

"I will." As Shamel went to hug Trinity, a group of police officers came charging out of the precinct. There were cops on foot as well as in cruisers speeding toward the projects. While Shamel looked on in confusion, he heard one of the cops say, "That Santana kid got shot."

Shamel's mouth suddenly became as dry as a desert wind. He told himself that he had heard wrong, but when he saw the tears in Trinity's eyes he knew that he hadn't. Shamel felt tears forming in his own eyes as he thought of his friend dying in some gutter. Before he could say anything to comfort Trinity, she took off running down the block. Shamel was right on her heels.

When they reached Columbus Avenue, the hood was in an uproar. Lights were flashing everywhere as the police and the EMS units tried to straighten out the mess. People were bowling and crying left and right. Some even went as far as to curse the police and throw rocks. Trinity looked at the chaotic scene and couldn't help but remember the warning that her dream had brought her.

People were screaming, but no one was really saying anything. Shamel managed to get ahold of a crackhead named Teddy and ask him what happened. "Ah man," Teddy sobbed. "This shit is all fucked up, Mel. They killed them, man. They shot Prince and his two sons dead on the street."

"Prince and his kids?" Shamel asked. Hearing this, he let out a sigh of relief. It was sad what happened to Prince and his boys, but at least it wasn't Rio. "How long ago, Teddy?"

"About fifteen minutes ago, man. Smoked em while they was just kicking it. About five dudes, man. Rolled up on the ride and popped it off."

"Damn," Shamel said. "That's messed up."

"Damn right. But that's okay though. When Truck gets wind of this, he's gonna turn it up on these niggaz."

"Hold on, I thought you said that Price and his two sons got killed?"

"I did, man. Melvin and Prince's youngest boy, Tito."

"Tito?" Shamel said, wide-eyed. "You mean Rio?"

"That's what I said, ain't it?"

"Teddy," Shamel said, grabbing him by the arm. "Are you sure?"

"Shamel, I know who Rio is. Tall kid with curly hair. He was one of the only ones who treated me like I was still a man. The rest of these ma fuckas act like I was born a crackhead."

Shamel released his grip and walked away. Rio was dead. He felt as if his heart was breaking into a thousand pieces. He sobbed heavily as he recalled his last moments with Rio. He could feel Trinity's eyes on him, awaiting the news, but he couldn't face her at that moment. He didn't want anyone to see his tears.

"Shamel," she said softly. "What's wrong?" Shamel remained silent. "Mel, is it Rio?"

"T," he said over his shoulder. "I . . . They said he's gone."

"Gone? No, Mel. It has to be a mix-up," she said, teary-eyed. "Rio isn't dead."

"Trinity, Teddy just told me he saw what went down. It was Rio that was in the car with Prince."

"No!" Trinity screamed. She began to cry and pull at her hair. "No, Mel! Tell me it's a mistake. Tell me that you're lying. Tell me something?"

"Trinity, I wish I could. I wish I could."

Trinity shook her head frantically. Her nerves were so bad that she didn't know what to do with herself. She tried to light a cigarette, but couldn't get her hands to stop shaking. She felt her breath shortening and the blood rushing to her head. She had to sit on the curb to keep from falling out. Rio couldn't be gone. Even though they weren't seeing each other like that, she would've known if Rio was dead. When two people loved each other as hard as they did, there was a connection. More than a physical one, it was like spiritual. Their souls were intertwined. If Rio was dead, she would know about it.

"Trinity," Shamel said, placing his hand on her shoulder. "I'm sorry. I loved Rio, too, ma."

"Shamel," she said, shaking her head. "This isn't right."

"I know, T. This whole situation is wack. I'm gonna make sure whoever did this to my man is punished."

"No, Shamel. That's not what I meant. I mean Rio being dead. I can't accept it," she said animatedly.

"Trinity, I know it's hard to believe, but Teddy saw it."

"I don't care what some crackhead said. I need to see it for myself. Which hospital would they have taken the bodies to?"

"Trinity, do you really wanna put yourself through this right now?"

"I need to see, Shamel. Please, which hospital?"

"Damn, Trinity. Okay, they probably took him to St. Luke's. But if you plan on going, then I'm going too."

Trinity didn't need Shamel to go with her, but she was glad that he did. He was a true friend to her and Rio. They headed for the intersection and flagged a taxi. All she could think about was Rio. There was so much that had gone unsaid between her and Rio. If he was dead, she wouldn't be able to live with it. All the times Rio tried to get her to let him in, she ended up just pushing him further away. Now she might not ever have the chance to let him in.

21

Truck staggered to his car, giggling to himself. He had really shown Cutty a good time. They drank and smoked until the wee hours of the night. The look on Cutty's face when the big-butt stripper lured him off into the back room was priceless. Truck had been with her before, so he knew just what Cutty was in for. She would keep him busy for hours.

So far his plan was going well. He needed to find a weak link in Rio's chain and Cutty had proven to be it. As soon as Rio brought Cutty in, Truck had begun sizing him up. Cutty was a loyal soldier, but probably would never rise above that level. He was more greedy than ambitious, so Truck knew that as long as he kept him happy, he had nothing to fear from the man. Rio was a different story.

Rio was always reaching for the stars. He was ambitious as well as smart. At first Truck didn't see the young upstart as a threat, but after seeing the kid work, he knew he was wrong. Since Rio had taken over the projects, the money was pouring in. There had always been money in Douglass, but not the way he was pulling it out. He had shown that he could turn shit to sugar, and that's why Price valued him so much. But Rio's most dangerous quality was his ability to make people love him.

Since Rio had been in power, everyone was eating. He made sure that whoever wanted a piece could get it. It didn't matter who you were or what your status was, if you came to Rio he would give you a job. Then he had the support of the people who lived in the projects. They knew who he was and what he was doing, but his good deeds outweighed his dirt. When he took over, he put some changes into effect. If you were a crackhead and got caught getting high in the building, you were gonna catch a beat down. If the weather was nice and the mothers brought their children down to play out in front, you had to move to another spot to bubble. If you didn't, you'd never work a shift for Rio again. The hood loved him for the moves he was making and would stand behind him. This made Rio a dangerous enemy. Truck had to plan his next move just right.

Truck was fumbling for his car keys when a cold gust of wind came through. A chill ran down Truck's spine as a sudden feeling of dread overcame him. At first he didn't know what brought the feeling on, but when he looked over his shoulder he understood.

"What's good, Truck?" Kane asked, stepping from the shadows.

"Man," Truck said, pulling his .357. "Fuck are you doing sneaking up on me like that?"

"Easy," Kane said, backing off. "I didn't come to fight. I brought you a message."

"Yeah, what's that?"

"The deed is done."

"You mean . . . ?"

"Let's just say that you got what you paid for."

"Well, well, the old man has gone on to his just reward?"

"Indeed. There were two more people in the car, but we won't charge you for them."

"Who were the other two?"

"One was the driver."

"J?" Truck smiled.

"No, it was another man."

"And who was the other person?"

"I don't know for sure. I know he works for your father because we've seen them together many times."

Truck racked his brain trying to figure out who Kane was referring to. Prince didn't associate with the grunts, so it had to be somebody important. But who? As he ran through the many faces of the organization, one in particular stuck out. Rio. That was the only person Kane could've been talking about. Truck couldn't believe his luck.

"The young cat," Truck asked anxiously. "Is he dead, too?"

"I'm not sure."

"You mean your boy didn't stick around to make sure the job was done?"

"Truck, you only paid us for one body. The others were just casualties."

"Fuck that! He should've made sure the little punk bought it with the old man. What kinda fucking so-called killers are you guys? You go and half do a job? You cats ain't killers, you're fucking jokes."

By the time Truck finished his sentence, Kane had closed the distance between them and had a grip on Truck's neck. Truck tried to overpower the young man, but his bony fingers were like steel bands. "You listen to me," Kane hissed. "If you ever speak to me like that again, I will break every bone in your body. Just because you've done business with us, don't presume to know us. You know nothing of me or those like me. If I wanted to, I could have you and everyone in your fucking bloodline put to death. Children and all. Don't test me, Truck. Do we understand each other?" Truck nodded as best he could, with the hope that Kane would let him breathe again.

Kane released his grip on Truck's neck and turned to walk away. On shaky legs Truck pulled himself up and drew his weapon. At the sound of the cocking hammer, Kane stopped short. "Go ahead, Truck," Kane said over his shoulder. "Show me your gangsta. Pull the trigger." Truck tried to pull the trigger, but his finger refused to budge. All he could do was stare at Kane's back and stew.

"Just like I thought," Kane said, continuing his stroll. "When you're ready to talk business, get at me, Truck. Until then, stay the fuck away from me."

Truck watched helplessly as Kane disappeared into the night. He was so angry that his eyes began to tear. No one had ever treated him like Kane had. Kane might've gotten away with it for the moment, but he would pay for it down the line. Truck would make sure of that.

St. Luke's Hospital had always made Trinity uneasy. The whole place held the stink of death and sorrow. The bruised and sickly people in the waiting area looked more like refugees than the citizens of a flourishing city. This was the very same hospital where Trinity watched her mother wither and eventually pass on. They were hard memories that would fade in time, but never go away.

Trinity walked up to a small window where a fat woman sat talking on the phone. Her blonde dye job did a poor job of hiding her black roots. She was clicking her gum and talking about someone's child being pregnant. She had to notice Trinity standing there but acted like she didn't. When Trinity tapped on the plastic, the girl raised a finger for her to wait. A whole five minutes passed before Trinity began to loose her patience. She tapped on the glass again, but this time the girl sucked her teeth and turned her head.

"Excuse me," Trinity said, getting loud. "I'm trying to ask you a question. This is the information desk, isn't it?"

"Hold on a second," the receptionist said into the phone. "Can I help you?" she asked in a stink voice.

"That's what I've been trying to ask you," Trinity said, matching her tone. "I'm trying to get some information on—"

"Look," the receptionist said, cutting her off. "I'm sure you can see that I'm on the phone. Take a number and someone will be right with you." Then she turned her back on Trinity and continued with her conversation.

"No, she didn't," Trinity said to no one in particular. Trinity had tried to be polite, but now it was time to get ghetto on her. "Look, bitch," Trinity said, damn near screaming. "My man got shot and you tell me to take a fucking number? You must've fell and bumped your head. Either you get on your fucking job or get someone down here that can help me."

The receptionist whirled back around. "Bitch? Who you calling bitch? Let's not get ignorant up in this piece. If you wanna get stupid, then we can get stupid."

"Well," Trinity said, taking off her earrings. "Ain't nothing between us but space. Bring ya fat ass from behind that plastic and we can do it up!"

"What's going on out here?" an older white man asked, wearing a pair of scrubs. "This is a hospital, not Madison Square Garden. If you wanna box then take it outside."

"I think you need to check your employee," Trinity said, staring at the girl.

"What's the problem?" the doctor asked.

"I'm trying to get some information on a shooting victim. He was in the shoot-out on 101st Street. He came in about an hour ago, maybe less?"

"Well miss, three people came in here from down that way. Two of which were DOA."

"Two?" Trinity asked. She knew for a fact that there had been three people in the car. Maybe God had been good to her and let Rio live?

"The one that lived," she began. "How is he?"

"Stable. We just removed a bullet from him. The other ones, well . . . I'm sorry. What was the patient's name you were inquiring about?"

"Darius. Darius Santana."

"Let me see." The doctor flipped open the clipboard that he was carrying and began to scroll through the names. He only took a few seconds, but it seemed like a lifetime. She knew that it was a long shot, but she had to keep the faith. Her boo was destined for more in life than to die in the game. Trinity's heart felt like it was going to bust out of her chest as the doctor looked up from his list.

"Santana?" the doctor asked. "Yes, that was him."

Trinity dropped to her knees and said a prayer of thanks. The doctor as well as the rest of the reception area looked at Trinity as if she was crazy. And she was. She was crazy with joy. God had finally chosen to smile on her and had spared Rio's life. If there was ever any doubt that they were meant to be, it was erased now. The fact that he had survived was a sign.

"Can we see him?" Trinity asked.

"Hold on," the doctor said. "He's just coming out of surgery. You can come back and see him tomorrow."

"Please, doctor. It's very important that I see him tonight. I won't stay long. I just wanna sit with him for a while."

"I don't know about that. It's against hospital regulations for me to allow anyone to see him besides the police or his immediate family."

"Oh, I am his family. I'm his wife," she lied.

"His wife, huh?" From the way that the doctor was looking at her, she could tell that he didn't believe her. But something about the pleading look in her eyes made him feel sorry for her. "Okay," he said, "I'll let you see him, but only for five minutes and only one of you can go up."

"Don't worry," Shamel said. "I'll wait for you down here. Just tell Rio that I'm here."

"Okay, Mel," she said, following the doctor through the double doors. Trinity could hardly contain herself as the doctor led her down a long hallway. It hadn't been that long since she and Rio had last seen each other, yet she had no idea what she was going to say to him. The doctor stopped in front of another door and held up five fingers. Trinity nodded and approached the door. Her moment of truth was at hand. Trinity pushed through the door and went to be by her lover's side.

Rio lay in the little hospital bed, looking up at the ceiling. His arm and side ached like nobody's business, but he would live. The medication that they had given him for the pain made it hard to stay awake. But every time Rio closed his eyes, Prince's murder played over in his head. His friend and mentor had been taken from him. There was still so much that he had to learn from Prince, but he would never have the chance. His adopted father had left him, just like his biological one.

If he hadn't seen it with his own eyes, he would've never believed that Prince was gone. Cats like him usually beat the odds. It just went to show that tomorrow wasn't promised to anyone. As he touched the bandages on his side, he realized how lucky he was. He could have been stretched out in the morgue next to Prince instead of in a hospital bed. Getting shot up was far from a good thing, but it was better than dying.

Rio heard muffled voices coming from outside the door. He figured it was the police. He knew they would come, but he thought that they would wait until the morning. See, when you go to the hospital for a gunshot wound, they have to call the police. As the door creaked open, Rio prepared to face his inquisitors. To his surprise it was a female who came into the room.

For a good while the two lovers just stared at each other. It had been a minute since they had been around each other, so it felt a little awkward at first. How could two people who were once so close feel like total strangers? It was like meeting for the first time all over again.

Trinity got tired of standing there, looking stupid. She didn't expect Rio to come to her, even if he wasn't lying there shot up and weakened, so she took the initiative. Moving one step at a time, Trinity made her way to Rio's bedside. He just lay there, staring at her. They had really done a number on Rio. His ribs were bandaged as was his right arm. His left arm was in a cast and suspended in a sling. When she looked at his bruised and bandaged body, she wanted to cry. The only thing that stopped her was that she didn't want to upset him.

"Hey," she said, touching his leg.

"Hey," he responded sleepily. There was another uncomfortable pause, but Rio broke the silence. "Been a while, huh?"

"Yeah," Trinity said. "Guess it has. How have you been?"

"Shit," he said, looking at himself. "You see me."

"Does it hurt much?" she asked, biting her lip.

"Nah. They got me pumped full of some shit. When I wake up in the morning, I'll probably wish that I had died."

"Stop talking crazy, Darius. You're lucky that you survived. You could've ended up like . . . Sorry about that," she said, turning her eyes away. "I know that the two of you were close."

"Yeah. The old man is gone. I'm gonna miss him a lot, but we know the ups and downs of the game before we play it. Prince had a good run while he was here."

"So what now?"

"I don't know. Just trying to focus on getting out of here."

"I know that, but I was talking about the other thing?"

"Oh. To be honest with you, I'm confused. This whole day has been crazy. I managed to get my ass kicked by the police and shot. All in less than twenty-four hours. I look at the madness around me and wonder what the fuck I'm doing?"

"That's life, Rio. We have our good days and we have our bad."

"I understand this, but look at me. I almost died just for being with the wrong people. A bullet ain't got no name."

"I feel you. You gotta be careful from here on, baby. This right here, hit too close to home."

"I gotta be honest," he said with his voice full of emotion. "I ain't no punk or nothing and you know this Trinity. But when those bullets started flying and I saw all of that blood . . . I don't know. I came that close to dying."

"What happened?"

"All I can call it is a miracle. After Prince went down the cat comes for me. I'm laying there scared and bleeding. I know that these will be my last moments. He puts the gun to me and I brace myself for the end, but it never came."

"What, did his gun jam or something?" she asked curiously.

"No, nothing like that. He just looked at me real funny and left."

"Damn, you got lucky."

"I was so scared, Trinity. I don't know if I'm built for this shit, T." Rio tried to stop his tears, but they came anyway. "I probably look like a coward, sitting here crying and shit. It was just so crazy, ma. I don't wanna die in the gutter."

"It's okay," she said, stroking his face. "Everything is gonna be fine. I'm gonna take care of you, Rio. I should've never let you walk away in the first place."

"I'm sorry, T. The argument that we had was so trivial."

"Don't worry about it, baby. Let the past be the past. What's important now is our future."

"Trinity, I don't care what my future holds as long as you're in it. It's messed up that it took me getting shot to check myself."

"Don't worry about it, Rio. Just take this experience and learn from it."

"You're right about that. From now on I'm gonna go about things differently. You know I've been thinking; I'm getting paper on the streets, but I realize no woman really wants a hustler for a man. I wanna do the right thing by you, Trinity. If it means giving the streets up and going straight, then I'm all for it."

"Rio," she said, patting his hand. "It ain't that serious. I know that the streets are dangerous, but I also know that you don't have a whole lot of options. You hustle out of necessity, not desire. If the streets are what's feeding you, then do what you have to until something better comes along. I know that you're not a career criminal like that fool Cutty, but you can't be expected to starve. I'm not thrilled about you being in the streets, but I accept you as you are."

"That's real, T, but Prince is gone now. Truck will probably be running things."

"Rio, what did I tell you about thinking so small? It's sad that Prince is dead, but it could be a blessing in disguise. Being that Prince isn't top dog anymore, the lane is wide open. Truck might be his son, but everyone knows who his favorite was. Rio, you can play the humble role all you want, but you know that Prince was grooming you to be the man."

"I don't know, Trinity. That's a big step. Truck isn't gonna just lie down for this."

"Pardon my French, but fuck Truck. You got soldiers just like he does. You should've seen the way people were tearing up the hood when they heard you got shot. They had to bring out the riot squad to break the mob up."

"Damn, it was like that?" he asked, feeling a bit flattered.

"Believe it. The people love you, Rio, and they'll stand behind you on this. The brass ring is there. All you gotta do is reach for it."

Rio thought on what Trinity was saying. Maybe she was right about it all. It had become painfully obvious that no one was gonna hire him, unless it was to mop a damn floor. Rio had the opportunity to become a rich man. He could get his mother and his lady out of the hood. Blow up or throw up, baby boy.

"You think I could do it?" he asked.

"Baby, I know you can do it. Whether you flop or fly, I'm with you. Now, you go ahead and rest. I was supposed to go take my GED test tomorrow, but I'm gonna reschedule it."

"Nah, go take your test, ma. You worked too hard for it."

"But you need me here."

"No, I need you to pass that test."

"Okay, boo. But as soon as the test is over, I'm coming to see you. I love you, Rio," she said, kissing him on the lips. Rio smiled at his lady as she walked out of the room.

Words couldn't express how happy he was. Now that he had Trinity back, he felt whole again. Now for the problem at hand. It was like J had told him, "You gotta be cold to play the game and win." At that point losing was the furthest thing from his mind.

Rio sighed heavily as he thought of everything that had gone down up until that point. The conflict, the bloodshed. Rio got in it to make money not war. Now he was in the middle of something that was sure to be bloody. Things were already out of hand when Prince was alive, but now that he was dead, it would get even uglier. Truck wouldn't let the crown go easily. The more Rio thought about it, he questioned how bad he really wanted it.

Rio had to laugh at himself for even dwelling on the issue. Not long ago, working for Prince was a part-time thing. Then it became the only thing. Rio wasn't big on the idea at first, but the deeper he got, the more comfortable he became with it. He got a rush from the power and the money sweetened the pot. Rio was finally able to provide for the people he cared about, without having to kiss anyone's ass. He had grown quite accustomed to the money he was making and wasn't sure if he was ready to give that up.

Rio never wanted any of it to go down. People had died and more surely would cash out before it was all said and done. He never wanted to live a gangster lifestyle. He was content to just live. But now he was in the thick of it and didn't have a lot of options. Even if he chose not to contest Truck, who's to say that Prince's oldest boy wouldn't attempt to have him killed anyhow? The way Rio figured it, he would have to play the game out till the end. The hustle was never pretty, but Rio had been chosen to play, and play he would. What he did from there on out would determine his future. It was a choice between life and death. Rio chose to live.

If it took a cold nigga to win, then Rio would bleed ice water. No more Mr. Nice Guy. It was time to take what was his and stop waiting on a ma fucka to hand it to him. Rio began putting a plan together for what was to come. He was in now. Till death do them part, Rio was one with the streets.

Shamel stood outside of the hospital smoking a cigarette. He was glad that his friend had lived, but until Trinity came down he had no idea how bad it was. He was pissed at the whole situation. Somebody should've been there to watch Rio's back, even if he was meeting with Prince. Cutty was slipping. Them cats in the streets really didn't love Rio. Cutty and Shamel were the only people that he could count on, besides Trinity. One of them should've been there.

As Shamel was tossing his cigarette, a taxi was pulling up to the curb. Shamel watched the car for signs of danger. The back door swung open and Cutty hopped out. Seeing his friend only added to Shamel's anger. If Cutty hadn't taken Rio on that fool hit, none of this would've come about.

"Yo," Shamel called out. Cutty noticed Shamel and headed in his direction. "What up?"

"Mel," Cutty said, giving him dap. "What went down?"

"The Prince is dead."

"Yeah, I heard. Said somebody popped him in the hood."

"Yep."

"Ma fuckas in the projects talking about Rio's dead."

"Nah, he just got shot up. I ain't sure how bad though. The doctor said he'll live."

"Can we see him?"

"Nah. They let Trinity go back there for a minute, but he can't have visitors until tomorrow."

"What's Trinity doing here?"

"She came to check on her man."

"I thought that Baron was her man?" Cutty asked sarcastically.

"You need to quit, Cutty. You know that shit wasn't about nothing."

"Looked like something to me."

"You ain't even right, dawg. But on a more serious note, where the fuck you been?"

"What you mean, where I been? I'm a grown-ass man."

"Nigga, you was supposed to be with Rio."

"Rio's ass was in jail. What, I'm just supposed to sit around and wait for Prince to spring him? I was uptown doing me."

"Doing you got Rio shot. We're supposed to look out for him, Cutty. Shit like this ain't supposed to happen."

"Mel, I'm just as tore up about this shit as you. But holding Rio's hand ain't my job," Cutty said, getting angry. "Maybe if I had been there, it wouldn't have gone down like that. Then again, maybe it would've been three corpses instead of two? That's not the issue here. The important thing is that Rio's okay."

"Cutty, that's some weak shit." Shamel chuckled. "If you wanna get technical about it, this whole mess is your fault."

"How do you figure that?"

"Because, this whole mess started over that little stunt y'all fools pulled on the ave."

"Man, that ain't got nothing to do with this."

"It does so, Cutty. Why the hell would you put the battery in Rio to kill that boy? Rio ain't no killer and you know it. Everybody ain't as fucked up in the head as you."

"Yo, I'm really not feeling how you're trying to come at me, Mel. We peoples, but respect my gangsta."

"Gangsta? Cutty, busting your gun in front of a bunch of ma fuckas don't make you a gangsta. That makes you stupid."

"What up with all that crazy talk?" Cutty asked, getting in Shamel's face.

"What, you act like I'm supposed to bite my tongue?" Shamel said, staring Cutty down with his good eye. "Ain't nothing sweet about me."

Before the argument could escalate any further, Trinity came out of the hospital. "What are y'all doing?" Trinity couldn't believe what she was seeing. Rio was lying upstairs, shot up, and his so-called team were about to tear each other's heads off. Trinity shook her head and readied her speech.

"Ain't nothing," Shamel said, staring Cutty down. "Just talking."

"Yep," Cutty said, matching his stare. "Just talking."

"Well," Trinity said. "I'm glad that the two of you are feeling so talkative. I need to talk to both of you."

"What's up, T?" Shamel asked.

"I have a message from Rio."

Baron sat on his cream leather couch watching the 106 and Park countdown. He blew smoke clouds in the air while the young lady that he had scooped up did hers on the oral level. The girl moved up and down gracefully on Baron's shaft, never missing a beat or coming up for air. Baron was on top of the world. His phone chirped on the end table, blowing his grove. Baron looked at the number before flipping the phone open.

"What up?" he said into the phone.

"What's good, youngster?" Truck asked on the other end.

"What's good, big man?"

"Ain't nothing. You know I had to holla at my dawg."

"Bullshit, Truck. We ain't never been like that. What you want?"

"I wanna talk a li'l business. Can you meet me one day this week?"

"If it's worth my wild."

"Oh, it will be."

"A'ight. Hit me back with the details, I'm in the middle of something." Baron closed the phone without waiting for a reply. He rolled his head back and continued to enjoy his oral. He knew that Prince had been killed a few hours prior, but Truck didn't sound too broken up. It wouldn't have surprised Baron if that slimy nigga had something to do with the hit. Truck was up to something and he had an idea what.

"What's wrong?" Joyce asked, wiping her chin.

"Ain't nothing," Baron said, caressing the back of her head. "Don't stop." As Joyce continued to handle her business, Baron thought about how he could use her to his advantage against Rio.

22

Truck and Slim hit the block early the next morning. Now that Prince was dead and Rio was stretched out in St. Luke's, Truck figured that the projects would be his by default. He wanted to come down and survey his new territory first hand. To his surprise the hood was deserted. He circled the projects twice and didn't see anyone. No workers, no crackheads, nothing. This struck Truck as strange.

"Fuck is going on out here?" he asked Slim. "Police raided the hood or something?"

"Not that I know of," Slim said, looking just as puzzled. "This shit is like a ghost town. Maybe niggaz is scared that the police are gonna crack down after the shooting?"

"Fuck that. They had better be more afraid of me than the police. Yo," Truck said, looking off to his left, "ain't that Shamel over there?"

"Yeah," Slim said. "That's his fat ass. Roll up on him, Truck. If anybody knows what's going on, he does."

Truck pulled the jeep to the curb where Shamel was standing talking to Knowledge. "What's up?" Truck asked, sticking his head out of the window.

"Truck," Shamel said, nodding. "What's good?"

"Shit, you tell me. I come down to check on things and ain't nothing popping. Did I miss something?"

"Oh, you must not have heard. Ain't nothing moving in the hood today."

"What you mean by that?"

"I mean what I said. Ain't nothing moving. We decided to close up shop for the day to mourn your father and say a prayer for Rio."

"Ain't that about a bitch. Who put you in charge?"

"Rio. He told me to watch over things until he can get back out in the streets."

"Shamel, I don't know who you think you are, but you better round these dickheads up and put they asses to work. Either that or you'll be back to snatching purses."

"Hold on, Truck. I know you're going through it because ya pops got killed last night, but watch how you talk to me. I don't work for you, dawg."

"Hold the fuck on," Truck said, hopping out of the jeep. "Who the fuck do you think you're talking to?"

"Chill y'all," Knowledge said, flashing the glocks under his jacket. "We don't need this right now. Why don't both of you just relax?"

"Ain't this about a bitch?" Truck said, looking at a shocked Slim. "Have these niggaz lost it?"

"It's like I told you," Shamel continued, "I don't work for you. Now that Prince is gone, I answer directly to Rio. Any problems that you might have, you need to take that up with him."

"Fuck is Rio? This is my shit now. I run the show."

"Don't think so, Truck. Everybody in the hood knows what Prince was grooming Rio for. You might have been Prince's oldest son, but you weren't his favorite. When Rio gets out of the hospital, we can settle this."

"Yeah, a'ight," Truck said, heading back to his jeep. "We'll see about this shit." Truck hopped in the jeep and peeled off down Columbus Avenue.

"He sure was mad," Knowledge said.

"Fuck that nigga," Shamel said. "Truck is a clown. We all know that Rio is Prince's rightful successor."

"True. But was it wise to upset him like that?"

"All part of the plan, Knowledge. Truck is a hothead. People like him always let their mouths write a check that their asses can't cash. Rio wants him to be upset. That way he'll do something stupid."

"So, Rio has a plan."

"Rio always has a plan, kid. Even shot up and in the hospital, that nigga is scheming. It's only a matter of time before Truck does something stupid. As bad as he needs to get hit, he's still a Capo in this. We can't just outright kill him without catching some kind of backlash from the rest of the crew. Our job is to make sure that we have the proper support before we make a move against that asshole. When that happens, Truck will die."

"You see that shit," Truck asked. "Them little ma fuckas raised up on me."

"I seen it, man," Slim said. "You know what that means, don't you?"

"What?"

"It's starting. Now that Prince is gone, things are gonna get crazy. You and Rio were Prince's most trusted Capos. The mantle of leadership will fall to one of you. As you've already seen, people are gonna start choosing sides. I know that there are a lot of the Capos that aren't feeling you, but they wouldn't be stupid enough to move against you directly."

"Damn right. My father built this shit here and it's only right that I step up."

"Not necessarily, Truck. Just because Prince built this doesn't mean that it will go to you by default. You will have the support of most of the Capos, but like I said, not all of them. Just because they wouldn't try to move against you directly, doesn't mean that you're safe. What's to stop them from backing Rio if he decides that he wants to step up?"

"Damn, Slim. I never even looked at it like that. We can't let that happen."

"You're right. But what do you think we should do about it?"

"Slim, I think it's time to take this little dispute to the next level. If the Capos don't support my push for leadership then they can get it too. No more games, Slim. If diplomacy doesn't work then we take it to the pistols. I will be king."

Detective Stark sat in the squad room talking to Officers Brown and Jenkins. From the look of things his little plan was moving along smoothly. He had thought that it was going to be hard getting Officer Jenkins into Prince's organization, but it had proven to be quite easy. Apparently Rio's peoples didn't have the good sense that he did. After Mikey dropped Shamel's name, School Boy had given him and Jenkins a play. Seeing how smooth things were going with the two moles, School Boy let them hold the block down every night. It would be a costly mistake on his part.

"So," Stark began, "what've we got so far?"

"They've got a pretty sweet thing going on over there," Jenkins said. "The first night that we got on, they checked at least ten grand."

"Ten grand ain't peanuts, but it ain't a staggering number either."

"But you're not seeing the bigger picture, Stark. That ten grand was made in about eight hours. Now you figure that there are about a dozen or so buildings in the projects, right?"

"Yeah."

"Okay. So imagine if every last building is checking in those numbers or better every few hours? Prince was probably checking at least a hundred grand or better per week, just in Douglass."

"Well, Prince won't be checking shit anymore. After all these years somebody finally laid that mean old bastard down."

"Yeah," Brown added, "things have been crazy in the hood over the last few days."

"Only gonna get crazier," Stark said. "Now that Prince is dead, they're gonna need another leader. Truck being his last remaining son, he'll probably be taking over."

"I dunno," Brown challenged. "There's another candidate that we can't rule out."

"And who might that be?"

"Rio."

"Rio? Nah, I doubt that. Truck's got seniority on this one. I'm betting that it'll go to him."

"Don't count Rio out, Stark. He's got what it takes."

"Brown, I don't care what kinda child genius you're trying to make this Santana kid out to be, it ain't gonna happen. What makes you think that Truck, or any of the other Capos for that matter, are gonna stand by and allow him to step into Prince's shoes?"

"Because," Brown said, "I patrol these streets every day. I know these people and how they think. The streets respect Truck out of fear. They respect Rio out of love. If Truck were to take over, everything would turn to shit. He'd end up getting the whole shit shut down. Now under, Rio they would prosper. He's smart and fair. A lot of the folks are gonna stand behind him."

"Brown," Jenkins said, "you're making this kid out to be the second coming or something."

"Might as well be. I don't agree with how Rio's moving, but I respect his wit. Cats like him only come around once in a great while. If Rio takes over we're going to have a serious problem."

"Don't you worry," Stark said, slyly. "This thing means too much to us all just to let it go to shit. Brown, in a day or so you're going to see Trinity. Drop the bomb on her, but do it smooth. When she needs that shoulder to cry on, you make sure you're there with a box of Kleenex."

Trinity came out of her building carrying a shopping bag with some of Rio's things in it. After three long days, he was finally being released from the hospital. She had about twenty minutes to get there and meet him, so she got on the good foot. When Trinity made it to the avenue to catch a taxi, Officer Brown was coming up the hill.

"Trinity!" Brown called. "Can I speak to you for a minute?"

"Hey, Officer Brown," Trinity said, not bothering to slow up. "I'm kind of in a rush. Can it wait?"

"Afraid not. It's about your father."

"My father?"

"Yes."

"Did you guys find him?"

"Well . . . yes and no."

"I don't understand?"

"Trinity, I really don't know how to say this to you."

"Oh, no. He's dead, isn't he?" Trinity's voice trembled.

"Well, we're not exactly sure."

"What kind of answer is that?"

"Well, we've found some of him. One of your father's hands was found in a meat warehouse out in Brooklyn."

"Oh my God." Trinity suddenly felt lightheaded. She knew that Rio had killed her father, but she never inquired about the details. She had already discovered that her lover was capable of murder, but not mutilation. Before Trinity could do anything about it, the bacon, egg, and cheese sandwich she had for breakfast came up.

"Are you okay?" Brown asked, patting her on the back.

"I'm fine," she said, wiping her mouth. "I just didn't expect something like this."

"I know, Trinity. I'm sorry I had to be the one to tell you."

"God," she sighed. "What are we going to do now?"

"It'll be okay, Trinity. I promise."

"Thanks. Officer Brown, I just want to thank you. I know I've been giving you a hard time, but you've still tried to help me."

"Trinity, you don't have to thank me. I do what I do because I wanna see you make something out of your life. I used to be just like you, Trinity. My father kicked my ass until the day that my mother killed him. I was a seventeen-year-old kid forced to take care of my six brothers and sisters. Believe it or not, I know just what you're going through."

"Wow," she said with tear-filled eyes. "How did you cope with it?"

"By talking about it. When you hold it all in, it can poison your system."

"Maybe you're right."

"I know I'm right. Take this," he said, handing her a business card. "I know you probably tossed the first one so I'm giving you another. If you ever need to talk, and I mean about *anything*, I'm here for you."

"Okay."

"Trinity, don't just say okay and blow me off. I want you to hear me on this. Whether you know it or not, it's about to get hectic out here. Prince is dead and he's left a multimillion-dollar empire up for grabs. The way I see it, either Rio or Truck is going to end up taking the wheel on this. The runner-up is guaranteed a proper funeral."

"Well," Trinity said, wiping her eyes. "I don't know anything about that. Rio's just out here trying to find honest work like everyone else."

"Trinity, you and I both know that's a lie. You can play dumb all you want, but you're only hurting yourself. I'm trying to help Rio, not lock him up."

"Like I told you, I don't know anything about that. I knew Prince through Rio, but as far as what he did for a living, your guess is as good as mine. Now, if you'll excuse me." Trinity turned to walk away, but Brown grabbed her arm.

"Listen to me," he pleaded. "The way that I figure it, Truck ties into this somehow. If he could have his own father killed, then imagine what he would do to Rio? Your boyfriend got lucky once, but how long do you think that his luck is going to hold out?"

"Well, I don't know why Truck would want to have his father killed, but I can assure you that Rio was just in the wrong place at the wrong time."

All Officer Brown could do was shake his head. Here he was trying to help Trinity and she was sticking to her story. When he first took on this assignment, it was just business. But as he got to know her, it became personal. He saw that Trinity wasn't a bad kid, she just made poor choices. "You're never gonna wise up, are you?" Brown asked sadly. "Listen, Trinity. What I'm about to tell you could possibly ruin my career, but I need you to listen to me. Regardless of what the reports say, you and I both know that your father's dead. It's messed up, but that's how it is. These people have a hard-on for Rio. They're even going as far as trying to pin your father's murder on him. Trinity, if you don't talk some sense into Rio, you're gonna lose him. If the law doesn't get him, then the streets will."

Trinity's face remained unchanged by what Brown was saying, but she was listening intently. Brown was smarter than she had first given

him credit for. He knew more about the inner workings of the organization than she did. Trinity had always felt some type of way about
Truck, but she wouldn't have thought even he was that vicious. If Truck
was really behind Prince's murder, then Rio was in danger.

"Okay," Trinity said. "I'll think about what you said." Trinity held
out her arm and an unmarked cab stopped for her. Before she got in
she had a last word for Officer Brown. "Thanks." Then Trinity got into
the cab and went to meet her lover.

Rio sat on the edge of his hospital bed, trying to occupy himself with the
news. Today was to be the day he was released from the hospital.
Couldn't say that he was sorry to be leaving. Rio's stay at the St. Luke's
had been a less-than-pleasant one. Hospitals had always made him feel
ill. There was something about being around all of these sickly people
that made him uncomfortable.

The few days that he had spent in the cast-iron bed did give him
some much needed thinking time. He needed to make some changes
in his life. The game was getting ugly and it was time to prepare for the
storm. Trinity had helped him see things a little clearer.

His first order of business was to move his loved ones out of the projects. He hadn't mentioned it to Trinity, but his connect came through
on the apartment. All Rio had to do was pick up the keys. He would
miss living in Douglass. Those old brown buildings were the only
home that he had ever known. But it was no longer safe there. Whether
he liked it or not, Truck was going to cause a lot of bloodshed over this
little beef they had going. If it were up to Rio they would share the pie,
but Truck was a greedy nigga. He would have all or nothing.

Rio hadn't been on the streets in a while, but he always kept his ear
to the ground. He knew how Truck was running around claiming the
throne for himself. He thought that by bullying people and try to lay his
pressure game down, it would make the transition easy. He was too stupid to see the error of his ways. People didn't work efficiently under
someone they feared. In the long run they began to develop a sort of re-
sentment. Pressure eventually burst pipes. Truck would end up getting
himself killed sooner or later.

Rio's thoughts were broken by a knock on his door. Before he had a chance to answer, it swung open. Detective Stark came in, wearing a yellow-toothed grin and a tired brown suit. Rio looked at the red-faced cop and sucked his teeth. The police had already been in to question him, so he knew Stark was just there to fuck with him.

"What's up, Darius?" Stark asked.

"Man," Rio said, "Fuck you want?"

"Just came to chat, kid. Looks like somebody tried to air you out."

"Like I told them pigs the other day, I don't know who shot me. I was sitting in the car and some cat came through dumping. I got hit and blacked out, I don't know what happened next."

"Oh, bullshit. You probably sold some bad shit and they came back to take it out of your black ass. Either that or some punk looking to take your spot tried to clap you."

"Whatever, Stark. I ain't got shit else to say to you. If you keep fucking with me I'm gonna have to call my lawyer."

"You got a slick mouth, 'shine.' That Jew lawyer of yours ain't gonna pull your ass outta every fire."

"Whatever, Stark. Is there a point to this visit?"

"Like I said, just came to shoot the shit. Heard it was just one cat."

"That's what I said."

"One cat took out you three tough guys? I can't swallow that, Rio. I know that at least two of you were strapped. We found two pistols at the scene of the crime and neither of them matched the bullets we pulled from any of you guys. What's going on, Rio?"

"I don't know what you're talking about, Stark."

"Yeah, okay. So let me tell you what I know. Prince was a large guy. It took someone with a lot of balls and a lot of money to pull this off. Another thing, how did the killer know when to move on Prince? My guess is that someone close helped out in that."

"What are you getting at, Stark?"

"You're a smart kid, Rio. Think about everything that's gone on over the last few weeks. Until recently Prince has never had a serious beef with anybody in the hood. Why would someone decide to try him now? If anything, I would think that Prince's boy Truck being home would've only solidified his hold on things. But as it turns out, things got worse when Truck came home. Tough luck, huh?" Stark winked his eye at Rio and left the room.

Rio sat there and thought about what Stark had thrown out there. He was an arrogant son of a bitch, but he did raise a good point. Things had been relatively peaceful over the last few years. When Truck cames home, things had started getting sour. The more he thought about it, the more suspicious he became. No doubt that was why Stark had told him.

Truck sat in his jeep on the corner of 155th and Broadway. He smoked a joint while he waited for Baron to show up. Truck had big plans for the young upstart. He planned to use Baron to help him remove Rio from power. He figured if he teamed with Baron and his little crew, it would give him an edge in the conflict. Baron would serve as his trump card.

Baron came strolling around the corner with three of his peoples. Truck could tell by how the chest of his jacket poked out that Baron was wearing a vest. The boy came ready to play if Truck got crazy. Baron spotted Truck waiting for him and headed in his direction. Before Baron made it to the vehicle, Truck hopped out to meet him.

"What's up, Baron?" Truck asked, grinning.

"Truck," he said coldly.

"What's with the security?"

"Ain't about nothing, Truck. Just a few of my homeboys."

"How about we speak in private?" Baron hesitated for a minute or so but he allowed Truck to lead him down Broadway. Truck waited until they were out of earshot before he began speaking. "Thanks for coming out to meet with me."

"Whatever, man," Baron said. "You said that you had some shit that you wanted to talk to me about?"

"Yeah, yeah. So, how's business up the way?"

"It's going okay. I'm eating, right?"

"I would imagine so, but just because you're eating doesn't mean that you're happy."

"I can't complain, Truck. I'm moving up in the world, but you know how the chain of command goes."

"True. Them cats that you're fucking wit still ain't gave you a hood of your own?"

"I got a li'l slice, but I can wait my turn."

"Yeah, but why wait when you could have it now?"

"Fuck is you rapping about, Truck?"

"Baron, I'm offering you a spot in my organization. Now that my father is gone, I'm in control. I'm giving the whole operation a face-lift. Things are gonna be a little different now."

"How so?"

"I'm getting rid of everybody who ain't reading from my page, feel me?"

"Yeah, but what's that got to do with me?"

"Baron, how would you like to have an entire project of your own?"

"Shit, it'd be better than what I'm holding on to now. But I thought that kid Rio was running things down that way?"

"Yeah, for the moment. Rio got that spot because my father wanted him to have it. If you ask me, the boy ain't built for the streets. I need a more qualified cat to hold that spot down."

"So you're telling me that I can have that spot?"

"If you're willing to take it. Let's talk business, Baron."

Rio was thrilled when Trinity came strolling through the door with his clothes. He had been wearing the backless hospital gown so long that he though he was going to catch pneumonia of the ass. When he leaned over to kiss her, she returned the gesture halfheartedly. From the look in her eyes he knew something was wrong. "Trinity," he said softly. "Something wrong?"

"No," she lied. "Just thinking."

"If you say so, T. Thanks for coming to pick me up."

"Don't worry about it. Better me than one of your friends. The first thing Cutty or Mel would've done was offered you some weed."

"Now that you mention it, I could use a blunt."

"Oh, no, Rio. You know that you aren't supposed to be smoking weed on top of those antibiotics."

"That's bull. The weed ain't gonna mess with the medication. Herb is natural."

"And your ass will be naturally messed up if you mix the two. Now, hurry up and get dressed so we can go."

"Yes, mother," he said playfully.

Trinity sat in one of the folding chairs and watched Rio dress. As she looked at his muscled body, she realized how much she missed being in his arms. Rio was the only man that Trinity had ever been with who had treated her right. He was so warm and sensitive. But there was also a dark side to her boo. When Rio was conducting his business in the streets, he was more cold and serious. She knew that he had a bad temper, but she had no idea of the things he was capable of when pushed.

Before Rio went to work for Prince, he had been so pleasant and full of life. As things became more intense in the streets, he began to change. All Rio thought about was getting money. If you had told Trinity a few months ago that Rio would become a killer, she would've laughed. Rio was too passionate about life to take it. The loss of her father showed her how wrong she was. Thinking about her father brought back the conversation she had with the officer. She didn't think Rio was capable of mutilation, but she had been wrong about him in the past. She had to look him in the eye and find out the truth.

"Officer Brown came to see me today," she said.

"Yeah," Rio asked, not bothering to stop what he was doing. "What did that cat want?"

"The usual. Wanted to talk about the shooting and stuff."

"You didn't tell him anything, did you?"

"I don't know anything."

"Good. Don't pay them people no mind, they're just fishing."

"I know, baby. But that wasn't the entire conversation."

"What else did he want?"

"Rio, I need to ask you something and I need the truth."

"Trinity, what's wrong?" he asked, concerned.

"Just promise me, Rio. Promise me that you'll tell the truth."

"Okay, T."

"Rio, the night that my father was killed, what happened?"

"Trinity, I don't think we should be talking about this."

"Rio, if you truly love me then you'll tell me."

Rio had known this day would come, but that didn't make it any easier. The memory of what happened that fateful night hurt almost as much as knowing he took his lady's father. As painful as it might've been, Trinity deserved to know.

"Okay," he said sadly. "I'll tell you. When I found out what Baker was doing to you, I was beside myself with rage. I wanted him to hurt just like you did. I was standing on the avenue when I saw your father going down the block with a young girl. When I set out to follow him, I didn't intend to kill him. I figured that I could scare him with the gun and beat him down if anything. Well, it didn't go like I planned. Your father reached for the gun and it went off."

"So," she began, "what happened after you shot him?"

"I ran and called Prince."

"So he died of a gunshot?" she asked, shocked.

"Yeah. What did you think?"

"When Officer Brown came to speak to me about it, he told me that they had located part of him."

"Trinity what the hell are you talking about?" he asked, feeling like he was missing something.

"They said that one of my father's hands was found in a meat warehouse in Brooklyn."

"Trinity, what kind of monster do you think I am? I'll admit, I killed your father, but I didn't mean to. But to think that I would cut off his hands?"

"I'm sorry," she said, wiping her eyes. "But I had to know, Rio."

"It's okay," he said, hugging her. "Let's just put all that behind us. You, me, and Billy are gonna build a nice life together."

Rio felt a little better after talking about what happened that night. He had held it inside of himself so long that he feared it would drive him crazy. What troubled him was that he had left Baker whole, but the police found a piece of him. Prince said that he would take care of the body, but he never mentioned dismembering it. Prince was a cold ma fucka in life. Rio wondered if he had what it took to fill Prince's shoes.

Rio was done dressing and ready to go, but there was one more question that nagged at Trinity. "Rio," she said, pausing, "one more thing?"

"What's that, T?"

"The girl, what happened to her?"

That was a question Rio hoped he would never have to answer. Every time he looked at a young girl in the streets, he thought about the precious young life he had taken. It was too much for him to talk about. "Trinity," he said looking her dead in the eye. "Some things are better left unsaid." On that note Rio led the way from the hospital room. Trinity could read between the lines. It would be the last time that she asked Rio about the murders.

23

Prince's funeral turned out to be a parade of stars. Hustlers, as well as a few politicians, were lined wall-to-wall, trying to catch their last glimpses and to bid farewell to the fallen kingpin.

J was taking it pretty hard. He and Prince had been friends since before most of the Capos had been alive. He blamed himself for not being at Prince's side. He figured that if he'd been there, Prince would still be alive. But no one could've saved Prince. Hound was among the elite as far as killers went. He had been bred and trained to take life. There was no escape once he had been sent for you.

Truck could've won an Oscar for his role as the broken son. He was ranting and crying over the twin caskets of his father and younger brother. Rio watched his little performance from his seat on the front row and shook his head. He knew Truck was full of shit. He just needed a way to prove it.

The service lasted about an hour. The preacher talked about how Prince was a respected businessman and a pillar of the community. It was all bullshit, but it sounded good. After everyone had paid their respects, they all filed out of the funeral home for the drive across the water to the cemetery. Rio was going to ride up with Trinity, but J informed him that he would ride in a separate limo with the Capos. Just as Rio had expected, Truck had called an emergency meeting.

The Capos limo was a stretch Escalade. Rio climbed into the backseat of the ride and was greeted by the other five Capos as well as J and Truck. Everyone wore faces of grief, but there was a mutual problem that needed to be addressed. Prince had left a vacant throne and it needed filling.

"Take a seat, kid," J said. Rio did as he was instructed. "Okay, you got us all here, Truck, so speak your piece."

"Thanks, J," Truck said, through fake tears. "I wanna thank all of you guys for coming out to pay your last respects to my father."

"Ain't nothing," said Jake, a well-built brown-skinned man.

"Yeah, brother," added Big Paul. "We all loved Prince. He brought a lot of us up from the gutter. We're gonna miss him." Paul stood out among the other Capos. Not because he was the only white Capo, but because he was dressed in leather pants and a leather vest, sporting his gang emblem

"I know," Truck said. "That's why we have to continue what he started. I think it's only right that we honor my father's memory by seeing his operation prosper."

"Listen," Marco said, running his hand across his shaved head. "We're all very sorry that Prince is gone, but he was the brain of this operation. He held it down for a good while. Who's gonna take over now?"

"Me, of course," Truck said.

"Hold on," Gino said, raising his lanky frame from the plush seat. "I know that you're his kid, but who says that you should slide into his spot? You've been gone for ten years, Truck. The streets are different now. Maybe someone with a little more knowledge of what's going on should lead us," he said honestly.

"Fuck outta here," Truck snapped viciously. "Prince was my father. If anyone should lead us, it's me."

"Slow down," J said. "It ain't as simple as that. Prince wasn't sure who his successor was going to be. You're his blood, but Rio was his student. Every knows that. It was a toss up between the two of you."

"Rio," Truck asked in disbelief. "He might've been my father's herb, but I'm heir to the empire. Ain't no fake-ass gangsta gonna slide in and take my spot. I ain't having it."

"Yo," Rio cut in. "I loved Prince, not for what he did in the streets, but for what he did for me as a person. Price looked out for me when nobody else would. Nobody was affected by his death like I was. I almost lost my life the night he was killed."

"Yeah," Truck said. "Mighty funny that when my father comes down to talk to you he gets killed."

"Fuck you, Truck. I got shot up that night, too. Do you think that I would have someone damn near kill me to get Prince out of the way? Truck, you're a clown."

"You watch your fucking mouth," Truck barked. "I don't have a problem kicking your ass. You damn —"

"Cut that shit," J said, interrupting "That man ain't even in the ground yet and y'all squabbling like a bunch of bitches. Man — the — fuck — up." He sneered, jabbing his index finger to drag out the last sentence.

"My bad," Rio said, lowering his voice. "I ain't mean to come across like that. Listen," Rio said, addressing all of the Capos, "I could give a shit about who gets control over what. Someone that I care about is dead. Whether Prince wanted Truck to run the show or me, I don't care. If it's that serious, Truck and me could share the responsibility."

"That doesn't sound like a bad idea," J said, thoughtfully. "What about the rest of you?"

"Sounds okay to me," said Big Paul.

"Fuck it," Jake said.

"I don't know about all that," Gino protested. "Rio's a good kid, but he just got down. I think that if it doesn't go to one of us," he motioned to the other Capos, "it should go to Truck."

"That might not be a bad thing," Breeze said, wiping beads of sweat from his round, chocolate face. "Truck is Prince's son."

"I dunno," Marco said, thinking the matter over. "Rio has proven himself. Maybe we should give him a play. If he fucks up, we can always kill him. No?" He made the last statement in a joking manner, but Rio doubted that he was playing.

"I don't believe this shit," Truck said, outraged. "We shouldn't even be having this discussion. It should go to me."

"Look," J cut in. "We could argue about this shit until the cows come home and it still ain't gonna pick a new general. I suggest that they share the title. At least until we can come to some kind of decision."

"Fuck that, J!" Truck roared. "It's my spot and you know it!"

"Regardless of what you think, Truck, we all have to agree. Until we can get this problem solved, you and Rio will run the show together, under the watchful eyes of the other Capos."

Truck didn't say anything else on the matter. He knew as long as they did things diplomatically, he was stuck. His only hope was to get the other Capos behind him. Once he was able to accomplish that, Rio would be executed. Little did he know, Rio was thinking the exact same thing about him.

The next few weeks were very tense in the hood. By then the dispute over Prince's legacy between Rio and Truck had become public knowledge. Some of the soldiers loved the idea of Rio taking over. He was always fair with them. But others wanted to see Truck in power. It was as if Prince's empire had split down the middle. Some of the soldiers even took to getting at each other in territorial-type disputes. For the time being they were isolated incidents. But it was only a matter of time before a civil war erupted between the two sides.

Truck sat inside the small restaurant talking to his partner Slim. "Shit is crazy," Truck said, taking a fork full of rice. "I should've been given the title, hands down."

"Don't worry," Slim said. "We're gonna work this shit out, dawg. That nigga Rio can't see you."

"I'm gonna fix his ass, Slim. Watch and see. But on another note, I need you to handle something."

"Anything, Truck. Just tell me who gotta die."

"That's what I like to hear, baby. I need you to take a few of the guys and go see that nigga, Kane."

"You mean that kid from the village?"

"Yeah, that's him. Old-boy done got beside himself. He needs to be put down."

"No problem, Truck. I never liked that creepy ma fucka anyway."

"You go down there and make that boy hurt. You hear me, Slim?" Truck asked emotionally.

Slim peeped the hostility in Truck's voice, but he held it. Whatever Truck's reason for wanting Kane dead didn't matter. The important thing was that Truck was his friend and boss of their crew. At least in his eyes. "Like I said," Slim said, standing. "Kane is a dead man. We'll get on that tonight."

"That's why I fuck with you, Slim. You about your business. Make it so that punk doesn't see the light of day."

Young Marv sat in the staircase of the building, moving stones. The flow was bananas and he was moving the crack faster than it was being packaged. Marv was a nobody from nowhere. He had no family and no home. Nobody wanted to give him a shot, but Rio had. He gave Marv a job and made sure that he was a'ight. Marv was forever grateful for Rio's kindness and gave him his undying loyalty.

Marv was snapped out of his thoughts by the sound of the staircase door to his rear creaking open. Marv relaxed a little bit when he saw that the person coming his way was a crackhead. "How many you need?" Marv asked. The crackhead didn't respond, he only stared. "You hear me talking to you? Look, if you ain't buying then move on."

"I didn't come to buy nothing," the crackhead said. "I brought you a message from Truck."

"Fuck kinda message you got for me?"

"Rio's fifteen minutes of fame are about over. Truck is gonna be running the show soon. He says that if you guys wanna keep eating then you had better come on over to his side."

"Listen," Marv said. "I don't have anything to do with Rio and Truck's beef. Truck didn't put me on, Rio did. So all that shit you popping don't hold no weight. I'm sticking with Rio."

"Have it your way." The crackhead pulled a .32 from his jacket pocket and fired a single shot. The bullet crashed into Marv's chest and sent him flying down the stairs. Marv looked on in shock as the blood squirted from his chest. As Marv lay on the pissy ground, bleeding out, the crackhead shot him in the face. Marv was dead at the age of seventeen.

Rio sat on the bench in front of 875 watching the fiends come and go. His arm was in a cast and his ribs still pained him, but that didn't affect his thinking abilities. Ever since the shooting, he made it his business to be extra careful. He carried a gun at all times. His attorney had advised him against it, but he wasn't trying to hear that shit. Epstein was from a world completely different from Rio's. At the end of the day, Epstein went home to his nice house and family, while Rio held sway over the unforgiven. The only law in the streets was survival of the fittest.

"How we looking?" Rio asked, giving School Boy dap.

"Everything is everything, boss," School Boy replied. "I got Mikey and Jenkins holding this down and two of the young homeys pumping across the street. We on, baby."

"Yo, Mikey used to run with the click, right?" Rio asked rubbing his chin.

"I guess so. He said he knew Mel," School Boy said.

"You check him or his man out?"

"Nah, Rio. Shit been so crazy that it slipped my mind."

"School Boy, I know that you know better than that? A mistake like that could catch you football numbers," Rio said seriously.

"Man, them cats ain't no police. They smoke too much weed to be the law."

"So, you vouching for them?" Rio asked seriously.

"Ah," School Boy stuttered, "I ain't saying all that. I'm just saying that they've been on the up and up so far."

"Fuck that. It's too much on the ball right now, School Boy. I put you on shift cause I know you're always gonna handle business straight. But don't let that fool you. Just like I gave it, I can take it away. Don't fuck me over."

"I'd cross my mama before I crossed you, Rio," School Boy said nervously.

"Ma fuck'n right you will. The time for games is over, dawg. Either you in it to win or you serve no purpose. The choice is yours, School Boy." Without waiting for an answer, Rio left School Boy to ponder his predicament.

School Boy was a little surprised by how Rio had came at him. Couldn't say that he blamed him though. The kid had been through a lot. Rio was becoming increasingly paranoid of the people around him. What he said did make a lot of sense though. Mikey and Jenkins proved that they knew how to get paper, but he really didn't know them like that. School Boy made a note to himself to dig a little deeper into the duo's background.

"What was that shit all about?" Cutty asked, catching up to Rio.

"Wasn't nothing," Rio said, lighting a cigarette. "Just trying to reacquaint myself with the hood. That's all."

"Fuck outta here," Cutty said, nudging him. "You act like you was in the hospital for a long time."

"I know I ain't been gone that long, but since the shooting I haven't really been in the streets like that."

"Scary-ass nigga."

"Fuck you, Cutty. It ain't about being scared, it's about being careful. Nigga, you wasn't the one laying in a pool of your own blood. That cat could've killed me."

"Fuck that nigga. He was a fucking pussy. When I move on a nigga, he ain't getting back up. He was probably more scared than you were."

"Nah, Cutty. You didn't see this cat. There wasn't a drop of fear in his eyes."

"So, why didn't he kill you?"

"I don't know, dawg. I just thank God every day for allowing me to live through it."

"God ain't got shit to do with it. If a nigga is pussy then he just is. I say we go find this nigga and put him out of his misery."

"Easier said than done, Cutty. We don't even know where to start looking."

"Fuck that. Somebody's gotta know this cat. He couldn't have just popped outta nowhere. If he's out there, Rio, we'll find him."

Rio admired his friend's determination. Cutty was hell-bent on finding the gunman and putting it on him. Rio wouldn't mind seeing the killer get what he deserved either. The Hound had taken someone very near and dear to him. Rio wanted him to pay, but seeing how the young killer moved, he wasn't too sure if he wanted to be the one to find him.

"So where you been all day?" Rio asked, changing the subject.

"Oh, I was up the block shooting dice wit Truck and them niggaz," Cutty replied.

"Truck? Since when y'all niggaz became so friendly?" Rio asked suspeciously.

"Ain't about nothing. Truck is a'ight."

"A'ight? Cutty, you act like you don't know what's going on."

"I know what's popping, Rio, but I think that all of this shit is stupid. We're all supposed to be on the same team, but we're fighting amongst each other."

"Because of ya man, Truck," Rio said, getting more agitated. "That nigga is the one wilding."

"Truck has been through some shit, yo. If my pops got hit up, I'd be tripping, too."

"Fuck, you siding with this nigga over me?"

"Never, kid. You my ace. I'm not co-signing for Truck, but maybe y'all should sit down and talk about this?"

"Fuck talking. Ya man made himself perfectly clear at the funeral. I offered a truce and he spit in my face. Truck isn't content to share, so I'm claiming it all."

"Just think about it, Rio." Cutty pleaded.

"Cutty," Rio said, his eyes becoming dark and sinister. "We've been friends for a long time, but never make me question your loyalty."

Cutty nodded his head dumbly and left the situation alone. His long-time friend had never second-guessed him or raised his voice at him before. All he wanted was to get Rio to listen to reason. If he could get Rio to back off a bit, then maybe he could get a little piece of the hood on his own. Cutty was loyal to Rio, but more loyal to himself.

Trinity sat on the bench in front of 845 with Shamel. Through everything that had been going on over the past few weeks, he had been the most helpful. He was her shoulder when she needed to talk and her pit bull when something needed to be handled. Shamel was a jack of all trades and that's why she had made sure that Rio brought him into the organization. He had been loyal to Rio and forever at his side. The only reason that he wasn't with him then was because Trinity had requested to speak with him.

"What's up, Mel?" Trinity asked.

"It doesn't look good, T," Shamel said sadly. "The word on the streets is that Truck has been trying to lay the pressure on all of our workers. He figures he can force them to chose him. I even heard that he had li'l Marv killed."

"Marv from sixtieth?" Trinity asked in shock.

"Yeah. He was barely eighteen," Shamel said solemnly.

"Rio really liked that kid, too. How's he taking it?"

"He doesn't know yet. Rio's got enough on him as it is. I'll tell him when I think the time is right."

"Yeah," Trinity said, nodding. "That might be the best thing for him. What's up with Cutty?"

"Still got his head jammed up Truck's ass."

"I don't know about that cat, Shamel. Do you think that Cutty can be trusted?" she asked seriously.

"I know Cutty. He can be a lot of things, but not disloyal. Honestly, I don't think he knows what kind of snake Truck really is."

"Still, he could be a weak link. Maybe we should only feed him info on the need to know basis?"

"You might have a point there, Trinity. Cutty means well, but his hardheadedness could blow everything."

"There's too much at stake to let it all go sour now, Mel."

"Don't worry about it, T. I'll handle Cutty."

"Okay, Mel. I trust you. What's up with that other thing?"

"Oh," Shamel said, smiling, "I got my li'l man on that right now. If Truck wants to play tit for tat, then so can we."

Jason came down the stairs of the tenement building followed by a body-guard. He clutched a duffel bag, containing two hundred grand of Truck's money, under his arm. Usually he didn't need a bodyguard, but in light of everything that was going on, Truck didn't want him taking his chances.

"Where'd you park?" Jason asked, looking at the bodyguard.

"I got the ride double-parked around the corner," the guard said.

"Good. I wanna get the fuck outta this hood and drop this paper off."

The two men continued to walk and talk, never noticing Knowledge hiding in the shadows behind the staircase. As Jason reached for the exit door, Knowledge made his move. He crept up behind the guard and leveled his silenced .22. The bullet pierced the guard's skull, making a chirping sound. The guard was already dead before Jason even knew what was going on.

"What the fuck?" Jason gasped.

"Shut the fuck up," Knowledge hissed. "Hand the bag over, nigga."

"Are you crazy?" Jason asked, not believing that the young kid had the balls to rob him.

"Yep," Knowledge said, looking at the dead guard. "Crazy than a ma fucka. If you don't pass that bag over, you'll see just how crazy I am."

"I don't think you know who you're fucking with."

"I know just *who* I'm fucking wit." Knowledge clocked Jason with the butt of the gun, knocking him on his ass. "I don't give a fuck about you or that faggot-ass nigga, Truck. Now up it, clown."

Jason reluctantly handed him the bag. "You're playing yourself," Jason said smugly. "When Truck finds out what you did, your life ain't gonna be worth dick."

"Probably not," Knowledge said, slinging the bag over his shoulder. "But who's gonna tell him?" Knowledge put two in Jason's head and ran into the street.

24

Kane sat on a bench inside Washington Square Park with a young lady. The girl blushed shyly as he fed her lies about how beautiful she was. He was a master at it. He would tell people anything they wanted to hear just to get what he wanted. At that moment, he wanted the girl.

"You say the sweetest things, Sean," said the girl.

"I say them because they're true," Kane said. "Why don't we get outta here and go someplace a little more private?" As Kane stood to leave with the young girl, he found himself surrounded by a half dozen angry men. Kane didn't know the other five, but he recognized their leader.

"Sup Kane?" Slim asked, grinning.

"What do you want?" Kane asked, sounding irritated.

"Truck didn't like the half-ass job you and your boy did. He sent us down here to show you the error of your ways."

"Fellas," Kane said, easing his hand into his pocket. "I'm sure we can talk about this."

"Don't think so," Slim smirked. "Business is business, dawg. I'm sure you understand?"

As the first man moved, so did Kane. He snatched a small glass ball from his pocket and burst it on the man's skull. The battery acid that filled the ball splashed over the man's face. As the first man howled in pain, Slim raised his gun. He clapped two shots, but Kane used the girl as a human shield and the bullets ripped into her torso. Kane used the moment of confusion to run for the park exit.

"Fuck is y'all standing around for!" Slim barked. "Kill that ma fucka!"

The remaining killers took off in pursuit of Kane. Kane had a good head start, but the men were fast on his heels. He zigged and zagged through the blocks, but he was unable to shake them. One of the men got close enough to grab Kane's coat, only to have his hand severed by the blade Kane kept concealed. The man dropped and clutched at his stump, but Kane never saw it. He just kept moving.

As Kane crossed Hudson Street, a slug slammed into his shoulder, just missing his body armor. He staggered a bit but didn't fall. The bullet wound could be tended to later. Survival was the first order of business. He ran through the streets, calling for the Hound. He hoped that his brother was still somewhere in the area, but it wasn't likely. Another slug hit Kane's leg, but it didn't do much to slow him down. He figured once he reached the office building he was headed for, he'd be safe.

When Kane reached the building, he didn't bother to slow down. He lowered his shoulder and crashed through the glass doors. A foolish security guard tried to stop him and was rewarded by having his throat slashed. Before the body hit the ground, Kane was halfway to the elevator.

"Don't let that ma fucka get away," Slim yelled, hopping over the dead guard. Slim fired three shots at the fleeing youngster. One went wild and shattered a window, the other two hit Kane in the back. Kane felt his strength fading from the loss of blood, but the need for survival drove him on. Just as Slim and his peoples were almost on him, Kane collapsed into the elevator.

"You," Slim barked to one of the men. "Try and find an emergency stop for this shit. The rest of you hit the stairs. That ma fucka can't get but so far with four slugs in his ass." The men went off and did as they were told.

Kane climbed out of the elevator at the fifth floor, which also happened to be the top floor. He knew it wouldn't take his pursuers long to find him so he had to act fast. Willing himself to move, he began to crawl for the rear stairs. If he could only make it to the back exit, there was still hope. That hope fled when Slim came bursting onto the floor followed by two other men.

"Where you going?" Slim asked, kicking him in the leg. "Made us chase you, ma fucka. Now you gonna die."

"Fuck you," Kane wheezed. "I'm a fucking warrior. Fear don't live here, pussy."

"Big talk," Slim said, raising his gun, "for someone about to die." Just as Slim was about to pull the trigger, he heard a howling. "Fuck is that?" Slim asked the other shooters.

"That," Kane said, laughing, "is death. Die bitches!!" As soon as the words left Kane's mouth, the hallway lights flickered and died. Slim placed his back against the wall and tried to get a clue as to what was going on. Through the darkness he heard an animal-like growling. The growling was followed by the most horrific screams Slim had ever heard. He quickly started firing blind into the blackness, not caring if he hit the attacker or his own men.

With all of his bullets spent, Slim dropped to the ground and crawled into a fetal position. As he cringed in the corner, something warm splashed against his face. As the warm liquid trickled down his cheek and across his lip, he immediately recognized the taste. It was blood.

Throwing caution to the wind, Slim got up and ran for his life. He had made it a few feet when someone grabbed him by the throat. He struggled against the grip, but was unable to break it. The backup lights kicked on and Slim wished that it had stayed dark. He found himself face to face with Hound. The killer's face and clothes were covered with blood, and he stared wild-eyed at Slim.

"Silly ma fucka," Hound snarled, drawing a large knife with ridges made to gut fish. "You come through our hood and lay hands on my blood?"

"Wait," Slim coughed. "It wasn't my idea! It was Truck! It was all him!"

"Don't worry about it," Hound said, leaning in close. "You two can point fingers at each other in hell."

On the street below, people were looking around nervously to see where the horrible screaming was coming from. It sounded like a cross between Axel Rose and a mating cat. Then Slim's headless body fell five stories and splattered on the ground.

Truck stood in the underground parking garage, talking to the last remaining member of the death squad he had sent after Kane. "Fuck is you talking about?" Truck asked in disbelief.

"Dead," the last surviving shooter repeated. "The whole squad, wiped out."

"I'm not understanding this," Truck said, grabbing the shooter by the neck. "I sent you ma fuckas down there with Slim to kill one little shit bird and you tell me that everybody got wasted?"

"Truck," the shooter said, gasping for air. "I don't know how it happened. We shot the boy up something fierce, but it's like he was too damn stubborn to lay down. We chased him into this building by the water and shit. Slim left me downstairs to try and find a stop button for the elevator. So, while I'm downstairs I hear this howling. I'm making my way up the stairs to see what's going on when I hear bullets and screaming. Now I ain't the smartest nigga in the world, but I know something ain't right, so I boogied. As I'm coming out of the building . . ."

"What else?" Truck asked, shaking him.

"Slim . . . his body came flying out of the window, but the thing is . . . his head was gone."

Truck released the shooter. "Not my nigga," he said, sobbing. "How can y'all let one cat lick you like that?"

"Truck, this kid was a fucking soldier. He had all kinds of tricks up his sleeve. Ma fucka Tim is still in the hospital with burns on his neck and face, while Jim lost his hand. I was lucky to get up outta there."

"Yeah," Truck said, eyeing the shooter. "Lucky or in on it."

"Hold on," the shooter said, backing up. "You know that I

wouldn't shit on you, in no kinda way, Truck. But this kid that you sent us for knows his shit. He murdered a security guard without breaking his stride. Truck, you picked the wrong ma fucka to put the finger on."

"Fuck that. Kane bleeds just like the rest of us. You think I just fell outta my momma's ass? You a lying ma fucka, yo," Truck said, pulling his gun. "There will be no weak links in this organization. You've out-lived your usefulness."

"Wait!" the shooter pleaded. "I ain't cross you, Truck! Just let me—" That was as far as he got before Truck put one in his head. The shooter slid down the wall of the parking garage, with his brains leaving a trail of goo. Truck hopped into his jeep and pulled off.

Truck was so mad that you could almost see steam coming out of his head. It seemed like everything was going goofy on him. Kane had proven to be more dangerous than Truck had given him credit for. But dangerous or not, that skinny bastard was gonna die slowly.

Then there was the issue of his two hundred grand. With the repu-tation that Truck had in the streets, none of the stick-up kids would've been crazy enough to try him. There was an unspoken law: If you fuck with Truck, you die. There were only a select few people that would've had the balls to pull that one off. Truck couldn't prove it, but he knew that Rio had something to do with it. The youngster had proven that he could be quite cagey. That was okay though. Truck was through play-ing nice. If Rio wanted to act like a big boy, Truck was gonna treat him like one.

Mikey strolled along Broadway lost in his thoughts. He couldn't understand how he could've allowed himself to get caught up in this fucked-up sit-uation. For the first time in his life he was getting money and it was thanks to Rio's organization. School Boy had taken him in and given him a way to get money, but Mikey wore a false face. Under the surface, he was nothing but a fucking snitch. Since the police had turned him, Mikey had been having some serious emotional issues. He had trouble looking at himself in the mirror while carrying the burden of what he was doing. As fucked up as it might've been, Mikey had to chose between himself or Rio. In the hood, it was every man for himself.

As Mikey crossed One hundredth Street, a green van came to a screeching halt in front of him. Before Mikey had a chance to react, two sets of arms snatched him into the van. Mikey was tossed roughly onto the floor and the door shut behind him. The van's engine roared once and took off. Mikey's first thought was that somebody had found out he was snitching and he was going to die. But when he looked up and saw Detective Stark smiling down at him, he knew he was wrong.

"What's up there, Mikey?" Stark said, flashing his yellow teeth. "We didn't scare you, did we?"

"Man, fuck y'all want?" Mikey asked as he tried to sit up.

"What kind of way is that to talk to a friend?" Stark asked, faking concern.

"Fuck you," Mikey spat. "We ain't friends."

"Whatever, kid. What do you got for us?"

"Nothing yet. I been slinging for them, but I can't catch Rio dirty. Now if y'all want me to give you School Boy, I can—"

"Fuck that," Stark cut him off. "We want Rio."

"Hold on," Brown said, making his presence known for the first time. "Maybe the kid is on to something? If we bring this School Boy in, maybe he can help us pin something on one of the higher-ups?"

"Nah, Brown. We ain't got that kinda time," Stark said, shaking his head. "If we keep bullshitting, someone else is gonna end up pinching that fuck Rio and taking the credit for our work. Look," he said, facing Mikey. "You get your ass back on them streets and get us something solid on this prick or it's back to the joint with you. Maybe you'll get yourself a nice boyfriend upstate."

"So," Brown said. "Now what Stark?"

"Now, we take it to another level. I don't know why I didn't think of it before, but I'm calling in a favor."

"A favor?" Brown asked curiously.

"Yeah. I got a pal downtown, by the name of Peterson, who worked on a case ten years ago. He was working for the NYPD when he locked up a mutual friend of ours. He works for the Feds now. The guy owes me a favor. It's a long shot, but it may put us a step closer to nailing Rio."

"What about the other Capos?"

"I ain't worried about those dickheads. They got about an ounce of good sense between them. Rio's the real threat."

"Have you forgotten about Truck?"

"You don't worry about old Truck. Our focus here is on Rio."

"Stark, why do you have such a hard-on for this kid? I know he's doing dirt, but the rest of them aren't any cleaner."

"Hey, I'm running this, *Officer* Brown. You let me worry about who's dirty and who's not. If you had been able to get anything from that cunt girlfriend of his, we might have an easier time of it," Stark said sharply.

"Trinity? I don't think she knows anything." Brown said honestly.

"Bullshit. That bitch is knee-deep in this shit. She's a slick one all right. I wouldn't be surprised if she had something to do with Rio killing her old man."

"Stark, we don't know for sure that Rio killed Baker."

"Oh, he killed him all right. He had motive and opportunity. Rio's a murderer and I'm gonna make sure he gets the needle for it. With any luck, we can get the girlfriend as an accessory. As a matter of fact, bring the bitch in for questioning."

"But why?" Brown asked.

"What the fuck is it with you and this broad?"

"Nothing. I just believe that she's a good kid. She might be a little misguided, but I don't think she's tied directly into this."

"Well, if she isn't, then we'll make sure that she is. You just do your fucking job, *Officer* Brown. Don't make me pull rank."

"Yes sir," Brown said sarcastically. Brown was getting tired of Stark and his obsession with Rio. He didn't mind doing his job and helping to bring the kid in if he was dirty, but bringing down innocent people wasn't what he signed on for. This shit was getting too deep for him. Brown knew he had a choice to make. He could either do his job or do the right thing.

Joyce came strutting from the building like she was the queen of Sheeba. It had been all about her for the last few weeks. Joyce hadn't been fucking with Alexis or Trinity for quite some time. She had made the mistake of getting drunk one night and confiding in Alexis what she had tried to pull with Rio. Instead of praising her for her attempt to shoot for the stars, Alexis beat her ass. What Joyce didn't understand was that, although she and Alexis were friends, Trinity was more like a sister.

Alexis had beat her something terrible, but she said that she wouldn't break her girl's heart and tell. "Fuck em," Joyce said to no one in particular. She reasoned that Alexis was just jealous that she hadn't thought of it first. Trinity, on the other hand, was a different story. If the dumb bitch had kept a tighter hold on that fine-ass nigga, then she would've never been able to lure him off. It didn't matter though. Joyce had her own sugar daddy now.

She and Baron had been seeing each other for a little while now. He would take her shopping and trick all kinds of paper on her. She figured that she had herself a winner. Sometimes she would be suspicious of Baron. Joyce was far from dumb; she knew Baron had girls on the side. But his interest in Trinity always made her leery. Lately he had been asking all kinds of questions about her. How's she doing, where she likes to eat, where she was taking her GED test? Joyce just figured that Baron hadn't gotten over Trinity yet. Joyce would have to get extra nasty with him to take his mind off the stuck-up bitch.

The black truck came to a rolling stop where Joyce was standing. Joyce snatched open the passenger side door and jumped in. She leaned over to kiss Baron, who was behind the wheel, but he pulled away. She should've been used to it by now. He told her it was because he didn't want any of his enemies to know who his *girl* was, but he really didn't want her nasty mouth on anything other than his dick and occasionally his ass.

Joyce didn't mind Baron's strange ways. She understood that it was dangerous on the streets. If people couldn't get at you then they would try for the ones you loved. Joyce thought that Baron really cared for her, but what she didn't know was that he had an ulterior motive for keeping her close.

"What's up, ma?" Baron asked, looking at the road.

"Chilling," Joyce responded. "I thought you wasn't gonna get to see me today?"

"You know I can't stay away," he lied. "Listen, I can't stay long, but I came down to ask you a favor."

"What kinda favor?"

"Don't worry," he said, stroking her cheek. "You know it's some paper for you."

"How much?"

"A few grand, for a few minutes."

"Look Baron, I ain't really wit that gang bang shit. I mean I did it two or three times, but—"

"Joyce," he cut her off. "You know I wouldn't share my loving with nobody else." *At least not now*, he thought to himself. "I just need you to do this thing for me. When you get done we can take that trip to Cancun you're always talking about."

At the promise of money and an expensive trip, Joyce was ready to play ball. "Okay, what is it?"

"That's my girl. Listen close, Joyce, cause I'm only gonna say it once."

25

That night Rio had three unexpected visitors. He was sitting in back of the center with Trinity when Shamel came looking for him. From the look on his friend's face he could tell that he had pressing business to discuss.

"What's up, Mel?" Rio asked.

"Need you on the ave, yo," Shamel said.

"Everything a'ight?"

"I don't know. There's some people here to talk to you."

"Who?"

"Just come on, Rio."

"A'ight. I'll be back, boo," Rio said, addressing Trinity.

"It's cool," she said, standing to leave. "I gotta run home to cook dinner for Billy anyway. Call me when you get done." Trinity kissed Rio and went her way.

Reluctantly he followed Shamel to the avenue to see what was going on. When Rio reached Columbus, J was leaning against a car waiting for him.

"Sup, J?" he said. "What you doing over this way?"

"Need to holla at you, kid," J said, pulling on his cigarette.

"Everything cool?"

"That all depends on you. Why don't we get in the car and talk?"

Something about the J's tone of voice was making Rio uneasy. He didn't figure that he had anything to fear from J, but the way things were going he couldn't be sure. He hated to think it, but if J did have something up his sleeve, the glock that Rio had in his waistband would start barking. To Rio's surprise, two other Capos were waiting for him. Rio nodded to the men as he slid into the ride.

"What's up, brother?" Big Paul asked from behind a pair of sunglasses.

"Trying to live," Rio said, still trying to figure what was going on. "What brings y'all down this way?"

"Business," Jake said.

"Yeah," J cut in. "We got some things that we need to talk about."

"What kinda things?" Rio said, resting his good hand on the spot where his gun was tucked.

"Well," J started, "we heard about the little tit-for-tat game that you and Truck have been out here playing."

"I'm afraid that I don't follow you, J," Rio lied.

"Rio, you can play dumb all you want, but I didn't just hop off the train from Georgia. We know you sent your boy to take off Truck's money. Just like we know that he's been trying to muscle your people."

"Okay, what if I did? Y'all came to do me in?"

"Hell no," Jake cut in. "It ain't even that serious. We know Truck can be an asshole. We came down here to talk to you about where you stand in the grand scheme of things."

"Okay," Rio said, relaxing a bit, but still keeping his hand close to his gun. "I'm listening."

"This is how we figure it," J said. "Since Prince got killed, this whole organization has been in a shamble. We're all supposed to be a team, but everyone is going for self. You got certain cats that we roll with trying to branch out and do other things, Capos feuding with each other. Prince is probably turning over in his grave behind this."

"Yeah," Rio said. "This shit has gotten crazy, but Truck is the one causing it all. I'm just trying to do what's best for my people."

"We know that, Rio," J continued. "That's why we're here now. We figured that it's time to restore some kinda order to this little thing of ours."

"How do you purpose we do that, J?"

"Can't you read between the lines, boy? We want you to step up and fill Prince's vacancy."

"Me?" he asked, surprised.

"Yes, you," J said. "Rio, you've always been a good kid. You follow directions and you know how to keep a low profile. You've been squeezing money out of a project that until recently brought in mediocre profits at best. You're running things down here accordingly while Truck is uptown acting crazy. We figure that you'll be the face of authority, but we can still kinda coach you on the sidelines. Advisors of sorts."

"So," Rio continued. "What do the rest of you guys think?"

"As far as I'm concerned," Paul said, "I'm cool with it. Truck is destroying what Prince has built and I don't like it. Prince was always good to me. The color of my skin never mattered to him. But Truck is a different case. Son of a bitch tried to send some of his peoples down to my bar and muscle me. They found out the hard way that we ain't your average white boys."

"And what about you and Breeze, Jake?" Rio asked.

"Breeze," Jake said, "that's always gonna be my nigga, but he thinks too much like Truck for my taste. We've had a good working relationship for a while now, but I ain't the snot-nosed kid that I was when we first hooked up. I need a spot of my own and if I can get it by voting in your favor, then so be it."

"Okay," Rio said. "What about the other Capos?"

"I spoke to Marco and he's with us," J assured him. "The only ones we might have some trouble outta is Gino and Breeze."

"Don't worry about Breeze," Jake said confidently. "He might not totally agree with the move, but in time he'll accept it. He's got no choice. Gino, I can't speak for."

"I hear that he's leaning toward Truck," Paul added.

"If so, fuck him," J snapped. "This shit has got to end. If Gino decides to roll with Truck, it'll hurt us, but it won't stop us."

"If worse comes to worse, I'll have a few of my boys roll through there and chain his ass to the back of a Harley," Paul joked.

"The way I see it," Jake said, "Truck could prove to be our biggest obstacle."

"Hmm, he's got a point there," Paul said. "Him being Prince's boy and all, we gotta handle him different. What do you think, J?"

"You know," J said, sighing. "Me and Prince been best friends since before most of you've been alive. When he died a piece of me went with him. Everybody's playing like they don't know who ordered the hit on him, but I got an idea. When I know for sure, that ma fucka is dead as shit!" J didn't say anyone's name, but the men assembled could read between the lines.

"I feel you, J," Rio said. "I loved Prince too and I'd like to see the ma fucka responsible for this put in a box."

"They'll be time for that later, kid," J assured him. "Right now we need to know what you're gonna do?"

"Okay," he said, getting serious. "I accept the terms of this agreement."

"Then it's settled," J said, pulling out a bottle of yak and four shot glasses. "You the man now. Rule wisely and justly. Remember those two things and ya might grow up to be somebody, Rio." J made sure everyone's glass was full before he continued speaking. "If Prince was here I'm sure he would've agreed with our choice of his replacement. Gentlemen, let us raise our glasses and toast to the new prince of the ghetto."

"To Rio," they all said in unison, before draining their glasses.

Rio wanted to shout with delight, but he had to play it cool. He thought that he would've had to do some maneuvering to step up, but it had proved to be easier than he thought. Soon the word would spread to every corner in the city that Rio had been named Prince's successor. Those who remained loyal would prosper. Those who sought to challenge him would be punished. Rio was one step closer to his and Trinity's dream.

Trinity was awakened bright and early the next morning by a knock on the door. She snatched her bathrobe and shuffled her way to the door. She was tired of all the traffic coming in and out of the house. It wasn't so much Billy, but her brother Richard. Crackheads loved to run in and out at all times of the night. She would be glad when the end of the month came. The lady had called Rio a few days prior to inform him that the apartment would be ready then. Wouldn't be soon enough for Trinity.

When she looked through the peephole she was surprised to see Officer Brown standing in the hallway. She wondered what he could want at this hour of the morning? Well, she wouldn't find out standing there.

"Hey, Officer Brown," Trinity said, cracking the door.

"Hello, Trinity," he said trying to muster a smile. "I didn't mean to wake you."

"Nah, it's okay. I had to get up anyway. What's up?"

"Well . . . Uh . . . I kinda need to talk to you."

"Oh God, what is it now?" she said, fearing the worst.

"Trinity, there isn't any easy way to say this."

"Just take your time."

"Trinity, they sent me here to bring you in for questioning."

"Questioning?"

"Yes, they want me to ask you about your father's disappearance."

"I told you that I don't know anything." she insisted.

"I know, Trinity, but Detective Stark thinks you do."

"That's crazy!"

"I know, but he's hell-bent on putting Rio under the jail."

"Officer Brown, I don't know anything about what Rio is or isn't doing in the streets," she said, trying to collect herself.

"Trinity, I don't think you understand where I'm coming from. This guy wants Rio bad. I mean, he was in his ass before, but since Prince is outta the picture, it's ten times worse."

"What does Prince's death have to do with Rio?"

"Trinity, whether you know it or not, Rio was being groomed to be the next big thing. Now that Prince is out of the way, he's a sure bet to take over his operation."

"No, you're mistaken," she lied.

"Trinity, you better wise up. If I were you, I would try convincing Rio to take an early retirement. If he doesn't, they're gonna make sure he ends up either in jail or the ground."

Trinity sized up Officer Brown, trying to figure out if he was playing on her. She looked into his eyes and saw genuine concern. "Why are you risking your career to help me?"

"Because," he said sadly, "I care. Trinity, you don't know how tired I am of seeing young black folks get railroaded. Now, I ain't no fool, so don't get it twisted. I know who Rio is and what he's doing. If he catches a bid, then he brought it on himself. But you're different. You're just a girl who got involved with the wrong kind of dude. I don't knock you for whom you've decided to love, but if you care for him as much as you say, then get him to step down."

"Okay," she said nonchalantly.

"Trinity," he said, grabbing her by the shoulders. "Quit saying okay and listen. Let Truck have his father's empire. Take your people and get outta here. When I go back to the precinct I'm gonna tell Stark that you weren't home. Take my advice, Trinity." Officer Brown released her shoulders and left her to think on what he had said. He hoped that she would listen, but in his heart he knew that she wouldn't. He just hoped that when the shit hit the fan they could bring Rio in wearing chains instead of a bag.

Trinity sat on the couch, her thoughts racing. If what Officer Brown was saying was true then staying in the game might be detrimental to both of them. Trinity wanted to get out of the projects more than anything else, but she loved Rio too much to risk losing him over something material. The last thing that Trinity wanted was to see Rio get locked up, but at this stage of the game, getting out wouldn't be that easy. Maybe it would be best to let Truck step up while she took Rio and left. It shouldn't be too hard to pull off. Prince's throne was vacant so let his bastard of a son fill it. As long as she and Rio could get away free. Little did Trinity know that the bargain had already been struck.

Truck took the remains of his crushed cellular phone and hurled them at the wall. The cracked plastic burst against the plaster and went flying all over the place. He had just gotten the word from J about the Capos nominating Rio for leadership. All the scheming and planning that Truck had done just to have it ruined due to a damn democracy. But what J and the other Capos failed to realize was that they weren't the government, they were criminals.

Truck was tired of playing games. If J and the others wanted to side with Rio then they could die with him. There was no way that Truck was going to let a billion-dollar-a-year empire slip through his fingers. He snatched his coat from the arm of the chair and headed for the door. When Truck snatched the door open, he was surprised to see a face from the past standing there.

Baron stood in the center of his team, giving them last-minute instructions. "Y'all make sure everything goes smooth," he told them. "I don't want my package to get so much as a scratch while you're bringing it in. Joyce," he said, looking at the shaken girl, "are you ready?"

"I guess," she said sheepishly.

"I don't need you to guess, ma. I need to know that you're ready?"

"Yeah, I'm ready."

"Listen," he said, stroking her face. "Don't worry about it. Nothing is gonna happen. Before you know it, this will all be over with and everything will be back to normal. I need you with me on this."

"Okay, Baron."

Baron watched the misguided girl leave and shook his head in disgust. Little did Joyce know she had almost outlived her usefulness. It was a shame what some chicks would do for a few dollars. Once she did this last thing for Baron, she would be cast out with the rest of the trash.

"Man, fuck do you want?" Truck asked angrily.

"Well, hello to you, too," Peterson said, inviting himself into Truck's place. "I just came to see how you've been."

"Bullshit. What you really came down here for, Detective Peterson?"

"That's Agent Peterson," he corrected. "I'm with the Bureau now. I hear you've been a busy little beaver though."

"I don't know what you're talking about," Truck lied.

"Come on, you know the Feds know everything. Listen, I'm not really here to trade lies with you. I need a favor."

"What kind of favor?"

"The same kinda favors that you used to do while you were locked up."

"Man, I ain't wit that shit."

"Oh, I think you are. Or would you like me to tell the homeys what you did to survive ten years behind the wall?"

Truck thought about what his life would be like if the word got out about his *extracurricular* activities and decided to hear Peterson out. "Okay, what do you need?"

"A bust. I think you'll like who the target is."

"Why is that?"

"Because I hear that Rio has been quite a pain in your ass for some time."

"Listen, nothing would please me more then to get that ma fucka outta my hair, but it ain't that easy."

"Don't bullshit me, Truck. I know that both of you worked for Prince."

"Yeah, but we can't stand each other. I've got about as much chance of earning Rio's trust as you do."

"Well, you better think of something. This thing that you boys got going has become bigger than just the local police. We caught wind of it, not too long ago. We were just trying to gather intelligence before we made a move. The locals just made it easier by alerting us to their operation. The moral of the story is, we're looking to pin a RICO charge on someone. Now, they want Rio bad, but they'll take you as the booby prize."

"I don't know what to tell you then," Truck said, beginning to waiver.

"Okay, Truck," Peterson said, pulling out his phone. "I guess you and me are going downtown then. Afterwards, I'll be sure to tell your father's crew how helpful you were."

"Okay, okay," Truck said, beginning to panic. "I can't get you Rio, but what if I got you someone close to him? Someone that could give you the goods on Rio for real. I'm talking murder and trafficking. Interested?"

"Okay, Truck. Start talking."

26

"Trinity," Rio said excitedly into the phone. "What are you doing right now?"

"What?" she asked. "I'm in the house. Why?"

"I gotta talk to you and I can't do it over the phone. Can you come and meet me?"

"Yes, but hold up. I got something I need to talk to you about, too. It's in regards to our plan."

"Good, cause that's what I need to talk to you about. Can you meet me uptown?"

"Yes, but what's wrong with you? You sound like you've just hit the lotto."

"Almost as good. Look, meet me inside of Crab Inn on 125th, okay?"

"Okay, Rio."

"Love you, ma." Rio hung up the phone and got back to join Shamel and Cutty.

"Was that T?" Shamel asked.

"You know it," Rio responded.

"Did you tell her yet?"

"Nah, I'm gonna wait until she gets uptown."

"I still can't believe it," Cutty said. "They finally bumped your square ass up."

"Bout fucking time," Rio said, excitedly. "I'm gonna change the game, fellas."

"A lot of niggaz thought that they can change the game, Rio."

"I know, Cutty. But I'm gonna actually do it. The time for all this madness is at an end. The drug game in New York is gonna change for the better."

"Fuck kinda sense does that make?" Cutty asked. "How you ever gonna make slinging poison a good thing?"

"Not the poison itself, Cutty, but the way we do it. With all of the money that we haul in off this shit, our hoods shouldn't be all messed up. I'm gonna do what the fucking government won't. These kids out here need something to call their own. It might take a while, but I'm gonna do my part."

"Fool," Shamel said, chuckling. "You gonna be a broke ass hell trying to help all these niggaz."

"Ain't about the money, Mel. It's about not wanting to see my people starve. My wife and my family are always gonna get first, but I'm gonna try and do something for the ma fuckas that ain't got nothing."

"Always the champion, huh, Rio?"

"If not me, then who? I'll see yall niggaz later." Rio gave his peoples dap and headed out.

"Man," Cutty said, "sometimes I wonder if that ain't the biggest fool to ever push a bundle?"

"Though he might be a fool to some, he's a savior to others. Later on, Cutty."

"I still say he's a fool," Cutty said to Shamel's back. Just then Cutty's cell went off. "Yeah? Oh, what up Truck? Huh? Yeah, I could take those off your hands. How much? Twelve hundred dollars for all three? Shit, yeah. I'll be there in a few." Cutty hung up his cell phone and headed for the cab base. It seemed like Rio wasn't the only person who had gone crazy. Truck had just agreed to sell Cutty two 9's and a .380 for short paper. If it had been anyone else, Cutty would've been suspicious of the low price, but this was Truck. He figured that he was getting the guns for so cheap because they were peoples. That's how friends did each other, right?

❑   ❑   ❑

Trinity was walking uptown on her way to meet Rio. She wanted to tell him what was going down but he refused to talk over the phone. She would just have to wait until she saw him to deliver the news. Trinity was side-tracked when Joyce came running up behind her.

"Girl," Joyce said. "I've been trying to catch up with you for the last few blocks. Where you headed?"

"Got something to take care of uptown," Trinity said without bothering to stop.

"So why you walking instead of taking a cab?"

"I felt like walking to clear my head."

"Well, I'm going that way, so I'll walk with you."

Trinity didn't really feel like being bothered, but she let Joyce walk with her. For the whole walk Joyce ran her mouth about this or that. Trinity was only half listening to the neighborhood gossip that Joyce was kicking. She was so wrapped up into her thoughts that she never noticed the van following them. When they reached 111th and Morningside, Joyce had a suggestion.

"T, cut through the block with me so I can get some smoke from this nigga," she said. Trinity thought nothing of it, so she made the detour behind Joyce. When they were well into the block, the van that had been following them pulled to a stop alongside the girls. Four men wearing ski masks hopped out and rushed toward Trinity.

When the first man moved on Trinity, she reacted more out of fear than bravery. Snatching the switchblade from her purse, Trinity swung her hand up and across. The blade cut through wool and flesh as the first man tried to keep the skin from falling from his face. When the second man tried to grab Trinity from behind, she caught him in the side with the blade. When he tried to jerk away from her, the blade remained lodged in his side. Trinity found herself unarmed.

Trinity took a fighting stance as the two remaining men came for her. With the odds being somewhat even now, they stood a chance. If Joyce could hold the other man off, they might have a chance. When Trinity looked over and saw Joyce standing off to the side, she knew that she was in it alone. She vowed that if she made it out of the situation, Joyce was gonna get her ugly-ass face cut.

One of the men tried to swing on Trinity. She dodged the blow and countered with a right cross. The punch staggered the man, but he kept coming. Trinity tried to run but the other man grabbed her by her blouse. She continued to fight and squirm until the fabric ripped, but she couldn't get loose. One of the men held Trinity by the arms while the other one squared off and punched her in the face. Trinity would've collapsed to the ground had the man not been holding her up. As the darkness set in, the last thing Trinity saw was Joyce running the other way.

Sally was coming out of the liquor store on 111th Street and Eighth Avenue clutching her bag tight. As she began the short walk back down to the projects, Joyce came flying past her. She was about to speak to the girl, but she was moving too fast. Sally scratched her head and wondered what had the girl so spooked. She cast a glance in the block and saw something wasn't right. Two men were hoisting a young girl into the back of a van. Sally wasn't the biggest woman in the world, but she could hold hers against most men when she was in her prime.

She jogged down the block screaming for them to stop, but she was too late. The men had loaded their cargo and sped off. Sally looked around puzzled as a small cluster of people watched the whole thing and did nothing to help. A flicker of color caught her attention. She picked the bag up from the floor and recognized it immediately. It was the Coach handbag that Rio had bought Trinity last Christmas. Trinity's initials were engraved on the clamp.

Everything started to click into place and Sally dropped the bag. Her mind raced in a million directions at once. She tried to calm herself, but fear for Trinity's life made it hard. Once Sally got her thoughts together she knew what she had to do. The police couldn't help in a situation like this one. She had to get to Rio as soon as possible.

Rio sat alone at his table inside the Crab Inn restaurant, twiddling his thumbs. He had been waiting for Trinity for almost two hours. It wasn't like her to be this late. Even if she had walked instead of taking a cab, she should've still been there. Rio was beginning to worry. As if on cue, Rio's cell went off.

"Hello?" Rio said into the phone.

"Darius!" said a frantic Sally. "Thank God I've found you!"

"Ma," Rio said, getting nervous. "What's wrong?"

"Baby, I need you to come home right away."

"Okay, ma. I'll be there in an hour or so."

"No. I need you to come now."

"Ma, what's going on?"

"Rio, would you please stop asking me what's wrong and do like I'm asking you!"

"Okay, okay. As soon as Trinity gets here, I'll come home."

"Damn it," Sally broke down. "She's gone. They took her."

At that moment the whole world seemed to go in slow motion. Sally continued to speak, but her words were incoherent to Rio. All he could think about was Trinity being gone. Without finishing his conversation with Sally, Rio hung up and called Shamel. "Yo, I need you and Cutty to meet me at my house, right now."

Rio hung up his cell and ran from the restaurant. He almost knocked three people over as he sprinted across 125th trying to catch a cab. His mind went wild replaying the different scenarios of what could've happened to Trinity. Sally had said that *they* took her, but who the hell was they? One thing was for sure, whoever had been foolish enough to lay their hands on Trinity was a dead man walking.

By the time Cutty made it to 139th and St. Nicholas, Truck was already waiting for him. As Cutty approached, he knew something wasn't right. The first clue was the fact that Truck was alone. Since the conflict between Truck and Rio had popped off, neither of them hardly went anywhere alone. Each man was paranoid about the other making a play for his life. The next clue was his body language. The whole time Cutty was walking in his direction, Truck kept looking around as if he was expecting something or someone. Cutty chalked it up as paranoia and went to greet Truck.

"What's good, Truck?" Cutty asked.

"Ain't nothing," Truck said, lighting a cigarette. "You dolo?"

"Yeah."

"Why you ain't bring Mel or one of them niggaz?"

"For what? I ain't got nothing to fear from you. Do I?"

"Nah," Truck lied. "Nothing at all." Part of him felt bad about what he was doing to Cutty. The youngster had always looked up to Truck as a sort of mentor. He was a good student and a valuable soldier. But fuck that. Truck was out to save his own ass. "So, you ready to do this?"

"Yeah," Cutty said. "Where you got em stashed at?"

"In the ride. Cutty . . . never mind. Let's go." Truck led Cutty and they both hopped in. After a brief look around, Truck pulled out the bag containing the police-supplied guns. "Here they go," Truck said, handing him the bag. "All clean and untraceable."

"That's what the fuck I'm talking about," Cutty said, examining one of the 9s. "Damn you been looking out for a nigga Truck."

"Ain't about nothing." Truck said, glancing into the rearview mirror.

"Say, Truck. It might not count for much, but I'm sorry that them niggaz voted against you. Rio is my nigga to the grave, but I got love for you, too. I think y'all both could've—" Cutty was cut off by the sounds of police sirens. He looked into the rearview and saw a fleet of squad cars approaching. "Rollers," he gasped. "Burn it, Truck." Truck sat completely still. "Didn't you hear me?" When Truck wouldn't look at Cutty, he knew that he had been betrayed.

"Ain't this about a bitch," Cutty said in shock. "Snake ma fucka," he howled, drawing his weapon. "Die, nigga!" Before Cutty could pull the trigger, he felt cold steel against his head.

"Go ahead," Stark whispered. "Gimmie a reason to smear your black ass." Cutty started to try him, but he knew it would be a fool's move. He just raised his hands and allowed the detective to pull him from the car. Detective Stark handcuffed Cutty and threw him roughly to the ground. As he was dragged away by the NYPD his last thought was how he was going to pay Truck back.

27

Rio and Shamel sat in the middle of his living room while Sally retold the story of what she had seen. No matter how many times he heard the story, Rio still couldn't believe it. Someone kidnapping Trinity didn't make sense to him. She wasn't connected to the streets and his promotion hadn't leaked out to the public yet. He just couldn't understand it.

"Is there anything more that you can tell us, Ms. Sally?" Shamel asked.

"I done told y'all all I know," she responded. "I came out when they were putting her into the van. They were wearing masks so I don't know who it was that took her."

"Ma fuckas." Rio said, his voice all choked up. "They gonna die. You hear me, Mel? I'm gonna ride on all them niggaz."

"Don't do anything stupid," Sally warned, fearful of her boy ending up getting hurt. "You're just talking crazy cause you're upset."

"No I ain't, Ma. I know just what I'm saying. The niggaz that touched my girl is gonna die. If I can't get to them, then I'm gonna murder their families. If I can't get to them, then I'll murder their friends."

"Baby, ain't no sense in hurting folks who ain't got nothing to do with it."

"Fuck that!" Rio shouted. "What about Trinity? She ain't have nothing to do with this madness out here."

"Just try and take it easy, dawg," Shamel said, patting him on the back.

"I can't, Mel," a teary-eyed Rio said. "This shit ain't right. Trinity never hurt nobody."

"We'll get her back, kid."

"What if we don't? What if Trinity's lying somewhere dead as we speak?"

"Don't talk like that."

"I couldn't live, Mel. If I can't have Trinity, I don't wanna live."

"It's gonna be a'ight. We're gonna find her. Ms. Sally," Shamel said, addressing her, "was Trinity alone?"

"Actually, I saw that girl running up the block."

"What girl?" Rio asked, paying full attention.

"What's her name, the one with all the weave?"

"Joyce?" he said in disbelief.

"That's her. I saw Joyce running from the scene."

"Come on, Mel," Rio said, hopping up. "We got some shit to take care of. I'll be back, Ma."

"Darius, maybe you should let the police handle it."

"That's a joke, right? Mama them pigs ain't got no love for poor ghetto kids. If we don't look out for our own then nobody else will."

Trinity was awakened by water splashing against her face. When she tried to focus on her surroundings, she realized that one of her eyes was swollen shut. Trinity's whole body ached from the beating that she had taken. She knew that she had hurt two of her kidnappers, but it still didn't keep her ass from getting snatched. She was fucked and she knew it.

"Glad to see that you're still with us," a familiar voice said. "I told my peoples not to touch you, but I heard that you were quite the scrapper."

Trinity knew the voice, but she couldn't quite place it. As the vision in her good eye began to clear, she was shocked to see who her abductor was. "Baron?"

"Oh, so you remember my name?" Baron said, stepping from behind the dusty iron desk. He had Trinity in an office of sorts; by the looks of it, no one had used it in a while.

"Why did you bring me here?" she asked.

"Nothing personal, ma. I got some unfinished business with ya man."

"What, you talking about that shit at the club?"

"Oh, nah. This is way bigger than that, Trinity. You see, he's got something that I want."

"Baron, I told you that I wasn't fucking wit you like that," she said defiantly.

"Bitch, don't flatter yourself. This ain't got nothing to do with you. This is about big business. Truck promised me all of Rio's territory if I take him out of the game." He grinned.

"Truck?" she asked in disbelief. "I know you ain't take the word of that snake? Truck is gonna snake you the first chance he gets."

"Probably," Baron said, touching her bruise. "That's why I'm baking a cake for his ass too. See, I got a secret. I got an uncle that works at One Police Plaza. Seems that Truck has been spilling his guts to the boys in blue for quite some time. Li'l J should be getting the package that I sent him real soon. Yep, they're gonna welcome me with open arms when I expose that snitch ma fucka. So you see, Trinity, I'll be getting Rio and Truck's turf."

"You're fucking sick," she spat.

"Not sick, boo. Just a master schemer."

"Rio's gonna kill you."

"Please. Rio has no idea who took you. If anything, he's gonna think that Truck snatched you and kill that bastard. If the Capos don't get him first. You tried to brush me off before, Trinity, but when I'm holding the cards you'll be begging to suck me off. Just like your little friend." Baron walked out of the room, laughing sinisterly. Trinity knew that things didn't look good for her, but she was more worried about Rio. He was alone out there in the cold world.

"Well, well," Detective Stark smirked. "Looks like we got your black ass, huh, Cutty?"

"Fuck you, pig!" Cutty shouted. "This shit don't phase me. You think I ain't never did a bid before?"

"Oh, I know you have. But this is a little different. See, this is your third strike. They're gonna put you away for a long time. Unless . . ."

"Unless what?"

"Unless you help us bring your friend, Rio, down."

Cutty began to giggle under his breath. Within a few minutes the giggling turned into a full-blown laughing fit. "You must be out of your fucking mind. You want me to snitch? I got a better idea."

"What's that?"

"Go suck ya mother. Bitch nigga."

"Oh," Stark said, grabbing him by the collar. "You think you're funny? We'll see how funny you are when they hit your ass with a basketball score."

"I don't give a fuck. I'd do a thousand years in jail before I go out like that bitch nigga, Truck. I'm a soldier, you doughnut-eating, cracker ma fucka. I don't break nigga. You hear me? You run and tell all these ma fuckas that Cutty don't bend. Fuck ya deal and fuck you. I'm a fucking soldier!" Cutty spoke his piece and went back to laughing.

"Shut up," Stark barked. "You hear me? If you don't quit that laughing, I'm gonna split ya fucking head open." When Cutty didn't stop laughing Stark kicked his chair out from under him, spilling Cutty onto the floor. "Shut up!" Cutty just laughed louder. "You shut up," Stark said, kicking Cutty. "Stop laughing," The more Stark hit him, the louder Cutty laughed. "Don't laugh at me!" Stark screamed, pulling his gun.

"What the fuck is going on in here?" Brown asked.

"This mother fucker thinks he's hot shit," Stark said, out of breath. "We'll see how hot you are when you're making wallets in Attica. Ship this fuck to the island."

Two uniformed officers came in to escort Cutty to the holding tank. Even as they helped him up, he continued to taunt Stark. "Ah ha, bitch. Cutty don't bend, ma fucka! That goes for all you fucking bitches. I'm a real fucking gangsta. Fuck you, fuck you, fuck you!" Cutty's little fuck-you segment lasted all the way down the hall. Brown waited until he and Stark were alone before he began speaking again.

"We've got a problem," Brown said.

"And what's that?" Asked the red-faced detective.

"Some asshole snatched Trinity."

"So, fuck is it to us? One less to worry about."

"You don't get it, do you? Rio is flipping the fuck out over it. The whole hood is saying that he's mad with grief and strapped."

"So, maybe he'll kill himself and save me the trouble."

"Stark, would you stop being an asshole for one minute? Rio is on the rampage to find Trinity. I'm guessing that he's gonna step to everyone who's crossed him and he ain't going to talk. Rio's got at least a hundred soldiers under him. All ready to kill and tear shit up on his command. What do you think is gonna happen if he decides to turn those cats loose?"

Finally the bigger picture started to register in Stark's head. An all-out war could erupt in the streets because of some lovesick kid. That wouldn't help the detective in his quest for a promotion. "We gotta find Rio. Send some units out. Every one of his soldiers that we've got dirt on, bring em in. The less soldiers that he has available to him, the better."

"What about Trinity? Should we call in the Feds?"

"Fuck her. She's on her own. But have Truck picked up. If Rio thinks that he had something to do with it, his life is *way* over."

Joyce sat on her living room sofa, watching videos. She tried not to think about Trinity, but she couldn't help it. Baron had said that his peoples were just gonna rough her up a bit to scare her, but the way those guys were acting, she figured he was lying. She didn't care for Trinity, but she didn't wish death on anybody. All she could do was hope that Baron kept true to his word and sent her home in one piece.

No sooner had Joyce finished her thought than the front door came crashing in. Rio came through the door followed by Shamel. Both of them were holding guns. Joyce tried to dive for the phone, but Rio had grabbed a handful of her ponytail. It wasn't really hers, and it came lose in his hand. When Joyce made her second lunge, Shamel clocked her square in the jaw. The blow staggered her, but she managed to stay on her feet.

"Where is she?" Rio growled as he grabbed her by the throat.

"Where's who?" Joyce asked, playing dumb.

"Bitch," Rio said, slapping her across the face. "Don't make me ask you again, Joyce."

"Rio, I don't know what you're talking about."

"Joyce," he said, kneeling over her and putting his 9 to her temple. "I know you were there. Where the fuck is Trinity?"

"Okay, okay. Just don't shoot me," she said, panicked.

"Joyce," Shamel said. "Tell us where Trinity is and you'll be okay."

"I'm sorry," she said crying. "He said that he just wanted to scare her to get back at you. I didn't know that he was going to hurt her."

"Who?" Rio asked, tightening his grip on her throat.

"Baron."

"Baron? You let that ma fucka take my girl?" he asked, sounding almost deranged.

"I'm sorry, Rio. I don't know what I was thinking. I was mad that you didn't want me and he told me that I was special and—"

"Joyce, where did Baron take my wife?" Rio asked, trying to remain calm.

"I don't know for sure, but I heard him talking to someone about an abandoned warehouse in the Bronx. Right off of Hunts Point."

"Are you sure?"

"Yes, Rio. That's what I heard."

"Okay," he said, stroking her hair. "You did good, Joyce."

"I'm sorry, Rio. If I had known . . ."

"Shhh," he said, putting his finger over her lips. "Don't worry about it. You fucked up, but we'll make it right."

As soon as Joyce began to relax, Rio put three shots into her face. It happened so quick that even Shamel jumped. Rio got to his feet and emptied his clip into Joyce's body. At this stage of the game life meant nothing to Rio. The only thing that mattered to him was getting Trinity back. Shamel didn't know that Rio planned to kill Joyce, but there wasn't much he could've done about it. That was his dawg and however he decided to handle it, Shamel was with him.

❏ ❏ ❏

J sat at his desk reading the transcript for the third time. Every time he read it, he got a little angrier. All this time the snake was in their own backyard. J was so hurt that he wanted to cry. But the hurt he was feeling at that moment wasn't shit compared to what Truck was going to feel.

J grabbed his phone from the desk and punched in a number that he knew by heart. "Yeah, let me speak to Larry or Lester." After a brief pause someone came to the phone. "Lester, this is J. I got something I need you and your brother to handle. Truck needs to take an extended vacation." J hung up the phone and turned his attention to the New York City skyline that loomed beyond the picture window. It hurt him to order the murder of Prince's son, but it was necessary. The weak must die in order for the strong to prosper.

Truck made his way hurriedly across 125th to the Metro-North station. Agent Peterson had complicated the hell out of his plan by making him rat Cutty out. There was no way to know if the word had gotten out about it, but there was no sense in taking chances. He had to get low until it all blew over. Just as Truck was about to cross Park Avenue, an unmarked car cut him off.

"What the fuck is going on?" Truck asked.

"We're taking you in, sir," the first officer said.

"What the fuck for?"

"For your own safety. Please, come with us."

"Am I under arrest?"

"No sir, but—"

"But my ass. If you ain't locking me up, then get the fuck outta here." Truck continued to the train station, but stopped dead in his tracks when he saw who was waiting at the station entrance. The Hound stood leaning against the stairs looking dead at Truck. "You know what," Truck said, turning back to the officers. "Maybe I should come with you."

As the officer placed Truck in the back of the car, he noticed Hound watching him. He winked his eye at the killer and they took Truck away.

28

School Boy and his girlfriend Sha came strolling through the projects. She had been harassing him about taking her out for some time now. With all that had been going on between Rio and Truck, he had to spend most of his time on the block. Sha wasn't having it this night though. She insisted that if School Boy didn't take the night off, she was cutting him lose. So School Boy decided to take the night off. The block wouldn't collapse without him for a night. Or so he thought.

School Boy had planned a nice evening consisting of dinner and a movie for Sha. The only reason he came back through the hood was to pick up some extra money from the spot. "Wait for me out here," he said, kissing Sha on the forehead. "I'm just gonna run up in there and get some paper from one of these niggaz."

"School Boy, you better not have me out here waiting long," she warned him.

"Yeah, yeah," he said over his shoulder. Sha was his boo, but she could be a pain in the ass at times. School Boy began his hike up the stairwell to where he knew he could find either Mikey or his partner

Jenkins. As School Boy got close, he heard Mikey and Jenkins having a heated discussion on the next floor.

"What do you mean the bust is going down today?" Mikey asked. "I don't wanna get caught up in that shit."

"Tough shit, kid," Jenkins said. "You work for us, remember?"

"This is some bullshit. You fucking pigs are all the same, no matter what your skin color. All you give a fuck about is screwing niggaz."

"Don't give me that 'I-have-a-dream shit,' kid. I came from the ghetto just like you. The difference is, I'm trying to rid the streets of ma fuckas like School Boy and Rio. You just do what the fuck you're told to do. Now, you better head back to the front."

School Boy couldn't believe what he was hearing. Two men that he had brought into the organization had turned out to be rats. This didn't look good for Jenkins or Mikey, but it looked even worse for School Boy. He was the one who put them on and trusted the men with his organization's secrets. Even after Rio had told him to, he still didn't have the men checked out and now that mistake was costing him. School Boy knew that his only way to live through this was to take care of the problem on his own.

Mikey didn't like what Jenkins was telling him. He thought that he would have time to make an escape before the shit hit the fan. It seemed that he wouldn't. Jenkins had informed him that there were units on the way as they spoke. Mikey's only chance to get up outta this shit was to leave *immediately*. As he rounded the corner of the staircase, he found himself staring down the barrel of School Boy's .38.

"Bitch, nigga," School Boy said. "I brought you in and you crossed me."

"Hold up, man. I don't know what the fuck you're talking about." Mikey pleaded.

"Lying-ass snake," School Boy said, cocking the hammer. "I heard you, nigga."

"Wait . . . they made me. What do you expect me to do?" he asked in a pleading voice.

"Die with some fucking dignity."

School Boy fired two shots into Mikey's chest, sending him crashing into the wall. Mikey clutched at his chest as if he'd be able to pull the bullets free. It was no use though. As Mikey's blood ran down the stairs, so did his chances of getting away.

Officer Jenkins had been listening to the whole thing from his spot around the corner. He had no idea that the young man was armed. Now it was too late for Mikey, but there might still be some hope for School Boy. Drawing his police special from his jacket pocket, Jenkins began the task of trying to reason with School Boy.

"School Boy," Jenkins shouted from behind the wall. "This is Officer Jenkins. Throw down your weapon and put your hands up."

"Fuck you," barked School Boy, slowly backing down the stairs. "I trusted you niggaz."

"School Boy, it's going to be okay as long as you cooperate with us. Just put your gun down and let's talk this out." Officer Jenkins poked his head out and School Boy tried to put a bullet in it. He quickly regained his composure and went to return fire. He came from his hiding place just in time to see School Boy making a run for it.

School Boy fired two wild shots over his shoulder and scrambled for the exit. Jenkins was hot on his tail, leaping down the entire flight of steps. School Boy was moving with the speed of a runaway slave. Sha went to ask him what was wrong, but School Boy ran right past her. By the time he reached the avenue, there were squad cars coming from everywhere.

"Drop it!" shouted a brave young officer. School Boy raised his pistol and split the officer's wig. When he turned to fire on the other officer he realized that he had made the mistake of not keeping count of his bullets. It was a mistake that would prove fatal. The police riddled School Boy's body with bullets while his boo, Sha, looked on in horror.

Shamel gripped the wheel of the stolen Cutlass, weaving in and out of traffic on the Cross Bronx. He almost crashed twice, but that didn't slow him down. They had to get to Trinity as soon as possible. Rio rode in silence with an AK47 on his lap. Shamel was beginning to worry about his friend. He had seen Rio angry before, but never like this. It was a sure bet that when Rio caught up with Baron he was going to air him the fuck out.

"You hear from Cutty yet?" Rio asked, speaking for the first time.

"Nothing yet," Shamel said. "I've been calling him for the longest and I keep getting the voice mail. I left a message though."

"Something is wrong, Mel. It ain't like Cutty to just disappear like that. I don't like this shit."

"You think Truck's got something to do with it?"

"I wouldn't be surprised. Mel, if that nigga touched Cutty, he's gonna die just like his little flunky."

Shamel was about to make a comment when his phone vibrated on his hip. "Yeah?" he said into the receiver.

"Yo, Mel," Knowledge said frantically. "Where you at, God?"

"I'm on my way to the Bronx with Rio. Fuck is going on?"

"Man, shit is going buck-fool out here. The police is snatching everybody in the hood. It's crazy out here."

"Damn, these ma fuckas tripping. You seen Cutty?"

"Did I? Man, I was coming from my girl's house on 137th and the police had that nigga hemmed up."

"What the fuck for?"

"Damned if I know. Him and Truck was together, but he was the only one wearing handcuffs. You know what time it is, don't you?"

"Yeah," Shamel said sadly. "Ma fucking snitch. I always knew that kid was funny style. Do me a favor. Get in touch with School Boy for me. Tell him—"

"That ain't gonna happen," Knowledge said, cutting him off. "Police laid that cat down about an hour ago. Shot him in cold blood."

"Damn," Shamel said, slamming his fist into the steering wheel. "This shit is happening too fast. Where you at?"

"I'm on my way to Port Authority. My black ass is on the next thing smoking out of town. I'll call you and let you know where I land, God."

"A'ight. Be safe, sun."

"You do the same, yo. Peace."

"Peace," Shamel hung up the phone and tried to make heads or tails of what the hell was going on. It seemed like everything was moving the wrong way at the worst time. He took a deep breath and prepared to break the news to Rio. "Rio, I gotta tell you something."

"I already know," Rio said without bothering to face his friend. "I couldn't hear what Knowledge was saying, but I pretty much got the gist of it. How bad is it?"

"Real bad. Cutty's in Jail, School Boy is dead, and Truck is a fucking snitch. Police are locking the hood down as we speak. Probably just a matter of time before they come for us."

"Shit," Rio said, stroking his machine gun. "This is bad. What the fuck went wrong with us, man?"

"Destiny, my man. Everything is going down hill cause of a fucking snitch. What are we gonna do, dawg?"

"We can't go back to the hood at, least not yet. They're probably tossing both of our houses trying to find us. You got access to any dough?"

"I got about two thousand on me and I can get up at least two or three more on the humble, but that's about it. What about you?"

"I got a few dollars on me, but nothing heavy. I do have another option though."

"What's that?" Shamel asked.

"When I first came into the organization, still part-time clocking, Prince showed me how to set up dummy accounts over the net. I've been putting a few dollars in it here and there for a little while. With that and what I got in my regular account we should be okay for a little while."

"Cool, but we're gonna have to figure something out."

"I know, Mel. What we gotta do is get Trinity back and get the fuck outta New York for a while. Once we're safe, I'll call J and he should know what to do."

"Sounds like a plan, kid. Let's do it." The two men continued to drive and make their escape plan. They were so engrossed in the problems that lay ahead of them that they never noticed the unmarked car following them.

❑ ❑ ❑

Hound came barging into the little coffee shop on West Broadway. He bumped past a patron and didn't bother to apologize. Seeing the look on Hound's face, the patron didn't bother to press the issue. Hound made his way to where Kane was sitting with two young ladies and flopped down in the booth.

"Why the long face?" Kane asked, trying not to move too much. His shoulder blade had been broken in the gunfight and he'd walk with a cane for a while, but Kane would live.

"I'm so mad that I could put my fist through a fucking wall." Hound snarled.

"What's wrong?"

"I finally tracked that piece of shit Truck to the metro station on 125th Street. I almost had him when the police picked him up."

"Oh, I thought something major had happened."

"You don't think that's major," Hound snapped. "That bastard deserves to die. I want him, Kane."

"Hound," Kane said, handing him a glass of red wine. "Try and calm yourself. You're starting to drool."

"Kane, how can you be so calm about all of this?"

"Because Truck is still going to get his just rewards. We have many friends in many different fields. Trust me on this one. Truck is in for the shock of his life real soon."

29

io and Shamel filed out of the car on a dark block in the Bronx. It wasn't hard for them to find the warehouse that Joyce had mentioned. The Vine had pointed them in the general direction and the rest wasn't hard. It was the only abandoned building with an entourage of luxury cars parked in front of it. Some people just didn't exercise common sense.

"There it is," Shamel said, clutching his 12-gauge. "I only see one cat at the door, but I don't know how many are inside."

"I don't care, Mel," Rio said. "Whoever's in there is gonna get it, too."

"Well," Shamel said, standing. "Let's go see if we can catch a felony."

"Hold on, man," Rio said, grabbing his arm. "You've already put yourself out there enough for me. I can't ask you to go any further."

"Check this out, Rio, we've been friends since I don't know when. We've done a whole lot of dirt together and not a lot of good. This here is a good thing. I love Trinity too and I wanna help. For the first time in my life I get to do something right. Please, let me do this with you."

The exchange almost brought tears to Rio's eyes. Shamel was a rare kinda dude. Friends like him didn't come along often, but Rio was fortunate enough to have one. He wanted to believe that everything would go smoothly but the reality of it was that they might not all make it out. Rio decided that if he were going to die, he was glad it would be with people he cared for.

"Fuck it," Rio said. "You ready to do this?"

"As I'll ever be. Yo, dawg," Shamel said, placing his hand over Rio's heart. "If I don't make it outta here, I want you to know that you're my heart. If fate has decided that I'm gonna die tonight, then let it be with you, my nigga."

"Thanks, Mel," Rio said, placing his hand over Shamel's heart. "You the realist nigga I know and I'm glad to call you my brother. Now fuck the dumb shit. Let's go twist these bitch niggaz wigs back."

Carl stood guard in front of the warehouse, bored out of his mind. Baron had said he had an important job for the youngster, but this isn't what he had in mind. Here he was standing watch over the warehouse while the rest of the crew was probably inside taking turns with the bad little light-skinned chick that they snatched. Carl got the short end of the stick as usual. He longed for something exciting to happen.

"Yo!" Shamel called from behind him. When Carl turned around, Shamel jammed the shotgun into the young man's chest and pulled the trigger. The game was afoot.

Trinity felt like death warmed over. Her lips were dry and cracked from dehydration and her muscles began to ache from spending all of that time sitting on the little metal chair. She didn't know how long she had been there, but she figured it had been a while because her deodorant was starting to wear off.

For the first time Trinity took notice of her surroundings. It appeared that Baron was keeping her in an office of sorts. There was a beat-up old desk off to her left, with yellowing papers scattered on it. The garbage strewn on the floor and cobwebs that coated the furniture, told her that the office hadn't been used in a while. Before Trinity could try and fit any more pieces of the puzzle together Baron returned to the office carrying a bag.

"I see you're awake," he said, setting the bag on the desk. "I figured you might be hungry, so I brought you something to eat. I hope you like McDonald's." Trinity didn't answer. "Come on, Trinity. You don't have to try and play tough with me."

"Fuck you, Baron," she said through swollen lips. "I don't want shit from you."

"Whatever. If you wanna play the tough bitch, then be my guest. It's your stomach."

"Keep talking, Baron. When Rio finds you, your ass is out."

"Please," Baron said, waving her off. "We're in the middle of west bubble-fuck. Rio's got a snowball's chance in hell of finding you." Baron smiled confidently as hope drained from Trinity's face. He truly believed that he had it all mapped out, until he heard gunshots.

After driving around in circles for a while, Officer Brown finally managed to track down the stolen Cutlass. When he examined the inside of the car, he found two AK clips and an empty box of shotgun shells. He knew that whatever the dynamic-duo were doing up there, it wasn't good.

Brown scanned the area, but found no signs of Rio or Shamel. He wondered where the two had gotten to. Something behind a beat-up warehouse caught his attention. He couldn't tell from where he was standing, but it looked like a shoe. Brown made his way over to the warehouse so he could get a closer look. Sure enough it was a shoe. But the shoe was attached to a corpse. A young man was lying on the ground with his chest missing. If Brown wasn't sure before, he was sure now. Rio and Shamel were up to no good. Officer Brown retrieved his police radio from his car and called for backup.

The sound of gunfire from outside the warehouse brought Baron's soldiers running. They were ready for war, but unfortunately so was Rio. Six men came charging down the stairs and were met by a murderous Rio.

He leveled the AK and squeezed the trigger. The hail of bullets ripped through the wooden steps as well as two of the gunmen. The remaining four scattered and tried to surround the duo.

One of the gunmen tried to hide behind a large crate. Shamel had a trick for his ass. He loaded two of the explosive shells into the gauge and cocked the slide. When he cut loose with the gun, it sounded like thunder. The explosive shells slammed into the crate, torching it and the man who used it for cover.

The two shooters took turns popping shots at Rio, but they didn't slow him down. Rio was a man possessed. He took his time firing burst from the machine gun at the men. One of the men was lucky enough to sneak up behind Rio. As if he was in an action movie, the shooter screamed as he charged Rio. This corny-ass stunt proved to be his undoing.

Without missing a beat, Rio pulled a 9 from his waistband and turned it on the shooter. The slugs hit the shooter in the neck and head, dropping him at Rio's feet. While Rio was preoccupied with the action-hero, another one of the shooters caught him in the shoulder. Rio was thrown face first into a crate, losing his grip on the AK. As he lay on the ground trying gather his wits, the shooter advanced on him.

Detective Stark paced the squad room, ranting. He had laid his plan out carefully, anticipating his promotion and all the other perks that would come with the bust. Now everything was going to shit. "Damn, damn, damn!" Detective Stark shouted.

"What's wrong?" Jenkins asked.

"Your stupid-ass partner, that's what's wrong. It just came in over the radio that he tried to play lone-soldier and go after Rio alone. Right now there's a goddamn Wild West shoot-out going on in the Bronx."

"What the hell was Brown thinking?"

"You tell me. That dickhead is gonna ruin everything. Come on," Jenkins said, grabbing his coat. "We gotta get to the Bronx before all of our plans go to shit." Detective Stark jetted from the precinct, followed by Officer Jenkins. They were on a quest for glory, but would only find carnage and death.

◻ ◻ ◻

Stan came bursting into the office where Trinity was being kept. "Baron," he said out of breath. "We've got trouble."

"What the fuck is going on out there?" Baron asked, getting scared. "What's all the shooting about?"

"That nigga Rio is here. He's down there lunching the fuck out. At least three or four of ours are dead already."

At the mention of Rio's name, Trinity popped her head up. It was a long shot, but her boo managed to find her. "Yeah," she taunted Baron. "I told ya punk ass that my man was gonna come for me. All of you ma fuckas is dead now."

"Oh, yeah," Baron said, getting angry. "If I'm gonna die, then your ass is checking out too," Baron gagged Trinity with a nasty old sock that he had found on the ground. "Stan, stash yourself somewhere. If he makes it past the soldiers, you're the last line of defense. Stan rushed from the office to find someplace to hide. Baron checked his gun to make sure it was loaded. He was scared to death, but he tried not to show it in front of Trinity. Truck's little deal didn't seem so sweet anymore. Rio coming for his head was definitely not part of the bargain.

"Got ya punk ass now," the shooter said, standing over a dazed Rio. "Bringing your head back to Truck is gonna guarantee me a block of my own. Later, nigga." Just as the shooter began to apply pressure to the trigger, his head burst open. Rio was pleased to see Shamel standing there, holding a smoking gun.

"Nigga," Shamel barked. "Get the fuck up. We ain't got Trinity back yet."

Before Rio could get to his feet, a barrage of bullets came sailing in their direction. He and Shamel were lucky enough to find cover behind some oil drums. Rio wanted to go for his AK, but it was too far away. They were pinned. Suddenly an idea formed in Rio's head.

"You got that other hammer on you?" Shamel asked.

"Yeah, why?"

"Give it here, dawg. I'm going for a touchdown."

"Rio, this ain't no goddamn schoolyard football game. These niggaz is serious."

"Me too, nigga," he said, taking Shamel's desert eagle. "Cover me, dawg." Holding his 9 in one hand and Shamel's pistol in the other, Rio charged in the gunmen's direction. Shamel laid cover fire with the 12-gauge, giving his friend the time that he needed. Rio leapt up onto a box in the center of his attackers' hiding places. When they looked up and saw Rio standing above them, both men took on shocked facial expressions. Unfortunately, those would be the faces they would die wearing. Rio dumped two shots into each one of their heads.

All of the gunmen lay in different positions throughout the ground floor of the warehouse. The only thing they had in common was the fact that they were all dead and stinking. But this did not slacken Rio's bloodlust. Rio screamed the name of his enemy at the top of his lungs. "*Baron!*"

When Baron heard Rio roar his name, he knew that his soldiers were dead. It was beyond him how two men could take out a half dozen soldiers? Baron didn't have time to ponder it at the moment. He had to prepare for Rio.

Baron began to drag Trinity's chair to a far corner of the room. Next he busted most of the lights in the office. The room was dimly lit and that made it hard to see clearly. As Trinity watched Baron running around doing this and that, she wondered if when Rio came through that door it would be their last time seeing each other?

Hearing that the gunfire had died down, Officer Brown made his way slowly into the warehouse. The sight that greeted him was a grotesque one indeed. The walls and floors were all coated with blood and entrails. Several bodies were scattered throughout the warehouse, but surprisingly enough, none of them was Rio or Shamel.

Brown cocked his pistol and proceeded with extreme caution. Judging by the vicious nature in which the men in the warehouse were killed, Rio was past the point of reasoning. He would leave with Rio in shackles if he could, but if it got crazy then Brown had to do what he had to do. Brown continued to search the warehouse, wondering where the two men had gotten to. When he heard the gunshots coming from upstairs, he knew.

"Be careful," Shamel said, leading the way. "We don't know where this little ma fucka is hiding out."

"All I wanna do is find Trinity, Mel."

"We will, kid. Just be easy."

"I'm trying." As Rio looked at Shamel in the dim light of the tiny hallway, he thought he saw something flash across Shamel's face. At first he thought it was the light playing tricks with his eyes, but then he saw it again. A red dot came to rest on Shamel's chest. By the time Rio shouted his warning, the left side of Shamel's chest was blown open.

"Mel!" Rio shouted. He grabbed the big man's shotgun and started dumping rounds into the darkness. There was a scream at the other end of the hallway, but Rio never heard it. The sound was drowned out by his own sobbing.

"Not my nigga," Rio pleaded as he dropped to his knees. "Come on, dawg."

"Damn." Shamel coughed. "Nigga caught me out there, huh?"

"Don't worry about it, Mel. I'm gonna get you outta here."

"Fuck that," Shamel said, squeezing Rio's hand. "Ain't no way I'm leaving here. Get ya wife, and boogie."

"I don't want to leave you, Mel."

"I don't want you to leave me either . . . but it is what it is. We had a good run, huh?"

"Yeah," Rio said, crying. "We sure did."

"I'm getting cold, Rio." Shamel began to shiver.

"Just hold on, kid. I'm gonna get you some help."

"Nah . . . I'll be gone by the time they get here. Just stay with me for a minute. I don't wanna die alone."

"Anything for you, kid. Anything."

❏ ❏ ❏

When Trinity heard Rio screaming Shamel's name, her heart wanted to break. A chill ran through her body and she knew that her friend was gone. She glared at Baron from her darkened corner, and her hate for him grew tenfold. She promised herself that if Rio didn't kill Baron, she would.

As Rio sat at his friend's side, he could feel Shamel's grip weakening. Within a few minutes his childhood friend had returned to the essence. Rio closed his friend's eyes and kissed his forehead. He and Shamel had come a long way together, but the last mile would be his to walk alone. Rio gathered up the two handguns and went to face Baron.

As soon as Rio's shadow appeared in the darkened doorway, Baron started shooting. Rio shot back, but he couldn't pinpoint Baron's location in the dim light. Trinity peeped what was going on and tried her best to warn Rio, but the gag kept her silent.

Rio was getting frustrated playing with Baron. He decided to do it smart. The next time that Baron fired Rio would just aim for the muzzle flash. Which is just what Baron wanted him to do. Baron positioned himself behind Trinity and popped two more shots. Rio followed the muzzle flash and let off two shots of his own. He could hear a muffled scream and a body hit the ground. He smiled sinisterly to himself, thinking he had just finished off the infamous Baron.

When Rio flicked on the lights, he was rewarded by a bullet to the stomach. He collapsed to the ground, but managed to shift his weight so he'd land behind a desk. He couldn't understand what was going on. He knew that he had just shot Baron. What kind of game was the kid playing? When Rio peeped under the desk, he realized that Baron was playing for keeps.

Rio saw his boo sprawled out on the ground with a bullet hole in the side of her head. His heart smashed into a million pieces upon seeing his Trinity dead. *How could God be so cruel?* An uncontrollable rage overcame him. Ignoring the pain in his left shoulder and gut, Rio grasped the desk by its edges. Using every ounce of strength left in his body, he hurled the metal desk in Baron's direction. The desk flopped over and smashed into Baron's knee. The impact was so great that it sent Baron's pistol flying from his hand. Baron collapsed into the corner howling in pain.

"You killed her," Rio said, approaching Baron. "This didn't have anything to do with her, Baron. She was mine and you had no right. Now you gotta die with her."

Baron started to try and reason with Rio, but the look in his eyes said, "don't bother." Rio's sanity had officially left the building. Baron tried to reach for his gun, but Rio was ready. He let off a shot with the desert eagle and blew three of Baron's fingers off. He looked Baron in the eye and saw nothing but fear coming from the tough guy. Rio swept his glance from Baron to Trinity and back again. Giving a heavy sigh, he emptied both of his guns into Baron's face and chest.

As his adrenaline rush faded, Rio's wounds started to take their toll. He collapsed on the floor next to his boo. "My precious, Trinity," he said, stroking her cheek. "I'm so sorry. I should've been there for you. Please, forgive me?" Rio heard footsteps coming up the stairs and grabbed Baron's gun. He was too weak to go on, but if it was more of Baron's soldiers then he was ready to go out in a blaze. Luckily it was just Officer Brown.

"Put it down, Darius," Officer Brown barked. "Put the gun down."

"They killed her, you know," Rio said sobbing. "My boo was only nineteen, Officer Brown."

"It's gonna be okay, Rio. Just put it down."

"I love you," Rio said, kissing her chilling lips. "In this life or the next. I love you, Trinity." Rio looked at the pistol in his hand as if he was seeing it for the first time.

When Officer Brown saw the grief in Rio's eyes, he knew the kid would never be the same. To cap it off he was about to go to jail for a very long time. Officer Brown would grieve for young Trinity, but at that moment he had a job to do. "Darius, I'm not going to tell you again. Put the gun down. It's over."

Rio tried to force himself to focus on what the cop was saying, but all he could think of was his lover and how she would never see her plans through. The streets had claimed another promising life and shattered yet another dream. "You're right," Rio said, chuckling. "Without Trinity, there ain't shit here for me. Now we can both be free, ma. Fuck it!" Before Officer Brown could stop him, Rio put the pistol in his mouth and painted the walls with his own brains.

Officer Brown's heart was heavy as he approached the two bodies. Rio lay across his lover's body, with blood oozing from the back of his head. Rio had gotten what his hand called for. He knew the consequences for his actions and he accepted it. Trinity, on the other hand, deserved better. She had so much promise, but her love for Rio made her blind to it. It would just be another sad story in the daily news.

30

"WHEN IT'S ALL SAID AND DONE"

J **had decided that** he'd seen enough death to last him a lifetime. Shortly after Rio killed himself, J decided to retire from the game and go back to Georgia to be with his family. It had been a while since he had seen his grandchildren. But before J stepped down, he had some last-minute business to attend to. He made sure Rio, Trinity, and Shamel were buried side by side. They were the happy trio in life and wouldn't be denied that honor in death. He took a good chunk of Rio's money and gave it to Sally to do with as she pleased. The rest he put into a trust fund for little Billy.

Unfortunately for Billy, BCW took him anyway. His sister was gone and his last remaining relative was a crackhead. Billy didn't mind though. There was nothing left in the Douglass projects for him. On the day that they took him, Billy received good news in the mail. Trinity's GED scores came and she passed with flying colors. Billy would always keep those scores with him, even through to adulthood. They were his last link to his beloved sister.

❑ ❑ ❑

It had been over a week since Truck had been picked up. The police said that he was under their protection, but he felt more like a prisoner. Truck had his own television and didn't have to eat the prison food, but he still couldn't go anywhere. It seemed that word of his activities had gotten back to the Capos and they weren't happy about it. He didn't give a shit. He still had his money. Once the streets died down, they would release him and he was on the next thing smoking to nowhere.

"Open cell four!" Shouted a beefy guard.

"Cell four," Truck said. "But that's my cell. I ain't supposed to have no company."

"Don't worry, Truck. It'll only be for the night. Besides, this guy is about one-sixty soaked. I know you ain't nervous?"

"Fuck it. Send him in." Truck said, trying to sound cool. When he saw who his roommate was, he wished he could eat his words. The beefy security guard took the shackles off Cutty and pushed him into the cell.

"Hold on, I changed my mind. I don't want a roommate," Truck pleaded.

The beefy guard laughed and said, "Kane sends his regards. You fucking rat!" The guard left the two men alone.

"What's up, Truck?" Cutty said, pulling a homemade shank from his work boot.

"Hold up, man," Truck said, backing up into the corner. "If you kill me, they're gonna give you more time."

"Like I give a fuck," Cutty said. "I'm a three-time looser, nigga. They're gonna give me life thanks to yo punk ass. It's okay, though. There's a lot of people who ain't real happy with you, snitch mutha fucka. I'm gonna live like a king in the joint. Time to die, nigga."

"Guard! Guard!" Truck screamed at the top of his lungs, but no one came to help him as the shank bit into the side of his face. Cutty cried for his fallen homeys as he carved Truck up like a Christmas goose.